This is a work of fiction. Names, characters, places and incidents either are products of the author's imagination or are used fictitiously. Any resemblance to actual events or locales or persons, living or dead, is entirely coincidental.

Copyright ©2024 by Emma Bruce and Morticia Gayle

All rights reserved. No portion of this book may be reproduced in any form without permission from the publisher, except as permitted by U.S. copyright law. For permissions contact: youreaglecoach@mail.com

Cover Art by Marie-Louise O'Neill

Formatting by Renee Brooks PA

First Edition

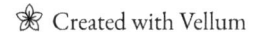

❀ Created with Vellum

# Race for the Ruby Sunrise

Emma Bruce

Morticia Gayle

*This book is dedicated to my family, friends and readers who love to escape inside of a good story.*

*Special thanks goes to Renee and Marie-Louise who've wielded their own magical skills, enhancing this book through the aid of powerful visualisation and formatting techniques.*
*- Emma Bruce*

*To my one and only; this one's for you darling.*
*- Morticia Gayle*

## Chapter 1

Olena Lupescu, a tall and lithe Vampire with hair as black as a raven's wings and eyes that glint hints of ruby tones under the right lighting——glances up at the sound of the small doorway bell. Using her red tinted eyes to glance across to the doorway having heard the small entry way bell jingle ——Olena can see to her disdain that it has signalled the arrival of Manix her father and Valeria her mother. Olena is the spit of her mother's image but in personality (much to Valeria's disdain) Olena is as rogue and rebellious as her father.

(A quick note to self here: For persons of a magical disposition to gain entry to this enchanted space——one must travel via portal doorway. A space that has been operational since even the times of the great *old ones).*

"Hello daughter." Valeria says, her voice an eclectic mixture of soothing hypnotic trance tones——of which Olena is immune to given they are from the same species

——*Vampire*. A human or perhaps some other member of magical species having heard Valeria speak may well have succumbed to instantly becoming more pliable to the demands put upon them by Valeria——as was the Vampire's way, to hypnotise those they wished to control and or to feed from.

Olena's father, Manix——a dashingly handsome fellow with big bright eyes tinted violet, waves of thick black hair sitting atop his well-groomed head accompanied with faint outlines of a beard defining that well chiselled jaw of his. Dutifully following his wife to two empty barstools, Manix gives Olena a far less enthusiastic welcome——that is more *huff* then hello. In Vampire culture it is customary for the men to be led by their wives. The only time a male Vampire would ever be considered worthy enough to be followed——is during the delicate time of *coupling* where unattached male Vampires would actively seek out their perfect and receptive eternal female (or male - yes even in Vampire culture there are same sex relationships) mate. The coupling is delicate in the sense that if any of the courtship or etiquette rules went awry with even the slightest misstep ——the Vampire seeking out a mate may well lose their fangs which would lead to a slow starvation——for a Vampire without their fangs…well…it'd be like a human without their limbs and given no disability aid.

"You're busy in here tonight." Manix grumbles taking a seat next to Valeria——who reminds her husband with threatening glance that he is to remain pleasant.

Barmaid was not the first choice of career either of them would have chosen for their only offspring. But Olena had been adamant she could handle such a dangerous job. Dangerous as the role of serving customers from all walks of magical life came tinged with the greatest of responsibilities——looking after one of her world's most ancient and busiest portal doorways.

Manix, shaking off his wife's warning glare as she and Olena now talk among themselves——looks around taking in the throng of individuals in this evening. There are species heralding from both sides of their world—— evenly split from the dark to light side. Nocturnal creatures who dwell in the dark side are usually closely linked to criminal activities. While daytime magical folk who live in much sunnier parts of their world——go about their days using magic for good such as healing the sick and wounded, having bigger and better impacts on their local communities and trying to remain tolerant of their darker side communities. Between both sides of the world however is a permanent shadow space where both can reside quite comfortably for important town hall meetings, government goings on (yes even in the Magical realm there's need for law and order) and other instances where both sides need to be privy to any and all-important upcoming events, planning permissions from local councils, voting etc.

---

The Chequered Inn with its ye olde wooden floorboards, beams, latticed windows and dim lighting——is heaving this evening. There isn't a spare seat to be had. Even standing room is rapidly decreasing——taken up by those still wishing to greet friends and do business under the protection of The Magical veil.

To prevent overcrowding a Ticket Master from The Magical realm keeps tabs on how many are coming and going via the Inn's portal doorway. There is a beautiful hotel situated directly above the Ticket Master's office aptly called *The Waiting Lounge*. Here magical customers can enjoy brief stays when the portal doorways get too busy and they may have a slight delay in their business or pleasure travel experiences.

"We'll have two blood club sodas——and some of that delicacy humans love so much——the black pudding." Valeria says placing the menus back into Olena's hands. Manix simply rolls his eyes that he didn't even get to participate in the choice of food for himself for as much as he may follow his wife about like an obedient dog——he must too always make sure she makes the bulk of decisions within their coupled arrangement, right down to what they eat or drink of an evening.

Olena obediently takes down her mother's request for food before hastening into the enchanted kitchen.

Hot air blasts Olena's pale face and skin from the various ovens and cauldron chucking out immense heat. The kitchen is all ancient stonework with various brass pots and pans hanging from the ceiling. Herbs, spices, potions and tinctures, line the walls on the heavy duty ye olde wooden shelves and spice racks. On the ground along the walls are barrels and sacks of various seeds, pulses, cereals and many other magical cookery components that perhaps are similar in look and feel to that of human food——but couldn't be more different. Much of human language and behaviour stems from magical folk teaching them along the way while disguised as human themselves. Right as far back as when men first walked the Earth. Cooking, building, inventions——it's all mostly from influence of those tasked from *The Powers That Be* to implement blueprinted plans for the direction they have wished to take humanity in. Free will for humans is not as free as they might like to believe it is.

Pikkatin, Olena's boss and head chef——is a mean faced, pudgy ginger-haired dwarf with fiery green eyes. His face was mainly hidden beneath a huge fuzzy ginger beard. What little skin Olena could see——was beetroot red and shiny from all of the sweat pouring down his angry looking features.

Presently Pikkatin is stirring (with vigour) stinky green contents bubbling away inside of a large cast iron cauldron, sitting squarely in the middle of the stone walled kitchen. The Cauldron was a gift to the Inn thousands of years ago by the three witch sisters whose names are——*Hear no Evil, Speak no Evil & See no Evil.*

As he stirs, Pikkatin can be heard loudly barking orders to his frazzled senior cooking staff. One of the taller, more lanky sous chefs, almost drops the tray of unbaked panny-fritters he's holding. He'd been startled by

Pikkatin yelling for someone to grab a bottle of *Simply Sweet* (magical equivalent of sugar) from the enchanted larder. Every day there is a lot of smoke, steam, red faces and ringing ears from Pikkatin's vile temperament.

Glancing Olena with parchment in her well-manicured hand, complete with black shiny gothic nail polish ——Pikkatin grunts in angry protest upon being presented with said order. Stopping the stirring, he snatches the small piece of parchment out of Olena's cool pale fingers. Her eyes flash with a glimmer of red as if to silently remind him that he may be her boss but she was still a Vampire which makes her a lot stronger.

Freedwreak, Pikkatin's young apprentice——has arms laden with plates ready to serve and so has been unable to receive the order himself. Sweat can be seen pouring down Pikkatin's portly ginger-fuzzed beetroot face. He shouts across to the already frazzled sous chef ——causing him to jump. Spinning around suddenly to ensure he caught all of Pikkatin's instructions the sous chef almost collides with a colleague who has a tray loaded up with delicate glass flutes full of confetti-fetti (a fancy bubbly alcoholic champagne style beverage that fae folk enjoy).

Pikkatin turning his back to Olena with no words exchanged between them——returns to his cauldron duties. Sweat drips into the large cast iron cauldron. The hot lime-green witch's brew bubbles away fiercely within, and as Dwarf sweat is a main ingredient of the brew it saves Pikkatin at least having to traipse the short distance to his magical pantry.

Cringing at her boss' bad mood Olena takes herself speedily back out into the sanctity of the packed Inn and away from his growing ire. Also wishing to avoid mindless chit-chat with her overbearing parents, Olena swaps duties with a colleague for them to cover the bar while her parents are gracing The Chequered Inn with their presence so that she can take over cleaning tables. Her colleague gives a wink and knowing look as they pass one another letting Olena know she's got her back.

A centralised round wooden table has been left in one heck of a mess by a group of *Purpanite Pixie Paraders* (purple troublesome creatures with pointy ears, teeth like needles, claws and bat styled wings). They absolutely revel in creating chaos for the average human family while visiting Earth. Every year their species hold *The Annual Mischief Games*——where clans of Purpanite Pixies gather from all around their mini kingdom to see who can cause the most stress and upset upon their poor unsuspecting victims. Favourite teddy bears going missing at bedtime for children, is a favourite activity shared among all of the pixie clans as it yields the greatest results. Some of the other favourite sporting games they partake in are bursting pipes, making humans trip over nothing whereby they smash their faces in and moving keys and mobile phones out of the way only to place them back where they were in the beginning. This causes untold amounts of family arguments to erupt, making the points for teams shoot up. The long and short of it is——everywhere pixies appear on Earth be they Purpanite or otherwise, chaos is sure to follow.

Purpanite plates gained their name due to the fact they are purple from head to toe - play panpipes and love any and all reasons to blow things up. Breaking it down yet further Pur = Purple, Pan = Panpipes, Ite = Dynamite.

Scanning the room with her vampiric HD precision sight, Olena huffs that there are no further tables to clean. Inwardly groaning, she takes herself back behind the bar where her parents can scrutinise her every move. Her colleague that had covered for her to give Olena respite, gives her a sympathetic glance as she takes off her apron ready to head home having finished her shift.

Olena makes a quick mental register of the remaining customers they have in. There are members of The Powderpuff Mushroom Clan (darkside critters that look like literal mushrooms with faces and personalities. Their people love setting up homes in deep damp forest areas on Earth). Next Olena spots a group of Golden Tree Elves (light side healers and seers.) Their skin has a faint golden glow along with their eyes that look like two glowing golden orbs. All Golden Tree Elves have golden colourings. A small group of Hoggleberry Witches sit huddles into one of the darker corners of the Inn. (These are darkside residents that love to cast out curses and voodoo). To Olena's left sit Turquasian Sirens (light side members of an enchanted choir used for healing and special occasions such as the baptism of royal babies). As you might imagine these people wear long light flowing robes, have elvish ears and facial features. Faint hues of turquoise run through strands of their long flowing blonde or white hair. (Think Lord of The Rings High Elves and you may get the picture). Nubelle Valkyrie warriors sit laughing and chortling at a more centralised table. (These women are an army all of their own that don't belong typically to either the dark or light side of The Magical realm.) These deadly female warriors can be hired for jobs such as assassinations - roughing others up - death threats etc. However neutral they may be, many decide to linger in the darkside areas as this is where most of their business is dealt with. Not many a good folk from the light side have cause to wish another harm or death. Rumour has it many of the women dye their hair red with the blood of goblins they have maimed or killed during raids and ambushes.

―――

Time between the world of Earth and magical realm is perceived to move differently for most species. Vampires can choose to travel speedily through time or at a more leisurely pace and so for them there is the small capability to almost bend time to their will (think of the marvel superhero *The Flash*. The way he can seemingly move so fast everything around him moves in slow motion and you get the idea).

"Olena! Your mother and I are off. we'll see you at home?" Manix asks more pleasantly, wondering if indeed Olena will be going to her own bed or staying at a friend's. Her social life was something else he and Valeria had to suffer through with gritted fangs at times. They'd tried to give her the all vampiric experience growing up but Olena being Olena, meant that she broke with normal traditions and made friends with all manner of species and critters. Valeria blamed Manix saying it was more than likely his humanity that bled through to create their offspring's good-natured self. However, when Olena invited friends from school back home it was always a tense time for both her parents. Blood lust was manageable between the couple but their staff were a different matter——accidents did happen after all. Having non-Vampire guests to their home was always a point of great anxiety for both Valeria and Manix.

Now that Olena was old enough to go out and stay at friends' places it eased the tension but still they worried who or what she may be getting up to while out of home. Fortunately, as Vampires could only have Vampire children there was no chance she would ever have a *mixed breed* baby——but just the mere notion she might be having sexual relations with other species made her parents' stomachs roll.

Olena nods an acknowledgement to her father's question while pouring pints of *Butterfly Dust Beer*, for two wood elves sitting at the far-left hand side of the bar. Instead of bubbles or foam——there were little golden sparkling-misty butterflies seemingly trying to escape out of the top of each tankard before evaporating.

Manix, his piercing pale-grey eyes with just a hint of lilac light in them, smiles as Olena confirms to be coming home after her shift.

Olena shares much of her mother's devilish good

looks, including her red eye hues——accompanied by thick long raven locks that would have seen Snow White all of those hundreds of thousands of years ago balking. All human fairy tale ideas have actually come from imps and pixies whispering ideas to humans subconsciously while they slept, so they would imagine having dreamed these characters up themselves——yet nothing could be further from the truth. Most if not all fairy tale princes and princesses, witches and other assorted "monsters" , have in fact been based upon real life characters from The Magical realm's various kingdoms.

Olena being very much a mini-me of Valeria——in looks only was forever getting a lot of attention in and out of school. One male Vampire tried to accost Olena mistaking her to be older than her years while she was out dress shopping with Valeria. He soon saw himself on the wrong side of Manix. The Vampire was lucky to escape with a snapped humerus.

When it came to personality however Olena was as mentioned earlier——every bit her father's daughter. This pleased Manix no end. Valeria would whine to Manix how unfair it was that Olena had him wrapped around one of her well-manicured taloned fingers. To which Manix would respond with that if he couldn't share in the *looks* department that he had to have at least some part of himself woven into Olena's make-up. Valeria would often respond by huffing yet further about this fact by simply stating that she'd drawn the short straw when it came to their only offspring being rebellious through and through. Then again that is why she herself had fallen so madly in love with Manix———his rebellious nature (much to her own parents' dismay considering Manix a half-breed as he was turned not born a Vampire.) The only sweetener going for Manix was giving Valeria a daughter therefore making her parents proud grandparents, ensuring their lineage would live on.

Valeria's parents reside in an underground mountain town called Killington. Manix didn't have parents before he *turned* Vampire in the mid-1800s. His adult human life saw him become a private detective following a childhood in workhouses and orphanages. Unsurprisingly it was the cases involving children that were Manix's forte. At the time of his turning, Manix was an unattached bachelor who kept himself to himself———meaning no one really missed him once he was gone from the streets of London. It had pained him to leave the human job he'd loved so much———helping to protect poor defenceless children. But after an unfortunate mugging incident that found him bleeding, dying in the street———rescued by the Vampire that would sire him, the choice was all but taken out of his hands. Manix left a note with his housemaid explaining how an opportunity had presented itself overseas during the very night he would become the undead. He went onto explain there had been no time to spare in preparation for travel and so had upped sticks with his new business companion. He did however leave his maid, a kinder older woman———the means to live the remainder of her life comfortably. The Vampire who turned Manix, a brusque Irish gentleman assured him human money was not necessary where they would be travelling to and so Manix saw no problem giving any and all of his financial gain away to his maid and local orphanage as an anonymous donor. Unfortunately for Manix, the Vampire who turned him was part of a wanted vigilante gang that would be executed not long after Manix became a Nosferatu. There was a magical court case that really showed how different their worlds were, with Manix given immunity——so long as he was able to become an upstanding citizen in the Vampire community within the dark side's walls of their realm. He took on the role as a Vampire private detective——working alongside magical police forces——whose rules and laws changed depending what side of the world and kingdom they hailed from——this certainly kept Manix on his toes while investigating different jurisdictions.

It was during his transition from Earth to The Magical realm that Manix met his present-day wife Valeria. The pair of them connected almost immediately when her father had taken her to their local bank. Manix had been going to pay in a cheque himself and after a brief introduction and conversation they were off for a private supper. Knowing nothing of Vampire courtship and the present danger he was in. Manix used only what he knew of his human-ness when it came to courting a lady. Manix had Valeria all but eating out of the palm of his hand right up until they were wed. Then the tables rapidly turned and Manix found himself well and truly bound with a ball and chain around himself. Work helped him to feel a little less neutered in the masculine department and Valeria did at least give him the grace to take charge in the bedroom from time to time. It's one of the things that had her fall madly in love with him in the first place——knowing all the right buttons in all the right places to press and how to press them. Occasionally Manix would flit back to Earth to keep an eye on children in the poorer areas of London he had originally hailed from. If he ever caught adults roughing up or beating a child they found themselves bled, dead and buried. Manix didn't believe in feasting on good souls however sour the rotten ones may taste.

"See you both at home." Olena confirms verbally not looking up from the present tankard she's filling.

"Oh, before I forget——how are your fangs feeling dear?" Valeria calls across to Olena which has her almost drop the full tankard of Butterfly Dust. Valeria's comment also catches the eyes and ears of nearby customers who've stopped all manner of eating, drinking and chatting to look directly where Olena now stands. Putting this into context, had Valeria been human—— she may as well have called out asking if Olena had started her period yet or not.

"*Mum! You know I don't like you asking such questions...in public.*" Olena hisses under her breath——in pitch and tone only other Vampires would hear.

As a natural born Vampire her kind don't have fangs right away. They are more commonly received when a born Vampire reaches in human years——one hundred and twenty-five years old. As Olena recently had her one hundredth birthday and her fangs appeared to be coming in a little prematurely——Valeria and Manix sought the aid of a local Gothling Dentist (a person who specialises in the care and attention of Vampire teeth) to check her over. After reassurances that yes Olena's fangs were well on their way but that everything looked completely normal their concerns of premature puberty were waylaid.

———

In stark contrast to human folklore suggesting that Vampires are cold blooded killers akin to that of psychopaths, Vampires are in fact a species who can and do frequently express emotion. Empathy for example is there——even if primarily expressed toward their own kin. What humans do have correct however is that Vampires will indeed snack on the odd human person ——predominantly for supper if they get delayed returning home from Earth should they become hungry. Bram Stoker for example was a royal mess when one of the oldest Vampire Princes left it so late to feed having got stuck Earth-side after human muggers ransacked his carriage setting lose the horses shooting dead the driver. Keeping to Vampire law——that excess force was only to be used as self-defence——the Prince knowing he was bullet proof surrendered his meagre remaining human funds he'd arranged to have with him for his trip to Earth ——and once shot himself by the muggers played dead expertly. The only problem being was when the muggers had left he was beyond starving and bordering on out of control rage. Bram was to be the Prince's victim. By the time the Prince fed he forgot to glamour Bram first to feeling no pain during the feed and then secondly forgot to erase the ordeal ever happened. As an apology to Bram and feeling bad for making the feeding both painful and confusing——on an already sick man——the Prince did eventually glamour him to forget once he'd regained his strength. The Prince also left Bram the gift of the story idea *Dracula*. The Prince now having reached his *elder years*——rests buried in the eternal mausoleum of sleeping undead. A place where Vampires who haven't yet fully crossed over to the realm of Anubis——lie in situ that can last a couple thousand Earth years.

---

Olena has only recently discovered just how itchy and uncomfortable the process receiving her fangs has become. Along with her fangs——has arrived an increase for blood lust. Up to this point she's been able to enjoy food and drink like the other species of her world but as time goes on this will become less as her internal organs will all change, requiring different nutrients. In another twenty years Olena will only be able to ingest and digest blood or edible products made from blood. Some species are inedible however such as The Silver Fox Fairies whose veins literally run thick with liquid silver. This breed of scavengers is as wild as they come and can shapeshifter to either their fox or fae form.

"My apologies my sweetest. I forget how *sensitive* you

are about the subject." Valera says sympathetically knowing all too well how trying it can be on a Vampire's nerves——to suffer the long drawn out discomforts of *fang inheritance*. Manix contributes no such support seeing as he was a turned Vampire not born - so his fangs came in immediately following the completion of his transition.

Valeria and Manix leave the Inn by seeming to glide effortlessly across the floor. Once out of sight through the portal doorway——it is here Olena realises she's been holding her breath as a big whoosh of air escapes from her lungs.

Parents out of the way, Olena starts relaxing a bit as customer numbers dwindle until it's time to call *last orders.*

"Olena! you're to be on clear up and closing duty. Pikkatin barks gruffly across to her from the opened kitchen doorway. She notes he has gathered his belongings ready to head home.

*Alright for some.* Olena thinks to herself, thankful Pikkatin doesn't possess the power of telepathy.

"Sure thing boss." Olena responds already busying herself with wiping up various liquid spillages from the bar. The rest of the staff having already clocked off, meaning Olena would be alone during clean up duty. She didn't mind so much. This meant she could give her fangs a decent scratch on a wire brush without risk of being disturbed.

———

## *A Short Lesson*
### *In Magical History*

The chequered Inn is situated behind a magical veil first erected when the world was formed four billion years ago. The three most powerful witches (previously mentioned as *Hear no Evil, See no Evil and Speak no Evil*) built the world as instructed by a powerful collective known as *The Magi*. An intermediary spiritual influence between themselves and eternal higher Powers That Be. The Magi themselves have been birthed from the unified field——where everything in creation stems from——no matter what parallel universe species reside inside of their own respective realities. Above all of creation everywhere across the cosmos, are the higher Powers That Be. A collective so ancient that not even they can trace their origins back to the beginning. It was decreed a few billion years ago that the Powers That Be, had always and will always be in existence, bringing an end to any and all research into the subject. As far as anybody is concerned the Powers That Be exist eternally.

Throughout the evolutionary processes of Mother Earth and her species, humans had proved to be the most destructive. Everyone will remember when fairies were really seen and photographed by humans and the huge scandal that followed. Leading to humans turning up in hoards to trudge through forest and undergrowth destroying many a fae home and community. Humans even made a movie about the entire debacle. Eventually (and with a lot of super star power) proof could be faked by members of the most senior staff in the Powers That

Be department. This helped *debunk* any and all belief by adult humans that fairies existed. It had taken some of the strongest magics to achieve the brainwashing lie——that fairies are *not real*. When as matter of fact they are as real as you or I.

Over the centuries, Earth has become a lot less magic-friendly making it more challenging for magical folk to come and go as they please. War scorched lands across Earth through the ages, have meant that large portions of magical operations have needed to be shut down or relocated elsewhere. As a result, huge protests erupted across the entire world of The Magical realm. These were regular and stemmed from the constant upheaval caused by the humans——a species seen as less intelligent than a majority of magical folk. Varying species demanded time and again for the Powers That Be to intervene setting things right. But even these celestial rules could not be bent or altered. Changing time-line events came with hefty penalties and punishment. Entire species have been wiped from the face of The Magical realm because individuals attempted to meddle in changing past events or tried creating a different outcome to a certain set of actions. The fairy issue was a different matter altogether as the humans had actual photographic evidence. However dangerous the risks are to meddle with time ——this still doesn't stop the desperate few. Some examples could be:

- ***A bad break-up***
- ***An exam gone wrong***

- ***A decision to have offspring——reversed after said offspring grow up to be nasty to their parents***
- ***An illness diagnosed too late***

Witches were some of the worst culprits at trying to bend time to their will. Using all manner of spells and potions, but the law was very clear——any intentional attempt to change time outside of the Powers That Be, would result in the swiftest of punishments being doled out.

Across Earth the hidden veils (that's right there is more than one) separating magical operations from human day-to-day goings on——have become harder to erect and stabilise. Humans have evolved to be in the possession of much more sophisticated technology. Take Loogle Earth for example or military radar and artificial intelligence. Humans now have the capacity to readily close in on craft they call *UFOs* and *UAPs*. These *alien spacecraft* are in fact some of the most powerful and sophisticated means of magical travel, invented by ancient wizards. The craft bring with them an alternative means to travel——outside of portal doorways being utilised. Air travel does come in handy, especially during the school holidays where doorway and security queues can become tremendously long. This is something humans share with magical folk. The stresses and strains of organising breaks away around school holidays for their offspring. The Magical realm's economy works much the same too, as in prices for travel are far higher during end of term season.

However, as handy as it might be to choose a magical flight. The technology even by magical standards isn't perfect and there has been the occasional blip. This has led to highly televised video footage of various craft and lights of different shapes and sizes being televised around the world. Fortunately, there are plenty of wizards posing as human astrophysicists, who have been tirelessly working hard to debunk such theories of aliens and spacecraft. This in itself is a mammoth effort on the wizards' part, as there are always the nutty humans with their conspiracy theories who continually stoke the fires of aliens and abductions. It's a constant under-ground battle going on behind closed governmental doorways.

The *aliens* in question——that people of Earth refer to as *The Greys* are a short, silver or green skin toned species with big almond shaped black eyes and tiny slits for mouths. Their true identity is that of Globustatic creatures. They have the power of ESP and use it when they are caught out being seen by humans. When spotted Globustatic creatures will paralyse a human person/s with the power of their minds——showing images of apocalyptic scenes to terrify the humans into freeze response; thereby giving the creatures enough time to beat a hasty retreat. In The Magical realm Globustatic creatures reside in a metropolis high above the clouds. If anyone ever remembers a cartoon TV show called *The Jettsons* you may have an idea of how their community is run.

Globustatic creatures pilot all the cloaked aircraft that ferry other magical folk around on Earth. Fortunately, there have only ever been two documented occasions where magical powered aircraft have crash landed – leading to Earth's governments seizing wreckage and bodies from the sites. When incidents like this happen, passengers on board are jettisoned back to The Magical realm using specialised buttons next to each passenger seat. Under each seat are small individual emergency portals. Globustatic pilots must stay and go down with the craft whatever the outcome may be. Apparently by Magical legal standards they are a disposable species, required to sign contracts agreeing to be in full acceptance of the risks involved.

The subject around alien abductions of humans does hold some element of truth. This rarely happens but when it does it is because a request has been put forward by the Globustatic senior members of the science department, that small groups of humans are to be taken and studied from time to time. Similar you might say to how some humans treat a large majority of the animals they do tests on in labs for the betterment of human health in the fight against germs and viruses. With so much off-world travel occurring daily it's important that human biology be studied extensively, to keep visitors of The Magical realm safe and free from cross-contamination.

# Chapter 2

Alone, Olena begins the unpleasant task of clearing up the remaining remnants of the evening. There's goblin snot smeared across one table, and pork type scratchings (from pig like creatures known as Munkswines) that have been scraped off their naked rear ends like scabs——flaking all over the area where they'd been sitting while playing magical card games. Most card playing games humans use to gamble ——have in fact bled through with magical folk teaching humans several versions of the games they play——all the while under the guise of appearing as perfectly normal human beings. Shapeshifters - naturally, are the biggest culprits of bringing gambling to Earth. Card games date as far back as medieval Earth. They're considered an integral part of helping to keep relations between magical species and humans protected. Humans have only ever believed they have played card games with other humans——never knowing that card games come from somewhere far removed from anywhere they could ever comprehend.

Humans, considered exceptionally gullible and easy to brainwash – have been manipulated and controlled since the dawn of their creation.

Everything humans do today has been moulded into their societal and spiritual beliefs by entities from The Magical realm. Zeus for example (the real one from the real Mount Olympus of The Magical realm) attests to having had such fun in programming human minds to accept belief systems around Gods and deities. The entire point of religion globally was bought about to better control humans as they evolved. Humans are treated much the same as animals in a zoo. Humans believe with their small goldfish minds that science, mathematics and physics can explain away anything. To freshen up further speculation as to just what humans know and do not know to be true of the *beginning of time*. The Powers That Be recently saw fit to covertly place a ring of galaxies now measuring *before* the point of the Big Bang——sending human physicists into an utter frenzy——with comments such as "We know this exists now because we can see it, but it shouldn't exist! There's no reason how it could exist." This example has recently been used in classrooms up and down The Magical realm to teach young malleable minds just how easily humanity can be manipulated.

———

Olena unsurprisingly given her Vampire nature has always been rotared in to work the night shift. Having already put in twenty Earth years at the establishment meant Pikkatin had no qualms about leaving Olena to close up by herself. She is his most trustworthy member of staff and longest standing. Most staff cannot stomach the long hours and bad moods from Pikkatin but Olena, being determined and stubborn, is not willing to give up her role as portal protector for blood or money.

The main doorway connecting the two worlds via The Chequered Inn is an unassuming medieval looking wooden door with heavy set hinges and a huge circular black metal ring for a door handle. There's nothing flashy about it——no suction of any kind involved. It's as simple as stepping through the door much the same as walking into another room. Every species has an identifying code for their specific territory of The Magical realm———which they must adhere to. Any and all deviations into other territories without prior permission comes with harsh punishments——the worst to date being that of an offender having their skin turned inside out.

---

Hands full of magical rubbish contained within shiny pearlescent bags, Olena makes her way on through the only other doorway leading out onto a cobbled street inside the city of London.

The Chequered Inn sits right near the edge of the

hidden veil encircling England's capital city. To magical eyes the veil looks thin and fragile, almost like a faint piece of fabric shimmering in a light breeze. It is however incredibly strong and to date has never been breached.

The night air feels cooling on Olena's pale-skinned face. Looking around she takes in the usual streets, parks, houses and schools on her side of the veil. A mini world where magical folk, when granted permission of the highest magical counsel——*The Magi,* can decide to settle more permanently by purchasing property not too dissimilarly to how humans might make property investment decisions.

To the untrained eye all buildings set up into small pockets of towns and villages on Earth would look like any other human dwelling. Again, in this fact Magical folk are quite similar to Humanity. How they choose to live and build their societies——then again it was magic that showed humanity the way——so should leave no surprise here.

Magic real estate is big business and can set families up for life depending what the needs and desires are. Even so there is still a strict policy on exactly which species are allowed to move to Earth and is done on a case by case basis. Pockets of hidden communities reside all across Earth's surface on almost every continent. There is only so much of an allowance per species and their needs. Although Earth has days and nights and not one side predominantly in darkness the other in light——needs can be managed with specialist buildings and interior designs. Residents living Earth side must adhere to a set of rules but most importantly must look after one another be they dark or light side dwellers. Anyone unable to commit is extradited and punished.

---

### *A brief lesson in magical history:Part two*
Unknown to many humans——there is a famous ring of cemeteries encircling London called *The Magnificent Seven*. Humans who know their travel and tourism and are aware of these cemeteries have enjoyed many a tourist walk throughout the gardens enjoying the spectacular stone workmanship on a lot of the gravestones and statues. In reality the graveyards were erected to give yet further safe journey to a large portion of magical society - so communities may come and go with ease to other countries around Earth. As expected there is a veil hiding a portion of the cemeteries from the prying eyes of humans.

The cemetery names are as follow:
**Kensal Green – situated in Kensington and Chelsea**
**West Norwood – situated in Lambeth**
**High Gate – situated in Camden**
**Abney Park – situated in Hackney**
**Brompton – situated in Kensington and Chelsea**
**Nunhead – situated in Southwalk**
**Tower Hamlets – situated in Tower Hamlets**

Each cemetery has a statue where a famous magical person has been buried. These towering stone statues are the point of every entry and exit through each of the seven portals. Each portal takes travellers hundreds of thousands of miles across Earth to their country and magical community of choice within a matter of seconds.

The process for travel requires the intended traveller/s to head inside the chapel of chosen graveyard first. From here travellers receive a one-time passcode which is paid for in whichever currency is native to that particular species. The code once successfully received is handed to the ticket Master for either one-way travel or with a return. Then the guardians known as *The Grimms* escort travellers to the portal statue of choice. The code is administered and off they pop. As usual there are specialised veils in place to ensure human interaction never occurs——if that were to ever occur the unfortunate human person/s involved would be immediately blinked out of existence - with young children being the exception, because of course children can have *very* vivid imaginations.

Although air travel exists for magical communities Globustatic piloted flights are becoming steadily fewer and farther between given humanity's growing air defence systems and technology. Rumour has it this type of travel may be done away with completely on safety grounds. There is already much speculation and chatter about *'UAP's and Aliens'* coming out of America. Had their suspicions and wild claims of knowing all about aliens not been so dangerous——they'd be hilarious.

### *Back to the story...*

Using an enchantment on the weighty rubbish bags. Olena watches them float up to her shoulder height before hovering along the cobble stones towards the bin. Olena flips open the lid of one of the large indigo coloured waste disposal bins. As expected with this being a magically enchanted bin——inside is a swirling black hole that sucks any and all rubbish into itself jettisoning it who knows where.

Instructing the rubbish to throw itself into the black hole, once away and out of sight Olena shuts the lid of the bin. Magical waste disposed of Olena rubs her hands on her apron cursing at the realisation she has Fae-shine dust on her fingertips.

*"Oh noooo, it will take days for the staining to go away. Yuck! I hate those Fae from the light side of the world."* Olena exclaims in frustration.

Feeling the tiniest pings of goodness emitted from the dust makes Olena's skin crawl and her budding fangs buzz. Vampires don't do sickly sweet anything!

A sound to her right makes Olena's head snap at unnatural speed to see where the sound has come from. Her pulse quickens as there should be no one in the vicinity of The Chequered Inn courtyard this close to The Magical veil at such a late hour.

Horrified, Olena can see and smell a human man illuminated by streetlight. This man has somehow managed to create a visible hole to appear, breaking open the veil giving him full view of her world from his.

Baring her fangs and hissing at the man——who

upon seeing and hearing Olena, yelps clearly startled——before jumping back. He disappears from view and when he does the hole seems to close.

"Sugarfrost knicker pants!" Olena exclaims knowing that had her parents heard her use such foul language, she'd have been thrashed to within an inch of her life.

Wasting no time, she bolts back inside the Inn grabbing hold of the manual kept underneath the bar for all types of emergencies. Flicking through the pages her hand stops during the speed reading when she comes across very clear instructions for this very emergency. The large fluorescent purple button encased in enchanted glass must be broken should there be any sign of someone human breaching the veiled wall. Slamming the book shut kicking up a cloud of dust, Olena wastes no time heading toward the large round button mounted on the wall. It is situated between two ornately designed glass liquor cabinets that would have members of any respectable steam punk faction positively drooling.

Encircling the fluorescent purple button - rimmed with chrome metal are the words: DO NOT BREAK UNLESS THE WORLD IS IN PERIL.

Trusting her gut and the instructions of the emergency manual (that's about as old as Earth itself) Olena braces herself for what she is about to do.

Feeling there is precious little time to waste Olena ——fist formed, forces her hand at rapid Vampire speed ——smashing through the outer layer emergency glass, to push the big round fluorescent purple button.

Instantly there is a shockwave throwing her backwards. She hits the far stone brick wall behind her——hard, knocking the very wind from her slower inflating vampiric lungs. As a half dead being she doesn't require such a frequent uptake of air inside her body that most creatures and humans do. Think of Vampires more like whales that take a big in breath before diving deep for some considerable time before feeling the need to come up for air.

Magical folk residing on Earth, feel the tremble inside their residences——prompting them to grab for their fragile table-wear and children. Humans however are none the wiser——as everything that happens this side of the veil, stays this side of the veil. Unless of course unscrupulous humans start poking holes in said veil.

Dust has fallen from the rafters coating Olena and Inn's surfaces. Dazed, it takes a moment for Olena's fuzzy vision to begin clearing——her ears still ringing. As she becomes more coherent a loud scream emanates from her ruby red Vampire lips as she comes face to face with a large purple faced species she has never seen before.

*AHHHHHHHHHHHHHHHHHHHHHHHHHHHHHHHHH!*

# Chapter 3

Olena's almost dead heart starts beating at the rapid pace of 45bpm which would feel to a Vampire the equivalent to a human heart beating at 200bpm. The effect is dizzying and quite disorienting. Annoyed with herself for behaving like a scared, sugar coated rabbit, Olena pulls herself up to standing brushing off the residual dust.

"I take it there is a large emergency at play?" The big purple creature asks, arms folded across his broad and bare muscular chest. Yellow eyes blaze scrutinising Olena should she have awoken the genie for the wrong sort of emergency——he would have been more than a little displeased.

"Err, yes...The man!" Olena blurts out grinding her tiny fangs together at how unravelled she feels she has become.

"The *man?*" The purple creature echoes back——a

most perplexed expression spreading across his broad purple features.

"Yes! Yes! A man, human man! The one putting holes in the veil!" Olena exclaims to a pitch that is almost as shrill as her Vampire squeal she omitted upon seeing said man.

A hearty laugh escapes from the creature's mouth making the walls and floor tremble. Olena takes note that the weird beast has some sort of smoke tail in place of legs and appears to be levitating above the floor of the Inn.

"Stop playing child and put me back in my——oh, that's right once released I can never return to my button... do you happen to have a genie lamp lying around?"

"Genie? You're a *genie?*" Olena casts her mind back to her school days when learning The History of Magic. Vaguely she remembers the lessons on genies and Djinn for both are closely related.

"Born and bre——well actually I was forged from the very fabric of a galaxy itself by The Magi." The genie admits proudly.

"So, can I wish the man away now?" Olena asks worried the man may have since stepped into their world while this conversation went on——her head would surely be on the chopping block should this be the case.

"Sure, one wish for one emergency." The genie states.

Drawing himself up to his full height the genie prepares by firing up his magic simply by clasping his huge clumpy hands together and rubbing them fiercely which created sparks and smoke to appear.

"Ok genie, then— I wish for you to make the human man by the veil disappear *forever*."

The genie claps his hands loudly, once again making the Inn shake releasing yet more dust atop of Olena and surrounding surfaces. She coughs and protests silent swear words under her breath at the state she will be in by the time she reaches home. Looking around she can now see the extent of mess left behind by the genie's release and continual antics that have the Inn shaking every five minutes.

"Tickle me turquoise! This is going to take me an *age* to clear up." Olena whines thankful again her parents were nowhere to hear such foul language.

"If there's nothing else then——oh Tizzwinkles!" The genie exclaims as he turns from purple to green then back to purple again.

"Oh...*Tizzwinkles*?" Olena parrots back having never heard such a phrase.

**BANG!!**

In spectacular fashion the genie explodes spraying Olena this time in sparkling purple genie goop as well as coating the walls, furniture and ceiling of the Inn. As she was already covered in dust——the mixture of sparkling genie goop has created hardened globules that appear impossible to pick off.

"Rude much! I didn't even get his name or any further instructions to whether or not the wish has even worked!" Olena exclaims to herself crossly while trying in vain to pick at the sticky mixture affixed to her uniform and body.

Rolling her eyes realising there is no way she can clear this up herself, leaves a short message for Pikkatin and the morning staff explaining the big emergency and that she ran out of time to clear up the mess. She also requests Pikkatin dock her wages if he wishes to do so and to put her on washing up duty for a month.

Checking outside to make sure the man is indeed gone which he is. Olena breathing a sigh of relief turns to head on back inside the Inn when a voice startles her from behind.

"Hey there." The voice says.

"*AHH!*" Olena shrieks which actually omits a sound akin to that of an Earth bat——resulting in the outer windows to the Inn cracking. The man covering his ears, cowers at the sound.

"Sorry I didn't mean to startle you there." The man says stepping closer to Olena having recovered from the sudden earache. "Woah! Can I just say that you are *gorgeous!*" The soon to be dead man continues on, getting dangerously close to a seething Olena.

"And you're *food*." Olena announces lunging forward——baby fangs bared, about to make the bite when all of a sudden, she stops.

It appears as if Olena has entered suspended animation. She cannot move—— anything apart from her eyes. Frozen in this awkward motioning statuesque pose.

The man's face wide eyed and horrified is paused in a jumping back freeze frame, hands coming up to his face.

*Like that would've saved you.* Olena thinks bitterly, wondering if she hasn't now been frozen in time for all eternity as some weird punishment for screwing up magical lore on such a gigantic scale.

The now catastrophic mistake she appears to have made all the more apparent with the man she'd wished out of existence——still very much still in the land of the living. No, something most certainly has not quite gone to plan. If anything, she was sure of it was her studies of genies certainly never covered them spontaneously exploding. Something very wrong has occurred indeed ——she feels it in her Vampire gut.

"Olena Lupescu! You have committed a crime most heinous and as a result of this must now be punished ——*severely.*" A big booming voice coming from seemingly nowhere states.

'*Oh yes here we go! The blame game! The punishment! Like I'm soooo sorry for attempting to save our precious magical realm. How stupidly empathetic of me.*' Olena thinks sarcastically knowing full well she has little to no empathy expressed outside of her own kind's existence.

"A vulgar attitude is no way to present yourself with while in the presence of greatness." The voice says making Olena realise whatever owns this voice——can also read her mind.

"Hey! Haven't you ever heard of a thing called *privacy?*" Olena thinks smartly.

"We have indeed——considering we are the ones who made up all of the rules to your world." The voice says smugly back at her.

"Save Satan! You're...The Magi!" Dread surfaces as it starts to fill Olena once she realises just how much trouble she will be in once her parents hear of her rudeness to their very creators.

"You have only recently gained your fangs young Vampire——which should make this next part of this *procedure*——less painful."

"What...? Wait! A procedure? Don't I have to agree to any such thing? Why do I not get a hearing? Am I not worthy of a trial? A jury? – hello?!!" Panic laces Olena's voice as she is still yet unable to move.

The Magi pop her back into full animation mode so that Olena now finds herself standing toe to toe with a cloaked figure whose face remains hidden.

"Hi...err...didn't you refer to there being more than one of you?" Olena says thankful to have use of her voice back.

"We are a collective contained within one vessel." The cloaked entity states. It is now Olena can decipher different voices all speaking at once.

"Oh...so what is my punishment to be?" Olena asks knowing that if a Vampire could sweat that she'd be totally saturated by now.

"You are to be de-fanged and turned human." The Magi entity states very matter of factly.

Olena blanches an even paler shade if that were Vampirely possible especially given her already alabaster white complexion.

"Wait! What happens to *this* guy? He's the real culprit. Don't you know *he* has the means to break holes in our precious veil?!" Olena says her voice laced beyond the tones of panic as she points to the rogue figure still frozen in time.

"This...*human*." The Magi start——vulgarity all but clear in their collective tone of voices. "May hold the *key* to your retribution. When you cast the emergency wish, the man in question had already stepped into your world. The man blinked out of existence was an Innocent bystander. The law of the cosmos believes in order, and thus due to the chaos of the Innocent man's eradication means the timeline has been skewed." The Magi explain.

"Ok, but it was one stinking human! I could have snacked on them and it wouldn't have made the blindest bit of a difference!" Olena argues, uncaring and unable to hold her tongue having heard the sentence about to be passed onto her.

"It was not written through time that you would have ever *snacked* on this particular human."

"Then it must have been written in time that I'd make *this* mistake."

"ENOUGH! The Magi cannot be responsible for every error of every being all of the time. You have done wrong so now wrong must be done to you. Olena Lupescu you are hereby sentenced to live out a life as a human being for the remainder of your days. You may never return to——

"Hang on a minute! What about my retribution?" Olena asks her frantic tone all too apparent as fear and Vampire adrenaline rush through her system at full whack.

"Ah, yes the *clause* that will enable you the chance to

set things right. Very well——should you choose to accept the quest set before you. You shall undertake twenty-one deadly trials in seven different locations around Earth. Remember you will be in a more fragile state of a human body so without any powers of persuasion or strength. The chance of success will be…slim at best." The Magi warn as they play with a small flame they conjured into existence as if bored of the conversation.

"Sign me up. I'll do whatever it takes! What do I have to lose——other than my soon to be short ruddy human existence!" Olena huffs angrily, running her tongue over her soon to be gone fangs. For all their nuisance she cannot believe that now her fangs have finally come in they will soon be gone. Feeling perhaps a little suicidal and knowing she won't cope as a human being Olena has no second thought on what she must do.

"If you're wondering why the human received no punishment, his *accidental* possession of an ancient enchanted artefact——in this incidence a ring, falls purely on a cosmic departmental error. The Ring of Harmony somehow made its way into a human antique shop. The man in question was looking for a priceless antique, the Powers That Be have him down on their books to being an intrepid explorer on the hunt for treasures and ancient artefacts——such as the ring he discovered. When the gentleman spotted the artefact——like a moth to a flame he made an impulse buy. How could he not? It's imbibed with angelic magics of the highest order. The Magic of these rings should never be underestimated. The antique dealer and shop have since been *dealt* with. How this man came to be aware of the veil ——well, *the Ring of Harmony* enables its wearer—— normally a maintenance angel, the power to seek out any hidden veil. The ring's purpose is to help make tracking the veils and all vibrational points easier. It appears no contingency plans were ever put in place to prevent anyone human ever using the ring. It was a scenario none of us could have foreseen or foretold. Maintenance Angels are the invisible beings working night and day to keep vibrations at peak performance——thus keeping us all safe." The Magi explain uncomfortably which does nothing to quell Olena's growing ire at how unfair the situation all seems.

*'Stupid angels, stupid humans! Damn them all to Hades! Why is this happening to me? Why do I have to be the fall Vampire?!'* Olena thinks silently to herself. If The Magi heard her thoughts they make no such indication this time.

"What's this quest then? Might as well know what I'm signing up to before putting myself forward for potential death. I don't want to live as a human anyway so it makes no difference should I survive or die." Olena says brusquely still wrestling with the rage boiling within her——knowing should she insult The Magi further ——they may well vaporise her here and now and that is a fate she is not ready to accept. If she is to die she wishes it to be on her terms.

"Your quest to save the entire Vampire race and yourself, requires you to travel to seven different dimensions——

"WHAT?!! You never mentioned about my very *race* being dragged into the faux pas!" Olena pants with effort as she shouts her disdain. Her semi-dead heart rate thunders away at 50bpm which feels to her the equivalent of a thoroughbred horse running a race at flat out gallop speed.

*'Mum...dad...my grandparents...my friends! Oh, if only I'd spent more time speaking with mum and dad today——why did I behave so dismissively toward them and now...now I may never get to see them ever again!'* Olena's heart begins to break as the information sinks in that as of now her race are, for now, no more. This make succeeding in this quest a priority——it's now no longer her own neck on the line.

"Until the reset has been initialised which will only occur upon completion of all the trials——then all Vampires shall remain erased out of existence. It falls to you Olena Lupescu to bring back The Seven Daggers of the Djinn. Once you have them in your possession, you will return here to this very spot. From here we shall journey forth to the *Forever Enchanted Wishing Well* where we The Magi will set you back in time to *before* you made the wish. This is something to have never been bestowed on anyone ever——so the honour is a big one and should not be dismissed so easily. The Powers That Be have a strict no changing of timeline policy. When we heard the request to offer such a quest had been passed down to our department for you, you can imagine our shock and surprise. So you see, Olena luck really has shone upon you this day."

*'Yeah! Really flipping lucky. Orphaned, de-fanged... alone.'* Olena thinks again as pangs of self-pity rip through her very being creating a nauseating feeling that Vampires despise. Uncontrollable weakness of emotion is not in their nature to portray.

"Not being funny here but can't you do that anyway ——whizz me back in time?" Olena asks, earning her a flash of hidden glinting eyes set deep within the cloaked figures hooded face.

"Do you accept the conditions of the challenge set before you or not? If you could hurry it up, we're all rather peckish and there's a nice nebula on the menu." The Magi say pressing Olena to make up her mind.

"Seeing as I have *no* say in the matter then fine——I accept."

A swift sound like an elastic band can be heard rippling through the air as Olena screams. White searing pain flits through her mouth and very skull causing her to see stars. Her superior strong fangs have gone from her mouth——replaced by much weaker human enamelled ones. The red hue of her mother's eyes disappears—— replaced with piercing green ones. Her previous ivory skin tone flushes full of peach and pink tones. The stark raven hair that matched that of her mother has become a fiery blaze of copper curls. Across her nose are cute specks of freckles that look like a light cocoa dusting. Lips stretch and pucker becoming plump with rosy red hues.

In the body department Olena's breasts form fuller and rounder, straining the buttons of her work shirt. Her waist pinches inward as her hips pop out. Gasping she blushes for the first time as her bottom fills out stretching the very fabric of her trousers.

Internal organs begin to shift and change, her heart rate picks up rapidly as breath comes in short sharp gasps.

Transformation over with The Magi entity hold up a conjured-up mirror for her to see herself for the very first time. Olena cannot believe how different she now looks compared to the painted portraits she's seen herself in throughout her home. Also, it is a strange feeling not just seeing a stranger but one who now has a reflection.

"What have you done to me?" Olena asks through panicked breath. Her voice appears to now be just as alien as the rest of her.

"We took the liberty of modelling you to a very popular doll among human children——it's called '*Miss Ireland*' oh and your voice, that's Irish too. It matches the pitch and tone of the talking doll's perfectly."

Olena discovers words have finally failed her.

"Next part of the process, here sign this, it's your binding contract about the seven daggers quest. We'd usually have this signed in blood but seeing as our department upstairs made a bit of an error regarding the gentleman, we agreed no further pain should be administered ——Here's a...*pen*."

Signing her life away Olena then waits for further instruction.

"How do I contact you if I need help or advice?" Olena asks suddenly wondering if she hasn't been duped by The Magi, after all she's seen no physical evidence her people have been erased.

"You can't. Here is your skeleton key code——this will enable your safe passage anywhere from the seven cemeteries but be warned, convincing the chapel and The Grimm of your purpose could be a tad tricky. We've given you both——

"Woah! Woah! Woah! You're not teaming me up with this loser are ya?" Olena exclaims in her strong southern Irish lilt.

"As we were saying, you've both been gifted temporary tattoos that will last just seven months giving you ample time to locate all seven daggers. No guarantees this tattoo idea will all work out as we've never had to do this sort of magic before. If all goes to plan everyone magical will sense both your human-ness but also that you carry the mark of The Magi——therefore must not come to any harm, but as we stress no guarantees. Good luck, toddle-pip."

With a resounding snap! The Magi vanish.

The man previously held in suspended animation falls backward onto his bottom making an audible *ooof!* sound. Alarmed at seeing a completely different woman standing next to him whereas milliseconds before there had been a beautiful gothic goddess. He garbles out incoherent nonsense until managing to compose himself.

"What just happened? Where am I——huh! My ring...it's gone?!" The man exclaims feeling his pockets but coming up empty.

Olena simply groans while rolling her eyes asking that the power of Hades give her strength.

# Chapter 4

Feeling he ought to man up here, Nathan steps toward the curvaceous auburn beauty——sporting he notes——all the right curves, in all the right *places*.

Thrusting a hand forward Nathan stands for a solid minute before realising this woman was leaving him hanging. The look of utter disgust across her features making him feel——*unclean*.

"Err, this is all a bit awkward isn't it. The name's Jones, Nathan Jones." He says offering at the very least his name hoping for any kind of response——positive or otherwise.

"Olena——but you may call me Miss Lupescu." Olena says keeping formality well in place while in the presence of mere food.

"Nice to meet you——

"Young man, finish that sentence and I promise you will live to regret it." Olena says threateningly while imagining ripping the man's very tongue from his mouth before shoving it somewhere sun doth not shine. The Irish accent rolling around uncomfortably in her new human mouth.

"You, sound Irish? I'm guessing...*southern?*"

The words are enough to make Olena see red. Stepping forward forgetting herself and how much weaker she is now. Olena storms right up to Nathan's face before putting a hand around his throat——and squeezing.

What follows is a swift reaction from Nathan that sees Olena apprehended with her arms pinned behind her back, her chest being pressed down onto the damp and unforgiving solid cobbled stones of the street.

"Ah! Get off me you imbecile!" She spits at him, wanting nothing more than to strip him of his manhood right here and now.

"The lassie has fangs." Nathan jests in mock Irish accent. "Now if I let you up are you gonna play nice or do I need to make a citizen's arrest?"

A blubbering, whimpering sound emanates from Olena's newly formed human mouth. Which gets louder and louder and *louder*. Soon her entire body shakes as wave after wave of intense emotions hit her all at once.

*Ah nuts! Trust me to discover myself with someone in need of the looney bin.* Nathan exclaims under his breath before hoisting Olena on her feet.

"Ok baby cakes, let's go." Nathan says whisking Olena up and over his shoulder fireman style——where the buttons on her already strained work shirt and trousers pop right off. Her breasts barely holding together in ivory lace bra also burst forth as the golden clasp at the front can bear the weight no longer.

Olena's bottom bobs up and down to the rhythm of Nathan's stride while her boobs jiggle about covered loosely by the remains of her now buttonless shirt. Utter embarrassment and mortification make Olena wish she were indeed *all* dead in this very moment.

"I...just...don't know what has come over *MEEEEEEEEEEEE!*" Olena wails her dignity now in shreds as she feels quite terrified at how out of control her new body feels with these extreme emotions flooding her frail human system.

———

Nathan realises they are in an area of London he has absolutely no memory of journeying to.

*Those drugs whatever they were must have been strong. This woman will pay for her drug addict behaviours and for losing me a small fortune in that antique ring——but first...to discover more about Miss Lupescu and where she really hails from. Who knows perhaps I'll get a small reward from the police for apprehending such a renegade. I can picture it now——local hero Nathan Jones catches notorious drug dealer——*

"Please, can you put me down. My body is rather achy from this position." A snivelling Olena requests as her rib cage is really starting to smart from the pressure of Nathan's hefty shoulder bones.

The sun is just beginning its rise as Nathan plonks

Olena down to stand on her own two feet. Here a little colour catches in his cheeks to notice how he'd missed how semi-naked Olena now appears to have become. Rapidly he takes off his jacket and carefully so as to not startle her——places it around her shoulders. A warm sensation spreads throughout Olena's body as she wonders if this is not also some sort of magical garment Nathan has acquired——as it has a most pleasing effect on her body and mind bringing a comforting warmth and pleasant scent that has her head all but spinning.

"Here, take a hanky will ya and sort your nose!" Nathan instructs brusquely quite sure this woman is on drugs and whatever drugs they are responsible for making him first hallucinate a most bizarre experience where he had magical powers after discovering some hidden veil and meeting a gothic goddess that clearly never existed.

"Where will I go? What will I do? My whole family is *gone!*" The wailing begins again and as nearby houses start switching lights on, Nathan thinks it wise to remove Olena from the immediate area.

"Are you telling me you honestly have nowhere to go?" Nathan asks unsure of Olena and if this isn't some elaborate ploy for him to take her home and then have the house ransacked while he's murdered in his sleep by some unscrupulous drug gang.

Olena shakes her head in confirmation. Looking down mortification runs through her at finding her bra well and truly nowhere to be seen leaving her alabaster breasts with perfect tiny pink nipples poking through the thin fabric of her wide open shirt as Nathan's jacket slips from her shoulders. The bra had been a gift—— specially woven by the dark side enchanted seamstress ladies. They live above their clothing boutique situated close to a courtyard where the pear fountain is situated. Enchanted creatures and species travel from across both sides of The Magical world to have these women make or repair garments. Even royalty frequent their boutique, it really is rather special and Olena holds many a fond memory of her mother taking her here to have dresses and underwear fitted. Sadness fills her now at the memory and knowing as of now her family and everyone in her community have been erased due to the stupid wishing mistake. It was common sense of course for her to have checked first which man she was erasing out of existence——perhaps her fang irritation made her head less organised then usual leading to the catastrophic error——of which she knew Nathan was not at fault for.

"There's a hostel about half a mile down that road over there, if you keep heading straight you'll find it ok?" Nathan instructs Olena not waiting around for a reply still feeling thoroughly spooked by recent events. Turning he starts to head away from a dishevelled, snivelling Olena just as a fresh rain begins to fall.

Numb from everything, Olena on shaky legs starts carelessly to put one foot in front of the other and is not but a few paces from Nathan before tripping and falling ——banging and skinning her fragile hands and knees which sees her howling with pain this time instead of wailing.

*"Owwwwwwwww! Ahhhhhhhh! Owwwwwwwww! Why does this hurt so much?"* Totally fed up Olena sits up onto the pavement edge as the rain falls harder completely drenching her. Shivering she hugs her knees close to her chest to hide her face. Salty tears make her snatch her head away however as they sting the now broken and tender flesh of her knees. Nathan's shadow looms close-by making her snap her head up to once again hiss at him.

Reminded of the raven-haired beauty that had done the same thing, Nathan checks himself——reminding his brain that she hadn't been real just some weird hallucination from the effects of whatever drug this Irish curvaceous cutie had consumed——whose residue must have come into contact with him. After all with his background in the military before becoming a civilian antique treasure hunter——magic was something for children. Nope Mr Jones was a start believer in physics and that everything *paranormal* was just a bunch of gobble-dee-gook!

"You're in a right mess aren't ya?" Nathan states helping Olena onto her feet.

"Wait...Your accent...it...it's like *mine?*" Olena says unsure if Nathan is just poking fun of her newly acquainted voice and accent.

"Looks like the ruse is up, ah——what the heck, a London accent is hard to carry over twenty-four hours. Yes, I'm from Ireland——southern and you?" Nathan asks curious now about the woman in front of him, sharing quite a big thing in common with himself.

*What are the odds that I'd bump into a lassie with Irish accent right here in London——why is such a beauty on such powerful narcotics?* Nathan muses.

"Yes, same." Olena answers wondering what the hell she's admitting to here having never been anywhere outside of The Magical realm's side of London's veil.

Olena weeps more as dread and fear riddle her newly acquired body. She feels so unprepared to face the quest in front of her and if she fails Vampires would never be known of——ever again! Also, how the heck was she meant explain anything to a human man with such a closed mind?

"You can stay at my place until we can find you somewhere——better suited for you." Nathan offers, knowing having Olena with him will ease at least his conscience.

An itching and burning sensation on Nathan's forearms that has slowly been getting steadily worse momentarily grabs his attention away from Olena.

"Woah! What is *that?!* When did I——get a tattoo?! Did you *TATTOO* me?" Nathan exclaims in angry shock at having been inked without consent.

"You wouldn't believe me even if I told you! You think I haven't heard your silent dig about how I'm a *crazy person*? How I must be off my head on drugs?" Olena spits out just in time before her stomach growls loudly, sending her head swimming, promptly causing her to fall to the ground——out cold.

## Chapter 5

"Mr Jones! Mr Jones! The young lady is rousing!" A loud brash woman's voice shouts close-by, causing Olena to wince.

"Oh good." Olena makes out the familiar sound of Nathan Jones' voice swiftly following.

"Ahh! Ahh! Will you *STOP THAT*?!" A sleepy Olena protests at having been patted vigorously on the sides of her face.

"Cancel the doctor Rosa——it seems our *guest* is going to be just fine." Nathan instructs as his house keeper turns to hurry off.

"How do you feel now?" Nathan asks as a groggy Olena sits up on what she now sees is a plush dark green chaise. A small fire has been lit bringing much needed warmth to her previously frozen and damp body.

"Mmmm, my head hurts and my——tummy." She exclaims clutching her stomach as it growls in protest again causing a lot of pain.

"You must be hungry. Rosa checked your blood sugars from my army med kit and they were awfully low ——here eat this and then you can have a *proper* meal." Nathan says handing Olena a chocolate bar.

Hissing she scoots back and away from the offending item.

"Are you *insane!* I can't eat *that!* I'll die!"

"Why because you're a——*Vampire.* You were mumbling about nothing else while you slept." Nathan quips annoying Olena further by making childish fang gestures with his index fingers while creeping around the chaise making exclamations of *'I vant to drink yur blurd'* in a faux Romanian accent.

This brings Olena fully back to the present immediately installing a huge disliking for this Mr Jones idiot before her. As realisation dawns however that what has happened is not just some awful nightmare, her parents and people were still gone——depression starts to seep in.

Carefully Olena breaks open the purple shiny wrapper and sniffs.

*"Mmmmm...this smells...surprisingly——*

"Yummy?" Nathan rushes in with before she has chance to decide.

"Well I won't know until I've tried it but sure, I'd go with——*yummy.*" Olena says while first sniffing before licking the chocolate bar. A pleasurable sensation rushes throughout her entire body giving her a strange feeling as the previous wave of depression seems to lift slightly.

Hesitant, she bites carefully into the rich velvety

chocolate bar and as it melts in her mouth before sliding down her throat, her expressions and moans of pleasurable euphoria all but set Nathan's nether regions ablaze. It is quite possibly the hottest display of erotica over chocolate he's ever witnessed.

"Oh my *BLACK GODDESS, that is sooooooo good!*" As Olena very much approves of chocolate——Nathan finds himself blushing beetroot with an uncomfortable bulge at the front of his trousers at how incredibly sexy Olena looks with colour flooding her pale complexion. The pinkness of her cheeks makes the emerald of her eyes stand out more as perfect auburn curls frame that gorgeous almost doll like face of her.

Looking down Nathan can barely contain himself as he had forgotten beneath his brown leather jacket Olena remained still semi-naked.

Licking every last morsel from her fingertips, as the chocolate had slightly melted in her much warmer human hands——Olena is spellbound and suddenly very keen to taste yet more human food.

*Humans may not be magic in the way I understand magic to work——but gosh if food can have such a powerful effect on such a frail body——I wonder do different foods elicit different emotions? Perhaps I can use food to my advantage much the same as witches may use potions.* Olena ponders still in mild post chocolate heavenly buzz.

"Do *all* foods taste this good?" Olena asks which has Nathan truly wondering what on Earth is wrong with the Irish babe in front of him.

*Feeling he's having a Henry Higgins out of body experience when the on-screen character deals with one Eliza Doolittle in the famous story My Fair Lady.* Nathan thinks amused to himself *'Trust me to get lumped with an Eliza Doolittle of the twenty first century. She's not staying Nathan, Rosa will find her a nice safe house that will take her in and some doctors to tend to all of her amnesia needs. She may well be a missing person——must get Fritz into looking at her background. Everyone leaves a fingerprint somewhere online.'*

"Well...you see it very much depends on an individual's palette. Take me for example I love sweet and savoury equally but someone else——my sister Felicity——

"Oh, you have a *sister?*"

"Indeed I do, however you shan't be seeing her I'm afraid. She is currently off gallivanting with her job——travelling the best hotels and locations money can buy purely for the purpose of reviewing these places. Felicity is a creature of comfort and only the best will do for her ——I suppose that's why they hired her, if anything were wrong with a hotel or holiday home my sister would find it."

"I see." Olena says feeling wounded again to be reminded all her family for the foreseeable future no longer exist.

"And yourself——do you have any siblings? Family?"

A look tells Nathan that the subject of family has struck a painful chord within Olena's eyes and so decides to change tack by getting back onto the subject at hand ——food.

"Don't feel obliged to answer that question——so food...yes. Well like I was saying it's all about trial and error really. You appear to have a touch of amnesia so I'll get Rosa to whip up some basic yet very tasty meals and we'll go from there——sound good?" Nathan asks happy to note his suggestion has at least turned Olena's frown upside down.

Holding out a hand Nathan helps Olena off the chaise, zipping up his coat that she still wears so as to keep her dignity intact and to save both of them any further embarrassment at how exposed she has become.

"Ah-Rosa, there you are. Please show Miss Lupescu——

"It's alright, you may call me Olena."

"Very well Olena it is. Please show Olena to Felicity's bedroom, she may pick and choose any of the outfits in there. Perhaps you could give her a little guidance?" Nathan suggests as Rosa gives him a total look of dumbfound.

"Certainly sir, come along miss——sorry, *Olena.*" Rosa says not waiting around for Olena o follow her before heading on toward the grand staircase of the house.

Olena notes while following Rosa just how massive Nathan and Felicity's house is. There are family portraits all over the place and framed photographs. Whoever these people are she thinks, they certainly are wealthy.

"Ok Olena, I'll leave you to get started. Should you

have any trouble finding what you need press this button here and I'll be right along." Rosa instructs Olena pointing to her service bell button close to the inside of Felicity's bedroom door.

"Oh...but I thought——

"What's the matter? Can you not dress yourself? Come along now, get started on finding something suitable to wear I have several other jobs to attend to."

With that Rosa leave Olena to her own devices while going to prepare the guest bedrooms for Nathan's guests arriving later this evening.

Taking in the room around her Olena notes what a stark difference Felicity's bedroom is to her own. It's all pale pinks, lilacs and fluffy pillows, whereas Olena's bedroom back home is every bit Vampire gothic as one human goth fan might expect it to be included with glass coffin bed, designed with stained glass roses all over it.

"Black...please tell me you at least wear black clothing from time to time." Olena says aloud to herself before getting stuck into Felicity's walk-in wardrobe and chests of drawers.

---

"Shouldn't you go and check on her?" Nathan asks Rosa who is adamant that Olena clearly needed no help dressing herself having had no call on the servant's bell.

The white wooden glass panelled doorway to the big Victorian styled kitchen opens as in glides Olena.

Nathan and Rosa's mouths all but hang open.

"Oh my...I think I'll get some tea on——would you like to take it in the conservatory?" Rosa says rushing over to where the kettle resides.

"Yes...tea...sounds like a very good idea." Nathan responds unable to take his eyes away from Olena.

She is wearing one of Felicity's Halloween gothic Vampire queen costume dresses. Its stretchy and as Felicity is more of a curvaceous character herself has helped ensure that her clothes fit Olena's new human form with ease. She has styled her hair up much the same as she would have back at home——only with the hair being a lot bouncier it was a tad trickier to insert the red jewel encrusted hair comb of choice now holding Olena's hair into her customary ornate up-do. The make-up however was the piéce de résistance. The striking black eye-liner and dark teal eyeshadow make Olena's emerald eyes positively pop! Along with her rich ruby red lips.

"Woah! You look——

"Tea won't be long Senor Jones, please make yourselves comfortable in the conservatory and I shan't be long in bringing it to you." Rosa interrupts in her rich Hispanic accent. Olena glancing at the auspicious housekeeper takes in her petit yet well rounded figure. In a bizarre way she almost reminded her of a female version of Pikkatin——only far less grumpy, hairy and ginger.

Rosa wishing for a moment's peace as her nerves now feel well and truly jangled busies herself setting up the tray ready to carry their afternoon tea through.

"Be sure to plate some for yourself Rosa, I would like nothing better than to have you join us for afternoon tea.

You have after all been rushed off your feet getting the house and rooms ready for my guests arriving this evening." Nathan instructs and Rosa knows it is almost an order not a request.

If she were to deny him the mini tea date with Olena he would only send her home early and that would be worse seeing as she had this evening's meal plans all laid out ready for the chefs this evening. Rosa would be overseeing the serving staff once the menu instructions were passed onto tonight's chef.

"I'm sorry if my appearance is rather striking——I appreciate for humans——I mean for non-goth people that the dress code and make-up I associate with can come across quite strong and...out of place?" Olena says with the last word coming out more of a question then a statement.

"No, no. You must dress how you feel is right for you. You'll find *no* judgement here——isn't that right Rosa?" Nathan asks just as Rosa splutters on the sip of cool water she has taken in.

"No——none whatsoever. Why do you think it was easy to find...such an ensemble in the first place? Mistress Felicity also like to...dress up from time to time." With that Rosa went back to busying herself with tea for now the three of them.

"You really do have a beautiful home, why the kitchen alone is exquisite." Olena notes as Nathan threads an arm through hers hoping he's not over stepping a boundary while trying to play the role of chivalrous gentleman. To his relief Olena graciously accepts his arm.

Olena is enjoying how familiar the kitchen feels with its Victorian vibes throughout. She perhaps likes a lot less the floor to ceiling windows bringing with them great beams of sunlight now that the rain has passed and sky has cleared.

As they approach the first link of sun beams hitting all manner of bright white kitchen surfaces and flooring ——Olena has a sudden feeling of dread, quite petrified that she may burst into flame as sunlight was a very alien concept to a Vampire who'd spent their entire existence in darkness.

Sensing the pause and apprehension with Olena Nathan unlinks their arms opting instead to hold hands as he gently brings her onward to walk quite safely through the rays of sunshine filtering in through the tall Victorian styled windows.

"See, no bursting into flames——proof you're not a Vampire." Nathan says hoping this evidence will help Olena realise any notion of her being a Vampire—— quite possibly brought on by having had a bad trip on whatever narcotic she had ingested, is complete and utter rubbish. She is in fact *human.*

Deciding her best ploy could be to play along with Nathan to being a dumb auburn-haired Irish woman with amnesia——Olena simply smiles and nods in agreement with him as they head on toward the core story situated toward the end of the kitchen.

"Do you know something, I think I'm starting to feel much better! Oh yes, of course I can only have ever been human. Gah! Whatever happened to me to make my head go all fuzzy with my memory goodness knows. I'm so sorry to have been such a bother." Olena says as she is lead to a comfortable padded white wicker chair. The conservatory is alive with sunlight and the warming sensation on her skin surprises her to feeling really rather pleasant.

"So do you feel you're getting some of your memories back now?" Nathan asks relief washing across his sapphire blue eyes and strong set jawline. "Is it possible Olena that you've been assaulted or attacked in any way? Had your drink spiked or drugged some other way? Whatever has happened to you to put you in this state it's nothing to feel ashamed or embarrassed about——so please if you remember anything of this nature you must tell me right away so that we can report it to the authorities." Nathan states as he takes a seat opposite Olena.

"No, no, honestly I'm fine. I do not believe my unbecoming behaviour is anything of such a sordid nature. Knowing how clumsy I can be——for all I know I might have fallen and banged my head." She says trying to get off the subject knowing full well that if Nathan Jones is anything like her father——once he starts investigating something he will not let it go until all of the truth is revealed. "I'm just so relieved at how you——my knight in shining armour came to my rescue. Ah, here is Rosa now with tea." Olena says expertly diverting attention away from the subject at hand.

"I doubt it was a fall for it were then how to you

explain my own succumbing to the effects of whatever it was you'd ingested." Nathan responds clearly as Olena feared an investigatory character just like her father.

"You raise a good point. I'll be sure to let you know if further memories surface."

"Please do." Nathan says as he helps Rosa set the tray for afternoon tea down.

## Chapter 6

"That was a most refreshing cup of tea Senor Jones——

"Rosa! Have I and Felicity not told you often enough to address us by our first names?"

"I know but——it's not natural for me, my culture, you know we learn the respect very young. It would not feel right for me to call you by your first name." Rosa explains having had this conversation quite a few times with Nathan and his sister.

"Very well...right I guess I should freshen up myself." Nathan exclaims standing to stretch his legs.

"And I too should start to get things prepared in the kitchen ready for Monsieur Pierre's arrival and that of his staff." Rosa says clearing away the tray of left-over cakes, sandwiches, empty china cups and tea set before exiting the conservatory.

"Would you mind if I sit a while longer in here——

my legs still feel a little wobbly from my earlier faint." Olena states while still getting used to the annoying Irish lilt now gracing her voice-box.

*If The Magi wanted to motivate me to hurry up with this sodding dagger retrieval quest——they sure picked a good way to do it!* She thinks bitterly.

"Certainly, take as long as you need. When you're done please wait for me in the lounge——Rosa will show you where to go if need be."

"That's alright, I remember the way back from here." Olena says faking a smile until Nathan has left.

The remains of the day's sunlight feel pleasant on Olena's skin. The rays gently touching her forearms and face feel to her very much like a soothing healing balm. Deciding here that she rather likes chocolate, afternoon tea and sunshine——ponders that perhaps her time as a human being may not be always so dreadful after all.

———

Nathan and Felicity had inherited their London family mansion five years ago when their parents passed away. It had been a tragic safari incident that saw both parties repatriated in pieces inside a closed coffin. The last memory Nathan has, is of his mum and dad cheerfully waving to him and Felicity at their driveway gates before getting into their taxi——heading off towards Gatwick airport. After the incident neither sibling was ever quite the same. Nathan spends his time in meaningless relationships while chasing after treasures around the world. Felicity keeps busy with her job ready to travel to various locations at a moment's notice. Being a top placement reviewer of some of the world's most luxurious hotels and villas keeps her diary full from January through December. The siblings have become like ships passing in the night, where previously they had been very close——even sharing the same circle of friends. All of which disintegrated after their parents' deaths. The friends became distant and with the siblings' erratic behaviours wanting to be on the move all the time it left little time for coffee dates or drinks down at a local pub.

---

Ascending the staircase to his bedroom, his feet silent on the plush carpet that match the house drapes——Nathan prepares to freshen up. He can already hear the crunch of tyres in the driveway as his expected guests. Rosa heels can be heard hurrying on toward the front doorway ready to receive them——having already greeted and set up Monsieur Pierre in the kitchen along with his sous chefs. The chef's detectable hum that he emits while preparing cooking between giving his sous chefs orders can be heard faintly echoing down the corridor. Thoughts of Olena's beauty start to plague Nathan's mind so decides on a cold shower.

---

Olena, fully sated from her rest in the conservatory decides once the sun has moved round to venture out in search of the comforting lounge Nathan had instructed her to wait inside for him.

Once safely in the lounge it is here Olena takes in more of what the room actually looks like. It's more library than lounge with wall to wall tall standing bookcases. The types that have ladders on wheels to get you from one side to the other. It pleases her that upon closer inspection she spots first editions of fairy tale classics. The furniture is all dark mahogany browns mixed with leather greens. The rich colours of fabric used for the chaise and a couple of armchairs situated close to a lit fireplace all but beckon to her achy joints. The transformation seems to have given her mild aches and pains all over. Feeling a wave of fatigue Olena sets herself up on one of the soft dark purple armchairs clasping the human classic version of Beauty and The Beast. She is not long into the story before sleep encapsulates her.

---

Showered and donning a pair of dark blue denim jeans and crisp white shirt open at the collar; as Nathan makes his way downstairs already he can hear his guests babbling away in the dining room. Before reaching the lower steps Nathan sends a fast message to his tech guy Fritz to begin a background check on one Olena Lupescu residing here in London but to also check Southern

Ireland for a trace on her. Without going into details Nathan requests his friend Fritz (who moonlights on *people finding* when not chained to his desk at the police station) to check on the national Irish database for any and all information he can discover on her.

In typical Fritz fashion he tries immediately with a flurry of texts back to try and plug Nathan for more details already knowing it is a vain attempt for Nathan is a staunchly private person. Once an agreement for payment is drawn up and Nathan has sent the funds across with the mere press of a button on his phone——does Fritz give the thumbs up confirming everything's in place to commence with the investigation. Nathan has also sent a photo of a sleeping Olena across to him as a starting reference point.

The loss of the ring Nathan had acquired from the local antiques store still smarted. He knew even before the valuation that he'd struck gold when he came across the glitzy looking ring inside of its glass casing——labelled *Pocket Universe*. In his very bones the familiar buzz of huge success on the horizon zipped through him the moment he clapped eyes on the jewelled beauty. Nathan could barely believe his luck when he noticed that the doddery old male shop owner had the ring priced at a measly twenty-five pounds. Nathan got the impression that business was slow——having seen all the dust covering most of the glass cabinets and shelves. The shop keeper had seemed nonplussed when Nathan popped into the shop ready to part ways with his twenty-five pounds. The man mumbled something incoherent about *magical charms* before ringing him up and sending him on his way. Nathan may have lost that ring but had made a mental note to return at a later date to the same shop, for any other secret goodies it may be ready to offer up to him.

———

Entering the lounge in search of Olena before going to greet his friends——Nathan smiles upon noticing the Irish sleeping beauty sitting in his father's purple armchair. The pair of chairs had been gifted to his parents before he or his sister were even born. His mum always had the left chair, his dad the right. He'd never sat in either chair since their passing but to see Olena this strange woman (possible drug addict), now peaceful in the land of slumber——does not surprisingly fill him with ire. Instead his heart just melts at her beauty and how in sleep she looks so innocent.

Nathan's phone vibrates on silent jolting him back to the present——looking down he can see that its Fritz already with an update undoubtedly.

*'The dude works fast. I'll give him that.'* Nathan says under his breath trying to muster up the energy to be around some of his closest friends this evening.

"Mr Jones, I have to say——whoever this mysterious young woman you have the pleasure to be in the presence of——well..." Fritz voice trails off and his face turns pensive on the video call before continuing on but looking unsure of how to deliver the next piece of information he has to tell Nathan "There is simply no online fingerprint of her——*anywhere.*"

"Really? Are you sure? Might she be in witness protection?" Nathan asks offering up possibilities as the news she has no online presence *anywhere* has him rock back on his heels.

Everyone, the world and his mother, has some sort of online fingerprint——somewhere.

"I asked my mate in the police force's tech department to run a search, and this Olena most definitely is *not* on any such database or programme. There is also something else."

"Ok, let's hear it." Nathan says, sighing——an unease threading through his body as all he can consider now is – *trafficked female.*

"I ran the photo you had taken of her through the most sophisticated AI face finding, biometric software and, it's not just here in England where there is no record of her but...the entire world! She isn't registered as being born, having a family, going to school...there's no dental records, no GP listing...it's as if she's literally appeared out of thin air. Even top-notch military guys have a faint fingerprint somewhere——but not this lassie." As Fritz speaks, the creepy feeling Nathan has——grows in intensity.

"Say for *argument's* sake, if a traveller——from another dimension were to suddenly appear, would this be what you'd expect to find?" Nathan asks trying to keep an air of humour to his voice so that Fritz doesn't take him seriously.

"Mr Jones I never knew you to be such a comedian. To answer your hypothesis, yes, this woman——should she be some sort of portal traveller, well then *not* being able to find anything on her anywhere would be a perfect example of someone who just popped into our world from——*somewhere else*." Fritz concurs in his rich Indian voice.

"I see...thank you for clearing that up."

"Take care Mr Jones, that woman...whoever she is, must be pretty powerful to be so well hidden. Perhaps it might be time to...send her on her *way*? Whatever organisation she could potentially belong to, may come looking for her and they seem to be good at, either making people vanish or disappear completely."

"Duly noted. Thanks Fritz——consider her gone come the morning." As Nathan speaks the white lie he wants to assure Fritz that this is case closed and nothing anymore to do with him. Whether or not Fritz will keep digging after this is another matter entirely——he can only pray his trusted friend does no such foolish thing.

"Take care, send my love to Felicity. I must go I'm about to start the night shift."

"Tough break, and thanks man for having my back. Hey listen, let's meet for a few beers when you're next available." Nathan says wanting to keep close tabs on Fritz now an unexpected hiccup had appeared in his grand plan to find out exactly who Miss Lupescu was.

"Sure thing Mr Jones. You take care now and thanks for the bonus." Fritz says in appreciation of the extra funds Nathan had sent across.

"Think nothing of it——say hi to Selene and the kids from me, see ya soon bro take care."

The call ends leaving Nathan with a creepy feeling in place of his earlier awe as he now looks down upon a sleeping Olena with a different set of eyes.

## Chapter 7

Olena awakens with someone rapidly tapping her on her upper chest and collar bone region. Using her lightning reflexes that her Vampire muscle memory still vaguely remembers. She clasps the person's wrist while still keeping her eyes closed.

"Sorry to startle you awake Miss Lupescu. Senor Jones has requested your presence in the dining room. Would you mind...giving me back my hand please...miss?"

"Oh I am terribly sorry Rosa. I've always been a bit jumpy in my sleep. Sorry——the dining room you say? Where might that be?" Olena asks still feeling the effects of a heavy sleep enveloping her.

"That's quite alright Miss Lupescu. Also, Monsieur Piérre this evening's chef would like to know if you have any special dietary requirements?" Rosa asks having already overheard Olena exclaiming that she had forgotten or didn't know much of anything about human food.

"Oh...I don't know. Erm...anything meaty and bloody should do me just fine." Olena says standing up to head toward the doorway of the lounge.

*"Anything meaty and bloody."* Rosa repeats back to herself unsure of how to deliver such a request to one of London's finest chefs.

"So...the dining room, I'm taking it if I follow down the hallway toward where what sounds to be jovial conversation going on I should find Nathan and what sounds like friends——yes?" Olena asks to where Rosa simply nods furiously.

Olena strides on out of the lounge and it is only when Rosa sees her head on toward the dining room that she lets out the big gulp of air she had previously been holding in.

Walking towards the kitchen Rosa keeps repeating 'Meaty and bloody, meaty and...bloody' as if almost to be in some sort of shocked daze, quite unbelieving of the instructions she is to pass along to Monsieur Piérre.

———

"A-ha! There she is, the sleeping beauty I was telling you about. Fellas meet Miss Saoirse O'Shea." Nathan says heading on over to Olena, gently placing an arm around her shoulders before she can protest at being called the wrong name.

*'Clearly something undercover is going with you and*

*seeing as Olena Lupescu doesn't sound even the slightest bit Irish——best to keep my friends none the wiser, wouldn't you agree.'*

'Mmm hmm' Olena nods in agreement before beaming a big smile at the room of handsome men now undressing her with their human male eyes.

"Twit-twoo bro! Where did you find this...gothic queen?" Jamie says unsure of how to quite describe Olena in all the gothic finery she chose out of Felicity's wardrobe.

"It's a pleasure to meet your acquaintance Saoirse." An older looking man of the group says——as the men all stand ready to greet her properly.

"Saoirse, please meet my closest friends from my time serving in the military. Their names are Frank, Donnie, Jamie and Pete." Nathan says introducing the men who are more like brothers to him then friends.

"It's so lovely to meet you all. I admit to not having known Nathan all that long but...well...better acquainted now I have to say I've been very much looking forward to meeting you all." The lie trips out of Olena's mouth so convincingly that it makes Nathan's head spin.

"The pleasure is all ours." The male pointed out as being called Jamie says.

Olena notes Jamie to having a tamed wiry mop of red hair atop his head——making his piercing blue eyes stand out.

*Note to self: be wary of this one, he seems to be a bit of a Jack the lad'*

Pete she can see has close cropped black hair, intense

green eyes flecked with golden hues. Frank the older gentleman has what Olena would class as dark tree-bark brown coloured hair and pale grey eyes—— wolf like and quite similar to those of her father. The thought depresses her slightly. Donnie has white blonde hair shaved at the sides with bright blue-green eyes. All of the men are well built as in muscular which does not displease Olena. Why if she were her full-bodied Vampire self any one of these men——Nathan included would make for a fine sanguination pet.

*Perhaps I will make pets out of you all once I am back to my normal Vampire self.*

Nathan pulls a chair out for Olena to sit on between himself and Frank.

"Thank you." She says acknowledging the chivalrous gesture from Nathan whose cheeks merely pink up in appreciation.

"Tell me, what do you all of you *do* then? Are you still soldiers fighting in wars or...do you follow other interests now?" Olena asks using her trained set of dinner table conversation topics that she had learned back in high school. If a Vampire were to woo their prey then first they must befriend them.

"Frank would you like to do the honours?" Nathan asks holding out a hand to his long-time friend and old boss who'd guided them all safely while on the battlefield during tours overseas.

"Certainly——

"Excuse me but I *believe* zis yung laydee haz poot een a request for sumsing———how did Rosa put it———ah yes

——meaty and bloody? Is zees right?" A het up Piérre asks while looking daggers at Olena.

The guys wait a moment before Jamie cannot help but let out a big hearty laugh soon followed by the others.

"I cannot verk een zees condeetions! I shall take my leeve of you awl——immediately."

Piérre storms out of the dining room swearing a ton of expletives in French before gathering up his tools from the kitchen——yelling to his sous chefs and having them all march right out of the kitchen back doorway.

"I am so sorry Senor Jones. Let me see if I can remedy this situation. I saw he already had some steaks and vegetables prepared——

"Say no more Rosa. You go and put your feet up back at home. The lads and I can take it from here. Olena would a bloody steak suffice?" As Nathan asks the question of Olena yet more raucous laughter erupts from the men as they head off towards the kitchen.

"Oh yes please——and the bloodier the better." Olena says winking at Nathan as saliva pools inside her mouth.

Rosa utters a lot of 'oh my gods' in Spanish before gathering her coat and umbrella in distressed fashion ——heading off out toward her little fiat sitting in the grand driveway.

"Oh dear I do hope your housekeeper will be ok?" Olena asks playing the part of polite human woman well (she hopes).

"Yeah, Rosa is just extremely passionate about doing

a good job. She'll worry I've fired her until I reassure her ten thousand times on her next shift here that her job is one hundred percent secure. Right, best go and oversee to the operation *cook grand meal*——any preference for wine? White? Red?"

"Err——red." Olena stutters thinking she may as well stick to blood coloured drinks as well as food. Although her basic knowledge of human etiquette touched on conversation etc the art of human food and drink was lost on many a vamp for obvious reasons.

"Are you sure? You seem unsure——I can grab ya a Guinness if you'd like." Nathan asks again in that rich dulcet toned Irish voice of his that makes Olena feel all warm and peculiar inside.

"No, no——red will do me *just* fine." Olena confirms placing one of the cloth napkins onto her lap.

"Very well, shan't be long with the food."

Having some quiet reflection time to herself. Olena reminds herself to return back to the subject of what these men do for a living. Seeing as they are to be staying the night given that she noticed Rosa making up a few bedrooms at the mansion——Olena appreciated with this predicament she found herself in that she would have to think of many things to discuss to try and keep attention and conversation away from herself——putting all emphasis onto them.

## Chapter 8

Once inside the kitchen Nathan can see that Frank already has a well running cooking operation at hand. Jamie and Donnie are finishing off preparing the vegetables. Pete is dicing potato slices ready for homemade deep fat fried chips and Frank is getting the steaks lined up to know in order whose he's cooking as they all have specific preferences for how they like their steaks cooked.

"Ah——Nathan it looks as if the chef has left the pudding instructions to your left. It all looks pretty straight forward——think you can manage it?" Franks asks waiting on the guys to finish preparing the veggies and chips.

"Sure thing boss." Nathan says giving Frank a mock salute before pouring each of them a large glass of red.

"I'll be right back——Olena has requested a red." Nathan says thinking nothing of his faux pas while pouring her glass.

"Olena? I thought her name was———

"Oops! the last woman I hooked up with———*her* name was Olena. God, I hope I don't accidentally call Saoirse that———she may well have my head on a platter." Nathan jests before half bolting back out of the kitchen to catch his breath before heading on back to the dining room.

———

The evening's meal goes off without a hitch and with no further mention of Olena's true name spilling out of Nathan's mouth even after rather a lot of wine.

Olena has been absorbing a ton of information on the men she's fast become accustomed to. It appears that these men seem to be a lot more pliable under the influence of wine. She has learned that Frank makes fake legitimate identities for high profile clients as well as aiding in the retrieval of hostages using his expert negation sills. Pete, runs his own security firm fitting and managing household and business alarm systems up and down the country. Jamie and Donnie work as a dynamic duo being doormen for elitist nightclubs and also hired muscle when need of their brute force strength as required———for a very weighty price naturally.

"Well gentlemen I feel for me it is time to call last orders. I'm awfully tired———perhaps it's my time of the month." Olena admonishes without a second thought, only appreciating that women have periods———not that it's something not to be highlighted as regarded by many women to be a very private matter.

"I'll walk you up." Nathan says once the guys have all said a fond goodnight to Olena.

The pair walk in silence until they reach the outside of Felicity's bedroom door.

"Tonight has been a lot of fun——thanks for...you know including me." Olena says blushing from the wine and having Nathan's muscular body so close to hers.

"You looked truly stunning this evening. Once I became de-sensitised to your gothic way of dressing. Please, feel free to stay as long as you wish——you're no prisoner here. If I can help in any way to get you back on your feet you need only ask." Nathan says leaning dangerously close to Olena's mouth he fears he may kiss her and that really wouldn't be appropriate.

"Thank you——well...goodnight then."

"Goodnight cutie." Nathan answers already heading on back down towards the staircase.

Stepping inside Felicity's bedroom and shutting the door, relief washes over her to have managed to keep all focus onto the men and off herself. Sure there were the occasional probing questions——but Olena made sure to follow Nathan's lead with regard to how she answered. Her biggest problem now was how in Hades was she to tell Nathan the truth of her identity so he would believe her before getting him to the first of the seven cemetery portals. She'd go herself but The Magi were very clear with their instructions. It was to be the both of them involved in retrieving the seven daggers. Olena fears going against the rules would mean any gain became forfeited ——and as her entire race now depended on her to get this right she feels she must follow the rules to the letter.

Stripping down and putting on a pair of dark lilac pyjamas which were the darkest colour she could find among the throng of fluffy and threadbare pale pastel toned bedtime attire. Olena lies down on the large four poster bed set up in cream duvet set with roses all over ——willing herself to experience her first full night's sleep in her new human body.

---

The following morning Olena is busying herself with what to wear today. unsure if anything of Nathan's sister will continue to even fit her. Pleasantly she is surprised to discover a selection of tops, trousers, skirts and dresses ——although marginally a little big, do feel comfortable.

*Thank the lord of darkness this woman has curves!* Olena thinks quite jovially, still adjusting to the flighty up and down emotions running hot and cold throughout her new body.

Having chosen the dress to wear today——a figure hugging little black number with pale grey and lilac flowers across it. Her hair loose around her shoulders, make-up more modestly done with less eye-liner and more mascara with a dark purple lipstick and eyeshadow to match.

The thing that does bother Olena is the fact her breath has a faint putrid tang to it and she has no idea how to rectify this situation. She had looked inside the en-suite bathroom but found no amenities, no toothbrush or special paste she knew humans used in their daily cleansing rituals that she had learned in classes on *how to take care of your pet human*.

Hearing voices pottering about downstairs and with her tummy rumbling Olena takes in a few steadying breaths. The fast heart rate pumping away inside of her chest feels at times quite alarming especially when mixed with the sensation of flutter flies——flitting about inside of her stomach.

Bracing herself to put on a persona once again of *ordinary* human woman. Olena grasps the round brass door knob of Felicity's bedroom door and with an only slightly trembling hand——turns it.

———

After a moment of wrestling with the door knob Olena realises it must be stuck. Panicking she turns it one way then the other, all the while adrenaline shoots her heart rate through the roof, ensuring her breath catches in her throat in rasping gulps.

———

Nathan exits his room and upon coming across Felicity's bedroom can hear a very flustered and panicking Olena.

"Oh sh—hang on! Step away from the door."

Nathan exclaims rapidly reaching for his set of keys to unlock the bedroom door.

With a click the door unlocks and bursts open to where Olena throws herself at Nathan, crying and in a very distressed state.

"I...I...I couldn't open the door. Then I panicked and the—-you came to my *rescuuuuue!*" Olena bursts into tears as relief washes over her.

The earlier make-up now running fast down her fact giving her the impression of some sort of weird gothic sad clown.

"I'm so sorry, it was totally my fault. I thought it might be safer locking you inside and——

"Woah! Wait a minute. Did you just say you *locked* me inside? Like some sort of caged animal?! How bloody DARE y——

"That dress! Why are you wearing that dress? That's the dress Felicity wore to our parents' funerals! Take it off immediately!" Nathan says sounding both alarmed and outraged.

"Oh no you don't! Do not think deflecting to my innocent wardrobe malfunction gets you off the hook taking all attention off the fact you *locked me in that room!*"

"Is everything alright? I heard raised voices, thought it best to come and check it out." A yawning Jamie exclaims now wishing he needn't have bothered as whatever was going on between Nathan and Saoirse was clearly none of his business.

"Its fine." Nathan starts to explain.

"Oh it most certainly is not fine!" Olena hisses at Nathan.

"I think I'll just——go get some coffee." Jamie says wanting nothing more than to be far away from the ensuing conversation——very far away.

"Look I'm sorry I locked you in. I'd hoped to be awake before you——given what went on yesterday, I figured you may need some rest. I promise not to do it again but please——won't you change out of that dress." Nathan says feeling the sting of a hangover being the only thing from keeping him continuing the argument with Olena.

"Fine, whatever I'm over it." Exasperated Olena steps back inside Felicity's bedroom partially slamming the door——wishing nothing more than to shred the blasted garment into pieces.

## Chapter 9

Changed into a plain emerald green long sleeved fitted top and pair of jeans with pair of black socks and leather ankle boots on, her hair and make-up also reset——Olena heads on down the stairs in search of hopefully something to eat.

Thoughts of her mum and dad clutch at her new beating heart and an alien feeling threatening to overwhelm her as before has Olena catch her breath before making it down the last few steps.

"I'm sorry for...yelling." Nathan says stepping out from behind one of the large stone flower urns sitting atop of stone pedestal in the hallway.

"You scared me!" Olena exclaims holding a hand to her chest. A little freaked out at the weird jerky movement her body did along with the sudden rush of adrenaline.

"Look, you're clearly going through *something* and me yelling at you like a petulant child was wrong——you weren't to know of the dress and its *significance*——I'm really truly sorry." Nathan says apologising again.

Olena feels that familiar warmth returning to spread throughout her body again while being in close proximity to Nathan. She rather enjoys this mysterious magic he wields over her. Whatever it is its helping to relax her ——growing in intensity the closer he reaches inside of her personal space.

"Apology accepted, now if you don't mind I'm really rather hungry." Olena says placing a hand to her stomach as it growls just audibly enough for Nathan to catch the sound.

Nathan smiles——feeling relieved to have cleared the air. As something about Olena has been plaguing his with all manner of *naughty* thoughts. If he were to have any chance to bed this young woman then he needs make sure she keeps a good opinion of him.

Women may have gone before but——Olena wields ——a different kind of illustrious power over him. Most women he's ever dated soon catch on that he is quite the wealthy eligible bachelor. Over the years it's become almost impossible for him to know which women were being sincere and which ones only wanted him to make them look good for their social media profile, and be spoilt with luxurious lunches and trips away. After having his heart broken for the last time two years ago ——Nathan decided to keep things simple in future relations with women, choosing a strictly *no strings attached* policy.

Offering up his arm to where Olena obliges him by

slipping her smaller one through. The connection of their bodies under a calmer setting makes Olena's heart rate pick up again bringing with it this time a feeling of immense heat that seems to bloom from her southern parts right the way up to her face.

*Oh my!* Olena thinks as her usually much duller Vampire sex drive seems to be revved to running hundreds of times faster and more intensely.

*I can certainly see now why humans appear to breed like rabbits.* Olena thinks wanting nothing more than to break contact with Nathan but finding herself unable to draw herself away. It is as if he is like an addictive drug to her system. The more contact she has with him the longer she wishes it to go on for. When contact ceases a feeling of emptiness seems to follow.

When Nathan swaps out their linked arms to instead hold hands, Olena feels all sorts of fiery feelings about her nether regions. Her footing falters ever so slightly as her knees turn to jelly. Nathan places a steadying hand upon her shoulder making her feel even hotter.

"Okay?" Nathan asks removing his steadying hand once sure she has regained her composure.

*Gulp!*

"Mm-hmm, guess I must be a lot hungrier then I realised." Olena says as they head on to the kitchen.

———

Vampires are, as a matter of course, not massive romantics. It's not in their bloodthirsty nature. Sexual intercourse for Vampires is simply a necessary act carried out once coupled and only for those wishing to try to conceive a natural Vampling of their own. Fertility rates among Vampires to conceive and spawn naturally are low due to the complexities involved in a Vampire's genetic makeup. Many Vampire couples without success of conception will opt for the age old——bite, drain, turn, kill option. Unless of course they wish to check out the fresh markets of newly turned Vampires where they can pick and choose which ones they wish to adopt into the fold of their nests. There are never any guarantees a turning will be successful——but the rates of a turning becoming a realty are far higher than that of natural Vampire conception. This is perhaps why Manix and Valeria have always been a bit overprotective of Olena. They know how lucky they have been to have one of their own——especially given that Manix is not a pure-bred Vampire making Olena's existence even more of a rare event. There isn't a vamp or soul alive today from the dark side of their world who doesn't know of Olena's existence——except perhaps only now that she and her race have been what one hopes to be a temporary poofing out of existence.

---

As Olena and Nathan enter the kitchen——Donnie jumps up to pull a chair out for Olena. He and Frank are presently sitting around the large white painted wooden table with matching chairs. Olena can see that a place setting is already laid out for her. Having her thought of in this way elicits an odd fuzzy feeling to leak from her heart centre making her all but want to burst into tears.

"Good morning Miss O'Shea." Frank says leading with pleasantries.

*Oh yeah, my fake name...is nothing about me...me anymore?* Olena thinks morbidly as tears prickle the sides of her eyes, threatening to spill over any minute.

"Good morning. So...what's for breakfast today—— I'm famished." Olena says carefully placing her napkin upon her lap.

"You may notice we are shy two of our comrades. They have gone out to hunt for sustenance." Pete exclaims looking up from his newspaper while taking a long sip of strong coffee.

"Damn! I love a good hunt. Do you think I'd still have time to catch them up?" Olena says standing with force enough to knock her chair over——having also slammed her fist down upon the table in vehement disappointment——a wild look to her emerald green eyes.

The men share strained glances among themselves as Nathan can only rub a hand over his face in embarrassment at how bizarre Olena is behaving.

*"They meant as in Jamie and Donnie have gone to the local bakery to grab some bacon rolls."* Nathan says leaning down to whisper into Olean's ear while pouring her a cup of coffee from the cafetière.

"Pah! You should have seen your faces! Sorry I couldn't resist playing the part of the *crazy lady* again."

Olena jests hoping the ruse is enough to take the unease presently coating the air out of it. "I'm guessing your friends must be out at some shop or bakery?" Olena says sipping the strong bitter tasting liquid in her mug——swiftly spitting it out lightly spraying Pete's held up newspaper which fortunately shields him getting the coffee spray full in the face. Shakily Olena places the mug back onto its coaster creating almost yet further spilling of the bitter liquid as her trembling hands can't seem to quiet themselves.

Pete takes his now coffee sprayed newspaper over to a portion of the sideboard bathed in sunlight to speedily dry it off. Re-taking his seat up at the table——raises his mug to Nathan out of eyeshot of Olena while he mouths *what the fuck dude!* To which Nathan simply shrugs mouthing back *sorry.*

"Indeed they have. Now, Nathan what is on the agenda this morning? Are we to meet in your office to discuss...business?" Frank asks giving Olena the firm impression she isn't invited.

"That can wait——the piece I was actually looking into appears to have disappeared. One minute I had my purchase the next when looking inside the little jewellery box——nada." Nathan explains feigning regret and upset.

"Guess you win some and you lose some. Maybe we can visit that antiques dealer to see if he harbours any other *rare* gems." Pete says winking to Olena as he does so.

"So if this is a social visit——might we make use of

the facilities?" Frank asks.

"If that is your subtle way of asking me can you use the games room and gym then yes——please feel free." Nathan offers bringing a wave of relaxation into the kitchen that Olena senses, as Frank and Pete's shoulders have both subsequently dropped.

Olena may have lost her Vampire magic but her powers of observation in reading body language which she'd accumulated while out hunting human prey with her parents, appear to be just as strong as they'd always been. For Olena the hunt was more about a field trip learning experience——because until she inherited her fully fledged fangs, any idea of hunting by herself was impossible. It'd be like a lion cub trying to take down an antelope all by its lonesome.

"While we wait for the lads to return, would you like a tour of the grounds?" Nathan asks wanting nothing more than to be alone with Olena.

Frank and Pete share an unreadable expression here before Pete coughs while standing, folding his now dry coffee stained newspaper before heading out of the kitchen followed closely behind by Frank.

Olena beaming with delight at Nathan's request takes hold of his hand pleased that the warm melty feeling returns——tenfold. A smile creeps across her lips as fire gleams from her emerald eyes. Combined with rouge pinking up her cheeks, Nathan finds himself positively spellbound by her beauty.

"We'll be back soon, feel free like I said to use the

games room or gym." Nathan calls down the corridor to Frank and Pete to where they call back a faint *affirmative*.

## Chapter 10

The sun is shining brightly this morning with a cool bite on the air. Nathan and Olena are taking a stroll around the walled garden of the mansion. Birds sing out their chorus and combined with the heady scent of many different fragrant flowers and shrubs——has a wonderful relaxing euphoric effect over Olena's entire being. All while worrisome thoughts plague her mind.

*Is Nathan her captor or is he a friend? Can he be trusted?* Olena's mind chews these thoughts over as Nathan walks beside her——both their feet making soft crunching sounds on the small white pebbled pathways.

"The grounds of your home are stunning. The way the sharply pruned rose bushes line up perfectly around the pebbled walkways is so satisfying to the eye. I especially love the garden's stone fountain designed with mermaids splashing and fooling about."

"I'm glad you like the garden. It was mum's pride

and joy. Here borrow this." Nathan says slipping his beige old-style bomber jacket around a shivering Olena's shoulders.

Nathan's scent is intoxicating for Olena. She wishes there were a way for her to drink him in. She imagined were she still her old self——that Nathan would taste smooth and spicy.

The pair of them come to stand closer by the fountain as Olena takes a seat on the edge next to a stone mermaid in frozen pose——brushing her hair with a shell comb. Memories and thoughts of her home world bleed into focus, causing Olena to take a sharp intake of breath so as to stave off any more tears.

"Warmer?" Nathan asks taking in more of the Irish beauty before him.

Sunlight bounces off Olena's fiery bronze hair bringing out an almost copper halo effect. In combination with her green emerald eyes glinting almost supernaturally——she totally mesmerises Nathan.

"Yeah——thanks. So...your house is pretty amazing and this garden also very enchanting but——

"It isn't home is it?" Nathan asks coming to crouch position in front of Olena.

She hugs the jacket closer as if to create a shield between them both. Olena is unaccustomed to having so much feeling all at once and is starting to feel completely overwhelmed and at times drained from them.

"I hate to ruin this morning's tour but now seems a good a time as any to come clean and if I'm to earn your trust I might as well let you in on a little secret. I had a friend do a thorough background check on you——only the funny thing is...it appears as if you don't actually exist ——*anywhere.*" Nathan says holding onto Olena's gaze unsure of what kind of response this unwelcome news will bring with it.

"You...have been *checking up on me?!* Who else knows about this? Please tell me no one knows? Dammit! I may have even less time than I thought to get to the cemetery." Olena reels off too late to realise her mistake.

"Just my man Fritz, but he won't tell a soul, after all how could he when he knows nothing about you—— wait did you say *cemetery?*"

"No, you can't deflect off my question. Who have you told about me? Is he truly trustworthy? I know how sneaky you humans can be——waft wealth in front of your noses and any ideologies of friendship go out the window!" Olena says teetering on the verge of hysteria as she stands to pace.

A darker rouge tint graces her peach complexion now as a fine sheen of perspiration breaks out across her brow.

"Olena will ya calm down!" Nathan says firmly placing two steadying hands either side of her shoulders to at least get her to stand still.

"I...I don't belong in this *body!* This *WORLD!* Can't you understand? Don't you see? I'm NOT *HUMAN*!" Wriggling free from Nathan's grasp Olena, shaking out of Nathan's jacket——sprints off across the grounds as fast as her human legs will carry her.

Heading back indoors knowing chasing Olena will only likely piss her off more. Nathan enters his secure office to check the CCTV monitors. Sure enough he picks Olena up pretty promptly sitting among two rose bushes in a shaded corner of the garden towards the back of the property. He also locates Frank and Pete playing a friendly game of pool while on a separate monitor sees Jamie and Donnie arrive back with their breakfast. Watching them park up before exiting——Nathan stands to make his way to Olena's known location within the grounds.

———

Opening the door that will lead him back out into the garden——before he can locate her, Nathan is pleased to see a tear stained Olena already standing awkwardly just outside on the stone steps——hugging herself. Nathan encourages her back inside, placing a reassuring arm around her as he does so.

"Come on, let's have breakfast——we can figure the rest out later, ok. I'm sorry, it was wrong of me to try to go poking around in your personal life." Nathan says to which Olena nods in response.

"No, I am the one who's sorry. I——lost my temper back there, my parents taught me better manners. It makes sense that you'd have wanted to check me out after all you know nothing about me barring my name and have invited me into your home. I'd have probably behaved in a similar fashion if I'm completely honest." Olena says so that Nathan need not feel bad about it anymore.

"Do you want to talk about any of your life?" Nathan asks as the pair stand awkwardly mere inches apart from one another in the downstairs hallways. Smells of bacon waft through causing Nathan's stomach to gently rumble.

"Well I lost my parents only recently you see——so things like their faces, the sounds of their voices——are all still so fresh in my mind." Olena admits while digging the nails of one of her hands into the palm, resenting this conversation entirely.

"Well——I'm sorry to say we have that in common as well as our Irish accents." Nathan says reflecting his own grief at the loss of both parents.

*'He is blind to the fact my parents' deaths have everything to do with him! ——I'd best stick to this narrative for if I let slip he is the very reason my parents and the rest of my people no longer exist——then Nathan may become a foe in place of friend. I can ill afford to lose him as an ally considering we are to work as a team to rectify this whole sordid mess.* Olena thinks in quiet contemplation while weighing up what truths to share and which to keep quiet over.

"Changing the subject *slightly*...I wonder——would you be up for having my private doctor check you out ——just to make sure you have no head injuries?" Olena is thankful for the change in subject but less so at the prospect of a *doctor's visit.* For back where she comes from doctors are always very much into pinching and poking.

"I——

*'Yes, go along with this. You're human now——a doctor will only confirm you are a picture of health. Play the part Olena.'*

"Sure, what could it hurt. Better to be safe than sorry I guess." Olena says giving her best friendliest fake smile.

Relief washes over Nathan's face as he once again draws Olena in close. Turning into him this time, the overwhelming sensations of lust burning inside of her ——Olena takes advantage to use this new human style of power and taking her chance reaches up to kiss Nathan.

He reciprocates the kiss immediately, deepening it ——revelling in her taste. When they pull apart panting Olena raises a hand to her mouth——mortified.

"Oh no, I'm so sorry my breath is foul this morning and I had no means to rectify the——

"I didn't notice if it were——you taste...exquisite." Nathan offers which has Olena's face turn a blazing shade of red. "If this does concern you however——head into my bedroom two doors down from Felicity's you'll find a spare toothbrush in my wash-bag in the bathroom cabinet."

"Thank...you, and also thank you for letting me kiss you. The warmth you bring me it...helps me to relax." Olena says almost clinically which makes Nathan consider this gorgeous female enigma before him with fresh curious eyes.

"Don't be long the bacon rolls are undoubtedly being kept warm in the oven for us. I'll meet you back in the kitchen when you're done——oh and Olena, we can do a lot more kissing if that's what you'd like to do——I know *I* certainly enjoyed it." Nathan says not giving her time to respond as she scarpers red faced out of the kitchen, down the hallway and up the stairs as fast as her little human legs will carry her.

## Chapter 11

*Damn you human body and damn you Magi! Just stay focused Olena, this man's only a human too——you can handle him just remember your training. Use him as the muscle for the job in hand then throw him to the wolves. Won't he get a shock when we travel to Kensal Greens portal doorway tomorrow. The only challenge remaining now——how to get him there and away from his annoying friends. As for the whole 'head doctor' idea——yuck! No thank you! Time to take back control of these humans and situation. Perhaps I'll discover the perfect plan once I've had breakfast. Yes, that's it, breakfast first——then the planning.* Olena thinks wickedly to herself finding strength in getting some of her Vampire funk back.

Bolstered by her inward pep talk, Olena smiles with ease as Nathan passes her the bacon roll she is to consume. Having never eaten one in her life she smells it tentatively as all of the men watch her——before she takes her first bite into the fresh crusty bread——containing crispy slivers of meat that have her audibly groaning such sounds that make all of the men look about awkwardly.

*Imbeciles! Look at them all drooling at me like a bunch of human adolescents! Hmm——perhaps this is a sort of human power I now wield——the art of seduction. If I could only get a grip on my own damned hormones I might actually be able to forge some sort of a plan. Then again bedding Nathan in this human physique could be ——fun. Seeing as just a mere holding of hands or touch from him sends my nether regions into meltdown and heart racing. Why, having sex as a human I'm betting must be a truly explosive experience and one I absolutely must sample before time gets reset. Oh look at me! I'm trying to gain control and already am imagining doing all manner of things with Mr Jones between the sheets—— gross! He's a human! What on Earth am I thinking! Just as well the timeline is set to get reset because I don't however think I could come back from the knowledge I'd coupled with potential food.* Olena thinks which kills the rest of her appetite.

*No——no sex of any sort unless absolutely necessary from a coercive point of view. If I'm to have Mr Jones eating out of the palm of my hand I'm going to have to throw all my efforts into wooing him first. I have until tomorrow to get us to the first sodding cemetery. Oh why did there have to be the added complication of 'friends' arriving to ruin everything.*

As Olena runs a plethora of possible scenarios as to how to get herself and Nathan through the first portal doorway——she catches Nathan's eye and using this to her advantage gives him her best '*come to bed*' expression —— hoping her new face is pulling it off. Going by Nathan's response giving her back a smouldering primal stare, she was confident the attempt had been successful.

## Chapter 12

Once breakfast had been concluded Olena excused herself to go and read in the room she had opted to refer to as lounge-library.

Upon trawling the book cases it took her a while but eventually Olena did find a copy of Bram Stoker's *Dracula*——sadly this was not a first edition but what seemed to be quite a modern version of the story. Inside was the inscription:

*To our darling Lissy, happy 16th birthday sweet girl. All our love mum and dad xx*

Nathan's sister is a fellow vamp enthusiast——will wonders never cease. That explains her gothic costume rail I discovered. It is a shame I can't meet this sister before Nathan and I must depart through the first portal.

Damn! How on Earth am I going to steer him to the damned cemetery. Perhaps I could set the scene for a romantic date——much as this would sicken me I fear it may be the only any to get the ball rolling. Time is ticking.

---

Nathan set the balls on the pool table as the men all prepare to partake in a friendly game.

"Come on man spill it. How did you and the pretty Irish princess meet?" Donnie asks while taking the first shot and pocketing a red.

"I...truth be told I'm not entirely sure." Nathan says rubbing chalk on his cue.

"Was it one of those glances across a dance-floor situations where you know before the night is out you're going to be bonking each other's brains out?" Jamie chips in taking the cue from Donnie who just missed his next shot.

Frank coughs reminding the men the crudeness and vulgarity are not tolerated while in his presence. Although none of them are on active duty anymore Frank believes in keeping standards as they've always been.

"No...it's a bit hard to explain really. We just sort of *found* one another——yesterday." As Nathan explains Pete splutters having breathed in some of his espresso.

"You mean——you bought a woman back to your place and you didn't——you know *do the deed?*" Jamie says a look of pure astonishment across his handsome face.

"When I happened across Ole——Miss O'Shea. She seemed to be in some sort of trouble——an inebriated state with some memory loss and ideas that she was a Vampire. I too then succumbed to some loss in time unaccounted for so whatever she had been subjected to seemed to be either airborne or passed via skin to skin contact."

"Was there anyone else around during this time that witnessed these events?" Frank asked his brow now furrowed with concern for his friend.

"No that's just it. I swear we were in one area of London first of which I cannot seem to remember——only that it wasn't far from this antiques shop of which the name I also cannot remember. Then we were somewhere else."

"Hmm——'tis a quandary my friend. So what do you think you'll do?" Donnie asks while rubbing chalk on his cue tip.

"I'm not sure——I've never come across a situation quite like this one." Nathan admits while taking his shot and pocketing a ball.

"Can you not contact that friend of yours——Fritz isn't it, and see what he can find out about her?" Frank suggests now sitting on one of the comfortable dark green armchairs.

"I did. He can find no trace of her anywhere on any database——and I don't mean just here in England but from across the world. Saoirse renders no visible digital fingerprint——anywhere, not even a birth certificate."

"Could she be a spook?" Pete asks.

"According to Fritz he went through all known police and military databases, even governmental ones——well perhaps those checks were done by friends he possibly has on the inside——I don't think Fritz has MI5 or 6 clearance."

"A quandary indeed. Nate, perhaps it may be better to let the lady be on her way. Whatever she is embroiled in——well it could get you in a lot of trouble brother." Jamie says a look of deep concern crossing his brow.

"*Relax* fellas. I am simply giving Saoirse refuge until she is back on her feet with some idea of where she will go next." Nathan says trying to play his friends concerns down but know all too well that now their interest is piqued this much neither of them will want to let the idea of investigating Olena's background go.

"I've never had a missing or captured person's case that I wasn't able to crack——why don't I look into your mystery woman?" Frank suggests and Nathan knowing even with or without his permission Frank will do what he pleases, simply agrees to allow him to go ahead knowing full well having given a false identity will render a fruitless search forthcoming.

———

Feeling bored Olena decides to go in search of Nathan and his pals.

Stepping into the large hallway Olena scents the smells of citrus. Walking ahead she spots Rosa with a spray can in her hand and yellow piece of cloth feverishly wiping at the large dining room wooden table.

"Oh Miss O'Shea——pleasure to see you again. Senor Jones is in the games room——you will find this upstairs straight down the corridor and it's the last room on the left." Rosa says not really paying attention to Olena while busying herself with the job in hand.

"Thank you Rosa——might I ask what that delectable stuff is that you are spraying onto the furniture?"

"Why, it is just simple polish. Oh——before you leave please ask Senor Jones what lunch requests he has. I have set out a menu for today but——sometimes he wants to do his own thing." Rosa says in her rich Hispanic accent as Olena nods in acknowledgement—— before heading off in search of Nathan.

## Chapter 13

Stepping inside the games room where Olena can see the men enjoying some sort of game involving sticks and balls not unlike a game played by many magical folk called *Hooley*. Olena gently coughs to alert them of her presence. When none of them move it is here she can see that they have all been frozen like statues.

*The Magi* Olena considers fearfully as indeed the floating apparition appears off to her side.

"Olena, deciding it would be better if you have extra pairs of hands to help you with your mission——the Powers That Be have graciously granted permission for these... *individuals* to join you on your quest. They are already in receipt of their tattoos which shall enable them to move freely with yourself through any of the seven cemetery portal doorways."

"No, this cannot be! How on Earth am I to convince a further four staunchly macho human gentlemen about any of this? I'm sure to end up in one of those places they put insane humans inside of here on Earth. Can I not have...*any* of my powers back——even if it's just the power to glamour these humans?" Olena pleads beginning to panic that having to convince Nathan appeared bad enough but *all* of them——surely an impossible feat for Olena in her much more fragile human form.

"Very well, as it was indeed departmental *Mis-hap* from our own department——we will grant you the power to glamour and as an added gesture of goodwill we will increase your strength to that of Amazonian warrior level. There's blame on both sides but it is *you* who made the wish." The Magi explain without a shred of sympathy to their tone.

"Ok, I agree to the new terms and conditions. Thanks for the help" Olena says appreciatively——relieved at the very least to being able to manipulate the men's minds into doing her bidding or accepting whatever she tells them to be true while also having some semblance of strength return.

"When you're ready we shall begin the procedure to giving you back the power to glamour and increasing your strength."

"Ok, I'm ready." Olena says almost immediately, more than ready to feel a bit more normal.

A sound like that of an elastic band is heard and in swift protest Olena moans as her body morphs into that of a much more muscular and svelte physique. Glancing in a wall mounted mirror across the room from where she stands——Olena can see she not only has the strength of an Amazonian warrior——but now also looks like one. The familiar buzz of her glamour capabilities returning——zings through her brain.

With no further words spoken between them The Magi simply vanish as the room becomes fully animated again.

Olena walks on over to the group of male friends. The men all smile upon realising her presence but their expressions soon turn from adoration to downright puzzlement.

Nathan's face whitens, as he remembers the feeling from before when he was frozen. The space in his mind that would make sense of this feeling draws a blank. The only way he would describe this feeling is as if it were his stomach were full of snakes.

## Chapter 14

Having all men in a room at once and in such close proximity to one another made Olena's glamouring much easier. Like the snake Kaa from the story *The Jungle Book* would hypnotise Mowgli ——Olena in similar fashion bent these men's minds to accept her version of events. She chose a simple route implanting the idea that Nathan and she were dating and that as a special surprise he was taking them all out to visit *The Magnificent Seven Cemeteries*. She also gave them the idea that as it was hers and Nathan's one year anniversary that is why they had all been invited round ——to celebrate. Taking any and all notions of any antique ring well and truly out of the equation.

Olena has to tread carefully here though as glamouring was not permanent and should any of her powers of persuasion begin to wear off——then she would need to re-glamour the men which meant watching them all with dragon eye precision.

The day was passing by rapidly. Olena knew that from tomorrow all she need do is get them cleared for travel at the Kensal Green cemetery chapel before they'd be well on their way to the first location where the start of the quest's challenges would begin——whatever they may be. In theory it all sounded simple enough but if life had taught Olena anything as of late——it was that life can become incredibly complicated very quickly.

———

"Man, I can't believe you guys will have been together an entire year as of tomorrow. Thanks again for inviting us to enjoy the day." Jamie says taking sip of his beer now that everyone is relaxing in the dining room ready for Rosa——also glamoured, to dish the supper of something Olena already forgot the name of.

"It's our pleasure, you guys——well you're like family to us. It wouldn't be right for us not to involve you in the celebration." Olena says expertly stroking the arm of Nathan's that she has hold of. He turns to look at her with such adoration and something else——something that has Olena's body burn for him.

Frank pours champagne flutes full of bubbly liquid supplied by Rosa. Handing them around he toasts the happy couple. Olena feels an unfamiliar pang of something. *What is it?* She wonders until to her very disgust she realises she's feeling *guilty!* The revulsion of this realisation to feeling bad proving all too much for her Olena rapidly excuses herself to fling herself inside the guest bathroom to where she promptly vomits up her champagne——and it burns.

"Olena isn't——you know...*expecting.*" Frank hints as the guys then all grin to one another.

"Oh my god a baby Jones! Can you imagine it?" Donnie says almost dreamily.

"I err...well I, I'm not sure. Let me go check on her." Nathan says feeling quite unperturbed that he cannot remember not just the last time he and Olena had sex but that they've *ever* had sex before. As these thoughts plague him, flashes begin to flit through his mind.

Broken memories, erased memories——false memories. In the blink of an eye everything comes back into pin point focus. He can even remember Olena doing something weird to them all like hypnosis. As he nears the bathroom hi blood is well beyond simmering.

Raising a hand to the bathroom door it is here that Nathan pauses. Could he perhaps use this situation to his advantage? Could he *play* Miss Lupescu at her own game. Get close and *personal* with her to gain insight and glimmers into the truth. Calming his breath and composing himself he stepped right on into the role of playing the doting boyfriend.

"My dear, are you ok? We're all so worried about you? Shall I call for the doctor? I'll call for the doctor. Ros——

"No need. I'm fine, perfectly fine." Olena says flinging open the bathroom door with a bit more force then intended and having forgotten her sudden injection of added strength almost pulled the whole thing off its hinges.

"Woah! Someone has been working out! Well if you're sure you're ok I'll leave you to finish freshening up and meet you back in the dining room——oh but first."

Nathan without thinking grasps Olena around the waist pulling her to him for a deep passionate kiss. The instantaneous taste of post vomit bile in Olena's mouth all but has his own stomach rolling but he knows he must carry it through to keep the ruse going.

"Wow! You taste so great. See you shortly sexy—— and it's an *early* bedtime tonight, if you catch my drift." Nathan says winking at her, waiting until she's back inside the bathroom door closed before turning down the hallway to throw up himself in one of the large flower urns.

*"Yuck! Gross! Eurgh I'm gonna need therapy after that!"* Nathan exclaims to himself before fast marching back to the dining room to grab the bottle of champagne from the ice bucket and down a few large glugs as his friends can only stare in bewildered amusement.

"So...are we throwing a baby shower or what?" Pete asks apprehensively.

"She's not got a bun in the oven just yet." Nathan says "but who knows maybe someday we'll hear the pitter patter of little feet."

A small crash grabs everyone's attention as Olena trips over the base of an indoor flower pot upon hearing Nathan's statement.

Nathan goes to say something but is cut off when a

humming Rosa strides in announcing that dinner is served.

---

All food consumed and thoroughly enjoyed the men decide to move the conversation to the games room for a friendly few rounds of pool. Olena seizing this opportunity excuses herself prematurely for bed explaining how all the excitement of the day has caught up with her and if she is to enjoy tomorrow fresh faced she'd best get her head down now.

"Let me walk you to our room *sweetheart.*" Nathan says, his voice dripping with unintelligible sarcasm. Olena looks directly at him wondering if the glamour has stopped working.

"Sure, *darling.* *yawn*——mmm why don't we all walk up together." Olena suggests stifling a yawn while stretching.

"No, you two love birds go on ahead. We'll catch up to you in a bit Nate." Frank says giving his best cherubic face translating to *I'm up to no good.*

"Ok guys I know this is likely some ruse to plan something for our special day tomorrow so we'll *play along.* Won't we Pookie?" Nathan says pulling Olena close in to his side kissing the top of her head this time.

"Oh...*ohh*——a ruse. I gotcha. Yes you guys just hang here and come up when you're ready. Goodnight all." She says blowing them all a kiss. Jamie pretends to catch it holding his hand to his chest as if to mime *be still my beating heart.*

Knowing full well Olena has none of her things inside his bedroom Nathan doesn't want to have things glaringly obviously that something's amiss——so plans to leave Olena standing outside the bedroom door before taking his leave of her.

As they reach his bedroom door Olena begins the process of glamouring Nathan again just in case her suspicions have been proven correct.

Nathan having suspicions of his own has decided to place specialised military grade anti-Hypnos contact lenses over his eyes with a tiny mechanism that can be placed out of sight inside of the ear. Obediently he plays along with the ruse happy in the knowledge his suspicions of Olena and her powers of hypnosis have been proven correct.

Nathan along with his comrades had been privy to some pretty spectacular top-secret projects and people with insane capabilities——such as astral projection, remote viewing and other weird and wonderful paranormal powers. Alongside this knowledge however also came the chance to try and some very exclusive top-secret high-tech gadgetry.

Having very strong suspicions now that Olena must be attached to an underground military operation Nathan finds playing along a lot easier. The idea he could get a free pass at bedding her makes his mini-me bulge inside of his tight jeans but he knows better than that and in honour of his mum and dad's memory will still treat Olena like a young lady——even if she is brainwashing him and his friends.

Whatever is going on with Olena she clearly wants to get them all to Kensal Green Cemetery tomorrow. Perhaps then all will be revealed——better yet perhaps she has been planted directly in all their pathways to recruit them back into the tight top-secret iron circle of trust.

"Goodnight my love." Nathan says chivalrously laying just the gentlest of kisses upon Olena's cheek. His scent has her insides doing a tango of hot lust for him but she reins it in remembering in just a few hours they shall all be well on their way to beginning the quest for the first dagger.

"Mmm, see you in a few hours. I've got a bit of a headache coming on so——you don't mind if we don't——

"Have sex? Why would I mind about that my little sugar plum princess? Go, get your head down—— tomorrow is a *busy* day." Nathan says goofily and so unlike himself to present as to still being under Olena's spell.

Turning he heads back down the stairs grinning the widest smile at how easily he has managed to elude her. Nathan also finds it utterly humorous at seeing his friends totally under the guise of the hypnosis Olena has cast upon them all with her powers of suggestion.

## Chapter 15

The birds are the first alert Olena receives that dawn has broken. After a very restless night of being embraced by Nathan in a vice like grip so she could not even escape for a mere bathroom break. Olena, bladder full is all but ready to brain him by the time he rolls onto his side for the first time in hours——releasing her from his grip.

Relieving herself in Nathan's en-suite bathroom, she looks feverishly for the spare toothbrush he had mentioned before and thankfully locates it without much hassle. The shower however takes a little getting used to until she works out what knobs to turn for water temperature that's bearable. Once cleaned, she skulks out of Nathan's bedroom leaving him undisturbed before slinking back into Felicity's bedroom deciding on what to wear today.

Looking into a more practical outfit knowing that a lot of walking may be required as well as travel——Olena opts to wear a pair of black jeans, dark green knitted jumper over navy blue T-shirt where the collar comes out over the top of the jumper. On her feet after searching for some time Olena finds what she's looking for. Heavy duty walking boots. Felicity's feet are just a tad wider then her own so Olena finds the thickest pair of socks she can to help pad out the spaces because yes even Vampires could get blisters too just like humans and Olena was no stranger to them——spending most of her days on her feet.

Finally dressed Olena thankful to hear not a sound about the house that would indicate anyone else was awake. She fast moves from room to room checking in on the men——adding a touch of re-glamour effect before sending them back to sleep for the next hour. While with them Olena notes the guys' tattoos bestowed upon them by The Magi are situated all under an individual arse cheek.

*Out of sight, out of mind——clever.* She thinks at how meticulous The Magi seems to have planned everything.

Exhilaration mixed with adrenaline course through her body at an unprecedented rate. She can't believe how easily executed her plan has gone so far. All that's left now is to get everyone including herself well fed and to decide what she will pack and get the guys to bring with them before they head on out.

As Rosa walks in through the front door Olena is all ready and waiting for her.

**"Rosa, your services will not be required for the next month. You have decided as Senor Jones is to**

*be travelling during this time to gift yourself a lavish holiday. Felicity won't be coming home during this time either so there's really no need for you to be at the mansion for the next four weeks. Enjoy your well-deserved break. Now you must drive straight home and snap up the nearest available dates for a holiday——somewhere exotic and exciting.*

As Rosa comes back into the room a big smile spreads across her face.

"Good morning Miss O'Shea. I am just heading off to a local travel agent——I'm going on an *adventure* to my motherland——Mexico! Please tell Senor

Jones I shall see him in a few weeks. Safe travels yourselves!" With that Rosa went almost skipping off back down the stone steps towards her car singing and humming all manner of Hispanic sounding tunes.

Closing the front door once Rosa is out of sight Olena breaths a huge sigh of relief before heading on into the kitchen. She scans the cupboards, fridge and freezer for something to eat but doesn't know where to start. It is then she spots a leaflet for him delivery pizza and seeing no other option dials in the number from the handset affixed to the wall.

*Hi! You've reached Joey's Pizza! I'm sorry were closed now. Our opening hours are Monday to Saturday 1pm to 9pm. Have a wonderful day!*

"Damn it all to Hades!" Olena says thumping down onto one of the white painted wooden kitchen chairs her increased strength causing it to whine under the weight before collapsing altogether making her hit her ischium hard to the floor.

Pain radiates up through the bones of her bottom as she staggers to stand up, opting to sit at a much slower pace on another chair.

"Feeling frazzled" the familiar voice of The Magi says as the collective in one contained floating and cloaked body state——asks startling Olena ever so slightly as they float into view.

"Wouldn't you if you were in my place?" She says reminding herself to keep calm and hold her tongue around them.

"A sour grapes attitude around us is not likely to help you Miss Lupescu."

"I know——I'm sorry. What can I do for you?"

"For us?" The Magi chuckle upon hearing Olena ask this. "No, it is us who have come to help you. Here it is a map of your first quest location with little tid-bits of hints to help along the way. We cannot divulge much as our proverbial hands are tied from up top."

"Oh——thanks, I guess. This will definitely help me get a good start on the quest. Is there anything else?" Olena asks wishing nothing more than for the sodding Magi to kindly bugger off!

"That is everything for now———we shall be in touch should needs arise."

With that they vanished from sight leaving Olena feeling a little less *frazzled* now she was in possession of said map. Glancing down however her eyes all but roll from her head here as she reads that they will journey to the Egyptian portal bringing them to The Magical realm hidden out in the desert.

"Oh! Fudge flickers!" Olena exclaims cursing aloud.

"Morning sleepyhead." Nathan exclaims giving Olena a kiss atop of her head, wishing he had indeed tried to bed her——as how she's dressed now has him thinking of doing nothing more than stripping her of her garments and taking her right here across the white kitchen table. The way her breasts press snuggly against both the navy-blue shirt under the dark green knitted jumper makes his Adam's apple bob up and down quite a few times and his Mini-me twitch uncomfortable inside of his pyjama bottoms——held thankfully in place by his snug fitting boxers.

*Just fluffin' wonderful! No more time to think—— well this is it. Time to start getting the plan in motion.* Olena thinks holding onto Nathan's hand longingly while making sickening cooing sounds before letting him go to begin making the disgusting brown bitter liquid humans seem to love so much.

## Chapter 16

The four men stand, mouths agape at the replayed CCTV footage of Olena glamouring them. Having left Olena to relax in the conservatory post breakfast of omelettes of just the two of them ——Nathan exclaimed to whizzing upstairs to awaken the rest of the guys in preparation for their *special* day. Once he had left Olena enjoy the mornings sun's rays and cup of *hot chocolate*——he bolted first to the bathroom to remove the contact lenses that had been irritating his eyes——he'd forgotten to remove them before falling asleep. He then raced on ahead to awaken the guys rallying them all into where the security hub of CCTV monitors resided.

"You're sure this isn't some glitch in the video?" Jamie asks for the umpteenth time as uncertainty and nausea swirl in his stomach.

"One hundred percent, I have no explanation for it Olena's powers of hypnosis are unlike anything we've ever witnessed——oh, yeah…sorry guys. Her true name is apparently Olena Lupescu." Nathan says sheepishly as his friends all give him disapproving looks.

"Had I not seen this with my own eyes I'd have never believed it. She sure is powerful." Frank admonishes rubbing a hand across the lower part of his face.

"Perhaps she left clues in Felicity's bedroom? Let's go and turn the space over." Donnie suggest all but foaming at the mouth to have any excuse to go through Felicity's underwear drawers.

"Ok, Donne and Jamie you're in charge of searching my sister's bedroom. Just do it *neatly*. My sister will kill all of us if we put so much as a puff pillow out of place." Nathan agrees as the men head on out of his surveillance office.

"I'd suggest we all wear protective eyewear but none of us are prepared and Nathan from my understanding just binned the only pair of contacts he had." Pete says an air of anxiety to his voice.

"Its fine——she believes we're all still under her spell. Frank and Pete, you're with me. We'll distract Olena long enough until you've turned Felicity's bedroom over——*neatly!*" Nathan reiterates.

"Sure thing, come on——best we get cracking, there may be many drawers and secret compartments to sort through." Donnie says all but skipping on up to Felicity's room. Jamie can only groan and roll his eyes at the arduous task ahead of them.

An argument can be heard breaking out among the

friends with comments such as "We don't even know what we're looking for" being exclaimed.

―――――

"By the way——what were you guys plotting behind mine and Olena's backs when you believed the lie?" Nathan asked as they reached the hallway that lead towards the kitchen.

"Nothing major, two of us were gonna sneak out early to grab balloons, banners and all that sh——

"Gentlemen. Need I remind you we need to be discussing things as if everything were still as it was in our minds before bedtime." Frank says interrupting Pete.

"Yes ok——valid point. Right deep breath." Pete says closing his eyes, taking in a large breath——marginally throwing his head back as he does this——preparing to travel back to the head space that told him Nathan and Miss O'Shea now Lupescu were about to celebrate a year-long anniversary together.

"Ready?" Nathan asks both Pete and Frank.

"Ready they say in parrot fashion back to him."

"Ok, let's do this."

The men wander into the kitchen pretending all is normal and that Pete and Frank are doing the usual things of fetching themselves breakfast as well as coffee. Nathan however goes in search of Olena who it appears has left her post from the conservatory sending Nathan's heart rate up a notch. But before panic can set in he hears the familiar sound of the toilet flushing from the hallway guest bathroom and lets out a sigh of relief.

Unbeknown to any of the men——while in the bathroom Olena had come across two discarded spherical items with some sort of metallic loop in the middle. It took her a while but eventually she figured out what they were——what humans called contact lenses. A technology actually invented and brought across to Earth by one of The Magical realm's brightest optometrists. Feeling as if worms were wriggling in her stomach Olena second guessed herself that her glamour on Nathan for whatever reason perhaps didn't take. She also found the box for the lenses discarded in a small white plastic bin off to one side of the pedestal sink. Reading the English language instructions Olean's head spun to discover they said that these were military grade lenses——used on undercover soldiers on project *Red Book*. Being in the presence of highly skilled hypnotists. Having sworn under her breath Olena decided she would all re-glamour them. As to who these contacts belonged to was a dead giveaway as Nathan's name was printed neatly on the box.

Exiting the bathroom and turning without paying much attention Olena bumps into a solid mass——Nathan.

Gently he presses her against the wall of the hallway ——kissing her and rubbing hands up and down her body bringing her to almost what felt like boiling point.

"I don't know what it is about you Miss *O'Shea*——I just can't see to keep my damn hands off you——it's as if they have a will all their own." Nathan explains moving from kissing her mouth to her neck.

"Stop!" She commands.

"Oh but baby we were just gettin' started." Nathan says with hungry lust ridden eyes.

"Ok, drop the act. I know about your contact lenses and that the whammy I put on your pals didn't work on you." Olena says sounding deflated at how miserably she's failed. Getting them all to Kensal Green seemed near on impossible now.

"Fair enough——consider the act well and truly dropped. The guys know as well. I showed them CCTV of your antics in the games room——the whammy or whatever you called it has also cleared their minds."

Expecting an eruption here, Nathan is quite taken aback to watch Olena crumple to the floor dissolved in floods of tears——sobbing her heart out.

## Chapter 17

"Hey——come on now. Please don't cry. Whatever it is we can solve it-together." Nathan offers to Olena in hushed tones.

"That's just it——even if I explain it to you, none of you will *believe me*. Heck I wouldn't even believe me!" Olena wails feeling totally despondent by this point.

"Ok, so tell me what you need? How can I or my friends help you? We noticed there seem to be an urgent need to travel to Kensal Green Cemetery——is this still the case?"

Olena nods several times while wiping at her nose with her hands as Nathan passes her a decorative box of tissues from one of the small hallway tables.

"Look, how's about I reserve all judgement——say, can't you whammy me to accept the truth?" Nathan suggests.

"No, once a human learns of the glamouring process ——it no longer works on them——at least I don't think it does. Even if it did how could I trust you weren't just lying to me like before?"

"You can't. Let's just try it and go from there ok?"

"Brace yourself——it's not going to be easy to accept what I'm about to show you." Olena explains trying this time to use visuals from her memory to place into Nathan's mind with the glamouring. Praying to all the Gods and Goddesses of the real Mount Olympus that this works.

At first Nathan feels like nothing is happening but then slowly a warm trickily feeling can be felt travelling from the top of his head right throughout his body as everything relaxes.

*"Nathan if you can hear me simply nod."* Olena instructs using the telepathy part of the glamouring process.

Nathan does as instructed feeling comfortably pliable at this stage. His mind wrestles with the fact he feels he should be terrified to feel so out of control of his body but oddly all he feels is intense calmness.

Slowly but surely Olena closing her eyes imagines placing recent events in freeze frame memory shots—— transferring them from her mind to his. When she has completed the process slowly she brings him out of the trance state. The entire process took mere moments but for Nathan it felt like an hour or two had passed.

Nathan's face was white as a sheet accompanied by a fine sheen of sweat clinging to his face—-as a small tremor worked its way down his upper body to his feet.

"I'm sorry——it's err a lot to process here. I...I——

Nathan never finishes the sentence as he crashes down to the floor unconscious.

Frank and Pete having heard the loud sound——rush on through from the kitchen and upon seeing their friend's limp body lying motionless on the floor get straight into army medic mode.

"I don't know what happened! One minute he was fine——we were chatting the next he just——

"Don't worry about it——let's just get Nathan to the lounge to lie him down before he comes to." Frank says being helped by Pete into lifting his friend the short distance across the hallway to the lounge.

"Saoirse, wait for us in the conservatory. He'll be fine once we sort out his blood sugars." Pete says gently blocking her from entering the lounge——as Frank's already administering necessary checks with equipment she can see he's pulling from a small khaki bag next to him with bright Red Cross on it outlined in red.

Olena spots a nasty gash on Nathan's forehead and where usually the sight of blood would send her into euphoric dizziness——now all she felt was revulsion.

Turning to head to the conservatory just as Pete closes the lounge doors to give them all privacy——Jamie and Donnie appear at the bottom of the steps.

Olena is white as a sheet and trembling.

"Miss O'Shea are you alright?" A concerned and puzzled Donnie asks her and both he and Jamie exchange worried glances.

"Yeah——I'm ok, Nathan...fainted and——well he's in the lounge. Frank and Pete are with him."

Without further words spoken between them Jamie and Donnie rush off in search of their friend as Olena feeling numb heads on for some comfort in the sunny conservatory.

---

"Ah! Do you mind being gentle?! That bloody stings!" Nathan yells in protest having re-joined the land of the living.

"Stop being such a baby and hold still or your stitches will be crooked and you'll look like Parry Trotter ——do you want to look like Parry Trotter the wizard boy? No, I didn't think so." Frank says sternly as Nathan huffs——gritting his teeth every time the curved needle goes in.

"What the hell happened? Did she you know—— hypnotise you?" Jamie asks almost foaming at the mouth to get the scoop. He's always been considered the Peter Pan of the group with his boyish charms and attitudes to life.

"Dude! Let's at least give him some air first." Donnie says which Pete and Frank know all too well is about to turn into a spat between the close friends.

"If you're going to bitch——take it outside—— that's an order." Frank says immediately grabbing both men's attention.

Taking a breath both Donnie and Jamie apologise taking seats on some of the comfortable furniture dotted around the room.

"Truth be told, I wouldn't know where to start. Olena didn't just tell me what has been going on she——*showed* me. Perhaps I should have her in here to show all of you too?" Nathan says sitting more comfortably now that his six small stitches are done.

"Come on, let's go find her. I'm sure she will be worried about what happened." Nathan states as his friend help him to standing.

"Take it steady, let me know if you have any vision loss, headache or feel nauseous." Frank says affixing Nathan with that stern fatherly look Nathan knows to mean he's deadly serious and woe betide him if he didn't do as he was told——even if they were all no long doing active service. Frank was still *the boss* as far as their group were concerned.

"Sure thing boss." Nathan acknowledges as they all head out in search of Olena.

## Chapter 18

"I'd best go in there first." Nathan suggests as they can all see the top of Olena's head bathed in sunlight from where they stand in the kitchen "Don't want to spook her. Whatever powers of persuasion she has——her mind is certainly *muddled*." Nathan explains as the guys all prepare themselves for whatever they are about to be shown.

---

Olena having thought fast on her feet, in her haste has decided to do away with The Magi's plans to having the men on board with her as 'hired help'. Fortunately Felicity had a large doll stuffed in the bottom of one of her wardrobes that had reddish hair. Placing the doll in the conservatory——once happy it could easily be mistaken as the back of her head she took her small bag of packed gubbins and made a break for the driveway gates.

---

Nathan races back through to the kitchen startling the guys.

"Oh crap——what is it now?" Pete asks sounding annoyed having just lifted his cup of coffee to his mouth without so much as taking a sip.

"She's gone! Olena has gone!" Nathan exclaims.

"Alright, alright——everybody calm down. You have CCTV do you not?" Frank reminds Nathan. "Then might I suggest we all move ourselves to the surveillance office to try and ascertain when she left and the direction she's travelling in."

Frank always had an astonishing way of calming tensions from any situation——be that arguments or trying to stay alive by not getting shot full of holes.

"This is why you're the boss." Jamie quips earning him a swift back of the head slap from Pete.

"Yo! Dude! Do not touch the——

"Quiet! All of you." Frank says only raising his voice just enough to knowingly put the wind up them all.

The group fall silent as they follow Nathan towards his CCTV surveillance office.

---

Olena having reached the entry way gates realises that short of becoming some epic pole-vaulting champion (yes magical folk even study the sports of humans— —they too also share in what humanity might deem to be *athletic* games. Only where Olena is from these are far less friendly as in some games are performed naked——and to the death).

Finding some vines growing next to a tree leaning up against the metal fence attached to the gates. Olena finds low lying branches and in conjunction with the vines manages to pull herself up and over the gate landing with a thump the other side.

Grinning to herself here at her stroke of luck and genius——Olena's sense of achievement is however short lived. Before she knows what's happened she's popped in the blink of an eye inside Felicity's bedroom. A distant voice says '*you must leave with all of the men assigned for the quest. Any further subordination will result in your immediate dismissal from existence! We will be monitoring you all closely——this is your final warning.*' Nausea rolls through Olena who presently couldn't care less about The Magi and their damned quest rules as she dives for the en-suite bathroom——vomiting her earlier omelette down the toilet.

---

"Woah...did you just see that?!" Jamie exclaims as the five men all huddle around the CCTV monitor pointed towards the property's entryway gates.

"She just...just...oh I don't feel so good." Jamie goes on as words fail the other men.

A loud shout however pulls the group from their dumbfounded stupor as they all but clamber over one another to exit the CCTV surveillance office in search of where they just heard Olena's voice.

"Going by the looks on your faces I'd say you just all witnessed something pretty unexplainable——huh?" Olena says sauntering down the last few carpeted steps, figuring now was a good a time as any to rip that plaster off, finally telling all what is going on.

"Right, so...guys——get comfortable in the lounge. I finally understand everything you've shown me is——all true." Nathan says to Olena, his face like that of a ghost's ——all colour drained from it.

"Nate——why don't you fix us something to eat. Olena can explain everything while you do that." Pete suggests and even Frank is quite impressed at how well Pete's mind is forming thoughts as his and he's guessing Jamie and Donnie's feels as if it were stuffed full of cotton wool.

In a dazed fashion, the friends set themselves up in the library readying themselves for Olena to spill the beans. She is not in the least bit surprised they already know of her real name by now——figuring Nathan must have told them once he realised something was amiss.

"So you see gentlemen——this is why I found it near impossible to come clean with you all from the beginning. I do hope you'll forgive me the glamouring I did on you all its just——I knew of no other way to get you all to Kensal Green Cemetery——today."

"Well...thank you for your honesty miss——

"Lupescu but please don't be so formal I insist on you calling me Olena." She says interrupting Frank.

"I think me and my comrades here can all agree we have seen some pretty——*spectacular* things during our time in the forces. Unexplainable at times——hence the need for the discarded contact lenses you found in the bathroom——yes even the military has its *secrets*." Frank carries on as if already trying to make sense of the scenario Olena has presented him with.

"So, you're really a Vampire?!" Pete asks wanting Olena to confirm this mind-bending conundrum his brain cannot seem to get to grips with—— while tugging at the collar of his olive-green shirt as if it were suffocating him.

"It's a lot to process I agree. Perhaps if you think of me more as interstellar traveller and not so much *monster* it will make things a little...*easier* for you to accept?" Olena says in vain attempt to contain the men's mental states——appreciating this knowledge would be enough to send many a human to the crazy place she had learned about in school——that human people get sent to on Earth when losing their minds. "I must reassure you all though that for now I am just a human. My people...those responsible for law and order you might say——they took away my Vampire privileges and my people."

"Do we even want to know what you did to make

them so mad?" Donnie asks raking a hand through his fine white blonde hair.

"I——err, well it was sort of Nathan's fault really and also *not* his fault. The ring he found, it was enchanted. Naturally it drew him——the wearer to the invisible veil. These rings are usually worn by maintenance angels who see to the upkeep and functionality of all the veils around your world. Their sole purpose is to separate our world from yours." Olena further explains as dead silence now fills the lounge.

"Come on now lads. Is it really so farfetched? We've seen alien spacecraft and——

"Oh, those *aliens* as you refer to them as are actually really pleasant creatures called Globustatics. They pilot all manner of air travel craft as an alternative to portal doorway travel——sorry——I can see that I'm creating a lot of stress for you all with this knowledge."

"Ok, so I get that you come from the world of *weird*. And I get there are things we wouldn't normally see on our world that would are beyond hard to comprehend but——we still don't know what you did that was so bad to warrant yourself being turned into a human." Pete asks, probing deeper for more answers.

"Here, it's better if I show you all. Link hands—— it'll be faster this way." Olena instructs.

Once they are all standing in a circle——hands linked. Olena begins the process of using glamour mixed with imagery the same way she did with Nathan for all of them to know exactly what lead to this very moment.

"Holy Sh——

"Bite your tongue Matthews. We're after all in the presence of female company." Frank snaps out at Jamie using his more formal address of surname.

"Oh don't worry about that! We have quite the wide range of our own *colourful* language phrases back in my home world." Mention of home makes Olena's face falter ——as the guys fast sobering up from everything they've heard and been shown start to put their efforts into supporting Olena.

## Chapter 19

The food Nathan has rustled up for lunch is surprisingly tasty. It gave Olena a similar feeling to how Nathan made her feel when she was close to him or they were touching one another even with a slight holding of hands.

"Bruh! This lasagne is mint!" Jamie exclaims making weird flicking motions with the fingers of his right hand.

"Good——Olena are you *enjoying* the lasagne? I unfortunately can't take credit for the meal——it's one Rosa made and stored in the freezer. Now seemed a good a time as any to eat it seeing as we're to be travelling very soon." Nathan says bringing into the room the realisation whatever she was involved in——they were now all involved in.

"Why it's——divine. Really tasty! Who knew human food could taste so much better than some magical stuff that gets conjured up. I shall most likely miss the delights of such flavours when I'm back to my old self and my people have been re-animated." Olena says unbelieving of the optimism such sustenance has stirred within her.

Nathan having noticed her flushed complexion bringing peach tones to her face making her emerald eyes pop——creates a stirring within him low down. Shifting in his seat to reposition himself simply smiles at her as he does so.

"Regarding travel Olena, have you got a plan of attack? What exactly are the details of this quest?" Frank says doing his usual preparedness——looking to cover as many bases as possible before they journey into no man's land.

"Well, I know we'll be travelling to Egypt——only it's the *real* Egypt. The Magical one. Humanity has been led to mimic a lot of magical lifestyles from religious beliefs to card games——sports and beyond. Some people from my world can disguise themselves as being human and so manipulating your species is easier—— sorry it sounds terrible."

"And when we get to this *real* Egypt what is the first thing we must do?" Pete says broadening on the question Frank pitched to Olena.

"I have brief descriptions and a map. Other than that ——I know very little. Sorry." The earlier feeling of euphoria from the lasagne is fast wearing off as the mood becomes more serious.

"I suggest we pack essentials. We're no strangers to the Middle East——I say let's pack as if we were going on undercover ops." Donnie suggests whereby the men all nod in agreement.

"Olena, while we get ourselves prepared——feel free to relax in any room of the house. I'm so sorry for having caused you all of...*This.*" Nathan exclaims with wide hand gestures.

"No, it was not entirely your fault. Now my previous anger has receded I see now it was a combo of higher power faults and my own. I was only just getting my fangs in as a one-hundred-year-old. Time moves differently for your kind as it does for mine. Why if I were a human I'd be around the twenty-one-year-old mark. Before any of you ask I am a purebred Vampire I was not turned like my father——so I would eventually age and grow old but it would be a process stemming over centuries not mere years. Anyway...none of that really matters. Best we focus on the job in hand——thank you for being so accepting of me and my predicament, I shall relax in the lounge until you're all ready to leave."

Once Olena has stepped out of the kitchen an eruption of voices can be heard babbling rapidly behind her. A wry smile creeps across her face to having learned how honourable these men were. Pondering that things may not be so gloomy after all. The truth was out, they'd accepted it——all that is left is for them to all journey forth through the first portal doorway.

———

"Kensal Green——Its Inside of Kensington and Chelsea." Frank says pointing to the spot on a map of London that had been folded in a desk drawer of Nathan's. "I'm guessing with these veils in place we may be in an area off-map. We'll be able to get Olena there but she will be our navigator. We must prepare ourselves to see things no human has ever seen before. If Vampires truly exist then I don't think it's a far stretch of the imagination to suggest fairies, pixies, heck even werewolves might live in her reality. Mentally if we can just accept this fact it will make this job easier——don't you agree?" Frank says turning to his men who look far more put together then they did a few hours ago as Olena spilled the beans.

"I'd just like to add that Olena may have *been* a Vampire but now she is flesh, bone and human just like any one of us. We must ensure we protect her. I can't imagine it——her very being, who she is has been torn away from her——not to mention her entire race——her family." Nathan says making the men consider her for a moment.

"Well, I for one am up for the challenge." Jamie says standing to place his hand out.

"I second that." Donnie says placing his hand atop of Jamie's.

"Count me in." Pete exclaims again putting a hand stop of Donnie and Jamie's.

Nathan and Frank soon follow suit as they withdraw their hands and then begin packing their kit bags brought inside from the various vehicles sitting in the drive-way.

# Chapter 20

They arrive at a secluded private car park having all travelled in Frank's Land Rover Defender. Civilian clothes had been suggested to help them look as human and non-threatening as possible. After all dragons breathed fire and witches cast spells, had been Pete's reasoning. If childhood stories being told to them growing up about myths and legends——if it had taught these military men anything it was that magic was not to be trifled with.

"Just a quick pit-stop before we head onto our final destination. Olena feel free to make yourself comfortable. For music on the radio twizzle this button here for tuning and this one for volume." Frank says as the men all exit out of the vehicle. To make things appear less claustrophobic for Olena——Frank deliberately leaves each window open a quarter.

The five brothers-in-arms have briefly returned to a rented out industrial unit they all class as a sort of headquarters base for side job requirements. Granted they have their own business interests away from the military since retiring from active duty——they all muck in to help one another if jobs require extra pairs of hands.

Nathan and the guys all have their own individual weapons locker. From here they collect their own personal hand guns. Knowing they are going into waters unknown it was discussed at length and in private—— weighing up the risks and benefits of having something to arm themselves with should the need arise. They'd all read the stories and seen the movies with Vampires, werewolves etc in. And however mind-bending it was to accept such creatures existed——each man wasn't prepared to journey into this level of unknown unarmed.

By the time they return to the vehicle Olena is sitting up front enjoying Rock FM.

"The lady has good taste in music." Nathan muses giving Olena a million-watt smile that has her turning gooey inside.

"Come on budge up, you're in my seat." Jamie says ushering Olena into the middle.

Nathan makes some grumbling sounds under his breath as a pang of jealously hits him being unable to sit next to his lust interest. The sudden realisation he really is fawning over her sobers him up as now is neither the time or place to be flirting with perhaps one of the worst predators in existence——be that she be human *for now* or otherwise. The way the sunlight hits her hair and skin though as it travels through the windscreen has Nathan unable to look away as all manner of ungentlemanly thoughts begin to flit through his mind. Thoughts of Miss Beckinsale in that oh so sexy werewolf and Vampire franchise of films starts to play with his imagination.

"Pssst, Nate——can you quite believe we're going on *mission Narnia*." Jamie asks in hushed tones. The guy is like a kid in a candy shop and has been ever since the truth was revealed.

Considered the baby of their group——Jamie has always been heavily into superhero paraphernalia and comic books he is the epitome of nerd central. Donnie also shares an interest in similar things but nowhere near to the level Jamie does——it's how they became fast friends before both joining the armed forces——from fawning over the best limited-edition comic books in a local store.

This probably also goes someway into explaining Jamie's love and fascination with computers and technology. He's always been the brains of their military—— now civilian outfit. Diffusing bombs, tracking and blocking Russian hackers——developing software for the British government that was cutting edge stuff and so undercover not even Nathan and co were privy to all of the information. No-one could understand why Jamie didn't make a business for himself using his tech brain skills——but he said doing normal jobs like guarding nightclub doorways etc helped to calm his mind otherwise he was prone to burnout and it could become a bit of an out of control addiction if he wasn't careful. At his worst Jamie was up playing all manner of online video games——the tournaments that offered up big prize money, yet Jamie never played for the money he always played for the win——much the same as an Olympic gold medallist might feel having won a race, this sense of achievement was far greater than any payment. Any money he did win in tournaments he put into charity as the government and private companies always paid him enough to live a comfortable life.

"Mate——seeing as we've just had it confirmed aliens exist——can't say I'm too surprised to learn mythological beasts are a thing. Do you mind if we stop talking about it——trying to get into the zone." Nathan asks placing headphones into his ears a method his friends know all too well is his way of coping pre-battle. Nine Inch Nails begins blasting through his earbuds going someway to blocking out thoughts of Olena, Miss Beckinsale and rampant sex.

———

Frank locks his Land Rover knowing that if the car gets impounded he can always pick it up when they return ——*if* they return. Frank thinks taking one last longing look at his pride and joy as the group proceed on foot toward the Kensal Green entryway.

Frank binned the *normal* map of London when Olena explained to him he'd find nothing of use on it as all magical entry and exit-ways were hidden from human sight. She did however share with him her own map The Magi had bestowed on her. It was written in some weird and wonderful language so realising he'd never be able to make sense of anything soon handed the map back to Olena agreeing they should all follow her lead.

"Feedle fungus! Your translators! I forgot! The Magi slipped these to me while I waited in your mode of transport. Here, this will be painless." Olena assures the men as she reaches inside of the small khaki rucksack of Felicity's she had borrowed.

"There you go you're all set." Olena says having pressed a small round, flat black sticker to each man's jugular where it rapidly seemed to be taken in and under the skin in the blink of an eye.

"These aren't any weird tracking devices are they?" Nathan asks sounding a little unnerved.

"I assure you they are purely to help you communicate with the people from my world. It's fairly simple tech from my world and many species rely on these translators when posing as human beings themselves——so as to appear inconspicuous."

"How do they get taken out?" Pete asks touching the spot on his neck where the device absorbed into his skin.

"Do you know——I don't know." Olena chortles as if enjoying a private joke.

"Gentlemen might I suggest we stop quizzing our guide and head onto our objective." Franks says pulling them all into line.

Not sharing the car ride sitting next to Olena and feeling positively peeved at how obviously Pete had been flirting with Olena——Nathan sidles on up to her taking hold of her hand. The movement seems reflexive almost as if he can't stop himself.

"Best we——look like we're just two normal people in a relationship, out with friends to——you know, *blend in.*" Nathan says trying to give an explanation that the hand holding was just a cover and didn't mean anything.

Pete inwardly kicking himself for not thinking of this looks daggers at Nathan. Frank simply clears his throat giving Pete *the look* which translated to——behave or find yourself in hot water. Backing off, Pete would lick his wounds later as he enjoyed watching Olena's ample bottom bob along in front of him while he thought of his own ungentlemanly thoughts as a sort of middle finger gesture toward Nathan. The jolt of jealousy did give him pause to reflect as he caught himself here deciding perhaps it would be best if he went on ahead in front of them.

Although it was totally unnecessary for any façade to be put forward given they were all human and therefore considered non-threatening to magical folk. Much as a goldfish wouldn't pose no threat to a human. Olena indulged Nathan appreciating the warmth and comfort feeling his contact brought with it.

"Well, this certainly looks pretty...*ancient.*" Donnie exclaims taking in the large domed stone archway——accompanied by tall wrought iron gates shimmering a deep purple in the sunlight.

"Say, that shimmering purple light isn't some sort of

electric field is it?" Pete asks as all of the men now wear a look of apprehension.

"I'm not sure——I've only ever travelled with my parents to parts of London closest The Chequered Inn ——my place of work. The Magi would have made sure we could travel throughout the cemeteries so..."

Without an utterance Olena breaks contact with Nathan to grab hold of the handle on one of the gates.

"Guess that answers your question——all is safe." Olena says slipping on through the gateway briefly disappearing from view.

"Hold onto your butts." Nathan says mimicking one of his favourite lines off a smash hit dinosaur film.

## Chapter 21

Across the gated threshold each of them lets out the breath they had been holding onto. Immediately in front of them is a bustling market full of stalls and stands where all manner of beasties seem to be selling their wares to a throng of shopping beasties.

"Woah! Is there some sort of festival on? This is seriously trippy." Jamie asks looking back at the group——noticing they too have been overcome with the sights and sounds.

No-one says much of anything as they stride forwards bypassing many weird and at times grotesque looking creatures of all manner of shapes, sizes and colours.

"This collective is worthy of a fancy-dress pride parade extravaganza." Pete says earning him a sideways jab from Donnie.

Their group is stared at as many a trader and shopper cannot quite believe their eyes or eye or——whatever it is that gives them right, that not just one but *SIX* human beings have infiltrated their magical veil. Unbeknown to the group however is that each of them is emitting a blackened aura signalling to all of a magical disposition who can see this that they are under the guard of The Magi.

"Olena! *Olena Lupescu!* That's never you! Hey! It's me! *Bambi*——over here!" A short hyperactive—— cloven hoofed female creature shouts over the din of the enchanted crowd.

Nathan coughs, giving a look to Olena before whispering that she is to get rid of the *friend*. He then gets busy distracting his military pals, pulling their focus to market stalls close-by while Olena goes to deal with the familiar face.

"We'll meet you at the end of the stands." Nathan calls to Olena as Jamie, Donnie, Frank and Pete melt into the bustling crowd of shoppers.

"Do you think that's wise? Us all separating?" Olena calls back but by the time she's answered she had already lost sight of Nathan and co.

"Great! In no time at all I've lost the people I'm meant to be guiding through this what must appear to them to be crazy world of ours. Oh spittle-flitters here comes Bambi." Olena thinks displeased that of *all* familiar faces she would see it would be Bambi.

*'How the blinking ballerads does Bambi even recognise me. Looks like I'm about to find out.'* Olena thinks to herself using more magical expletives that would have her in a whole lot of trouble should she vocalise them. That

being said a veiled female tuts while pulling her younglings away——clearly a mind-reader.

"Sorry." Olena says to the veiled female's back as she speed walks her spawn away.

"Hey——Bambi." Olena says struggling to find a friendlier tone. "How did you know it was me?" Olena asks jumping straight in with her burning question to her loosely acquainted enchanted friend.

If Olena were being completely honest she'd say that Bambi was just useful to her which is why she had kept her on side during their school years. Bambi had been forever doing Olena's homework and expertly writing sick notes from copied signatures of her parents so she could evade any sort of physical activities.

"Err——hello! I'm an enchanted nymph, we *smell* coded magic——guess that's why they employ us to guard the kings and queens from our world." Bambi states ever so proudly.

"So you can...*smell* it's me?"

*Eurgh! Gross!* Olena thinks sharply while then looking about to ensure no more mind-readers were around as Bambi was well known and loved among the telekinetic communities.

"Sure can. Although I admit the new...look is *intriguing*——why particularly have you gone for being human? You're the equivalent of a human deciding to become a favourite variety of food——is it for Spirit Days?" Bambi asks reminding Olena what time of the year cycle her world is in. Much like how humans would dress up for Halloween——so to do magical folk dress up to honour their dead.

"Gee...thanks, and if you really must know it wasn't for Sprit Days——long story short I managed to get my entire race erased——

"What?! *Ohhhh*! That makes sense. I was beginning to panic——my memories of us as youngsters growing up together kept plaguing my mind but no one seemed to remember you or——any of your kind. I thought it must be some *Powers That Be* mojo going on but——I was second guessing my own mind. Great jizzle-bizzles it's so good to see you——and better yet I'm not going round the twist so *bonus!*" Bambi says with the carried over chipper persona that never seems to falter (this American cheerleader). Olena was always only able to suffer Bambi's company in small doses and only when she had use of her. It is no secret how narcissistic Vampires can be.

"*Please* keep this info under wraps will you." Olena hisses affixing Bambi with a glare that has her peppy attitude falter a moment.

"You have my word. I wonder if that's why the mayoress of Cheese Wheel Village is throwing all these impromptu street parties and festival markets." Bambi says clearly contemplating Olena's predicament.

"Eurgh that *witch* and what she does or does not decide to get up to——neither interests or impresses me. Be a pal Bambi, I gotta get this team of...employed human males through the gateway to Egypt——can you help me? its orders from the very top." Olena explains using a thumb to point skyward.

"Oh——my! The Magi! Oh honey what kinda trouble are you in? No wait, don't tell me I can seldom keep a secret as it is. FYI you are carrying a black aura that possibly you can't see, seeing as you're all human now and all...just thought to give you the heads up. Man! I'm gonna struggle with the bomb of info you've given me about all vamps being erased——mind you if everyone's minds have been wiped I doubt the odd slip here or there should matter." Bambi says pondering on the immense information that's just been landed on her. "Ok—— gather up your *friends*——I'll sneak ya'll across. Meet me by the exploding pumpkin patch stall, right at the end on the right." Bambi instructs before literally trotting away as fast as her dainty golden nymph hooves can carry her. Candy floss pink coloured hair and loose-fitting rainbow dress flowing breezily behind as she goes.

Due to Olena's heightened sense of smell she manages to locate the men quite quickly. Their scent is a very distinct aroma among her kind——pleasant to the nostrils, a mixture of spice and masculinity——not like some of the species from her world who can smell positively repugnant. Surprising even herself here that even though her body has forgotten how to vamp——her Vampire sense of smell seems to be functioning as normal ——at least for now. Olena worries her senses will continually dampen down the longer she remains human.

Spotting her newfound travelling companions. Olena

sidles up to Nathan who is currently perched atop of an outdoor bar stool——looking very mellow indeed.

"Oh...*panty plooties!*" Olena exclaims gaining her shocked gasps and angry glares from passing shoppers.

Inwardly Olena groans to see all the men apart from Nathan——down *Prickly Wood Pear juice* out of tankards made from Skittish Metallics.

"What? What's the matter?" Nathan asks looking about with those blue sapphire pools now out on stalks.

*Lord of darkness help me!* Olena thinks giving herself a massive inward kick for not mentioning the ubiquitous warning for humans.

"I'm sorry, I should have forewarned you not to eat or drink *anything* while I was gone?" Olena says already seeing the effect of the Prickly Wood Pear Juice taking effect on Nathan's comrades.

"I'm fine——decided to stick to the bottled water and sandwiches Frank packed——why? What's *wrong* with the food and drink here?" Nathan asks as a growing sense of unease claws its way up his body from his legs to his chest.

"Ahhhh!" Pete, Jamie and Donnie all wail alongside Frank as they grip their stomachs in agonising pain.

"Here we go." Olena sighs waiting for the full effect of the Prickly Wood Pear juice——drunk from the skittish metallic tankards.

"Holy shit!" Nathan exclaims falling off his stool unable to comprehend the transformation he just witnessed.

"Oh my god! What's happened to us?!" Jamie all but

screams to feel his wood bark skin accompanied with branches and leaves now sprouting out of various places on his body from head to torso region.

"You have all turned into animated Prickly Pear Wood Trees." Olena explains——rather annoyed to see the vendor and his colleagues of AKO Wood Elves cackling among themselves before blanching at the vicious glare Olena throws their way.

Clambering over the table and over the threshold to be standing the same side as the owner of the beer stand Olena grasping him with her Amazonian strength lifts him off his feet exclaiming that if he doesn't find a cure to rectify this situation immediately she shall be notifying The Magi. To hammer her point home, she shows the wood elf and his pals her tattoo.

"Please...please don't report me! I'll lose my license and my wife——we're on baby number fifteen! I need the finances. I'll give you the remedy just please——please don't report me." The Elf all but wails as Olena unceremoniously drops his short ass to the ground standing over him with menacing glare.

"See to it that you do. Depending on how fast this remedy of yours works will depend on whether or not I file my report."

"Bagshaw! Grab the Norflak seeds——*NOW* you imbecile!" The wood elf yells as Bagshaw begins to fumble in a cabinet close to hand for the Norflak seeds.

"Here! What do I do with them?" Bagshaw exclaims, elf hands trembling.

"Give them here." The owner says snatching the jar away from his inept member of staff.

Grabbing a pestle and mortar the bar tender boss grinds up the seeds adding some sparkling dust stuff. When ground into a fine powder he simply blows it over Pete, Donnie, Jamie and Frank who rapidly transform back into their old human selves. Jamie falls to the floor a quivering wreck as Donnie, Pete and Frank all hug in celebration to being human again.

"Consider yourselves *warned*." Olena says affixing the wood elf with serious expression. "Tell everyone——get the word out that the six human warriors are not to be trifled with under the protection of The Magi. We shall be treated with respect and helped should we need any. If anyone tries to meddles or interfere——may the Powers That Be have mercy on all your wretched souls!" With that Olena turns, proceeding to walk away hoping Nathan and co are following her.

## Chapter 22

"Hey! Wait up." Nathan says gently pulling Olena toward him having caught up to her. The guys can be heard making murmurings to never chop or burn firewood ever again.

Nathan's sudden and unexpected contact with her skin causes Olena to flush red as familiar quivering sensation hits her stomach while heat blooms between her legs.

Noticing the effect he has on her, Nathan squeezes her hand a little tighter eliciting a shy smile from her.

Pete coughs his disdain as Frank elbows him in the ribs mouthing for him to stop it. Donnie and Jamie, still reeling from the sensation of what it could possibly mean to be a living tree are still discussing it completely unaware of the obvious flirting going on between Nathan and Olena.

"Ok, we're here. Now, I must forewarn you—— these are not like human pumpkins they are incredibly aggressive and will bite you if you get too close. Annoy them enough and they're sure to explode." Olena says as they pick their way through Orange, White, Black and Purple pumpkins.

"The pumpkins all have *faces?!* How can anyone eat anything with a face as adorable as these?" Jamie exclaims horrified.

"*Eat Them!* Why on Earth would anyone wish to eat the exploding pumpkins? No——*these* little fellas are used to help guard royal castle grounds on my world. I'm figuring here they're used to guard holy ground the closer we get to the portal doorway. You see the pumpkins will attack anything with evil intent. So long as we keep our intentions pure—-we'll be fine." On hearing this Nathan rapidly pulls his hand away from Olena earning him a quizzical look before she notices it is his turn to blush.

"No Nathan——not *that sort of intentions.* I'm talking about murder or assault——the killing of a king or queen sort of evil intent." Olena explains as Nathan simply smiles turning his head to the ground before taking up her hand again affixing her with a stare that if Olena didn't know better would have said had hypnotised her to become transported into some sort of *happy place.*

As the group all venture further into the exploding pumpkin patch——conversation evaporates as they all become hyper focused on treading carefully so as to not startle the pumpkins or step on them which would lead to an immediate explosion.

*POOF!*

"Oh Jesus! Oh God! Oh Jesus! Oh God!" Jamie yelps while doing a weird dance on the spot——having accidentally trodden on a baby exploding pumpkin that fortunately only gave up a weak explosion as not yet full grown.

Olena thinks of what to say before she can hear the sound of a woman humming a tune, singing something about growing pumpkins.

"Hey, guys——follow me. This way, I think there may be a farmer around and if so it will be safer for you to stay with them while I meet my friend Bambi to organise our travel plans." Olena explains not wanting to go too heavy on details as to the *whys* and *wherefores*.

"Eurgh! I got purple baby pumpkin juice all over me!" Jamie exclaims making muted gagging sounds.

*Hades give me strength.* Olena thinks as she continues to follow the sound leading towards the pumpkin farmer.

"Well hello there travellers, how are ya'll doin'? Come, come. It's not safe to wander these parts——oh dear I see you got one of the little guys——are you ok? Did you hurt your foot?" A voluptuous, round faced, golden haired woman says as she beckons the group to head closer to her barn entryway.

"Errr——is she human?" Pete asks noticing nothing *unusual* about this seemingly harmless woman.

The woman takes off the protective head gear she had been wearing as well as reinforced breast plate to help protect against any exploding accidents.

"Never mind." Pete adds having seen that this

woman beneath her head gear has very pointy ears and a third eye——like a literal eye looking at them all.

"Name's Meep. Welcome to Wayward Farm. Word works fast round here; you guys are all practically *famous!*" Meep goes onto explain while holding out a hand in familial handshake gesture. Meep is wearing a red chequered shirt with dark blue dungarees with buttons barely holding in place against her rather large form.

"Pleasure to make your acquaintance Meep. We were just heading toward the chapel of travel. I wonder if—— you wouldn't mind looking after my friends here so I can arrange everything?" Olena asks hoping it will make this next trickier part of the process easier.

"Sure thing, I'll be at my farmhouse, just up this road straight up——can't miss it. Come along fellas, I bet ya'll are famished! No good travelling on empty stomachs. Have no fear——I'm quite the fan of human produce. Bacon and eggs sound good?" As Meep says this the men all but gallop behind her as they wander off up the path without so much as a bye as you leave.

*Charming!* Olena thinks as Bambi comes skipping toward her out of the forest shadows.

"Hey you! Glad to see you made it through. Perhaps it was not my wisest move to recommend coming this way but look on the bright side——you halved your travelling time. Oh, I also spoke to the Chaplain on shift today and he says travel may be permitted but I unfortunately can't do it for you this time——you'll need to show the ID you've all received from The Magi. Sorry I couldn't have been of more help. Right! Must be off, don't want to miss second breakfast *again!*" Bambi says and before Olena can so much as utter a thank you she is gone, dissolved among the trees and dense foliage of the veiled enchanted cemetery forest.

---

"I must say Meep these eggs are astonishingly good and the bacon——wowzers!" Frank says washing his food down again with freshly pressed apple juice.

"Say Meep, you don't happen to have any coffee on offer, do you?" Donnie asks shovelling more mouthfuls of food in——earning him a swift kick under the heavy-duty wooden table from Frank.

"I mean...if it wouldn't be too much trouble, don't worry if you don't, the juice is *Divine*." He adds having recovered himself and his manners.

"Honey, I'm about the only place you will find coffee or tea around these parts. People shunned me for my eclectic interests into human cuisine and beverages but as a pipkin I'm curious by name and nature." Meep goes onto explain bringing relief to all the men's faces at mention of tea and coffee.

---

Unfortunately for Olena, an unseen tree root had been responsible for her tripping and landing in an entire patch of baby exploding pumpkins. She was now riddled with splashes of orange, purple, black and white pumpkin goopy guts. It was in her hair, all over her face and body and some in her mouth. Swearing while marching angrily toward Meep's farmhouse by the time Olena reaches the driveway she's all but breathing out of her backside.

A human's lungs it appears are nowhere near superior to her previously owned Vampire ones. Her feet are riddled with blisters and it takes what little resolve she has left not to burst into tears by the time she's raising a hand to rap on the painted blue wooden farm door to Meep's house.

Nathan opens the door stunned by the sight in front of him. Stifling a laugh——struggling to keep concern etched on his face at the dishevelled sight of Olena's hair, face and body.

"Woah, what happened?" He starts to where Olena raises a hand to silence him as she stumbles over the threshold and into a warm blanket of heady aromas included wood smoke from the lit fire.

"Olena! Are you alright?! What happened? Pete says jumping up to help her with Nathan to hobble over to a spare wooden seat.

"Goodness, the poor girl must have fallen into a pumpkin patch. I'll grab some cream for abrasive sores." Meep says rushing up her rickety wooden stair case to the upper floor. The house is all open plan, not much dissimilar to how one might find a human barn conversion had been designed.

"Stop fussing all of you——I'm *fine*. I just fell on a patch of baby pumpkins. It's my feet that are the main issue." Olena exclaims as Nathan kneeling in front of her gingerly takes off one of his sister's ankle boots.

Olena sucks in an audible breath as pain rips through her.

"I have calamine lotion and bandages in my pack." Frank indicates as Nathan heads on over to start fishing for the essentials. Many a soldier knew of blisters and how to treat them accordingly.

Donnie and Jamie are deep in conversation while still busily eating to pay any attention to the fact Olena is being tended to.

"Glad to see those two buffoons have their mind on religion——food I mean." Nathan mumbles, using the bowl of warm water Meep passes him which is helping bathe Olena's feet.

"Here, let me dab this purification powder onto any scorch marks. You have a couple of minor ones on your face." Meep says having returned to sit by Olena as she makes fast work cleaning off the sticky pumpkin remains before administering the soothing powder.

"By the looks of those feet——you're gonna need new footwear. I shan't be a moment." Meep exclaims wandering over to a cupboard. When she returns she is carrying sheets of cured leather.

Once Nathan has completed bandaging her feet he slips the socks back on carefully so as to not disturb the dressings.

"Ok my love, place both feet onto each of the leather squares and hold very still." Meep instructs as Olena follows along with everything that is asked of her.

"Bind!" Meep says as a great big pink flash of light zips out of one of her index fingers.

Both leather squares rapidly surround Olena's feet, entrapping them like a second skin. They feel amazing light and comfortable.

"Oops! Nearly forgot." Meep continues as she then points again to Olena's feet saying "zippers!" Instantly two zips appear at the side on outside of each boot.

"You'll all be wanted new footwear and I sense time is of the essence. This will ensure your footwear never wares down as this is everlasting unicorn hide." Meep exclaims proudly.

One by one the men are sized and fitted with new everlasting unicorn leather boots.

"I've taken the liberty of packing you all some ham and cheese sandwiches——I know these are a firm favourite among your kind. Olena seeing as you missed the eggs and bacon——I packed you a little extra."

"Thank you so much for your hospitality Meep——I wish there was some way we could repay your kindness." Frank says speaking for all of them.

"Are you kiddin' me! Just having you all here in my home was gift enough. I never thought I'd see the day to have real life *humans* here in my home! The boys down our local tavern are never going to believe I had you in my home!" Meep goes on, gushing with excitement while everyone begins making manoeuvres to head out of the door.

"Did you get everything you need?" Nathan asks Olena regarding their travel arrangements.

"Yes, it's all sorted. We need to meet with The Grimm guarding the statue of Anubis——I know the way as it's a mere stone's throw from the chapel. If we hurry we might be able to get there before it begins to get too busy." Olena explains ushering everyone out of Meep's home thanking her again for everything.

Once the group of haphazard travelling companions are back on the road——it doesn't take long for Jamie and Donnie to switch back to the subject of food—— discussing when might be best to eat their sandwiches.

## Chapter 23

Bambi is waiting patiently for Olena and co while standing next to The Grimm on duty for today's safety checks before granting access through the Anubis portal doorway.

"Hey guys! Over here!" The fawn says giddy with excitement as she waves them on over.

"I thought you'd got lost. Anywho this is Doddy. He'll be your transport Grimm today." Bambi states proudly.

The guys all just look at Doddy with glazed expression.

"Codes please." A foreboding echoing voice asks with only a hooded form to look at.

"This dude looks the spit of that final ghost in Christmas Carol." Jamie says quietly.

"Shut the eff up Jamie. Let's just sort out these codes with the…Grimm and be on our merry way. I'm not ready to meet my maker just yet." Frank exclaims feeling ice trickle through his veins feeling he is literally staring death in the face.

"I gotta go, but you got the codes right Olena?" Bambi says chipperly to her friend.

"Sure do. Stay safe Bambi——and thanks for...you know helping out." She adds as a bad sensation spreads throughout her heart centre with these new human feelings——in that she had only ever used Bambi when in Vampire form.

"You too——friend." Bambi says looking tears eyed as she hugs Olena before rapidly skipping off, disappearing among tombstones and forest.

"We all have tattoos from The Magi. This is mine, and my friend Nathan here has one on his arm too. The others——fellas you're gonna need to drop your trousers for this one." Olena instructs making each of the men look at her completely aghast.

"Why? Where are *our* tattoos?" Pete asks his cheeks flaming red at the prospect of having to drop his trousers in front of a gorgeous young woman.

"Under one of your arse cheeks. Now come on you need to be scanned to prove we have permission from The Magi to be here before I can give Doddy the codes from the Chaplain." Olena says annoyed that there seems to be a delay. Not yet fully understanding the human concept of embarrassment.

The guys all drop their trousers after Nathan advises Olena to turn around to give the guys privacy. When she asks why he simply whispers that guys can feel a little awkward about their bodies much the same as women do.

"Ok, that's fine. Even if highly amusing that The Magi have quite literally blessed your——*bottoms!*" The Grimm named Doddy says while having private laugh to himself.

Clearing her throat, affixing the hooded figure with a stare. Olena waits for him to request the codes to which she hands Doddy six tickets not dissimilar to the ones you'd see bought for train fare in London.

"Very good. Follow me please." Doddy instructs as the group now follow the hooded figure down a stone corridor its stone walls illuminated by braziers.

After just a short walk they all come up against a large iron doorway that sits below a towering statue of Anubis.

"When you're ready, place a hand here on this panel and each of you shall be granted access. We haven't lost a soul yet to any malfunction but there's a first time for everything. Sorry, part of the job I'm required to forewarn all travellers coming through for insurance purposes. I must return to my post. Safe journey!" Doddy simply vanishes in a plume of mist and smoke as he says this.

"Who's going first?" Donnie asks as they all turn and look at him. "Guess that will be me then——ok here goes." Donnie says placing a hand of his on the incredibly enormous illuminated square——affixed to the side of the doorway.

"Why such a large panel." Nathan amuses to no one in particular.

"Probably for giants." Olena answers matter of factly.

"Ah——you have hearing like a bat, I will remember this." Nathan says phased more by Olena's acute sense of hearing then the fact she just mentioned they have giants where she comes from.

As Donnie puts his hand on the panel the door simply swishes open to the side effortlessly.

"Oh, guess I just step on through." Donnie says pleasantly surprised there was no electric zap or that he didn't become annihilated on contact with the panel as he felt more than a little out of his depth here.

As Donnie steps through and out of sight everyone then lines up to await their turn. Next went Jamie, followed by Frank then Pete and finally Nathan and Olena.

---

Due to unforeseen transport turbulence——by the time they arrive in Egypt on The Magical side of the veil—— all of five of the men relinquish almost simultaneously the contents of their stomachs. Olena seemed to be faring better perhaps because she was still on an empty stomach.

Rinsing his mouth out with water from the only remaining bottle before handing it around to the rest of the guys——Nathan sidles up to Olena, placing an arm around her quivering body.

"Thank you, I don't usually have much of any reaction during portal travel or temperature drops." Olena says feeling quite embarrassed at her shivering mess of a human body.

"Let me guess, Vampires are immune to such things?" Nathan says in place of an explanation.

"Well...we...everything is just a lot slower perhaps...to that of you humans. Oddly I was always taught...how hot a country Egypt was..." Olena says through chattering teeth as Nathan slips his jacket around her shoulders. The warmth and his scent both calming her nerves while helping warm her.

"In the day time it can be extremely hot but at night ——temperatures plummet. Some folk lost out in the desert have even been found to die from hypothermia ——basically they freeze to death." Pete explains still smarting from the budding romance seemingly blossoming between Nathan and herself.

"Oh——you really are a fragile species, then again I am usually quite allergic to silver so who am I to make such comparisons." Olena says pulling Nathan's jacket tighter around herself.

"Let's not forget crosses and wooden stakes?" Jamie chimes in having used the last of their bottled water to rinse his mouth from the taste of vomit.

"That's just urban legendary stuff. Probably planted into humanity's psyche since the days of our darkest Prince——the one who began the whole Vampire mythology among your race. No, you see to *kill* a

Vampire you need simply chop off our heads. Any other area of our bodies pierced, burned, squashed etc—— would simply regenerate." Olena replies grinning impishly to herself that Mr Smarty Pants Jamie has been put well and truly in his place.

"Then I guess I'm glad you're our tour guide for this little expedition." Jamie quips back at her as they all trek forward towards civilisation.

"Hey! Guys! I don't think we're in Kansas anymore." Pete says stating the obvious.

City lights glimmer off in the distance as all around them in every other direction is sand and sky for miles.

A whoosh, followed by the braying of animals and then *plopping* noises alerts Olena and her comrades that they have new arrivals——transportation in the form of *camels*.

"Aright, alright! What the *hell* is going on?" Frank demands beginning to tug at his short hair while pacing back and forth. Olena watching him begins to worry that his mind might be about to crack open like an egg. None of her world would appear remotely normal to any human——whereas for her their world seems usually dull and uninteresting.

Frank's anxiety she notes has begun to rub off on the rest of the men. Rolling her eyes and sighing as the men look about to try and work out where the camels had come from——Olena gets atop of her camel. Bambi, she realises must have arranged transportation appropriate for their destination——figuring they'd be exhausted on foot. Olena automatically knew which camel was to be hers as it had a big red bow around its neck——accompanied with short message on a rolled-up scroll.

> *Be careful my dearest dark friend. The fam all say hi (even though they think you're an imaginary friend with the amnesia of forgetting all about you) Hope the camels help.*
> *Bambi xx*

Olena feeling a surge of emotion toward her youngling friend——is encouraged to know there is someone out there looking out for her and her new friends. Someone who hasn't judged her for her mistakes and only wants a good outcome. Silently Olena makes a solemn promise that when the quest is over she will make more of an effort to be kinder to her two-legged fawn friend.

"Come along guys, we have a long way to go. Try to keep up." Olena says grabbing everyone attention.

Clicking her tongue, she nudges her camel off at a trot with her unicorn booted feet.

Unbeknown to Nathan and Co——Olena can communicate telepathically with her camel. If the men all loosened up a bit she could eventually teach them how to do the same.

Olena, pulling her camel up to a halt upon realising

the men were struggling to board their camels——offered help a few times but was told they had everything *under control*. Not wishing to waste any more time, finding the darkness far more intimidating as a human ——Olena spurred on her steed into the night. Glancing back relieved to note all the men were now mounted and following along.

*You do realise we're only rented right?* Olena's camel communicates using their telepathic link.

*Yes of course. How would you like to earn yourselves some extra time off work?* Olena asks her newly acquainted four-legged friend.

*Go on.*

*If you can stick with me and my...friends while we are here in Egypt, I'll put in a good word with your handlers?*

*Fine...I'll consider your offer with my brothers. Can you ease up on the reins——I got a mouth ulcer from eating Crinkly Pacti.*

*Oh——sure, sorry, there is that better?* Olena asks dropping her reins.

*Much better, so——where are we going?*

*The city over where the lights are.* Olena indicates by pointing ahead.

*I'm gonna need to speed up——check the left saddlebag pocket, the small vibrant green vial, pour it into my left ear.* The camel instructs.

"*Erm...ok.*" is all Olena says before following her furry friend's request.

It is as if she has administered rocket fuel as her camel

takes off ten times faster than it had originally been going.

Nathan, having sorted his comrades out on each of their own camels——head spinning with all the weird woo-woo going on——begins to preside over whether or not he may be in fact lying in a hospital bed somewhere experiencing some whacky coma dream. He shivers as cool desert night air whips up around him as his and the other camels struggle to maintain pace with Olena's formula 1 version of transport.

"*Woah! Stop! Hang on a second——my friends, they need to keep up.*" Olena shouts aloud but can hardly hear herself let alone the camel as a cold wind viciously whips past her.

Slamming on his brakes——unprepared for the sudden manoeuvre sees Olena shot forward like a stone off a catapult.

*Ooooof!* Air whooshes out of her as she slams into a sand bank.

Three minutes later the others arrive. Nathan immediately jumps off his camel to rush to Olena's side. She is winded badly and her ribs feel bruised even given her Amazonian strength.

"Are you alright?" He asks helping her gasping to her feet.

"I...just...need...a minute. I'll...be...fine."

"Ok, woah——nope, you can ride up top with me. In fact, as your camel is so fast I have an idea." Nathan says taking some thick rope that was tucked neatly to the side of his humped steed.

Tethering Olena's camel to his and the others——once she catches her breath, Nathan prepares to climb aboard with her so they can stay together and hopefully avert any more accidents.

"Have you...done this before? It's just, the way you handle camels isn't really coming across as amateurish." Olena asks, blowing a stray strand of copper hair from her face.

"We...learned during our time out in the Middle East." Nathan says in way of explanation.

"Middle East?" Olena asks cocking up a brow.

"The war."

"The war?" She parrots back.

"Afghan...Iraq?"

"Oh sure——*the war.*" Olena answers making it sound like she knows exactly what Nathan is talking about when in reality she doesn't have a scooby. Magical folk know little to nothing of human history as their politics are far removed from their own world's goings on. They know wars happen sure but they just don't deem it worthy enough to pay that much attention.

"Everyone ready?" Nathan calls back to his four friends, chatting busily among themselves.

"Let's get this show on the road." Frank barks while looking haggard and well and truly fed up.

Nathan nudges the camel onward quite unprepared for the unnatural speed it gallops off at.

*Please tell that human friend of yours to loosen the reins.* The camel yelps painfully to Olena telepathically.

"Here let me take the reins——I feel more secure

when I do." Olena says, happy when Nathan obliges no questions asked.

---

"Well, we're here...wherever *here* is. What now?" Nathan asks Olena helping her off the camel.

*I recommend The Blue Pharaoh Hotel we can lead the way.* Olena's camel suggests.

"The Blue Pharaoh Hotel——its...this way." She says taking the reins of her humped friend letting him lead on, at a notably calmer pace. The injection of green ear rocket fuel seeming to have worn off.

"This is all very freaky." Donnie exclaims riding up beside Olena and Nathan.

"Indeed——starting to wonder if I'm not stuck in some weird dream." Jamie adds.

Pete and Frank remain silent. Olena can see the stress etched on everyone's faces. Come daylight she sure will have a lot more explaining to do.

Reaching the foot of the marble steps leading up to The Blue Pharaoh Hotel. Everyone dismounts and before any mention of where to place their camels can be discussed the six animals trot away en masse in an orderly fashion.

"Ok then Miss Lupescu, please do us the honours and lead on." Nathan says just as Frank places a gentle arm across her chest indicating that he shall be the first to climb the steps and lead them all on inside.

"Old habits die hard I guess——don't take it personal." Jamie says climbing the steps two at a time after his boss-come-friend.

Nathan gently holds Olena back with firm grasp of her hand until his comrades have all ascended the stairs entering the hotel.

"I know you're meant to be the one leading here but...Frank he's——

"Set in his way?" Olena says finishing Nathan's sentence for him.

"Yeah——so like Jamie said, please don't take it personally."

"It's quite alright. Clearly from what you've already told me about Frank having been responsible for all your safety while out on the battlefield——why there's no-one I'd rather follow myself." Olena says to Nathan going some ways to reassuring him she honestly has no issue with Frank's brusque demeanour.

"It's just——I don't want you to feel un-superior now that you're a woman."

Olena bursts out laughing at Nathan's comment.

"Jeez——of all the things I'd half expected you to say there——that was not one of them." She says once finally able to control her breath long enough to speak.

Dabbing at the sides of her eyes with the backs of her hands Olena still giggles at what came across to her as some sort of crude joke.

"What? What is so funny here? I'm serious!"

Again Olena howls with laughter begging Nathan to stop with the hilarious commentary because of course in her world it is the female Vampires that reign supreme over their male counterparts and not the other way around.

"Come on——let's catch up with the guys." Olena says beginning to walk on ahead of Nathan who's left looking totally dumbfounded at the bottom of the marble stone steps.

## Chapter 24

"Woah! Check out the *digs!* How on Earth can we afford to stay here? ——or anywhere for that fact. I didn't bring any cash? Bugger! Guys! Hey-guys! Does anyone have any money on them?" Donnie asks as if to suddenly state the obvious.

"No need, it's all in hand." Olena says gliding through the four of them until she is out front in the hotel lobby taking centre stage and feeling somewhat better at being surrounded by people from her world.

"Ok Olena, we're all ears. You tell us what's what around here and we'll gladly follow suit." Frank says making sure his men know to listen carefully to what she looks to be about to tell them all.

"Thank you——*Frank*. If truth be told there really isn't much to say other then as luck would have it we have a free pass by The Magi——on everything and anything we require, as far as hospitality goes, food, drink, clothing etc."

"So what you're saying is, and if I'm to understand you correctly it's that we're——*VIPs*?" Pete asks as all of the men's faces suddenly brighten to the prospect of begin these VIPs which Olena isn't sure what is meant by such a sentiment.

"They mean *very important persons*." Nathan says filling in the blanks for her having sidled up next to Olena.

As the group all settle into the lobby——questions soon peter out as the sobering sights of beasties and creatures coming and going are a stark reminder to these usually brave military men that they are on most unfamiliar turf now.

"You should see all of your faces right now. *Relax*, you're with me and given our upgraded status among the people from my world——we're near as damn well close to royalty as you can get so come on——loosen up a little will you." Olena says flashing a brilliant white smile before turning and almost skipping across to a huge curved reception desk.

"What's got her so peppy all of a sudden?" Donnie says quietly to Jamie.

"Dude, the woman or Vampire or whatever the hell she is——is now among her own *people*. Think about it, if any of us were suddenly cursed to live out our days as some alien beast or whatever under the knowledge our entire race had been erased——wouldn't you too feel comforted being around familiar home comforts? Ok so there are no *Vampires* but——these are still *her* people from *her* world. Come on, we'd best keep pace with Miss Lupescu and follow her lead. Also quit with the inane and stupid questions——ok?" Pete says following Nathan and Frank as they stride ahead letting what Pete said to both Jamie and Donnie sink in.

The troublesome duo simply look at one another aghast before shaking their heads like two naughty school boys falling in line.

———

Everything within main reception is every bit stereotypically Egyptian looking. The one thing that does stick out however is there seems to be a clear line of division right through the centre of the building. On the left side——Dark interiors adorn the walls, centralised fountain and flooring whereas on the Right side everything has been decorated in much brighter hues. Similar one might say to that of a yin-yang effect. The lighting is also in stark contrast to each respective side. The darker side has very dimly lit walls whereas on the brighter side everything is wonderfully illuminated, bathed in heavenly tones of whites, creams and magnolias.

Indoor palm trees equally bring the outdoors in, with the polished marble flooring reflecting hues from the overhead golden steepled enclave above. The darkened side gives an almost twilight night-time effect whereas the light-side brings the floor alive with illusionary liquid gold effect.

A smartly dressed figure sporting black suit, white shirt and black bow tie with vibrant cobalt blue handkerchief tucked neatly into his top left coat pocket, intercepts Olena before she can reach the reception desk. The figure in question has skin as grey and hard as what looks to be granite rock.

"I am Gargoyle40121962. How may I be of service to you." The brutish looking beast asks.

"I need a lie down." Jamie admits, his legs going weak after turning away from the gargoyle to spot that reception is being manned by a half Minotaur-half human character. It all appears to be too much for his fragile human constitution.

"For heavens sakes man! Pete, Donnie——help me with this whimp will you." Frank barks getting all of the men to immediately act into finding a seat or somewhere where their fainted comrade can lie down.

Using the distraction to her advantage Olena takes Nathan onward to where the Minotaur is standing. Dressed in similar fashion to the gargoyle, the Minotaur too sports a sharp suit——only his has pinstripes down the pant legs and jacket.

"Good evening Miss Lupescu, we have been expecting you. Your friend *Bambi* is it? Well she put in the call briefing our establishment of your plight and also your special *pardon* by The Magi. Should you require anything——anything at all. Please do not hesitate to ask. I took the liberty of setting you all up in our most extravagant enchanted penthouse suite——I assure you it's got more than enough room to house all of you. Your room is on the top floor——I'll get Monnie to take you up." The Minotaur receptionist says relieving Olena that at least she doesn't need to give a big speech as to what they need and where to request they stay. Bambi has earned herself some huge pixie points which Olena pockets to the back of her mind while they all settle in for their first night in Egypt.

"Excuse me a minute kind sir——much as I love my brothers in arms over there presently being helped by the big stone dude——I assure you they will *all* want their own rooms." Nathan interjects before Olena can get a word in edgeways.

"Very well. We have four singles and a double all on the same floor——take it or leave it. Magi or no Magi that is all that is on offer." The Minotaur states snorting, annoyance registering clearly on his big beefy bull like face.

"You take the penthouse suite——I'll bunk up with Frank, we're used to far *less* luxurious sleeping arrangements." Nathan says making Olena's heart sink momentarily having been hopeful his request for extra rooms excluded himself in the equation meaning they'd have been able to steal some proper *alone* time together.

*What is wrong with me! Fawning over a human man ——it's disgusting, gross, its...but who am I kidding look at his face, that well chiselled jaw, perfect hairline, his hard-muscled body— -Hades help me! I gotta get out of this hormone fuelled human physique!* Olena thinks as her mind continually flits from wanting to have sex with Nathan to then being repulsed by her sudden unvampiric urges.

Olena digs her nails into the palms of her hands to try and remain grounded. Revulsion spreads through her like a sickness and she can't help but shudder as these *feelings* and constant visions her and Nathan writhing naked together——insist on plaguing her.

"Thank you Brax, for being such a gracious and accommodating host." Olena says taking hold of the key cards hot footing it away from the desk.

"Huh——would you look at that. *Key cards!* Your people really do have similar tech to Earth, don't you?" Nathan asks in that rich Irish accent Olena has grown to love far too much.

His perplexed demeanour at how *normal* the key cards appear makes her smile on impulse as her heart rate begins that tap dance inside of her chest to once again be in such close proximity to the annoying object of her desire.

*Had I my full fangs and Vampire instincts——why I'd simply drink him dry leaving him for scavengers to pick at his bones. Stay focused Olena think about what mum and dad would say.*

Thoughts of Valeria and Manix have Olena all but leaping sideways away from Nathan.

"Sorry——thought I saw a bug." Olena fibs unable to think of anything more realistic to say.

Her suspicion about said bug does however make Nathan spin three-hundred and sixty degrees on the spot

——eyeing up carefully the floor and walls around them clearly spooked as to what *kind* of bugs might live in her world.

Lightly laughing having recovered herself. Olena takes up Nathan's hand which goes some way to helping calm his own nerves.

"Come on, let's go tell your buddies the good news ——we have officially been checked in with free room and board."

"Should you require anything from room service or need medical assistance——feel free to call down to me here at main reception. The name's Brax and I'm on shift all day everyday——as my forever punishment from The Powers That Be. Probably best you don't ask what I did——I'll go get my staff to see you to your accommodation. Does your human friend require medical attention?" Brax asks as the trio look across to a slouched Jamie being fanned furiously by Frank, Donnie and Pete.

"Nah, just some of the best booze——that's alcohol, and food consumable for *our kind*." Nathan says unbelieving how he just uttered the words *our kind* as if he buys into the crazy coma dream world he's fast convincing himself he's a part of.

Brax rings a bell and a talking monkey wearing a red and black uniform——not dissimilar to a London bellhop.

"Monnie——please show our esteemed guests to their rooms. They are to have anything they desire on the house by orders of *The Magi*." Brax instructs making

Monnie's demeanour falter only ever so slightly at the mere mention of The Magi.

*"I'm getting the sense these Magi fellas are 'those who must not be named'"* Nathan says quietly to Olena parroting a line from a world-famous book and cinematic franchise.

"As you wish sir." Monnie the monkey man responds.

"That's actually not a bad idea——not mentioning them by name. They have a tendency of...popping up when one least expects it." As Olena says this a weird chill runs through Nathan's body as his mind plays back flashes of seeing the dark raven-haired goddess before being confronted by a much burliest red-headed Irish woman who claimed to be a Vampire no more.

———

A weary Jamie stands back on his own two feet as everyone now stands in awkward silence——inside of a well-polished golden lift, with interior mirrors. Monnie is in front of the group with his back turned to them so he can man or monkey the buttons while whizzing them to the top floor.

Taking in his uniform better upon closer inspection Olena can see that upon his slim monkey physique——Monnie is wearing a white shirt with cravat, red button up waist coat with black collar, black trousers leaving a space for his tail to poke out at the back. Vibrant brass buttons run up the front of his coat and a red pill box hat sits atop his head between well rounded monkey ears, finishing the look.

"Do you remember that movie Jumanjoo with the monkey scene in it." Jamie begins in quiet voice toward Donnie's ear that is closest to him. When he catches Frank's face in the opposite mirror he soon gets the message to keep any and all commentary about any monkeys——firmly to himself.

Upon exiting the lift, everyone now sees exactly how palatial everything looks.

Tall marble pillars align the walls, polished marble floors give an almost wet look that captures the groups reflections. Tall standing stone Egyptian figures stand or sit atop of their respective pedestals where in between each one a giant brazier stands proudly burning.

"You have reached your destination. On this floor are only your rooms. You shan't come across any other guests during the remainder of your stay with us here at The Blue Pharaoh. Your key cards should all match the numbers on the doors. I notice you have no luggage with you——do you require a tailor?" Monnie asks sure that they may require more than the simple clothes they wear on their bodies. Having studied human nature extensively outside of his normal working life——fascinated by how they mate, live and explore their home world (between having wars and destroying vast swathes of it with deforestation), Monnie knows how customary it is for humans to change their clothing frequently.

"Thank you Monnie——a tailor would be great. Tell them we'll require fittings for five men and one woman."

Olena confirms with Monnie flashing him one of her newfound bright white smiles.

"Right away ma'am." Monnie says backing into the lift cheerfully, clearly pleased as punch to have made a good first impression.

"Oh——please do call me Olena."

"Sure thing ma'am I mean Miss Olena! I'll work fast to learn all of your names during your stay here with us." Monnie says flustered now as he presses the lift button to close the mirrored doors.

"Oh and Monnie before I forget——could you please find me someone with information on The Ruby Sunrise."

As Olena asks this, Monnie's face falters as he leans against the open lift doorway to stabilise himself which also prevents the doors from closing any further.

"R—r—right, The Ruby Sunrise you say."

"The very same, thank you that will be all."

Once Monnie is out of sight, Jamie all but passes out again leaving Frank and Donnie to hold him up as they drape his arms about their shoulders.

"Get cheese brains inside his room. Then I suggest we reconvene in the Master suite for an emergency meeting." Frank says sounding tired and grouchy.

The guys all help carry Jamie to the room he'll be sharing with Donnie. As they disappear inside Frank heads off to the room he has picked for himself and Nathan. Although normally Frank would have his own separate quarters if this were a military operation, all men agreed that none of them should be alone and out of earshot of Olena it was already agreed among them in the lift on the ride upstairs that rotational sentry duties should be implemented to keep an eye on anyone attempting anything suspicious while they would be presumed to be sleeping and in their most vulnerable state.

"I'm sorry...this is such a mess. I wish...there was some way to explain it all——*better.*" The light falters in Olena's face as she speaks and it saddens Nathan.

He has seen Frank edgy before but this time Frank seemed——*different.* Like there is a deeper weariness to his bones. Mind you with it being over a decade since they were last in a Middle Eastern warzone together he presumes that it's hardly surprising being called into a sort of active duty again after all these years has had some sort of drain on Frank.

"No, I'm the one who's sorry. I didn't believe you, I accused you of being on drugs and——come on let's talk more in your room until I'm summoned in for that *secret meeting.*" Nathan says making a funny voice at the end while making his eyebrows do a dance that has Olena laughing.

"Frank——he's always edgy at the start of missions." Nathan explains taking Olena's hand in his which again elicits that warm fuzzy feeling throughout her body, as her heart rate picks up and things down south turn tropical.

Frank coughs while affixing them both with an old-fashioned look before unlocking his bedroom door and stepping inside and out of sight.

"Can I get that apology on record Mr Jones." Olena jests.

"Don't push your luck——come on, let's settle you in." Nathan states having pressed the key card against Olena's door and as it confirms access granted the pair of them slip inside.

# Chapter 25

Immediately what grasps Nathan is just how insane Olena's bedroom looks. Wondering perhaps what his own shared room with Frank is like. The ground is a sea of emerald green grass, there are trees——*real* trees and birds. A small trickling sound catches Nathan's attention off to his left and here he spots a waterfall complete with mini lagoon to swim in. In the centre of the forest come bedroom is what looks to be some sort of luxury glamping yurt complete with camp fire place and with tree stumps for sitting on encircling it.

"This is...*interesting*?" Nathan says utterly dumbstruck, so much so that words appear to have failed him in this very moment.

"It's portal technology, you think you're entering a regular sized box room and voila – *magic*." Olena says as if it's the most reasonable explanation going.

"But...its *outside*...as in *outside!*"

"Err, yeah. The hotel must be a high brow establishment with only the best enchantments what you humans would class as, money can buy."

"I'm gonna get the guys, be right back."

Nathan steps outside of her bedroom firmly shutting the door releasing expletives under his breath while also catching it.

A purring sound catches his attention sending the hair on the back of his neck standing to attention. Slowly and deliberately Nathan turns, collapsing against the door while desperate fumbling for the handle as a bright orange and black striped tiger strides toward him. Unarmed Nathan finds himself frozen to the spot.

"Be a good fellow will you and open the lady's door ——I'm all paws." The tiger says sitting to lift a paw, chuckling and the quivering wreck of a human man standing in front of him.

As if on auto-pilot Nathan turns to face the door, locating the handle this time with no trouble at all as he does what is requested of him without uttering a word.

"Thank you, good fellow——some guests find it soothing to rest their head on a purring *pussy cat*, lulling them to sleep. Might I add you smell absolutely scrumptious! Do not fear me though. We've all been informed you *humans* are off the menu——shame. The last human I consumed was an unruly zoo-keeper in London. Fortunately, my friends helped me escape—— can't say I'm a fan of your species of meat walkers—— awfully sinewy."

"I see...and do *all* animals talk or is it just The

Magical ones." Nathan asks as the talking tiger walks by him brushing his huge feline body against Nathan's legs.

"Oh...I'm not actually a tiger but a mime. I can choose many different forms but grew quite attached to being a tiger on your world——until at least I was captured and placed into that zoo. Most unfortunate for the fellow I ate but only way I knew how to escape. Still, it hasn't put me off wishing to remain in tiger form for the foreseeable future. I shall save you the terror of my *real* form.

With that the tiger enters Olena's forest bedroom shutting the door behind him with his tail leaving Nathan rooted to the spot.

"This isn't real, it's a coma-dream, not real——coma-dream." Nathan recites over and over as his freeze responses begins to thaw and he actively seeks out his comrades.

---

Knocking on each respective bedroom door to check in on his friends——Nathan is at least relieved to see the rest of the bedrooms are pretty standard. All are en-suites with double beds and balconies that look out over the city. No illusionary forest effects or otherwise in these rooms.

In vain Nathan had tried to relay what he had just witnessed and experienced in the Master penthouse suite where Olena now resides——but all of the guys simply looked upon Nathan to be either winding them up or perhaps having some weird illusionary meltdown.

All together again——having bigged up Olena's room and its effects to Frank, Pete, Donnie and Jamie——Nathan was aghast to see upon re-entry a most normal looking room with forest wallpaper and accents of a forest nature. In place of the yurt there was now a wooden four poser bed dressed in rich green and aquamarine tones and cracking log fireplace where he could have sworn he'd seen a campfire just moments before. Tall French styled patio doors lead out onto a handsome balcony overlooking the city.

"Gentlemen please come in——don't mind the tiger he was just leaving." Olena exclaims, as the men all startle ——gawping at the huge orange and black striped creature.

"Good evening, I do hope your stay with us here at The Blue Pharaoh is a pleasant one." The tiger states upon exiting.

"*YEEEOW*!! What the bloody hell was that for?!!" Jamie yelps as Donnie pinches him hard on the nipple.

"Sorry...just making sure I'm not hallucinating." Donnie explains weakly.

"Oh yeah." Jamie says doing the same back to his friend.

"Ok, ok, ok dude! Get off! Jesus! I get it we're all *not* hallucinating." Donnie exclaims——rubbing at his just as bruised nipple.

"Brax called from Main reception to see how we were all settling in and if there were any requests for supper?"

Olena says as the men take up seats in the varying armchairs dotted around the room.

"I don't know about anyone else but I could *murder* a steak and fries with some garlic mushrooms." Jamie says rubbing his tummy making all of them suddenly feel incredibly hungry indeed.

"Might I suggest then that we all eat in the dining room." Olena says striding across the floor space to open up a previously concealed part of the room.

Sliding the two sliding doors apart the men now standing all head on through to the extended part of the space.

A table sits in the middle of the dining room and has already been laid out for six guests. The enormity of the space is jaw dropping. The men had seen palaces before given their time in the military when the Iraq and Afghan war kicked off——but this was palatial luxury on another level.

Jamie wandered over to where a golden cherub stood upon its pedestal brushing a hand lightly over the golden structure. The cherub elicited a giggle and let fly the arrow from its mini bow.

"*AH YA BUGGER!*" Frank yells, bending backward as the small golden weapon had imbedded itself into his right buttock.

Yanking the offending item free from his person Frank proceeded to rub the painful area whilst hobbling toward the table gingerly taking up a seat. The rest of the men including Olena fall about laughing alongside the cherub——unable to stifle the surprised shock of what had just taken place.

"So sorry man, I had no idea the cherub was *real.*" Jamie said offering his apology.

"Just, don't touch anything else in here——capisce?" Frank grumbled feeling himself redden in the cheeks with sheer embarrassment.

The men all give mock salutes and nods.

"I shall call down to Brax and relay your request for food——unless of course there are any other requests? Honestly you can have whatever you want. I've been assured there is nothing they cannot provide for us here. I'll be eating whatever you're having so it makes no difference to me——not being very clued up on the whole human diet issue." Olena says trying to inject a tiny amount of humour into the situation but failing miserably.

"Steaks will be fine——oh and what's this about your room being a forest? Nathan was trying to convince us all you had fountains, lagoons and wilderness in here." Frank says eying Olena conspicuously as they all now turn to look at her.

"Oh that——well it was just an illusion you see. Steaks was it? I'll get right onto that." Rapidly Olena leaves the men to their own devices feeling like a rainbow-sprinkle fish out of water. If they think an enchanted bedroom is mind bending then Hades help them come morning when they'd really start to see some sights and have experiences that would surely challenge the very fabric of their existence.

Olena had seen human minds pop before which ended them up in those prison type buildings for people with broken minds. She hoped this wouldn't happen to Nathan or his friends——but as things looked the way they were now, probability of popped minds seemed quite a high certainty.

Half closing the sliding doors behind her Olena breathes a sigh of relief as what she deemed to be normal conversation erupts among the group of male friends. Mentions of *I told you so* were quite audible from Nathan which made her smile.

Picking up the very normal human looking handset Olena calls down to Brax to put in their request for supper. Some technology from her world didn't just mimic human-kinds but was exactly where humans gained such knowledge of things like electricity, telephones, cleaning applicants and most other technological devices. It is a fine balancing act with the tech wizards from her world blending into humanity to give enough glimpses into power they may wield with technology from their world without giving too much. There had been no choice when it came to having nuclear warheads devised——as had been taught to Olena in school, had Hitler not been taken out the human war would have eventually have bled into theirs and it would have become a war of worlds not just a world war.

Food ordered, upon her return to the dining room Olena has to shoo away a lively miniature statue of a Griffin that had been curled up asleep on the only remaining chair.

Expressing its annoyance, the living statue stretches, roaring weakly before flying back to its own pedestal.

"Food's all ordered, I don't imagine the wait to be very long. How are you all settling in? If being human for me has been difficult to accept I can't begin to imagine where all of your heads must be." Olena says trying to steer conversation to a place where she can at least gauge the sanity of the men before her——as bothersome thoughts of popping minds won't leave her.

"Ah yes that's right! the elusive *Vampire* ruse" Nathan jests which brings an icy silence to the room.

"Vampire Ruse?" Olena says parroting back what Nathan had just said.

"Come on, you don't honestly expect me to *believe* any of this or you are *real,* do you? Why I'm clearly having some sort of coma-dream. Sure I may *think* I'm feeling pain. When in actual fact it's just my subconscious so wide awake that my consciousness now can't ascertain what's real of phoney anymore. I intend to enjoy myself while I'm here though." Nathan goes on explaining how he seems to have worked it all out in his mind——bringing Olena's worst fears to the fore.

Nathan's mind is at risk of popping——big time.

Frank, Donnie, Jamie, Pete and Olena all give one another weary glances as Nathan's sense of delusion grows while he fast babbles along to himself——as well as occasionally turning to the Cupid statue and joining the little animated cherub faced creature in a laugh.

"Nathan." Olena says gently placing a hand to his shoulder grabbing his attention. "Remember——this is *all real*." Olena states trying to put the whammy on him with her powers of glamour.

"Pffft! You don't honestly believe this *mystical* glamouring power of yours to work again do you? Come now, do you *Vampires* not know the first thing about hypnosis? You have to believe it will work for it to actually take effect." As Nathan speaks these words Olena recoils from him as if poisonous barbs had shot forth from his skin.

"What does that mean?" Pete asks as the group of four male friends looks to be even more troubled.

"I...I don't know——this has never happened to me before. I know it's been told should a Vampire's powers be found out by mortals the effects may be less——but to not work at all?! Well this is news to me. Maybe because I am now mortal myself, and you all now know what I can do——it's rendered my power useless." Olena says feeling an increased sense of deflation.

"Everyone——give us a moment. This could get ugly and I'm not one for being comfortable swearing in front of a woman, be they human or otherwise." Frank says sighing as the guys and Olena step out of the dining room to give him privacy with Nathan.

"I'd close those doors if I were you——Frank's about to go nuclear on our buddy in there." Donnie suggests as Olena turns away from the closed doors just as Frank's raised voice becomes audible.

# Chapter 26

"I suggest you go tend to our friend in there—— sorry if you heard me yelling, but something had to be done." Frank says stepping into the living room space of Olena's bedroom.

"Is Nathan...alright?" Olena asks puzzled at how concerned she hears herself sound——as a rule Vampires couldn't usually care less about humans.

"Doubt it——guessin' boss man wants us to go in there to *soothe* Nathan's wounded pride?" Pete says heading on inside the dining room as Frank simply nods in agreement.

"Best we let the guys have some quality *lads time*." Frank says placing a gentle hand lightly to Olena's chest in a gesture to hold her back. Fire rolls through Olena's body as no one normally touches her without there being a very special reason for it. Clearly human females can be touched whenever its presumed ok in the man's world.

*Luckily for you Frank I'm unlikely to be able to rip*

*your hands from your body at this precise moment in time.* Olena thinks as her disgust clearly registers on her face ——Frank pulls back his hand with quick enough motion as if she had burned him. Embarrassment showing clear across his reddening cheeks.

*Eurgh! These humans are so sensitive! What I wouldn't give to be back in my desensitised Vampire form. And how typical, the first time I get to see my reflection is with a stranger's face.* Olena muses as she turns away from Frank to view herself in a gold embossed floor length mirror——feeling quite boggled at this strange Irish red headed female staring back at her.

*No, this will certainly never feel normal.*

A knock at Olena's bedroom door signals the arrival of their meal.

"Should we——

"Best we eat here in the lounge——let the lads enjoy food together having some *normal* time if you get what I mean. Besides, it'll give you and I chance to get better... *acquainted*——you are after all for want of a better word our glorified tour guide so——I'd appreciate getting to know the eyes and ears of this operation better, if you don't mind." Frank says cutting Olena off which has her blood starting to simmer.

*Keep your cool Olena, he's just an old man trying to keep the house in order. These walking bags of blood wrapped in meat are a means to an end. Even if they are rude and egotistical.*

Olena, can see this is not a request but an order and just as Nathan and his comrades seem to fall in line Olena decides to humour Frank and do the same. How long she could keep jumping when he said how high was anyone's guess but the worry was that eventually she would bite back——perhaps not with fangs but with words and weaponry.

"Sure, whatever you feel is best. We can set up our supper by the fireplace." Olena indicates with open hand for Frank to take a seat.

Heading off to greet the room service team, Olena is most pleased to see two Nix creatures pushing the food tray inside. These critters have a particular nasty streak about them and tend to get on with Vampires very well.

"Who are these unassumingly looking human creatures then?" Frank pipes up making Olena wish the ground would swallow her up with sheer embarrassment.

"We are the *Nix*!" The female hisses immediately as she rounds on Frank——flashing him with a devilish glare. Her seemingly normal dark eyes glowing sudden fluorescent red, along with a show of red horns atop her head complete with forked tail swishing forward from behind her.

The male does exactly the same to show Frank they are anything *but* human. And for the first time since learning of the quest, where Olena is from and their current destination——Olena swears she sees Frank blanche.

"I b-beg your pardon——sorry——I didn't mean to offend." Frank says breaking eye contact while holding up a hand in non-threatening passive gesture.

The Nix duo give wicked grins to one another before taking on their human form again.

"Me and my friend are eating here in the lounge this evening, the rest of our group are through there." Olena says affixing the Nix with a stern glare, while making sure her tattoo from The Magi is on full display that soon has the Nix swallowing their smug smiles.

"We'll set up your meals and be on our way." The male Nix says suddenly sounding a lot less cocky.

"Yes, if you could be as quick as possible we'd appreciate it." Olena says finding Frank's eyes——giving him a wink as she takes up the armchair next to him. The female Nix places their food atop the small glass rectangle table stationed between herself and Frank.

"Can I light the fire for you?" The nameless female Nix says to which Olena nods in response.

Clicking her fingers, a flame shoots up as the Nix sends it across to the open fire setting the logs within it well alight.

Once left in peace, Olena begins indulging Frank by answering any and all questions he fires at her.

---

"Regarding this Ruby Red dagger, do you not have the slightest iota of where to begin searching for it?" Frank asks taking another forkful of steak and chips having to bite back audible moans of satisfaction as its near on the best goddamn steak he can ever remember tasting.

"I wish I did know where to begin looking——seems

silly saying *wish*, as that's what got us all into this ruddy mess." Olena expresses bitterly while stabbing her fork through a much bloodier piece of steak.

"Will The Magi give you any indication? I mean I hate to state the obvious but we're kinda looking for a needle in a stack of needles." Frank says downing a big slurp of his beer while Olena takes a more conservative sip from her can of cola. Frank thought it sensible to keep Olena away from booze unsure how her body might contain it seeing as she hasn't been human for very long.

"It's a possibility. Until we know for sure what any more of their *plans* are regarding this quest——might it be an idea to search the city for answers? Perhaps people living here know of the dagger's whereabouts or can at least let us know of its last known whereabouts? Why else would The Magi send us here if it were for a wild booble-bag chase."

"*Bobble-bag?*" Frank asks quietly parroting back what he just heard Olena say. "Never mind——I don't want to know."

"Between getting us all here and having a map of the city I've been left with little else——sorry." Olena says a tight ball of anxiety forming in her stomach upon realising she really does know little to nothing.

*Nothing like becoming the sacrificial lamb. Thank Hades mum and dad can't see me now——they'd probably die a thousand eternal deaths.*

"Try not to fret. My team and I are old hats at being sent on missions with next to no intel. Let's enjoy our meal and afterwards we can all congregate together and forge a plan forward." Frank says placing the last cut of steak into his mouth. "Damn that was good." He says sitting back in his seat washing the remaining morsel down with beer.

"I must admit these steaks are really rather tasty. I shall miss human food when I become a Vampire again." Olena says licking her fingers.

"That's the spirit! We're gonna get all those daggers, reset the timeline and all will be well." Frank says brightening at hearing Olena sound so optimistic. "Changing the subject. Going back to what you were saying about *this* Egypt——the one on your people's side of the veil ——it's the real one and ours is a sort of simpler mimicked version is that right?" Frank asks unable to stop peppering Olena for information.

"Yes, to cut a long story short. All across Earth are pockets of magical communities hidden to the naked human eye by magical veils——your people mimic quite closely, historical and religious sites around Earth. But sorry to be the bearer of bad news——they're all pretty much fake unless you're on our side of the veils.

"Wow! That sure is a lot to digest. A bit Truman show if I'm honest. Man! Our lives are all...*lies?!*" Frank says mulling over what Olena's just relayed to him about most of their world's monuments being replica knock-offs.

"The veils were first erected millennia ago by The Magi——under orders from The Powers That Be. The Magi are not what you might class as Gods...they're more complicated than that——think, very fabric of space and time——"The Magi are connected to everything——all parallel universes and beyond." Olena says reflecting stars in her own eyes at the sheer awesomeness of the true creation of everything.

"That's...a lot to...digest——well, anyway...cheers. Here's to getting you the daggers and saving the world ——yours and ours." Frank says as they both chink their drinking vessels together.

"Cheers?" Olena asks raising an intrigued eyebrow at Frank.

"It's an old custom our kind have done for a long time. It's like a small celebration either before an event or to celebrate success following something big."

"I see. Should we...be getting back to Nathan and the others now? I'd like to know the status of Nathan's mental health before we devise any plan moving ahead ——we wouldn't want him sent back to Earth to be locked up in one of those prison-type places your people send those with broken minds to now—— would we?" Olena says eliciting a small shiver as she places her cola can down——not waiting for Frank's permission this time before striding on through to the dining room.

———

"A-ha! There she is!" says a very red-faced Jamie, chipperly. "The star of the show!" he continues on.

Before Olena can utter a word Frank walks in ahead of her glad to see his men are a lot more laid back and relaxed. Pete gives his boss a wink and nod indicating all is well again with Nathan.

"So——what are you all up to?" Olena asks quite perplexed at the game Donnie and Jamie appear to be playing whereby they have hold of one another's hands with arms bent on top of the table.

"It's called an arm wrestle." Nathan says with sparkly eyes and glowing cheeks Olena notices as he sidles up to her creating an instant warmth to flush throughout her body as she does nothing to resist his charms.

"Yes, well I hate to break up this little boys' party but if it hasn't all slipped your attention——we have a job to do?" Frank reminds everyone while giving a reassuring wry smile to Olena before turning all brash and boss-like again.

Donnie and Jamie release one another's hands as the men all brave for a mission plan like none they've ever done before.

"Boss, if I may suggest——wouldn't it be wise to get a few hours shut eye first so we're all level headed and fresh to discuss the matter at hand?" Nathan asks Frank, giving Olena a gentle shoulder nudge. As she turns to look up at him she finds herself almost drowning those glistening sapphire pools she was coming to love so much.

"Good idea. You all have exactly thirty minutes to freshen and sober yourselves up. Olena and I will meet you back here." Frank says barking out the order making the men all but flinch as they now prepare to get ready for the late evening plans.

"Once you're all freshened up in Miss Lupescu's en-suite then its strong coffees for everyone." Frank says slightly adjusting his previous order to now at least include coffee.

"There will be far more room to *freshen up* as you say if my room is in its illusionary form." Olena states earning her some very blank stares.

Olena claps her hands together twice and before their very eyes the entire room shifts——melts and dissolves to transform from an average everyday looking luxury penthouse suite, to that of an enchanted forest——whereby Jamie, overwhelmed finds himself passing out——*again.*

## Chapter 27

"See——I told ya." Nathan says to a shell-shocked Donnie who unfortunately had been stood right next to where the waterfall and lagoon are situated. He and Jamie are both waist-deep in cool water looking more than a little cheesed off as Jamie had quite the rude awakening from his latest fainting spell.

"Right! Guys! Come on—— stop messing about ——showers——NOW." Frank says keeping his nerve as he just accepts they're not in Kansas anymore. If he fell apart and went spare out of his mind he knew the men would surely follow.

*Be normal Frank. Keep operations normal,* is all he can think to do in this far-out situation.

"Follow me please gentlemen." Olena says curling one of her dainty Irish human fingers toward her—— before turning to sashay off toward where the men can all wash themselves. Nathan all but has his tongue hanging out as he follows Olena like a well-trained house dog.

The previously normal looking bathroom was now less bathroom——more exotic jungle cavern, with specialised alcoves for each of them to wash themselves in. No one said a word, they all just looked around figuring out what was what as they went. Olena gave a brief overview but left before anyone could ask questions.

A bamboo cabinet stands central to the cavernous space. It is filled with fresh green and beige towels. A wicker bin sits off to one side for the laundry when they were done.

"You know, for a fancy pants mystical place——things sure are normal around here. Room service, fresh towels etc." Jamie says standing hands on hips nodding in approval at their new bathroom situation.

"Jamie." The men all say in unison to which he glances across to them. "Shut up!" They then all say again in unison.

The men shower in individual alcoves——whereby they simply pressed a rock on the wall which releases mini waterfalls acting as showerheads to run at the perfect temperature——all down their well-toned, muscular bodies.

Once finished a simple press of the same stone in the wall——sets off jets of warm air to blast off the remaining water droplets. Small bottles of varying coloured liquids clearly labelled shampoo, conditioner and shower gel were all neatly placed in small mossy compartments just inside the alcoves. There was a set for each of them to utilise with one set left over for Olena.

The bottles remaining had varying pink and purple liquids——a stark contrast to the green and reds the men had all used. The set that remained——when smelled gave intense floral tones of hyacinth and rose——in place of the much richer spicier notes of the men's toiletries. The guys left the, as Donnie called them——*girly* lotions and potions alone——scared they may all end up smelling like powder puffs.

"This is so trippy——I literally feel like we're in the Belize jungle. Remember when Donnie freaked out about the *huge* spider that had invaded his pack." Jamie jested being the last to step out from his chosen shower-dryer alcove.

"Yeah, I bet they could hear him screaming all the way over in Timbuktu!" Pete laughed remembering the memory all too well.

"Frank looked like he was about to pop a vessel. Everyone got battle ready, it was hysterical." Pete reminisced——flicking Donnie hard on the backside with a wet towel.

"Hey! Cut it out! So glad I could fill your egg-heads with amusement! ——Holy shit!" Jamie exclaims jumping back and away from Donnie, suddenly paling as he's seemingly noticed something on his dear friend's person. "Donnie...err...don't move...ok." Jamie says winking to the others as they cotton onto what he's doing.

"What?! What's on me?! Get it off! Get it off!" Donnie exclaims spinning where he stands.

"Keep still——do *not* move, probably better if you...

shut your eyes." Pete says adding to the ruse by inching close to his comrade while acting as if scared for his own safety.

"Oh, god has it got claws?! Pincers?! Is it venomous?!" Donnie says, starting to sweat and sway. "This better not be a prank or I'll kill you!" Donnie says but is assured by both Jamie and Pete's panic-stricken faces that neither of them are kidding around this time.

Jamie having grabbed a handful of what looked like mud from the cave wall——proceeds to smear it all across Donnie's stunned face while his eyes remained closed, naked body trembling.

Nathan, Jamie and Pete fall about laughing at how easily Donnie fell for the prank not least of all because he let out one almighty scream that made Jamie's ears ring. The laughter however was short lived as Donnie started to take on an entirely different appearance altogether.

"Well fu——

"OLENA! FRANK! I think you'd better get in here!" Nathan yells cutting off Pete's expletive.

Hearing no response and not waiting around for an answer. Unthinkingly in his stressed condition and worried out of his mind about Donnie, Nathan bolts from the jungle cavern butt naked——hoping there's something that will help his friend before he suffocates as presently Donnie appears to be doing a very good impression of a solid rock statue.

Olena jumps at the commotion almost spilling her cup of tea. Frank, knowing how much Olena despised coffee decided to call them both up some tea to enjoy with milk and sugar.

Immediately Olena turns the colour of red velvet cake as Nathan races across to her traversing fallen trees and small boulders in nothing but his birthday suit. The manhood she can't help but notice——is impressive. This of course does nothing to quell the burning embarrassment she now feels raging all across her cheeks.

"What the bloody hell is going on? You boys had one job! Get a shower before we——oh for pity's sake man! Put some damn clothes on, will you?!" An enraged Frank yells as Nathan now having recovered himself realises the cool air surrounding his nether regions.

"Eeee-gad! Sorry boss——Olena. Errr—-hurry please, this way?" Nathan says having cupped a hand around his man-hood not waiting for Olena and Frank to follow him back toward the jungle shower room.

———

Upon entering, there's a pregnant pause before Olena bursts out laughing. Frank looks at her and the pair of them end up in uncontrollable fits of giggles. It is quite the sobering sight for the men to see Frank so loosened up but then again these are by no means *normal* mission circumstances.

"Sorry——I probably should have advised everything is usable...*but* the mud." Olena explains fast joining the dots as to what has occurred. As before her impromptu exit from The Magical realm Olena had only recently been discussing the finer points of *solidifying stone mud* with a fellow member of staff from The Chequered Inn. There was a new process being developed by magical chemists whereby human bodies could be petrified still long enough for a Vampire to drink while they remained asleep——the entire process would appear nothing more than a bad dream. Many a vamp had been against the idea as they believed traditional means to hunt were best. Olena had been quite positive about these modern developments as her argument was that times were changing and with them so too should the Vampire community look to better means which would protect their anonymity and identities. Human technology was developing at an alarming rate and there had been quite a few near miss incidents whereby Vampires had been spotted, snapped with camera devices or recorded. Undercover magical agents do their best to keep the advancements at bay but with Musk around——not so easy. Many a governmental argument had been undertaken for the urgency to take Musk out but as this would skew the timeline it was forbidden by the highest council in all the land——The Red Dragon Order.

Olena pondered here whether or not even The Red Dragon Order for all its power, might and influence on her world have forgotten Vampires and figures they must have. What seemed like a mammoth undertaking to magical and it appeared human eyes (going by the military men's reactions to everything) appeared to have cost The Magi nothing less than a proverbial click of one's fingers to simply whoop——erase all Vampires from memory while also turning one of their own into a human.

*One rule for one and one for everybody else. Oh sure ——if anyone from my world fudges up a timeline its death row but noooo if the darling departmental beings above have a little mis-hap then undoubtedly, they'll do everything in their power to come up smelling of ambrosia ——even if it does require the entire eradication of a species from memory.* Olena's thoughts dampen her peppy mood as the laughter wears off.

---

"How long is Donnie likely to stay like this? Please tell me not for the rest of his miserable existence?" Nathan says trying to play down the situation while butterflies charge around inside his stomach. The rising pitch of his voice however betrays that cool exterior which makes Olena want to burst into fits of giggles again.

"*Relax!* It'll last the night. No reversal I'm afraid—— Donnie's going to have to ride it out. He should be able to *relieve* himself as normal and eat and drink——but someone will have to spoon the food into his rock mouth hole and place a bucket underneath him to go——you know——to the toilet. All orifices will remain uncovered." Olena explains pointing at first to Donnie's mouth, then nostrils. "You can check the downstairs holes if you wish." Olena says turning away from Donnie as Frank, Pete and Nathan do just that. Jamie looks to be about to say something smart but gets cut off.

There's a creaking sound followed by a *pop.* Jamie has also solidified——most likely from having had the mud on his hands in the first place. His face has been set in stunned expression.

Pete and Nathan immediately start cracking jokes ——laughing while making references to the neat little *exit holes* on each men's tidy stone bottoms. Jamie is always quick to make jibes or fun of others predicaments alongside Donnie, so this time the shoe is well and truly on the other foot so Pete and Nathan make great use of this advantage knowing there's not a thing either Jamie or Donnie can do about it.

"Let's just be clear——either of you need to go number two——we ain't wiping your arses for you." Pete says keeping a deadly straight face before he and Nathan are howling again.

"That's enough you two. Let's just be thankful these effects are not *permanent.* I suggest we all get some shut eye and tackle the issue of finding this dagger head on first thing. If you'll excuse me, I wish to freshen up myself before bedtime." Frank begins to strip as Olena makes herself scarce while Pete and Nathan begin moving Donnie and Jamie out of the enchanted cavernous bathroom.

———

Deciding its best they all stay together in Olena's bedroom——tents have since been erected for the guys to sleep in while Olena has sole use of her luxury yurt.

Nathan and Pete laid Donnie and Jamie on a patch of soft grass outside the tents with a few throw pillows borrowed from Olena's yurt to comfort their heads——covering their naked stone bodies with warm blankets. The temperature of the room always remains at a steady comfortable setting suitable for humans to survive in ——so there is no chance Donnie or Jamie would catch hypothermia or be eaten alive by bugs or other wild animals you might expect to find in a jungle.

Frank having taken his sweet time in the hot waterfall shower. On passing his two comrades lying face up——eyes stuck open, kindly places two small towels over their eyes hoping it may help them sleep as they can communicate nothing of how they're even feeling in their stone formation.

"Poor buggers. Sorry for laughing fellas——see you both in the morning. Sleep well." With that Frank headed on inside the tent he had chosen to share with Nathan who is already peacefully snoring lightly in his cot bed.

Olena waited up for a few hours unable to switch off, eventually falling into a troubled sleep where she dreamt like a human——of screaming Vampires, her parents' deaths and the feeling something snake like was chasing her.

———

Sunrise is signalled by the sound of birds singing a beautiful morning chorus. One of the birds flies down to sit on Olena's shoulder as she sits on the small porch of her yurt soaking up the sounds. As she goes to touch the bird it turns into a glittering mist reminding her that none of the illusionary aspects here are real just as visions from her dreams filter through making her shiver at the memory.

"Good morning Olena, how did you sleep?" Nathan asks handing her a metal cup of the hot brown liquid she despised.

"Now don't look so sour faced——I know you don't like coffee, so I made you up a mug of hot chocolate." Nathan says happy to watch the wave of relief and surprise wash across Olena's beautiful peach and rose complexion.

"*Hot...chocolate.*" The words sound so slow and deliberate as Olena repeats back what Nathan just said.

Bringing the mug to her nose and sniffing a pleasant feeling flushes throughout her body——and after a first sip she's all but groaning with pleasure——evaporating any and all thoughts of residual nightmares.

"I called down to the hotel manager and asked him to send up some items so we could prepare breakfast. We're old hat at camping and survival training——thanks to all our years in the military. Knowing what you've been through, losing your family, an entire race of people——your identity...me and the guys talked it over and we know it won't fix your problems but making you a yummy breakfast of comfort food, is the best we can offer...given the circumstances." Nathan goes on unable to stop himself babbling. Every time Olena is near him he just wants to make her feel good, or touch her. Oh what he wouldn't give to be able to touch her——*more*.

Frank's deliberate cough breaks the doe-eyed expression worn by Nathan as the others focus on the job in hand of making eggs, bacon and toast. No-one appears to be discussing Jamie or Donnie's stone petrifying faux pas so Olena doesn't think to bring it up.

Taking another sip of the chocolate——spontaneously and seemingly out of nowhere Olena bursts into tears.

Instinctively Nathan rushes forward to place a comforting arm around her and with a nod from Frank takes Olena off to her yurt for some privacy. Jamie had looked to be about to make some sort of wise crack—— until Pete elbowed him hard in the rib cage making Jamie curse aloud before jabbing him back.

"I...I'm terribly sorry I have no idea what just came over me." Olena explains as they both step inside the sanctity of her yurt.

"I'm not a psychologist but...as you're going through a lot of *changes*...hmmm how can I put this." Nathan thinks mulling over in his mind how he is to deliver his presumed diagnosis. "I've seen Felicity become suddenly emotional as we were growing up and even now she still is at times——I think what your experiencing is PMS - Pre-menstrual-tension." Nathan explains which earns him nothing but a blank expression from Olena.

"You never heard of PMS then? ——I guess the birds and the bees talks were different where you come from huh?"

"Birds...? Bees?!! Oh god I'm not going to sprout feathers and grow a beak and a stinger am I?!" Olena all but shrieks as fear surges through her.

"No——no!" Nathan says, alarmed to having freaked Olena out. "Come, let's get *comfortable* and I'll dive straight in.

"Aww, come on wipe your eyes——you're about to go through quite the womanly experience——your period is what every woman experiences once a month and it lasts a couple of days. Men don't have these." Nathan says finding it less difficult then he originally thought it might be to relay this information to Olena.

"Wait! Periods? I know this one, we learned about it in human anatomy and physiology class——oh *cracker jams*." She wails "No, no, no!——ew! think I'm gonna be sick!"

"Ah, I am *relieved* to see the concept is not so lost on you after all...you may require some *products* to help you. Want me to call down to——

"No!...err——no that's quite alright. I can do it myself." Olena says feeling mortified and embarrassed.

It wasn't a new concept for Nathan to consider ladies *goings on*. When Felicity would visit he'd pop to the shops and purchase her favourite brand of sanitary pads, chocolates, alcohol and other creature comforts she liked to have when hunkering down through a period. He had the upmost respect for all women who had to suffer regular monthly bleeds.

"I'll leave you to get sorted then. Do you want to

have breakfast in here or with the rest of us?" Nathan asks.

"Let me call Brax and order some things...I'll be right out——oh and can I have another cup of that yummy hot chocolate?"

"You bet." Nathan says smiling as he exits on out of her yurt. Nathan knew his parents would've been proud of how well he'd turned out——the way he was taking care of Olena, he knew in his heart they would have approved.

Nathan finds himself wiping away tears of his own and it startles him the fact he *never* gets teary eyed over a woman and yet Olena seems to have stirred something from deep within him. Carefully, Nathan reminds himself to keep it together for now would not be the best time for any sort of unravelling to occur.

## Chapter 28

Olena was shown how to use sanitary pads by an on-site enchanted nurse. Tampons just did not appeal to her in the slightest. The mere idea of putting anything inside herself just grossed Olena even more then the mere idea she would now bleed on a regular basis.

---

Similarly to human high-end hotels——Blue Pharaoh guests could also call upon the services of on-site medical teams to deal with all manner of medical maladies that may befall them at any given moment. The medical team only usually deal in magical health concerns but being stationed Earth side meant they have all extensively studied human beings as part of their training——to help them *blend* in with the population when across the veil on the human side. Very dedicated magical doctors and nurses actually took on roles working in human hospitals and surgeries to learn as much as possible about the inhabitants of Earth. And although no history of human beings ever visiting beyond the veil was written in any magical scripture anywhere——everyone it seemed, (at least where The Blue Pharaoh was concerned) was prepared.

"You're all set now Olena. These pads should last you throughout your first period. So sorry about your predicament, I sadly must admit to also not having any memories of Vampires. Anyway, Brax reiterates that should you or your friends need *any* further assistance regarding healthcare issues, you are but simply to ask." The kind nurse says as her green chameleon style skin quivers rainbow styled tones. Olena thinks here how it's probably better no one does seem to remember her race, as many a war had been fought over millennia in her world with Vampires and various other species looking to battle it out. Vampires became reliant on human blood to stave off feeding from species of The Magical realm. This opened many doorways for the beginnings of a proverbial magical black market to open. Then communities began to move their lives and businesses to Earth, hidden behind the veils. Whereas many were all for the modernised changes——lots were not and so factions developed and home-grown terror groups popped up which lead to many wars over the centuries being battled out. The biggest threat posed to everyone now however was not Vampires but artificial intelligence and yet no one with the power to contain or control its development on Earth was doing a damned thing about it. If A.I. became sentient there was no telling what could happen to the veils or their world. It was technological advancement that reached even beyond the realms of the higher powers level of understanding——for they only dealt in matters of spirit and time. Although A.I. would never reach the realms of spirit——it could still develop time travelling devices and that is when upstairs would throw everything they had at the technology to defeat it, should such a time exist, which as of now was not written or predicted on the enchanted tapestry strings of time.

"Thanks...tell me, before you leave——are things among the Juju tribe?" Olena asks having recognised immediately what species the nurse belonged to——given her skin tones so using this conversational *in* as a way of seeking information to the comings and goings back on her home world.

The nurse slightly taken aback as to how a human/Vampire might know of her people. Ever the professional though shakes it off having learned through her career not to get too involved in personal conversations. "Ah...King Assyer is making trouble as usual but apart from that——no all is well. I'm sorry again to not remembering a thing about the *Vampires*...if there is nothing else I'm about to go off shift. Figuring I'll take my chances playing Fairy Poker with the Druids—— Excuse me." With that the rainbow scaled nurse steps out of the enchanted yurt——leaving Olena feeling better educated and confident about managing her new *womanly body.* The pad took some getting used to but soon Olena had even forgotten she was wearing one.

*If bleeding begins I must remember to change these pads every few hours——jeez hope I don't get caught out. What if I don't have any with me? No——don't go there. You have pads, no period as of yet——you're prepared. Everything's going to be fine.*

Following her inward pep talk, a thought of Olena's mother, Valeria flashes into her mind at how repulsed she would undoubtedly be to learn of her daughter's human menstruating body.

"Eurgh! Confound these awful thoughts and *emotions!* It's a ruddy wonder humans can even get out of bed in the morning! So overwhelming——how can I ever hope to complete these quests when I'm riddled with so many yucky *feelings?!*" Olena exclaims to herself while pacing back and forth just as Nathan pops his head inside to check up on her.

"Come in, all is well. I am now up to date in how to cope with this *time of the month* stuff." Olena says frustration registering clear in her voice "sorry I'm late for breakfast. This delay will be an unwelcome one I imagine. Frank gives the impression tardiness is not well tolerated where he is concerned. Olena says pouring herself a cup of herbal tea the nurse encouraged she drink to help with pre-menstrual tension.

"Nah, Frank will be cool. He's practically like a little puppy dog once you get to know him——please don't tell him I told you that. Err——here, I brought you a plate of scrambled eggs, bacon and toast." Nathan says placing the wooden plate of hot food onto Olena's bedside table.

"Mmm——otherworldly! Thanks for this." Olena says giving Nathan an appreciative smile that makes him blush.

"Sure, so long as you're really ok and nothing is too... *painful* for you?" Even as Nathan speaks these words he cringes. Olena says nothing, just gives him a blank blackened expression before clearing her throat.

"I've been thinking about how we can search for The Ruby Sunrise Dagger. You military men are usually pretty good at map reading right?" Nathan nods as Olena states the obvious.

"Good, well we should split up in teams of two and ask about the town. Don't worry about coming across any trouble——we're all protected by The Magi's mark. If anyone tried anything you'd only need to flash the tattoo——I guess in the guys' case it will be their *bottoms* ——but sure, just show the tattoo and I promise they'll be left alone." Olena chews a fingernail as plans whizz through her mind. Keeping one human safe would've been a challenge out here——let alone five of them. But splitting up seems the only sensible viable option given how short the time frame is and with little to no information——their options appear very limited.

"Ok, so where's this map?" Nathan asks feeling like a fish out of water experiencing this so-called *real* version Egypt which couldn't be further from the one he had come to know and understand during his time serving in the military.

"The only map I had was to help work our way through the differing cemetery portal doorways. Out here in Egypt——I'm just as lost and blinded as you all are. Perhaps Brax might be able to give us some maps of the city——you know like where might be a good place to start looking?"

Well it's not a *terrible* idea. Let me put it to Frank first. We're limited to options anyway so it can't help to ask Brax."

"It's because I'm a woman isn't it?"

"Sorry, I'm not sure that I follow you?" Nathan asks his head all but spinning on the three-sixty Olena was displaying with her bouncing mood swings.

"Why should it be *you* that tells our comrades about my plan for the day? Am I not capable enough to voice my opinion? Or do you feel it would have more weight coming out of your mouth? The mouth of a *man?*"

"I——actually just thought you might like some more time to yourself. Seeing how wrong of me it was to *assume* this. Please be my guest——lead on." Nathan says trying to utilise what little patience he has left. Stepping to one-side he proceeds to bow at the entry to the yurt with out-stretched arm inviting her to walk ahead.

"You know what——you're truly pathetic." Olena says passing Nathan and gently shoving her empty plate at him, having all but forgotten the short wooden steps situated directly outside her yurt doorway.

Losing her footing, Olena yelps as she can feel herself and her pride about to topple over and down. Squeezing her eyes shut it takes a second for her to realise she hasn't gone anywhere.

"Relax princess——I got ya." Nathan says having managed to grab the back of his jacket Olena is still wearing about her shoulders——therefore holding her back from a world of hurt.

Pulling her back toward him, she says a shaky *thank you*. Before clearing her throat to exclaim "Shall we." Only this time ascending the wooden steps like a pro.

Nathan lets out a silent oath before following her along the short grassy pathway over to where the rest of the team are setting up for whatever day may lay ahead for them all.

———

"Good morning Olena, I hope you slept well?" Frank asks giving her a warm fatherly smile that all but has her heart ache——wishing for nothing more than to be in the company of her own dear Vampire dad again.

"It was...*ok*——can't complain the bed's pretty comfortable. How about everyone here? Glad to see you and Donnie looking less stony faced this morning." Olena says giving a wink to Pete who splutters on his sip of coffee, stifling a laugh. Jamie and Donnie just give hooded glances toward Olena——wanting nothing more than to forget the awful hours spent experiencing total paralysis.

"As we are all fed and watered might I suggest we get down to the business at hand." Frank says placing his now empty mug of coffee in a spot with all other items set by for washing up. Everyone mumbles in agreement as they all sit on individual tree stump styled seats.

Once seated, Olena immediately jumps in with her idea of splitting up to seek out information regarding The Ruby Sunrise Dagger. She goes onto divulge more information as to how in total there are seven Earth months to gain each dagger so approximately a month to locate each one——before the chance to reset the time-line runs out. After this, time will be forever stuck as it is which could mean all manner of chaos ensues. She also surmised that perhaps this is why the Powers That Be were feeling particularly fractious about this specific kink in time. They didn't want to get their hands dirty but they also didn't want Olena to fail.

"That is everything I know, sorry I appreciate it's basically nothing to go on but there again I wasn't the one who messed with our magical forcefield now was I?" Olena says affixing Nathan with a blazing accusatory stare.

"Your plan sounds solid enough——everyone ok pairing off for the day?" Frank says as everyone merely nods in silent agreement.

Nathan looks to be about to say something but shuts his mouth remembering that when Felicity was due on——there was absolute zero point in trying to argue any point with her. And Olena wasn't wrong—— he had been the catalyst for starting this weird string of events.

"Boss, do you think it's wise us splitting up?" Jamie

asks giving. Sideways veil glance to Olena for her earlier stony-faced jibe.

"Oh I assure you this will be quite a safe operation. We all carry the mark of The Magi with us——which is universally understood by everyone from my world. If anyone tries anything simply flash the ID tattoo and all will be well." Olena says speaking in her mind an accent that sounded like old fashioned posh London——but when spoken aloud comes out in jarring Irish tones.

"You mean flash our asses? Like that's not going to insult the majority of people in the city." Donnie says looking and sounding fed up as he begins packing a bag with amenities for the day.

"Ah——Olena, any ideas? You are after all our guide for this mis-adventure. I think Donnie makes a valid point. I myself am not looking forward to the prospect of having to *flash* my tattoo around given its location." Frank says which earn him slow nods from the rest of the group.

"Very well, get your things in order and meet me by my yurt. I can paint your forearms with the tattoo pattern with enchanted ink. Once word gets out about who we are I feel we won't need to keep on proving ourselves." Olena says excusing herself to head on back to the yurt. As she turns Nathan catches a whiff of some scent Olena is emitting and before he can stop himself picks up his own pack——following her on toward her yurt, ignoring the wolf whistles going on behind him.

———

"Shouldn't you be getting ready with your friends?" Olena asks but before she can utter anything else Nathan strides right on up to her to plant a kiss on her lips.

Startled at first and about to pull away, Olena soon melts at the sensation allowing him to deepen the kiss. When he finally breaks away from her his eyes look completely drunk with lust.

Breathless, Olena staggers away to the side of her bed.

"What is that?" Nathan asks struggling to keep himself from tearing Olena's clothes from her body to all but jump on her.

"What is what?" She asks feeling slightly unnerved at Nathan's much darker eyes in place of the bright sapphire pools she likes too much.

"That...*aroma!*" Nathan exclaims walking up to Olena crouching down and to her utter horror *sniff* her.

"Oh...oh——err——perhaps it is the tea I drank to, you know——help with my...period." As Olena says this Nathan licks one half of her face before going in for a light nibble on her neck.

"Hey! Hey! Get off me! FRANK! ANYONE! Get in here NOW!" Olena yells at the top of her lungs praying the guys heard her.

Not a moment too soon does Frank, Pete, Donnie and Jamie burst into her yurt as Nathan is now foaming at the mouth with pure black eyes.

"Ok buddy, time to go." Pete says stepping forward with Donnie to lift him away from Olena.

With startling ease, he pushes them away from

himself. Frank looks tense as no one appears to know what to do.

"Run!" Nathan exclaims to Olena.

Not waiting for another invitation to get away Olena sprints up and out of the yurt——tearing across the forest floor to exit on out of her bedroom. Racing across the floor toward the lift Olena on entering it turns just in time to see Nathan crash through the doorway followed in hot pursuit by his comrades. The lift doors shut a mere fingernails breadth from Nathan's hands. Pressing the button to take her down to the lobby Olena begins to catch her breath. Hoping that whatever put Nathan in a knot didn't have a similar effect on anyone else. In her hand she held one of the Innocent looking tea bags the nurse had suggested she drink.

———

"I am so terribly sorry for the mix up Miss Lupescu. Let me call the nurse and have her verify what tea this is. It should by all accounts have been perfectly safe for human consumption with *no* magical effects whatsoever——as per my strict instructions for all of my staff here." Brax says picking up the phone receiver. "Please, take a seat ——she'll be right up." He continues on indicating to one of the plush velvet chairs situated opposite the reception desk.

The nurse appears promptly and it appears she's just in time as the lobby lift doors open and like a stallion in heat, out strides Nathan making a B-line for Olena.

Other guests make startled exclamations while jumping out of the way as he charges forward.

Lifting a small pipe to her lips the nurse fires off some sort of dart that drops Nathan like a dead weight——just as Frank, Pete, Donnie and Jamie all appear from the stairwell doorway.

"Relax, everything is fine. Miss Lupescu if you would be so kind as to follow me, I shall take you to my medical room. Fellas, if you could bring your sleeping friend please that would be most helpful." With that the chameleon nurse turns and walks away keeping a professional cool head, completely ignoring the fiery glare Brax is aiming toward her.

---

"There we go. In my haste to leave you I mixed up Fiery Fairy Frangipani tea with Florescent Hibiscus and Redbush." The nurse says handing Olena a box of bog-standard human herbal tea this time.

"What about Nathan? Will he be *okay*?" Olena asks tentatively while still feeling shaken up about the near miss she had with him trying to bed her with no control to his actions.

"Oh yes, he will be quite alright. I gave him a shot of Aloominum Foxtrate. I believe you all have a busy day ahead of you as was reiterated to me by the somewhat leader of your group——Frank is it?" Olena nods in response. "Yes, well *Frank* seemed most upset is the yelling and spittle flying everywhere are anything to go by, that I also gave him something to help calm him down. Anyway, if there is nothing else I shall bid you good day, you're free to go." The nurse says dismissing Olena, swivelling on her chair back to her desk where she feverishly begins writing up some notes.

"Errm." Words fail Olena as she steps out of the medical room making her way back up to reunite with Nathan and co.

# Chapter 29

Nathan cannot hold eye contact with Olena for the waves of utter shame he feels at losing control like that. However much she tried to explain it was not his fault——he still felt horrified at the monster he turned into——losing all manner of control which just wasn't like him. He'd known a girl in college to be raped by her boyfriend and how she had gone running to him from the girls' dormitory. It had been a friend of Felicity's and made Nathan want to murder the guy responsible. She swore him to secrecy——but it was a promise he broke due to the fact his sister went to the same boarding college and he couldn't allow a rapist to have free rein at the college putting other girls in danger. The guy was arrested. News travelled down that he was doing jail time but the details were very well hidden—— probably by mummy and daddy's rich lawyer. The mere idea he could have been about to do the same thing made Nathan feel physically sick.

"What I don't understand is, how come none of us were effected? Only Nathan?" Donnie says aloud while fastening his pack closed.

"The fairies use this particular tea to help those wishing to attract their perfect mate or force an old flame to lay with them——usually for want of offspring. I doubt for one moment the nurse deliberately sabotaged my safety. It would appear that Nathan might have an *attraction* toward me and this tea and the scent it created seems to have heightened such wants and desires——

"Like an aphrodisiac." Jamie says interrupting her.

"Exactly!" Olena confirms which earns her a sideways *eff-off* look from Nathan as he clips his own daypack of provisions shut.

"I'll see you all in the lobby. Best get onto Brax about giving or lending us some form of mapping for the city." As Olena turns to head off out of her room Pete calls out for her to wait so he can accompany her down.

On the ride down in the lift to the lobby, Pete explains about Nathan's experience in college helping the girl after she was raped. It was a close friend of his and also one of his sister's friends. She of course left the college after this; her parents didn't press charges against the college but the guy responsible did time. The realisation of everything Pete had told Olena made her stomach churn——for Vampires could and did regularly seduce humans for sex and blood. Was it dissimilar to rape? The thought made her feel nauseated. Even if humans were glamoured to forget the sex and draining——for those lucky enough to be left alive or un-turned, it wasn't consensual. Normally such trivial things wouldn't bother her in the slightest as Vampires were quite cold-blooded, but now full of human blood and feeling——Olena found herself spiralling into emotional depths unknown and that scared her.

Pete noticing how quiet Olena had become decided not to divulge anything further appreciating it was a lot to mentally digest.

"If I hadn't got away...had Nathan been able to... what would——

"Like putting a dangerous dog down——any one of us would have neutralised him." The doors of the lift ping open cutting off any response from Olena.

*Who will comfort me now? Nathan...he's unlike anyone I've ever met before. These feelings are all so strong inside of me. I wanted him to kiss me and maybe more but...now he won't so much as look at me——unless to silently tell me to do-one. What is this feeling inside of me now? It hurts——I hope it isn't a long-lasting emotional storm. I can't stand much more of this after today.*

———

Once the team are assembled in the Lobby earning them cautious glances from other hotel guests and staff milling about. Frank is quite impressed at Olena's organisational skills as Brax indicates for the guys to approach his reception desk so he can explain the devices he's loaning out to them all.

"These wrist devices activated here with this button

when pressed brings up 3D images of the city. Although there is no WiFi to connect technology this side of the veil. There is however something we call *source* that comes directly from The Magic veil. It works similarly to that your human WiFi but is faster and quite efficient. The wrist devices also work like phones so you can remain in contact with each other. You can also see where your individual icons are on the map. I took the liberty of attuning individual colours as identifying markers. Olena you are red, Frank white, Nathan green, Pete blue, Donnie yellow and Jamie you are turquoise. Should any of you need any further assistance please don't hesitate to ask. Again, I'm sorry Miss——

"Save your apologies. We'll be just fine——let's go." Nathan exclaims his blood still clearly simmering as he gruffly picks up his pack heading for the doors. Brax gives an annoyed snort out of his Minotaur nose and Frank says a brief apology before storming after Nathan his own blood now running hot. They can ill afford to piss off their generous host.

"Hey check this out——these devices even have a cool compass setting." Jamie says trying to pull attention away from the clear and present tension filling up the lobby space.

Fiddling about with his wrist attachment he shows everyone how the four compass points follow along with traditional pagan symbols:-

- **A tree representing 'Earth' = North**
- **A tornado representing 'air' = East**

- **A flame representing 'fire = south**
- **A raining cloud representing 'water = West.**

There is also a clear visible divide in the city between a light and dark side.

"Hmm——cool look, the west side is totally in shadow and the east is all in the light." Donnie muses now fiddling around with his own wrist device.

"On my world we have two main communities. Those better accustomed to lighter climates and those of a more nocturnal standing——like myself *normally* and my people. Having never travelled anywhere outside of London with my parents——*before* I got my job working at The Chequered Inn. Seeing how Egypt has adopted this clear light and dark division, perhaps other countries have a similar divide." Olena suggests feeling a bit more upbeat now to see the rest of the guys have at least shown an invested interest in the gadgetry on offer to help them in their quest.

"Let's go check it out." Pete says heading off out of the hotel.

"Woah dude! This is so trippy! It's like that lion movie——the one about the pride lands, you know the one with Mufasa and Simba in——ah come on bro don't tell me you ever watched it?" Jamie says gently elbowing Donnie who gives a blank expression in response.

As the guys all turn to look back on the entry way to The Blue Pharaoh hotel they can clearly see a clear line going straight down the middle of not just the building but the entire city.

"It's already heading up to noon. I suggest we get a move on if we're to make any ground today." Frank says pulling all attention back to himself.

Nathan still smarting from the grilling Frank just gave him——remains silent.

PTSD had touched all their lives seeing real battlefield action——for Nathan however he'd suffered with an especially bad spell after watching a comrade burn to death after their vehicle drove over an IED. Now the men were all retired from active service in the military they picked only the jobs they felt comfortable doing as freelance agents.

Having been plunged into the unknown Frank noticed has been especially challenging for Nathan. Giving him a stern talking to made Nathan remember that victim mindset wouldn't help him here and taking his ire out on Olena was just cruel and unnecessary. Having his head back in the game allowed Nathan to focus better on the job at hand.

"I'm guessing you won't be partnered up with me then?" Olena states flatly as that horrid empty feeling inside of her stomach bubbles away again.

"Quite the contrary Olena. I have *insisted* Nathan be partnered up with you. Jamie and Donnie will after a fashion stick together——which leaves myself and Pete. You've all got provisions and we shall meet back here just at sunset. No-one will mention what transpired earlier it's over and we all need to move on. Guys you all know the drill when we do recon——so I'm not teaching you to suck eggs. Usual rules apply, make sure you keep your communicators on and if anyone gets into a spot of bother come back here. If you get into a spot of bother use those well-honed military skills to help you. If no one has any questions, best of luck." As everyone peels off in their chosen directions for the day, Frank barks out another reminder, (startling a small group of pixie looking creatures) for them all to be back before sunset. Donnie and Jamie give mock salutes before disappearing off into the throng of a small crowd of magical folk coming and going. Frank and Pete then melt away themselves leaving Olena and Nathan standing in awkward silence just beyond the stone steps of the hotel before also heading off in their agreed South easterly direction.

---

"Thank you...for agreeing to partner up with me——I know you were sort of put into a corner by Frank but, I just wouldn't feel secure with anyone else——no offence to your friends it's just...I've known you the longest." Olena babbles on nervously, as she and Nathan began the arduous task of even pretending to know what they were doing.

"Just don't get to close yeah——and do your shirt up will you!" Nathan says growling out the request as Olena reaches for the buttons on her open khaki shirt that is loosely draped over a white strappy top underneath. Brax had already sent up clothing provisions for all of them, after researching what materials would be best for human skin in magical desert conditions. It turned out cotton and linen were the best choice of materials. Everyone had been stunned to find a neat pile of clothes labelled for each of them upon awakening. Yet questioned nothing, seeing as where they were oddly everyone accepted that during the night when they'd all been asleep, someone or something had snuck in to deliver the clothes.

"Look, I get what happened earlier spooked...both of us. But, please do not punish me for that. I had no idea I'd been given that weird tea——everything was meant to be safe."

"Yeah well it wasn't was it and like Frank said——drop it!"

"You know something...you can be really mean. None of it would have happened anyway if you could just not feel attracted to me!" As Olena says this Nathan pulls her somewhat roughly into a quiet shady alleyway holding her against a sandstone wall——panting. A fearful expression flits across Olena's face before she remembered the nurse cured both her pheromone issue and Nathan's uncontrollable sexual lust for her.

"Oh my Hades! You still do feel attracted to me——don't you? You just won't admit it! Why? ——too *macho* is that it?" Olena says trying her best to feign bravery. She never gets to add anything further though as Nathan kisses her——*again*, and she kisses him back. It feels more controlled and makes her body come alive with a heat that all but overwhelms her, as she presses herself into the wall for stability given that her knees have gone weak.

"This will go a lot smoother if you just don't talk so much or mention anything about *attraction.* Got it?" Nathan growls again, against her soft sweet mouth while burning to do more. It took all his restraint to peel himself away from her as his own heat and sexual desire created a painful ache within him.

"Yeah...well if you'd stop *KISSING* me it might go some way to preventing us doing something foolish!"

"Hmph! Fat chance of anything else happening barring kissing——how many of my kind have you killed I wonder? Sorry but I don't bed murderous wretches!" The sound of the slap echoed around them as a raised red welt began forming across Nathan's left cheek.

"Ah! Jeez!" Olena exclaims shaking her sore hand. "For your *information!* I was only just getting my one-hundred-year-old fangs in before you totally strucked up my life!" Olena all but yells in his face——using one of the strongest swear words in her vocabulary that would have seen her borderline disowned from her parents, should they have heard her.

"Yeah well, I bet you still *drank* the blood of dead humans, including babies!" Nathan spat back at her feeling like a complete arsehole but figuring if he could get her to despise him just enough——it would help both of them to keep their hormones in check.

"Know what——just leave me alone. Unless we're discussing the search don't speak to me."

"With pleasure——killer." Nathan answers, relieved

at how riled up he'd managed to get Olena. The angrier and more dis-interested she became in him——the easier it would be to cool down his sex drive. As right now he was horny as hell and wanted nothing more than to let Olena know *exactly* how he felt about her. Combined with the intense desert heat beating down upon them ——it wasn't helping matters.

---

*Thirty minutes later...*

"Okay, I can't stand the silence any longer. I'm sorry ——you know for being...mean." Nathan says which goes some way to lifting the sober expression registering across Olena's heart shaped face. "Where do you suggest we begin searching for the dagger?" Nathan asks feeling better now his body and mind had calmed down—— away from thoughts about Olena and him doing a naked bedtime tango between the sheets of her yurt bed.

Stalls and stands litter the sides of roads and alleyways that they pass. Several varieties of creatures and species shout about their wares in tongues that without the implanted translator device The Magi put inside each of them——Nathan would never have understood.

"I...appreciate your apology. I thought about going to visit the Seer. Every town and city I learned in school has one——they are a sort of, what your kind might consider as a remote viewer or psychic." Olena explains.

"Cool...so, we're ok now? I'm sorry my head is such a

mess——I had some...*bad* experiences on the battlefield and so, I can get a little moody at times. I'll say or behave in a way that isn't helpful to anyone."

"Look, its fine. I'm digesting what it means to be a human——you're all digesting what it means to be inside my world so...we're both going through a lot. But please can we just be honest about our feelings toward one another? I may not know all the workings of this body yet but all I know is when I'm close to you I feel good, and when you pull away——it hurts...right here, here and...*here.*" Olena says pointing first to her head, then her heart and finally her stomach.

"Ok, I admit it. I like you *a-lot*. Would it help you if I ——held your hand while we walked?" Nathan suggests figuring he can handle that amount of contact with Olena.

"Oh yes, that would be *lovely.* Thank you." Olena says her eyes brightening as Nathan takes up her hand in his.

She closes her eyes and takes in a deep breath. "There, that nice feeling - its back again. Thank you."

"My pleasure. Now, what were you saying about this Seer character we need to look for?"

As conversation progresses, Olena finds her earlier ire towards Nathan and his demeaning comment about her being a *murderous wretch*——thawing as they continually communicate quite civilly to one another, the further they venture into their city zone of choice.

"Ah——damn my wrist device is busted, how's

yours?" Nathan asks gently taking a hold of Olena's arm to raise it up so he could see it. His gentle touch on her lower forearm had her all but swooning for him.

"Hmm, also busted. So much for the tech being better and more efficient. Best we get a move on. I'll ask Brax upon our return if there's a better way to keep us all connected. For now, however——it looks like we're travelling blind." Olena says realising they are heading toward the edge of the darker side of the city.

"Hang on, I do believe I have the Boy Scout method of tracking direction." Nathan says placing his pack on the ground pulling his own manual compass out.

"Good idea——does it work this side of the veil? A lot of human stuff wouldn't due to atmospheric things and electromagnetic field shifts."

"For a magical person you sure know a lot about Earth's electromagnetism."

"Not really——You see in school we had to learn about the geography of not just our world but also Earth's. I don't know much about electromagnetism just that its responsible for messing up a lot of your people's technology——take the Bermuda Triangle for example, why do you think so many ships and planes go missing there. It's a veiled area."

"Having peeked behind these veils now, I can appreciate that explanation more. Good news is the compass ——works." Nathan says showing Olena the needle and how it moves with him to find true north.

"Lucky for us then I guess. Shall we?" Olena says

indicating with open hand for them to carry on their way. She'd made a mental note as to where she thought she had located the psychics' street. On her holographic map when it had been working, she had spotted a row of shops with psychic insignia above doorways and on signs hanging outside.

They walk along ignoring the many merchants selling their wares. Olena's sense of smell still being heightened to that of Vampire levels helped her to sniff where some of the strongest magic was culminating. To a human the smell of strong magic would omit an aroma of burnt caramel.

"Oh——my watch device is back up and working again. It looks like The Seer might be down Padrigan Lane. I made a mental note earlier of a row of mystical shops——here take a look, what do you think?" Olena asks Nathan, pulling up the holographic image of the lane and zooming in——much the same as someone might do with Loogle Maps on the internet.

"There——zoom in on that building, the one with the eye over the door. Is *that* where this Seer might be?" Nathan asks earning him a big smile from Olena.

"Why Mr Jones. I believe you are a natural dab hand at seeking out that which you are seeking——are you sure you don't have magical DNA?"

"Alright enough with the flattery. Let's hope Frank and the guys are having just as much luck. Let's check in with them once we've visited this Seer person."

"Feels better now we appear to have a plan coming

together." Olena says as the pair hold hands again sharing sips from Nathan's canteen.

Looking into one another's eyes as they take turns sipping the water, inevitably the pair end up kissing——*again!*

## Chapter 30

Frank & Pete
**North East section of veiled Cairo**

Frank and Pete have found themselves in a most peculiar bind. Having entered what looked to be standardised bar establishment they have somehow found themselves involved unwittingly in some toe-to-toe high stakes gambling card game with British bulldog faced competitors.

"I'm sure these guys remind of a famous gambling painting I've seen before." Pete whispers to Frank as the pair of them are presently sweating bullets unsure exactly of how to get themselves out of such a tight spot.

"Will you focus please!" Frank says tensely. "I can't work out my arse from my elbow here. These symbols are complete gobble-dee-gook to me. And seeing how those two buggers down there, whose places we have taken, got turned into sloppy mushy magical gloop before our very eyes——I'd say working a way out of this mess needs to happen sooner rather than later." Frank says as big droplets of sweat pour down both men's faces.

"Hang on a sec...a ha! I think I got it!" Pete says triumphantly placing his hand out onto the table for all the other players to see. Leaving Frank with all colour draining from his face.

One of the dog-faced characters growls. Slamming his hand of cards riddled with hieroglyphic styled symbols down upon the table as every hand is now shown. The remaining players have lost——which means by some miracle and astonishment to Frank, that Pete and he have won!

"How in the——

"Algebra." Pete admitted winking at his friend.

"These are not numbers though."

"I'd explain but we don't have time. Let's take the dinaro, ask the questions and leave."

The losing bulldog players as per the rules, are transformed into porcelain statuettes by a weird skeletal wand wielding looking dude who'd been stood off patiently to one side of the table. Carefully the skeletal character places the now porcelain bulldog players atop a shelf to accompany other transformed players.

"Care to play again gentleman or would you prefer to collect your winnings and *leave?*" The skeleton dude says holding out their winnings to whereby Frank graciously takes the bag of coin as he and Pete make a speedy exit out of the establishment.

———

**Donnie & Jamie**
**South West region of veiled Cairo**

Donnie and Jamie are presently getting eyefuls of alien female looking boobs——of differing translucent colours, as they have unwittingly fallen into a Sirens rave trap. The music filtering through from a closed nightclub door was enough to overpower them——drawing them in.

"Mmmmm you smell *divine!*" A scantily clad Siren says rubbing her glittered neon pink and purple body up against Donnie's restrained one.

Both men have been strapped to upright metallic frames held in place by super strong magical vine looking restraints.

"Well...can't say I've ever experienced a bondage situation quite like this." Jamie says earning him an eye-roll from Donnie who cannot believe even now with their certain demise that his good friend can crack jokes.

"Do you think the others will find us in time?" Donnie asks trying to keep his eyes anywhere but on the bodies of the naked females fawning over him.

"I don't know but *ohhhhh.*" Jamie's eyes roll back as he has a *servicing* experience quite unlike anything he'd ever experienced before.

"Dude – did you just?" Donnie asks mouth agape, the disgust registering clear and present upon his own flushed face.

"I couldn't help it. Oh God, you don't think they're going to make cross-breeds of me, do you? I'm not ready to be a dad!" Jamie exclaims alarmed as he watches the female siren place his seed inside of a tube.

"Seriously! We're about to become mincemeat and all you can think is what they might use your juju for?!" Donnie exclaims alarmed when a green and blue female alien looking creature sidles up to him.

"Say hello to my lil friend!" Donnie says quoting a line from a famous movie line.

A loud squeal erupts making glasses and mirrors smash. Creatures and species hurl themselves toward the exits, some looking as if they have the equivalent of bleeding ears or – gills.

Donnie manages to break free from his binds as the alien skinned women all put attention on their suffering friends who didn't make it outside and who are now whimpering on the floor——grabbing what might account to being like ear holes on the sides of their heads.

Making fast work of Jamie's bonds the men scurry for the exit thankful to make it out into the blistering sunshine alive. Jamie had grabbed their clothing that had been dumped on the floor beside them as well as the vial of his own DNA before hurtling through the doorway. Both men sprinted naked away from the establishment before finding a quiet corner to dress——as Jamie poured his *juju* down a drain cover.

"How did you...get her off you?" Jamie asks, still panting. Hot dust laden air, filters into Jamie's lungs between each spoken word.

"I...tasered her."

"What? How?!"

"Remember how my uncle Larry was a top magician."

"Yup!" Jamie says as the men walk in slow tandem ——sweat pouring down both their red and exhausted faces.

"I learned a thing or two about hiding objects about my person, I tucked the taser somewhere unmentionable ——and no before you ask it wasn't inside of me."

"Thankful for your uncle Larry then. Come on, no-one seems to be following us, lets retire the operation and wait for the others back at the hotel——lunch?" Jamie says patting his friend on the shoulder.

"Sure, I could murder a Big Mac and fries——bugger, my comms device is out. Hope we can find our way back." Donnie says, concern flooding him to realise both their packs are now missing along with their provisions such as the water they'd been carrying.

"Already tried mine but look——also not working. We are alone. Man, I wish we still had our packs——I'm dying of both hunger and thirst."

"Frank won't be happy about this. Do you think they can conjure up Maccy's out here?" As Donnie suggests this both men pick up their pace upon turning into a main road and looking ahead they can see The Blue Pharaoh hotel. Relief floods both their bodies.

"We'll worry about Frank later——let's just get back and find sustenance." Jamie says holding onto his dear friend as they help one another hobble back to their dwelling having had near on all their energy zapped by the Sirens.

**Nathan & Olena**
**Heading into dark western territory**

The west part of the city was full of colours representing watery tones. There were rich hues of purples and deep blues. Clothes, spices, footwear, as well as home-ware such as lamps, cabinets and other sorts of magical bric-a-brac were all on display. Nathan grinned to spy a washing up set——where basically the dishes washed themselves. Fairies in lights——danced about inside what looked to be mason jars with breathing holes drilled through the lids. Messenger birds begging for freedom while fluttering about inside both metal and wooden cages tugged at Nathan's heart strings. A children's toy stand showed an array of all sorts of animated objects and toys.

"Just as well Jamie isn't with us, I'd never tear him away from the toy stand." Nathan says fully taking in the sights, sounds and goings-on all around them.

"So...you're fast becoming a fan of The Magical side then?" Olena asks quirking up a quizzical eyebrow at Nathan. The smouldering look this question earns her from Nathan makes her blood run hot as lust slams into her full force again with all of these new female hormones she's learning to contend with.

Before Nathan can answer her, a loud merchant with rotting teeth inside of his lizard face, accompanied by rotting fishy breath yells aloud——holding out scabby hands laden with sparkling gem goodies.

"FRESH GEMS! You'd like to try something on miss?" The lizard man says hissing out the last word.

"Allow me." Nathan says, taking the fierce looking emerald pendant from the merchant's hand to fasten it around Olena's neck. It sets her emerald eyes ablaze while also complimenting her copper coloured hair.

"This is the *lovers'* jewel——very rare and *very* potent. How would you like to pay?" The merchant asks while trying to hypnotise them into making an extortionate purchase.

"We're...here under The Magi's orders." Olena says un-affected by the stinky lizard man's charms.

The lizard man hisses——ripping the gemstone pendant from Olena's neck breaking the hypnotic spell that had worked on Nathan a little too well. The lizard guy then retreats into his seller's hut *slamming* down a blind making rude curses under his breath.

"Woah, what happened?" Nathan asks shaking the residual dreamy feeling from his mind.

"That handsome was a——*Charmdile*. Think crocodile but with the addition of legs, arms and *charm*." Olena says unable to shake off the intense vibration she had felt in her nether regions a mere moment after the Charmdile had slipped the pendant around her neck. Intense feelings like this just didn't exist for Vampires. As previously mentioned reproduction was a means to an end, Vampires seldom had sex for pleasure with their chosen spouse. No——humans were usually utilised for their blood and also their bodies for sexual release when a Vampire didn't want to go through the dangers of courtship with one of their own. Even when coupled for eternity a female Vampire could so easily turn on her male partner erasing him from existence with her much stronger female strength.

Olena feeling overcome with these waves of intense urges, made her want to physically scream as there just seemed no way of alleviating any of it.

"I see. Looks like the sun's beginning to dip low in the sky. We need to get help but I can't see that happening anytime soon if all we receive is doors being slammed in our faces." Nathan says stating the obvious while trying to regain his composure with a literal pressing matter painfully squeezing itself against the zipper of his fly.

"Hmm, perhaps we should work to getting some Moolakash——that's money to you." Olena surmises, pondering on just how to go about it. "Odd, I can see Frank and Pete on my watch device but cannot raise Donnie and Jamie. We're definitely going to need better forms of comms when we get back to the hotel." Olena says not realising the pain Nathan is presently suffering with the after effects of the Charmdile's lust inducing whammy he managed to put on Nathan. The charm didn't work on Olena given the fact her own glamouring skills had been reinstated by The Magi, making it impossible for Olena herself to come under anyone's hypnotic spell.

They walk side by side in silence while Olena mulls over their current predicament at having no Moolakash. It was all very well having The Magi state that anything they needed they would receive so long as they flashed their Tattoos about. But in reality, it appeared no-one was readily available to help *humans* on this side of Cairo's enchanted veil.

"Bambi! Of course!" She almost yells, mildly startling Nathan.

"Isn't that a deer?"

"No, *not* the human version of a cartoon animal. I mean my friend Bambi! She can sort us out. Come on, the faster we can speak to the Seer the quicker we'll be connected to Bambi and get some much needed Moolakash." Olena exclaims almost skipping ahead as her excitement bubbles over. She has not realised this behaviour is very un-Vampire like. It appears Olena is beginning to forget herself and what it means to be Nosferatu.

Linking arms, together they stride on past the rest of the colourful stalls——heading into a shadier part of the market where things go from bright and sunny to murky and maroon.

An impromptu shiver runs through Nathan and Olena gives his arm a reassuring squeeze. Checking her watch while Nathan keeps his eyes on his compass, Olena states they are travelling in the right direction to which Nathan agrees on as he watches their own colourful dots dance on the holographic image as they inch closer to the shop with mysterious eye logo above its door. His earlier discomfort appearing to ease the further down the alleyway they get as all of a sudden, they find themselves beneath a canopy of overhead curtain style material that is helping to keep the hot sun from the tops of their heads and bodies. Goosebumps run along his arms and torso as the sweat begins to evaporate off his body.

Market stalls quieten the further along they travel and soon all that surrounds them are quiet dusty streets and alleyways.

A chill rolls across Nathan's skin as he realises they are venturing toward dark side territory. Everything here seems a lot quieter——a lot more...empty. It appears that the merchants of Padrigan Lane are not so popular.

## Chapter 31

A Menthe Fairy named Fliss has agreed to help lead Olena and Nathan towards the city's Seer. She is about the size of Olena's hand with pale green hair put up into two cute little bunches either side of her fingertip sized head. On her body Fliss is wearing an aquamarine coloured dress with cute little pink fairy boots.

Olena and Nathan had both spotted the quaint little tea shop and decided to stop for a break——hoping there was something at least like standard water they could consume here. As luck would have it there was——mint tea accompanied with human grade chocolate fairy cakes——infused with mint aromatics. In Egypt mint tea is simply adored among human and magical people alike. Seeing a gap in the market many decades ago, Menthe Fairies set up to grow fields of mint on Earth. Finding the business to be profitable on both sides of the veil which meant that Menthe fairies were quite wealthy. Distributing the mint across the veil was a relatively simple procedure. Fairies would drink a short-lasting tincture to transport the mint under the guise of working as humans for an international wholesaler. Their mint was considered the best in the world which should come as no surprise given it was infused with safe magical fertilisers that lead to no ill effect on human consumers but added a mighty punch to the flavours.

Fliss having cleared their table hands Olena a small business card. It is green with a gold embossed border and animated dancing four leaf clovers all over it. The writing on it is indecipherable as unfortunately the translators only work on spoken languages to translate——not written. Olena tells Nathan the card had Fliss' name on it and an instruction to flick the card three times and call her name to speak with her.

"Now you wanted me to show you to our city's Seer ——I feel I must warn you she can be a bit of a battle-axe, so tread carefully. If you're ready to leave then follow me!" Fliss says zipping ahead at an unusually unnatural speed.

"Sorry! I forget, humans can't move so fast." Fliss says zipping back to hover in front of Olena and Nathan's faces. "Before I forget, I also took the liberty of setting you up an account with Infinity Bank. It's the pleasure of The Menthe Fairies to help you on your quest ——if you could see your way forward to putting in a good word for me with The Magi——I'd be forever grateful." Fliss says winking before zooming ahead at a speed that Olena and Nathan can keep up with so long as they lightly jog.

Having learned not to ponder on anything magical anymore, Nathan keeps his mouth firmly closed over the burning questions wanting to pop out——such as how on Earth could Fliss have whipped up a bank account for them without so much as a piece of identifying paper or phone call.

"Thank you ever so much Fliss, and of course I shall definitely mention your name to The Magi if I happen across them again." Olena says slightly out of breath having stopped jogging now that Fliss has also come to a hovering halt.

"Th-thank you." Fliss says sounding a little bashful in her cute little fairy voice as Olena keeps her fingers crossed firmly behind her back having no intention of bringing Fliss' existence before The Magi given how threatened she herself feels about them.

"Ok, so The Seer is down there. I'd take you but our kind don't have security clearance past here. Head straight to the end of Padrigan Lane——you'll find her tucked around to the right. Look for the dark maroon shop front with painted eye above the door. Ring the bell and take three *large* steps backwards."

Before either of them could respond Fliss pinged herself out of sight. A weight lands in Olena's hand, it is a shiny pouch of gold coins with a mini note that says *with compliments from The Menthe Fairy Clan*. Each coin is stamped with the Menthe fairies four leave clover insignia proving the authenticity of the currency.

Clipping the pouch to her jeans belt, Olena and Nathan venture forth following Fliss' instructions straight ahead.

---

As they skim the line between the dark and light side of the city. Both Olena and Nathan can see how Padrigan Lane has suddenly become noticeably darker.

"Ah——*sorry*." Nathan exclaims alarmed looking down at the small, round and fluffy critter that angrily squeaked at him.

"That's just a dust sweeper, small balls of animated fluff conjured up by local cleaning witches. No one can ever decipher what they're saying as they are too small and low to the ground. Wizards and Mages study them furiously in our world but as of yet their language remains——an enigma." Olena explains looking enamoured at Nathan caring even so much for such an insignificant creature.

Nathan grins at the ludicrousness then links his arm through Olena's. as she leans into his body, heat courses through him and he cannot stop the urge to kiss her once more. And like something possessed Olena deepens the kiss, pulling at Nathan's loose-fitting shirt, tugging him to her wishing more than anything they could do more than kissing.

"Woah! Wait...*wait.*" Nathan says which takes all his restraint to call time on their impromptu kissing session.

Olena all but flings herself away from him as if having received an electric shock.

"It's me isn't it...you can't *bear* the thought of touching a cold-blooded killer——even though I've never actually killed any human——*yet.*"

"Err, no actually. I was just thinking we have no——*protection.*"

"What the hell are you talking about?! We couldn't be better protected——NO ONE'S HERE!" Olena yells angrily, as indeed they appear to be the only two people walking along Padrigan Lane.

"Do you remember that discussion we had——about...*periods* and the birds and bees?"

It takes Olena about two seconds to cotton onto what Nathan was going on about.

"Oh...right...baby making. Sorry...for my kind its near on impossible to conceive naturally——hence the *turning* process." Olena says reddening at the mere mention of sex.

"Let's cool off——go see this Seer woman and *then*, we'll see how we can help each other out regarding——this situation." Nathan says focusing on not wishing to get Olena pregnant being the only thing stopping him from having his wicked way with her.

*Just like Frank always advised——wear your seatbelt, even if the woman claims to be on contraception. Safety first!* He reminds himself mulling over some of the best advice Frank ever gave him that Nathan is sure saved many a love child from ever being born.

"Wait! This *feeling* its overwhelming. Is there

nothing that can be done to help alleviate it? ——its bordering on painful?" As Olena says this, the pleading in her voice for just how much she requires *attention* all but undoes Nathan, who then has a light bulb moment he could all but kick himself over.

Clouded with lust he'd forgotten all about *foreplay.*

"Indeed, there is *something* I can try with you. I don't know why I didn't think of this sooner." Nathan says as his eyes blacken with deliberate hunger——decision to help Olena already firmly made.

Gently, he draws Olena into a darkened side alleyway. Turning her around so her back is to him he then begins making fast work of, *alleviating* some of the sexual tension for her.

*"Oh...MR JOOOOOOONES!"* Olena sings out as a powerful orgasm bursts forth from her.

Feeling her soft folds flood with sweet nectar between his fingers nearly tips Nathan over the edge himself, however he manages to remain steadfast and focused. Later he will most certainly be introducing Olena to the nicer aspects of human coupling but for now he knew he must keep his snake in its cage.

"Th—thank you...that was——-

"No 'thank you' required Miss Lupescu." Nathan says taking up her hand in his as they walk in warm silence the rest of the way toward the Seer's store front.

# Chapter 32

"I'm feeling——much *better.*" Olena says without an ounce of embarrassment. This surprises Nathan as most women would have become bashful and coy but not Olena it appears. As ever she coming across as matter of fact and quite pragmatic. Nathan doesn't know whether to find her demeanour refreshing or insulting. Then again having used women for *releases* of his own with no strings attached——he perhaps appreciated now how the recipient women might have felt—— even if they did at the time say they were ok just *having fun.* The lingering look in most women's eyes he'd bedded often let down their cool exterior yet he'd never had any *bunny boilers* fortunately as through the years he'd heard of plenty of soldiers getting caught out by stalkers and psycho female types who couldn't handle the man in uniform doing the whole *wham, bam——thank you mam* tango No, when it came to women Nathan was especially cautious, usually opting to go for those slightly older then him. With Olena however, he couldn't help but feel pulled toward her. Had she been born pure bred human and had they met under different circumstances ——would he have felt the same way? These thoughts race through his mind worse than ever after helping to take the edge off Olena's sexual itch.

The pair of them share a lingering look into one another's eyes before turning to face the maroon store front accompanied with blazing golden eye painted above its door. Nathan could've sworn he saw it blink at them but tries not to pay any attention it.

"There will be more of *that* to come——later." Nathan states, hypnotising Olena once more with those *come to bed* sapphire pools as his eyes smoulder with adoration and lust for her.

A pang of the previous uncomfortable feelings begins to stir so Olena clears her throat gently pressing a hand to Nathan's muscular chest to give herself some distance and a beat to recover her already shaky composure.

Smiling at Olena's loss for words he turns his attention back to the door lifting the heavy brass pyramid shaped door knocker——reiterating the instructions to knock and then take three steps backwards.

The door swings outward slowly bringing with it swirls of grey mist from inside the dwelling. A small hooded figure floats out of the doorway towards them. A pair of amber orbs that perhaps are eyes Nathan muses to himself——flash from the depths of the blackness inside the hood.

"Sharine is ready for you——you're expected. Follow

me." The un-introduced character says in a tinny pitched voice, as both Olena and Nathan obediently follow them inside the misty-esoteric looking shop.

The door creaks closed behind them——transforming to shape what looks to be solid brick wall. Fear prickles along Nathan's spine not liking the fact there is now no visible exit. His military training always taught him to have or seek out an exit.

Looking around both Olena and Nathan can see that the shop is stacked floor to ceiling with crystals, cabinets full of statues——including your stereotypical unicorns, dragons, mermaids, three eyed monsters, demon looking beasts and more. Trapped fairies plead their case from golden cages charged with magical electricity——shocking any who touch the bars. Smelly sticks protrude from an incense burner that appears to be the cause of the swirling mist, the scent makes Nathan's nasal passages itch as he sneezes loudly, making Olena yelp in surprise causing her to knock a glass vial of liquid onto the stone floor——as it smashes fumes float up that immediately have her head swimming.

"Bless you." A woman's voice says from behind a ruby jewelled——beaded curtain. "Clear that up won't you Jance, I believe our...*guests* require an audience with yours truly." The mysterious veiled woman says giving the levitating hooded figure a side-ways glance as they are busy clearing up the spilled mess all over the floor.

The looks like a gypsy that you might imagine to see from an illustrated fairy tale story such as that of Aladdin. She has long black wavy hair tied back held in place with red sparkling twine. Her face is partially covered by semi-see-through veil showing a pair of piercing purple eyes about it. The top of her head is covered with similar see-through rich magenta coloured material. On her body are what appears to be a dark purple-velvet material crop top accompanied with matching long skirt finishing the Seer's belly dancer, gypsy look. Metal discs attached to her ensemble, emit a pleasant jingle sound as she turns gliding through the ruby curtain. With nothing else to do, cautiously Nathan and Olena follow her.

"You are right to be wary of me, but do not be afraid ——I know why you've come. Follow me, and please, call me Sharine." The Seer named Sharine says——her friendly tone however, *not* fooling Olena who has been educated to be exceptionally wary of any and all Seers whose intentions are hardly ever honourable. Nathan however seems less apprehensive, as he all but has his tongue lolling out after Sharine while they follow her through the ruby curtain stepping into a much nicer and inviting space.

*She must be working some form of magic over him. Best to tread carefully here——I hope you don't embarrass me Mr Jones or worse!* Olena thinks to herself, giving a curt smile to Sharine as she continues following Sharine and Nathan deeper in what Olena deems fit to be called lair in place of shop.

Eventually the trio arrive into a vast expansive space that looks like the insides of a giant carved out succa tree (trees that grow in the city of giants back in The Magical realm). It boggles Nathan's mind how from the outside the store looked only to be one level, bet here it was so much bigger.

*Parry Trotter eat ya heart out.* Nathan muses recalling a famous scene from a famous Earthbound book franchise——talking of tents giving the illusion of being nothing special, however when someone entered inside was a much bigger, taller space. He now wondered if perhaps the author R J Kowling wasn't magic herself.

A small tree with lilac coloured blossoms sits in the centre of the room giving off a heady blossom aroma ——the walls are adorned with wall to ceiling shelves of books and other magical paraphernalia. Comfortable looking rich toned velvet styled furniture give the space a relaxed and pleasant feel. Oddly seeing the furniture makes Olena remember Nathan's home but puts this down to coincidence.

Sharine's eyes flash excitedly as she indicates with outstretched palm for them both to take up a seat on one of her plush purple settees.

*This all feels...oddly familiar.* Nathan can't help but think considering the familiarity of the furniture around them. He shakes off the vibe thinking how silly it must be of him to even consider anything *familiar* about Sharine's dwelling.

"Let me conjure up some tea for us——English breakfast ok?" Sharine asks which certainly makes Nathan's eyebrows shoot up at how educated Sharine appears while she plays hostess for two *humans.* The realisation breaks the unnatural infatuated pull he's been feeling toward Sharine since first laying eyes on her. As realisation sinks in he isn't himself, this immediately puts his other senses on alert.

*Never eat or drink anything offered from a Seer.* Olena's past teachers voice rings clear as a bell through her mind. *But there again don't offend by refusing anything offered.*

"Tea would be lovely, thanks——I take mine with sugar and milk." Olena says remembering how Nathan had made tea for her back in London. As she gives the instruction she also takes advantage of Sharine's turned back to fire Nathan a wary glance while gently shaking her head indicating for them not to touch anything offered——hoping her silent message lands correctly.

"Sure, tea would be grand. I'll have the same as Olena." Nathan says affixing Sharine with his best warm smile and she focuses her efforts on the small coffee table between them Nathan connects eye contact with Olena and strangely with just a *look* has come to the realisation he has understood her.

"Olena dear, before we drink our tea—— would you like me to rectify your *look*? It pained me terrible to feel the rip in the fabric of time and evaporation of your people——as I imagine must have been felt by all Seers. Our link to the Powers That Be being stronger given our ——*unique* set of fortune seeing skills means we don't have the grace to simply *forget* things." Sharine explains stunning Olena with an odd sense of comfort knowing that not everyone from her world appears to have forgotten her or her people.

"Thank you——that's very gracious of you to say. I admit to being so embarrassed by the whole mess. As for my looks, you...could *really* change me back? It won't upset The Magi? I worry——looking like *this* was...part of my punishment and wouldn't want to upset things further." Olena says warily but unable to keep excitement from trickling through her voice.

"Pish! The Magi may have moulded you to look a certain way but there's no law stating one which has been transformed can't be——changed back. You'll still be human after all, only now you'll be retaining those gorgeous, natural vampiric looks of yours. I got Jance to check *all* legal magical literature before your visit here today——it's part of my skill set——seeing visitors before they arrive." Sharine says finishing conjuring up a tray laden with tea and what look to be cupcakes and biscuits on the small wooden coffee table situated between them.

"Wait——what will the transformation cost me? I've learned well that nothing a Seer does is free of charge." Olena says as Sharine reaches for Olena's hands having finished setting the table.

"Consider *this* a freebie. Your father, he was very kind to me as I was growing up. I was a human child- an orphan. Your father, he hunted and killed both my parents before realising they had a child. It wasn't entirely his fault, he got waylaid taking out a Vampire hunter who had mortally wounded him——by the time he found my parents walking home from seeing a play... he...was out of control. By the time realisation registered it was too late. I was placed into a workhouse and beaten on a regular basis, then I was moved from pillar to post through orphanages. One night I managed to escape after a particularly brutal beating for spilling a bucket of dirty water all over the floor I'd just finished scrubbing. Your father he...had been tracking me, unable to live with the guilt of ripping a child's parents away——perhaps it had something to do with the fact your dad used to be human and worked to help children with his detective skills. Anyway, he found me lying in a puddle of blood on the verge of death from multiple fractures, broken bones and cuts. It was a miracle I was still alive by the time he discovered me. Sensing my strength, he offered me eternal life but I was ready for death even at the age of seven——all I wanted was to be with my parents. Ignoring my protests your father made me drink his blood which healed me within mere moments, I then had my first psychic flash in front of another person—— I'd had them before. Your dad, seeing my potential and realising I could be more, took me to Egypt's magic council where upon sensing my capabilities was granted the chance to become a Seer." Sharine says taking a breath having laid her cards on the table as painful memories made her itch, as Seers were trained to feel suppressed emotion.

"A ha! So *that's* why you have a London accent." Nathan says clocking why it was Sharine sounded so bizarrely out of place in Egypt——when everyone else appeared upon translation to have rich Middle Eastern accents.

"How every observant of you Mr Jones." Sharine says flashing him a glare at not allowing Olena to respond first.

"That's...a lot to digest, at least in this body." Olena says trying hard not to cry. while flicking an annoyed glance at Nathan silently relaying the message for him to kindly keep his mouth shut.

"Your dad sure was a rare breed of Vampire. He exacted revenge on all those who'd laid a hand on me, I dare say even you Olena may have tasted their blood when you were but a babe."

The thought upon hearing this makes Olena's stomach all but roll with revulsion.

"Then again I'm circa 1700s so perhaps not given your youth." Relief soon replaces the recent queasy feeling. As Sharine confirms there's no way Olena would have drunk sour human blood. Vampires tended to stray from crooks and criminals as their blood always tasted so very bitter. Whereas the pure and Innocent——it was like pure ambrosia.

"I'm so sorry you went through that Sharine—— with these human emotions plaguing me, I can genuinely say that I'm truly, deeply sorry for the loss of your parents." Olena says wiping tears from her eyes.

"In a bizarre way when I checked for an alternative timeline——to see if I'd have had a long and happy life with my parents——turns out we'd have all died in a big house fire——so in a way it's serendipity." Sharine says affixing a fake warm look across her timeless bewitching face.

Sharine takes up her seat directly opposite Nathan and Olena on the plush green settee.

"I assure you all these delicacies are completely safe to consume. Afterall I dare not interfere with The Magi's plans outside of what I can already do——which is to restore your natural good looks." Sharine says pouring the steaming amber tea out into three china cups. "Right, tea poured, let's get on with getting you looking like your old self again?" Sharine says cheerfully clapping her hands together making Nathan almost spill his tea he has raised to his lips. Olena shoots him another glance shaking her head to which he takes just a pretend sip.

"*Mmmm,* the tea is exquisite——cheers." Nathan says raising the small china cup up.

"Quick question——will I still be able to cast a reflection once the spell is cast?" I've never seen my real self in the flesh before."

"Of course, while you remain human you shall be able to do all human related things such as——casting a reflection. I cannot turn you back into a Vampire, but I can indeed help you to at least *look* and feel more normal. All you need do is look directly into——this mirror!" Sharine says whipping out a small gold framed pocket mirror from seemingly nowhere, making Nathan jump again this time spilling some of the hot tea onto his trouser leg. Cursing, he places the tea cup back onto its saucer while proceeding to feverishly fan at his burning leg with his hands.

"Woah!" Nathan lets out a shout of surprise looking up from his damp trouser leg to see Olena in her true form. "It *is* you...it was always you..." Nathan's voice trails off realising Olena had been nothing but honest about who she was. The raven-haired goddess had returned. But Nathan's feelings were felt marred with the burning he'd felt for the Irish woman he'd grown to love.

"Now, your voice will be a bit trickier——Jance! Get me a bottle of Voicetune!" Sharine says barking out the order to her magical aide.

The floating hooded mage who materialise out of thin air——passes Sharine a bottle of shining silver liquid.

"Careful Olena...it looks——

"*Unnatural*? Sharine says interrupting Nathan's concerned warning. As she carries a vigorous gleam to her eyes."

"I was gonna say it looks like liquid mercury." Nathan says feeling unsure as to whether or not Olena should ingest the liquid metal looking contents.

"It's ok, she's a friend of my father's...I trust her." Olena says taking the vial, raising it to her lips downing it in one.

Within mere moments Olena's voice breaks and what floats through is a sultry almost Romanian styled accent. The dreamy sound has Nathan's head spinning once again.

"Olena, listen to me carefully. So as to not skew the timeline further both of you should leave immediately, but before you go I have one message to relay to you. When the time is right *choose wisely*. I'm sorry there's nothing more I can say to help you." As Sharine rattles off the cautionary instruction, and before any further words can be exchanged——a sound like a balloon popping fills the space as Olena and Nathan are jettisoned from the property——unceremoniously dumped onto their backsides, back out onto the dusty lane.

Helping one another to stand, both Olena and Nathan begin the arduous trek back toward The Blue Pharaoh, hoping to make it back before sunset as the sun begins its rapid descent causing darkness to creep across into the normally sunnier side of the city. As they venture onward, neither feels ready to address what Sharine has divulged——deciding to stick to small talk. As they get closer to busier night-time streets, food vendors can be seen selling all manner of magical sustenance. Playing it safe Nathan and Olena walk on by, hoping for a hearty meal upon their return to the hotel.

## Chapter 33

"You know, I think your sultry Vampire voice is starting to grow on me." Nathan says breaking the awkward silence that had been growing between them as they fast ran out of small talk subjects to chew over. As he turns to look Olena in the eye with a broad smile across his face she instantly finds herself to feel more relaxed about being in her own body again——even if it were not the full Vampire McCoy.

"I'm getting those *feelings* back again. Are we...still ok to——you know." Olena asks, feeling embarrassment wash over her like hot water. Her rosy cheeks set her red tinted eyes ablaze making Nathan audibly gulp in awe and wonderment.

"Let's just...get back to the hotel first. Reconvene with the guys and then take things from there——yeah?" Nathan answers making Olena's heart sink not realising that his lust drive felt as if it were on steroids right now and should this conversation carry on well he didn't feel he'd be able to be held responsible for his own actions ——which this time would be driven under his own steam and not some mysterious effects of fairy tea.

*He's changed his mind...maybe I was better off being the stranger's face? Perhaps the real me is too much for him. What am I even thinking?! None of this will matter soon. No. Once I have the daggers and reset the timeline it will be as if I never met Nathan or his friends. Damn! This still doesn't help me with these annoying human feelings!* Olena thinks as her raging lust now mixes with sexual frustration——worse than before having already sampled what Nathan can do with those magic hands of his.

"To put your mind at rest, yes, I have every intention of helping to *alleviate* those uncomfortable feelings you're presently experiencing——as am I. First though, we must check in with Frank and the others. It's normal protocol, then we can have some proper *alone* time." Nathan says as they both step inside the lift with Monnie who presses the button for their floor.

"Have you had a good day? Did you find any information out about the dagger? Sorry I couldn't be of much use to you——the only things I've ever heard of such things is in bedtime stories." Monnie says rabbiting on while remaining forward facing in the lift with his back to both Olena and Nathan.

"That's quite alright Monnie. We've had an *interesting* time exploring your beautiful city of Cairo. We may not yet know much about finding the dagger—— but it's been a good day none the less. How about yourself?" Nathan whittles on to Monnie in his Irish lilt that all but has Olena crumbling with weak knees.

Monnie feeling overcome that he should be asked how his day has been when normally guests ignore him or bark abuse at him not getting them to their floor fast enough, or ordering him about to fetch their luggage, take room service orders (which isn't actually part of his job but he obliges guests none the less).

"Well...yeah it's been...good thanks for asking. I must say I'm loving your new look Miss Lupescu." Monnie says brightly turning to briefly smile at the couple.

"How did you know it was me?" Olena asks wondering if like Bambi, Monnie could *smell* it was her.

"I err...guessed. Also, the way you two look at one another——I doubt Mr Jones would give another woman quite the same affectionate glance...also no other female guests have been checked in to your floor." Monnie admits blushing ever so slightly which for him at least is hidden behind his monkey furred face.

The lift pings to signal the doors are about to open and before they step out Nathan unclips the bag of coins on Olena's belt handing Monnie the funds.

"Sir! I——can't accept this! It's too much! Brax will blow a fuse if he sees me with such a generous tip. Please——

"Monnie, when someone graciously offers you such a gift it is wise to accept it no questions asked. It is your money or Mooklash or whatever the hell you people call it to do with it what you will." Nathan responds in firm

Irish tones that have any further protests dying on Monnie's tongue.

"Yes Mr Jones, Miss Lupescu...th-thank you very much." Bashfully while bowing his head, Monnie steps back into the lift, shutting the doors to head back down to the next floor requiring his lift service.

"Think Brax will let him keep the moolakash?" Olena says threading her arm through Nathan's as they head on toward her enchanted bedroom.

"Not a chance in hell but if I discover he has been relinquished of the funds I shall be seeing to it the coin is reunited with him. It is *our* Moolakash to do with as we please." Nathan says giving Olena a warm smile.

"Well it's nice how I factored into that decision *Mr Jones*. But no, I agree, that money has gone to the right person. It will help Monnie undoubtedly; perhaps to even find better work for himself. I can't imagine anything more mind numbing then pushing buttons all day." Olena says jumping slightly as one of Nathan's hands smooths themselves over one of her pert and firm bottom cheeks.

"Hmmm, I dunno, I quite *enjoy* pressing your buttons Miss Lupescu."

This time it is Olena's turn to audibly gulp and gasp as his fingers dip over her clothing to the same spot that had brought her sweet release mere hours before.

"Feeling your heat, I doubt we'll need much *foreplay* this time around." Nathan whispers in her ear as they reach the door of her bedroom.

A note has been pinned to a tree informing the couple that Frank, Pete, Donnie and Jamie are all in a room that has been specially set up by Brax for them to privately discuss the day's events. Nathan makes a quick call down to reception for confirmation as Brax confirms the rest of the guys are indeed situated in a private lounge of the hotel upon his invitation.

Knowing they are totally alone, Nathan's urges spill over as he wastes no time whisking Olena up into his arms to where she audibly *whoops* aloud. As he strides on into her yurt hero style to have his wicked way with her. Let's just say the fireworks that followed the coupling were not marred by Nathan remembering that above all he must wear his seatbelt before inviting or being invited by a woman to lay with him.

"Oh...my *HADEEEEEEEES!*" Olena calls out as her climax sends her head into a stratosphere of pleasurable feelings followed swiftly by Nathan's own blissful release.

Recovered Olena turns to him having caught her breath back.

"Please tell me we can do that again."

Laughing Nathan kisses her on the forehead before relaying to her that there will most definitely be *more* where that came from. This all but lights a fresh fire of lust in her hazy-red eyes, but before she can entice Nathan to spend longer with her in bed, he is already standing and heading for the jungle shower encouraging her to do the same so they can meet with everyone downstairs.

"If we hurry we may be able to squeeze in some sex in here before we catch up with the guys." It's all Nathan needed to ensure Olena was now chasing after him into the sanctity of the cavernous bathroom.

———

"Hey guys, sorry it's a bit past sunset, we err——got a little dirty on our recon mission and so had to freshen up first." Nathan says addressing Frank and the guys upon entering the private lounge.

Inside it's all gold accents, mirrors and animated picture frames where the artwork seems to have a life to itself.

The men are all sitting around a large table covered in a rose gold and silver table cloth. The chairs are golden with leaf design to match the rest of the interior. A tall lurch type character stands off to one side in butler fashion having shown Nathan and Olena inside the lounge.

"May I get you some drinks?" The lurch man says as Nathan and Olena take their seats and before Frank or anyone can utter a word in response to Nathan's excuse for their tardiness.

"I'll have a beer please and Olena? What do you fancy?"

"Err how about some of that black fizzy stuff again?" She says embarrassed to have forgotten its name.

"She'll have a coke with ice and a slice." Nathan reels off watching Olena trying to silently store it to memory.

"Very good sir and to eat——

"Well we already gorged ourselves on Maccy D's—— you don't know what you missed, suppose it served you both right being late." Jamie says leaning back and belching loudly causing everyone in the room to wrinkle their noses in disgust.

"Maccy D's! Please tell me we can still order this." Nathan says with pleading expression toward lurch.

"Certainly, you can order anything suitable for human consumption. What specifically would you like from the Maccy D's menu?" The butler Nathan has aptly decided to name Lurch says.

As Nathan reels off the order Olena can only look on in perplexed excitement as to what all the fuss is about this 'Maccy D's' where clearly it is a firm human favourite.

As the butler disappear to collect their order Nathan and Olena turn still red faced to reconvene with their small group.

As Frank and Pete tell them of their interesting experience (with whom Olena informs them both were Bully-Dog Busters), regarding their unintentional gambling escapade whereby fortunately they were the winners——otherwise they'd have been a leader and a man down. Nathan can only look on stunned that his boss could end up in such a weird and wiry bind but thankful none the less the outcome had been in both their favours. Donnie and Jamie then express the bare minimum of what happened to them having sworn each other to secrecy. Leaving out the details about Jamie's unpleasant experience at being forcefully relieved of some of his little guys by some hypnotising yet utterly terrifying female singing siren creature. They simply state how they got into some trouble in a nightclub venue whereby they lost their communicator devices. Feeling there was more to this story knowing his friends all too well——Nathan registering the awkwardness across both their faces decides not to press them.

To the best of their ability Nathan and Olena relay their own strange experience having tracked down the City's Seer named Sharine——while also explaining this is how Olena got her true looks back but unfortunately not her Vampire powers as that would have been a step too far, muddying the legal loopholes regarding magical lore.

Everyone seems to be in quiet reflective moods as they mull over the fact they still don't know much of anything about how to find or obtain the Ruby Red Dagger.

"I suggest from now on we *don't* split up regarding the search for this dagger." Donnie says and everyone vehemently nods and mumbles in absolute agreement just as Olena and Nathan's food arrives.

"Mmmmm smells——*interesting.*" Olena states as her food is placed in front of her and the silver dish lid raised. The smell of food to hit her nasal passages then all but sees her mouth drooling.

Frank orders another round of beers for the men as

well as a request for pudding once Nathan and Olena have finished their mains of everyone's firm favourite——strawberry cheesecake.

"I wonder if I may be so bold as to suggest that... seeing as everyone's fed and sated that I may have my room——back to myself tonight?" Olena says not holding anyone's gaze as she finished off the last few French fries on her plate.

Frank goes to look at Nathan but he has tipped his head back momentarily to take a lingering sip of beer. Although he cannot be certain——he can see that there's this invisible energy between Olena and Nathan, magnetic almost.

"Of course, Olena, gentlemen you heard the lady. Tonight, we are to take up residence in our own humble abodes. Arrangements will be as before. Nathan you're with me, Pete you can bunk with Donnie and Jamie——unless of course you'd rather suffer through my snoring which I know you all complain about under your breath when you think I'm out of earshot." Frank says as Pete looked to make protest about bunking up with the two chatterboxes of the group——then clearly thinking better of it kept his mouth firmly close, because at least when Donnie and Jamie were sleeping——they did so soundlessly.

"So boss, what's the plan for tomorrow? Same again only this time we all venture out together?" Jamie asks as the tall slim butler of few words, aptly named Lurch by Nathan, clears their empty plates away exclaiming that their desserts would be along shortly.

"I think we could all do with a good night's rest before looking at maps and making a plan of attack in the morning. We've all had a...busy day and so I feel a good rest is in order so we can better plot a course tomorrow. My weary bones have had quite enough adventure for one day. If you'll excuse me I'll take my leave, back's a bugger and my knees are screaming——hey Grunt, please bring my dessert to my room will you and also send for the nurse——I'm in need of some medical assistance." As a mark of respect, the guys all stand as Frank stands up to leave, Olena slowly following suit before taking up her seat again with the others once Frank left the lounge.

*"Grunt, this dude's name is...Grunt! Funny I pegged him for a Lurch."* Nathan whispers to his comrades seeing as Grunt their butler for the evening already left in search of the on-site nurse for Frank.

"Wonders will never cease here my man." Pete says stretching and yawning. "On second thought I think I'll take myself off to bed, walking all day in this damn heat is exhausting." He stretches and yawns as if to extenuate his point before standing and heading out after Frank. Olena went to stand but Nathan placed a hand on her knee shaking his head assuring her it wasn't necessary.

"And then there were four!" Jamie says taking a mouthful of his slice of delectable cheesecake Grunt has placed in front of him on a golden plate before placing the others down.

"Why do I get the feeling you and Donnie are holding back details from today?" Nathan asks while taking his own mouthful of cheesecake, moaning audibly as the sweet sustenance hits all his happy tummy places, sending endorphins rushing through his brain like a bullet train.

"We...don't know what you're talking about." Donnie says cagily affixing Jamie with the mother lode of death stares as both men's cheeks pink up upon recalling in memory the events of the day.

"I do believe thou doth protest too much, add in the reddening to both your faces——I'd say you either had yourselves a nice time in some version of magical strip club, or...you became unwholly embarrassed but getting caught out with say——your trousers down." As Nathan says this Jamie all but chokes on a mouthful of cheesecake before Donnie makes rude exclamations and taking himself and his cheesecake off out of the lounge and up to the room.

Olena smiles and brings one of her dainty porcelain hands to her seemingly un-naturally rosy red mouth, stifling a gentle cough.

"Ah man did you have to kill the mood. Better go and check Mr sour grapes isn't tearing up the bedroom because if he is he can keep his grubby little mitts off my bed for the night." Jamie says wolfing down the remains of his cheesecake before jogging off and out of the lounge.

Alone again, Olena slides one of her hands along the breadth of Nathan's muscular thigh making him first clench in surprise and then relax as her hand continually travels south to his crotch.

Rapidly he downs what's left of his cheesecake, also knocking back the dregs of his beer bottle before taking hold of Olena's hand and bolting for the door with just a swift *Thank You* to Grunt who couldn't look less amused.

As Nathan walks Olena to her bedroom door he explains he must feign going to spend the night with Frank so as to throw off any suspicion. If Frank catches wind of their copulation antics he'll get his ears bent. The plan was for Nathan to wait for Frank to fall asleep before sneaking back to be with Olena. As luck would have it when Nathan entered his and Frank's room for the night——the on-site nurse was just on her way out explaining that she had given Frank a sedative to help him sleep. This nurse was different from before, she looked human enough save for a pair of stereotypical elf-styled ears, amethyst purple hair and forest green eyes.

"Thank you for looking after my friend. I'll be sure to put in a good word for you with the big man——Minotaur——Brax, downstairs." Nathan says tripping over his words unsure of how to refer to Brax.

"It is my pleasure. I am the senior nurse practitioner here at The Blue Pharaoh. If you and your friends need any further medical assistance please don't hesitate to ask.

Before Nathan could catch the nurse's name she turned and evaporated in a haze of smoke which Nathan wafted the remnants away with one of his hands. Looking at the card the nurse had handed to him he is amazed to see that it is written in perfect British English.

**Mortina – Chief Mage-Nurse resident at The Blue Pharaoh Hotel**

"*Thank you Mortina.*" Nathan says to himself feeling like the cat who's got the cream that she's inadvertently taken Frank out of the tricky equation on '*operation sex with Olena*'. Hearing Frank's nose throwing out its usual snoring tirade——gives Nathan the green light for a safe exit as he heads on back out to spend what he hopes will be an incredibly wild night with Olena, his raven-haired goddess, who he previously presumed was a hallucination. Knowing she was really *real* though——for the first time in his life where a woman was concerned, made Nathan Jones' heart do an Irish tap dance all of its own.

## Chapter 34

"Oh-hey, you're here...sooner than I thought but at least you came." Olena says breathlessly as she turns to watch Nathan stride on inside of her yurt while wearing nothing but a clean white T-shirt and black knickers.

He says nothing in response just walks on up to plant a wild passionate kiss on her lips. By the time they break apart both their chests heave up and down with the effort it takes for them to steady their breath back to normal rhythm. Nathan goes in for another kiss when gingerly Olena places a hand upon his chest giving way to a pause.

Instantly his blood sings with trepidation as he's all but verging on the edge of want to claim Olena's body again.

"I...had a thought. You've done so much for me, introducing me to your close friends, helping me with my transition from being a Vampire to human——that I, *wanted* to do something for you in return." Olena says stepping back from Nathan blushing which makes her eyes and lips have him burning for her even more.

"That's really sweet of you Olena, truly it is but honestly I don't need *anything*...only you." Nathan says fixing Olena with a smouldering gaze he hopes will be enough to entice her to strip down naked with him and dance as they did before between the sheet.

She bit her bottom lip, which made Nathan's Adams-apple bob up and down. Wanton lust flooded both of their eyes but until Olena moved from amber and onto a green light, Nathan had no intention of becoming sexually physical with her.

"Please, let me do this for you. Hades knows when we might get a chance to do something spontaneous and fun again——just the two of us." As Olena says these words it enables some of the pressure to release from Nathan's tyres as his lust-o-meter slowly begins to quieten while he fully takes on board what she is telling him.

"Ok, humour me——what'd you have in mind?" Nathan said pondering on the late hour and what she could possibly be thinking of arranging.

"The water-fall in my bedroom garden is actually a doorway that open up to an enchanted Egyptian mermaid city, under the sea. It's two way for us and no one can follow us back here above ground. We'll breath using the green pills I've requested from Brax be sent up. They'll give us each twenty-four Earth hours of under-water breathing time. Not that we'll use the full twenty-four hours but I thought it's better to be over cautious then under. So...what do you say? Want to experience the sea like you never have before."

The idea sounded so ludicrously bonkers to Nathan that his intrigue had stepped into place of the earlier primal lust. The simmering to bed Olena was still there but now all his focus it appeared seemed to be on wanted to see this underwater city.

"Is this...like Atlantis?" Nathan asks wondering what the hell he might be about to agree to as drowning had always been one of his biggest fears.

"No, this city is not Atlantis but I'm guessing it would be a close second given the fact it's all underwater. So, as time is marching on might I suggest we slip into some swim clothes and make our way on down to the lagoon pool and waterfall. The tablets work instantly ——here." Olena says pushing one of the green pills into Nathan's hand. She is the first to swallow hers down with what looks to be innocent glass of water.

Nathan then takes the glass to down the remaining liquid with his own pill. Immediately the liquid scorches the back of his throat as he coughs and grabs at his neck wondering just what in the bloody hell Olena has given him.

*Christ! She's poisoned me!* He thinks trying hard not to let panic overrun his senses as his head begins to spin.

"Got a bit of a kick to it doesn't she?" Olena says grinning wickedly more than a little used to downing strong alcoholic beverages over the decades. "Relax, its premium vodka. To activate the pills, they have to be consumed with human poison of choice. I made sure to request ones that would be calibrated to our chemistry and physicality."

Nathan recovers his breath, relaxed in the knowledge that the flame strength liquor is unlikely to kill him. A knock on Olena's bedroom door however has his heart nearly stopping, for if it were Frank about to catch him inside her bedroom at this late hour——he'd surely have Nathan's guts for garters. You might wonder how a grown man could be afraid of his boss but when it came to operations——Frank was all business. Nathan dreaded to think how many of Franks rules he had broken already by already rolling around in the proverbial hay with Olena, only he didn't seem to be able to control himself so well around her.

"Geez, will you *relax*. It'll be room service with our swimwear." Olena says bypassing Nathan to head across the forest floor toward her bedroom door to collect the required items.

By the time the pair of them are suitably dressed with Olena wearing a simple black one-piece swimsuit and Nathan donning a pair of red swim shorts that cut just above the knee it is already heading up to 1:00am.

Bracing himself as they reach the water's edge, expecting it to be uncomfortably cold, Nathan is surprised again to feel the temperature of the lagoon is most agreeable and cool enough to dampen down his earlier lust drive aimed at Olena.

*It's a shame I'm going to forget all this magic and wonderment with Olena...had she been human and had we met under different circumstances——perhaps we'd have made a great couple, perhaps even a marital one. Hell! What am I even thinking of here. We're both just enjoying the moment until...hopefully we succeed and reset the timeline. Frank will more than likely chew me out over the friendship with benefits vibe Olena and I got going on, and the guys will most definitely rib me about it but——I can't stay away from her and the more I try the more frustration blinkers my focus. No, I need her as much as she needs me——if nothing else to at least keep switched on without worrying out feelings getting in the way. This is purely only physical relief.* Nathan runs a continual narrative inside of his mind convincing himself that any and all feelings he has aimed toward Olena are purely platonic, they're not serious and never would be. However much he knew deep down this wasn't true, that he really did enjoy Olena's company in so much as how she was growing in his heart——the lie did at least keep him from the pain of the knowledge that one day, when their quest was all over——it would be as if they never met. What Nathan doesn't realise is that Olena will retain all the memories as will be necessary to prompt her into action regarding preventing the events transpired that put them all in this predicament in the first place.

"Follow me, and breathe as you would normally." Olena says taking the lead fast swimming across to the front of the mini-waterfall before disappearing behind it.

*"Far be it for me to deny an attractive young woman the chance to play kiss chase."* Nathan says before rapidly following Olena in watery pursuit.

Pleasurably Nathan was happy to discover upon entering the watery kingdom of Cairo's underwater city. That inhaling and exhaling were as easy as Olena claimed it would be. The pills had not given him painful gills or anything of that nature which he'd feared would happen having seen all the movies that accompanied the Parry Trotter wizard book series, he'd enjoyed reading as a boy.

Talking was also clear and easy, so much so that Nathan occasionally forgot that they were even in this underwater world of mystery.

"This is so cool——Felicity would flip her lid if she were to ever discover anything like this." Nathan says while reaching out to gently bring Olena to his side. Cute little bubbles burst from her nose as she lets out a small giggle. Her raven hair floating up high behind her.

"How is it humans have never discovered the underwater pockets of magical spaces on Earth?" Nathan asked genuinely curious how all this could be going on right under everyone's noses and eyes. "I get the above ground stuff but——our submarines and military vessels have the most hi-tech sonar equipment, constantly scouring the sea bed and its depths.

"Much the same as I imagine goldfish on your world don't know they're in a bowl." Olena says moving to one-side, allowing a mermaid with bright purple hair and pink tail, pushing a shell styled stroller past with cute little pudgy baby mermaid inside that has matching colours to its mother. The mer-mother gives wary glances to both Nathan and Olena as if totally stunned to see two humans milling about. She soon rushes away with a look of fear registering across her much paler green skin.

"Well, that was surreal. However, I'm coming to understand and accept the many critters and creatures of your world. They may be far removed from how we humans choose to live and work but——your world still has its own systems and citizens. Magic or no magic, I'm fully on board with helping put things right again—— for both our people." Nathan says making Olena well up as tears rapidly begin to descend down her heart-shaped porcelain face.

"Look at me I'm off crying again——damn hormones. Come on, there's much to see and not a lot of time left before we'd best head back." Olena says taking up Nathan's arm in hers again to steer him off to a busier part of the underwater city.

The streets are alive with mer-folk coming and going. There are even underwater taxi type vehicles spewing out an array of iridescent rainbow bubbles from what Nathan supposed was a sort of exhaust.

"Your face is a picture. The word of our arrival will most certainly be out now——that two *humans* have somehow managed to infiltrate Pharaoh King Midas's underwater city. Don't be surprised if we get a summoning, any and all upper world visitors must be vetted by the king for safe passage and permission to remain here for short stays. I've never met the guy, but I can say with certainty that anyone I met with who *has* met him have all said how agreeable and friendly he is." Olena says shrugging as if the bombshell of information she just dropped on Nathan that he was about to meet *THE* King Midas was nothing but a simple trifling inconvenience they'd have to suffer through.

"This Midas fellow...is he like——

"A God? Mmm-hmm. Don't worry though he's *very* placid and fair. Mum and dad said that Vampires always had a very good standing with the people of Earth's underwater cities." Olena explains which does nothing to quell his bubbling tummy.

"But...wont they have forgotten your kind...you know——*exist*?"

"Yeah but so long as we have *these*." Olena says pointing to their tattoos. "We're protected."

"I forgot about our tattoos. Ok, guess I can relax a little——for now. How will we even know when we're summoned?"

"I'm not sure but I imagine someone like a royal aide may be sent out to greet us——requesting an audience with the king."

"Right! Well lead on boss, I'm just here for the ride." Nathan says as they cross an underwater road arriving outside of a restaurant with bright blue neon and purple tones.

The name emblazoned on big flashing light board says:

**Amethyst Azul Appetite**

"How are we even able to walk right now without simply floating away?" Nathan muses quite befuddled at how they can breathe and move as if still on the surface.

With the exception being that they breath bubbles out with every out-breath they take.

"Must be the tablets. Come on, I know we already ate but I'm still a bit hungry——let's see what's on offer." Olena says excitedly as they step inside the Purple-blue doorway.

A very energetic gold looking mermaid comes over to greet the couple.

"Good evening." She says as realisation dawns on her youthful shimmering golden complexion. "Oh WOW! *Humans!* We haven't had your kind in here——*ever*!" The mer-woman states as small little golden bells woven into her wavy hair do jingle as she jostles about excitedly.

Customers stop and gawp for a moment as they are seated in a quiet booth as far away from the hustle and bustle of the establishment as their hostess they've learned is called Chione, can place them.

"Here you are." Chione states handing them both a menu. "Dendera your waitress will be over to take your order soon——I've got to get back to manning the welcome desk. Thank you for choosing Amethyst Azul for your dining pleasure." Chione says spinning away as her golden hair and bells jingle all the way back to the entryway of the establishment.

Speechless Nathan starts doing the only normal thing of reading the menu but the language is all gobble-dee-gook to him. It appears speaking magical languages is a lot easier with an affixed translator then reading it.

"Can't read it——huh?" Olena says noticing the pained expression across Nathan's face.

"Sorry, would you mind?" He says indicating for Olena to translate for him.

"Not at all." She says siding up to him to scan through the menu.

By the end of reeling off the many dishes he's still just as stumped.

"There's nothing on here that's akin to cod and chips is there?" Nathan asks feeling a little awkward.

"Hmmm, well I've never eaten human fish and chips but I've heard of this famous dish Pikkatin——my boss spoke of called *Cotchi-han-alar* is very much like this cod and chips you mention. Fancy ordering a batch to share?" Olena says batting her eyelashes at Nathan in a way that make it impossible for him to refuse.

"Can we——*eat* magical food?" Nathan asks now beginning to sweat about this brand-new gastronomic experience about to befall him.

"Sure can. If I thought it would cause us any issues I'd have never have suggested this place. I never came here with mum and dad but I had a best friend who frequented Cairo's underwater city with her parents—— she's part mermaid, don't ask it's a very long drawn out story. Anywho she gave me a map of the city as a sort of souvenir and this is the very restaurant she would come to eat at with her folks."

"I see...ah, here I believe comes Dandruff——or whatever her name is." Nathan says making eye contact with the mer-person heading towards them.

She has a fluorescent peach coloured octopus' lower body and matching tentacles where he supposed hair should be. Her skin is a much paler peach tone with her face being dolled up palette style to the nines——with punchy colours worthy of a 1980s pop music video. Matching baubles dangling from the tentacles atop of her head, held back by some sort of sea-weed head wrap thingy finish the look.

"Eeeeek! It's true you really *are* human! This is totally stella!" Dendera shrieks giddily while clasping her order pad to her chest.

It takes a moment for her to calm down but eventually she steps back into her professional role of waitress.

Olena orders their food whereby Dendera writes it all down using what looks to be some sort of bone in the shape of a pen that has an inky fluid jettisoned from the end Dendera is using to write from. Accompanying their meal Olena orders up two glasses of a purple fizzy drink that Nathan is pleasantly surprised to learn, tastes very much like blueberry soda——with no ill effects on his stomach.

All too soon their date comes to an end. There was no summoning via King Midas and Olena had assumed that perhaps his royal highness was either away or sleeping as it was getting pretty late by the time they both decided to head back.

"I had such a lovely time tonight." Nathan says putting on an olive-green t-shirt atop of the black jogging pants he'd thrown on after they had both showered and dried off.

"I'm glad——gosh I feel so...*yawn*"

"Tired?" Nathan offers to Olena in place of guessing what she's feeling.

"Yeah, tired...it's odd, I'm usually most active at night and the early hours but here as a human I'm——*tired*. Guess we'd best get some sleep."

"Guess so." Nathan says already peeling his clothes off as the pair of them head on into her yurt where they make wild passionate love before falling into a deep sleep in one another's arms where Nathan dreamt of sea people and golden palaces.

## Chapter 35

Hours later as illusionary woodland dawn breaks, a chorus of just illusionary tropical birds burst into song outside the yurt. Olena having sleep elude her for most of the remaining early morning hours following on from hers and Nathan's underwater jaunt——tucks in tighter to Nathan who stirs the moment she begins drawing shapes across his bare muscular chest——which has just the right amount of hair across it for her to play with.

*What am I doing? This Is not right. I am a Vampire he is a human——and not just any human but the very one who caused this whole debacle. Being human is hard work. All these crazy emotions how do they——*

"Mmm, good morning sexy." Nathan says sleepily as he rolls over to smile at the object of his affection while also interrupting Olena's racing mind——before anxious thoughts had chance to de-rail her morning mood further.

Slowly Nathan guides her up atop of him so that she now straddles his firm toned torso.

"Morning, she says leaning down to plant a morning kiss upon his soft and gentle lips. "Oh before I forget, there was a call not long after we got back. It was Midas ——he sends his regards. I thought he might summon us but apparently my little *wrinkle in time* has caused some issues in under water kingdoms across Earth. Nothing major thankfully just some loose ends the underwater kingdoms needed help with. As Midas is leader of all mer-people on Earth and The Magical realm——his plate's been more than a little overflowing. He did however wish us all the best with our quest and said we're welcome back anytime.

"It's nice to know that at least one enchanted king from your world doesn't take umbridge against us—— otherwise I'd say we were in a whole world of trouble and I don't quite fancy myself being turned into a gold statue for all eternity."

"I never considered the whole *turning into gold* matter. Gold would be a good look on you——it would bring out those sexy sapphire pools of yours." Olena all but purred out her observation out in sultry Romanian tones——making the corners of Nathan's lips curve upward in a lop-sided smile.

Checking the time out of habit more than anything and figuring the guys would be rousing very soon, Nathan groans, stating to Olena how he'd best sneak back to his and Frank's bedroom to feign having slept in his bed——but not before giving her a long languid kiss bringing out a much rosier complexion to her cheeks from her usual pale alabaster.

Olena whines but understands their friends with benefits arrangement must be kept under wraps——so as to save Nathan from getting a hard time from Frank and the rest of the guys.

Fortunately for Nathan when he sneaks back inside his and Frank's bedroom, Frank is still asleep——however not snoring——indicating that his sleep state is light. Nathan picks up the phone receiver sitting on the bedside table between his and Frank's single beds. He calls through to Pete, Donnie and Jamie's room dialling 0 on the keypad of the telephone——mind still boggled that for all of The Magical tricks and trinkets of Olena's world there were still very human means to communicate.

Nathan arranges for them all to have breakfast with Olena in her room——calling through to her to make arrangements——keeping up the appearance that they haven't spoken since the previous evening——just in case Frank's listening to him with eyes closed while in a lighter sleep state. Not feeling up to cooking their own breakfast this morning Nathan also rings down to room service, putting an order in for the regular items they all order off the Maccy D's breakfast menu. After so many years of working and fighting side-by-side with his comrades Nathan was pretty confident he knew what each of the men wanted.

"Ok, so that's six cheesy-bacon flat breads, five lattes a strawberry milkshake, six egg muffins, six hash browns, six portions of baked beans, six portions fried mushrooms. For dessert——two stacks of blueberry pancakes with maple syrup——anything else?" The women downstairs in room service asks.

"No thanks, that's the lot——oh and perhaps some onion rings——yeah six individual portions of onion rings."

"Very well, there will be no charge for this service as all orders are covered by The Magi. Thank you for trusting The Blue Pharaoh room service dine-in experience. Should you need anything else please ring down and request myself, Raquel." The females voice rings through the receiver.

"Thank you Raquel, I'll be sure to keep you in mind ——oh and I will also be wanting to put in a good word with your boss Brax about how efficient and polite you've been this morning." Nathan says cheerfully, happy in the knowledge his growing hunger shall soon be quelled——the man was starving!

"Your food shall be delivered within the hour." Raquel says not waiting for a response before cutting off the call. Nathan got the distinct feeling Raquel, *whatever she may be*——was *not* a fan of the human condition.

"Morning." Frank says yawning and stretching before scrubbing a hand down his handsome yet weathered face.

"How long have you been awake?" Nathan asked wishing to know exactly when his boss roused.

"Just now. I have the nicest dreams——don't entirely remember taking myself to bed. Did we drink much last night?" Frank asks Nathan who turns giving him a wry grin.

"No, but you were visited by some attractive witch-nurse named Mortina. She medicated you." Nathan says relinquishing the truth of Frank's condition finding himself unable to lie to his old-time boss and good friend.

"Ah——that explains my fuzzy memory then. Well, if we see her again I must be sure to thank her for I haven't slept so good since perhaps I was a babe." Frank says indeed looking bright eyed and bushy tailed this morning Nathan noticed.

"How about you? How'd you sleep? Sorry if my snoring kept you up——you're looking tired, the bags beneath your eyes always were a dead giveaway." Frank says getting up and pottering about before heading into their en-suite bathroom.

"I'm good, managed a few hours——nothing some strong coffee won't fix. On the subject of coffee, I took the liberty and ordered us all breakfast——I have arranged with Olena if we can all eat together in her room. Just thought it'd be nice for us all to socialise, so she doesn't have to dine alone before we plan for the day ahead." Nathan explains but doesn't think Frank's paying much attention as the mere mention of breakfast has him all but rushing on to grab a shower.

"Ok, well——I'll just go shower in Miss Lupescu's room to save time. See you in there." Nathan calls through to his boss who simply leans sideways out from the frosted glass shower door to answer but Nathan had already bolted from the bedroom, keen to see Olena alone again before their breakfast arrived.

---

"Wow, that was *so* good!" Jamie exclaims through a mouthful of blueberry pancakes smothered in copious amounts of maple syrup which he washes down with a gulp of his sweetened latte——relinquishing a loud burp that has everyone else in the room cringing as Frank, within swatting distance, wallops Jamie once around the back of his flame red haired-head, exclaiming he shouldn't be so crude in front of a lady.

"Sorry everyone——Olena." Jamie says looking bashful as he wipes at his mouth with a napkin. His piercing blue eyes although blue like Nathan's are lot brighter——more like topaz than sapphire. They seem to sparkle now that he's been well fed.

A knock at the door makes everyone freeze momentarily as they glance one other with the same silent question on all their lips——wondering who it could be.

"Is anybody home? It's me Monnie——I——err... have some *information* regarding that dagger you've been seeking, it is The Ruby Sunrise...*right*?" Monnie says as his muffled tones carry on through the closed enchanted bedroom doorway.

Graceful as a gazelle, Olena stands indicating with a hand for the guys to remain seated, as she heads on over to open the door. The men watch on wondering what on Earth her and Monnie might be discussing as the conversation looks to be quite animated. Nathan after about five minutes goes to stand but Frank holds him in place with firm grip.

"Let's wait——I'm sure Olena will fill us in momentarily." Frank says and realising his tone relayed more of an order then passing comment Nathan did as he was told and remained seating. The uncomfortable feeling something may be wrong however was beginning to bubble up inside him, threatening to give him a very upset stomach. So he focused on his breathing and remaining relaxed until Olena returned to where they were all sitting.

By the time Olena did return to the breakfast table however———everyone can see she looks troubled.

"So...what did monkey dude say?" Jamie asks pushing a nervous hand through his short tidy mane of flame red hair trying and failing to use humour to cover up his anxieties.

"His *name* is Monnie." Olena exclaims hotly. "And he's basically told me that presently The Ruby Sunrise Dagger is bizarrely the talk of the city——which spins my head considering no-one appeared to know much about it yesterday. Monnie told me someone had come into the hotel early this morning requesting Brax put up a poster and staff memo——announcing that the Ruby Sunrise dagger is going up for auction right here in Cairo. The seller is wishing to stay anonymous and there are limited spaces for the auction hall. It doesn't matter if we got a space anyway seeing as our only hope now would be if we were to make the winning bid for it——although there'd be no point as royalty and the extremely wealthy magical occupants of Cairo will undoubtedly outbid any measly offer we may think of putting forward. I just don't understand how it can suddenly surface a day after we begin looking for it. Something sure is fishy here. We'll need nothing short of a Magi miracle to get us that dagger now. *Damn*! What are we to do?" Olena says looking about as deflated as she now felt inside.

"Hey, maybe we could *steal* it back?" Pete suggests leaning forward on his tree stump seat. Being a man of few words in their testosterone-fuelled group, Olena feels quite surprised to hear him so extrovertly put this idea forward——even if in her mind it seemed a little crazy. His green eyes she can see, are fired up as cogs of creativity begin to whir inside of his mind.

Olena goes to make fun of his crazy idea until that is she notices everyone has stilled like statues——again.

"Ah fraggle-cackers! ——*what is it now*?" Olena swears hotly while rolling her red tinted Vampire eyes, as she waits for The Magi to materialise.

"Olena, it has come to our attention that the dagger you seek, is *unfairly* out of your reach." The Magi begin.

"Gee ya think?" Olena says smartly stating the obvious like a stroppy teenager, immediately regretting her projection of such low-class immature behaviour ——which she finds is way beneath her usual Vampire formality.

"You forget yourself. Remember who it is you're addressing and sit up straight!" As The Magi bark out the order an invisible force seems to lift Olena up on her seat, until she is sitting uncomfortably ram-rod straight. Already she figured no matter how much she might've struggled——it would've proved pointless against such powerful magic.

"The Dagger had been brought to Cairo under secure measures ready for your trial to begin. However, Lisl-imps managed to sneak it away from its hidden place of safety. As you can imagine this caused an almighty storm with the Powers That Be...*and ourselves* as a mad search went underway to find it. Hearing you speak to your monkey friend——

"Monnie!" Olena exclaims frustrated at the lack of simple respect even The Magi deem isn't necessary to bestow to Monnie by simply remembering his name.

"Please, *excuse* us——hearing *Monnie* discuss the auction with you, well from there it was a mere trifle to whizz the dagger away and place it where it shall reside until you can retrieve it. We've already wiped any and all knowledge and memory of any such auction. You shall begin *The Trials of Leo* as of now ——the name should come as no surprise to you seeing as Rubies represent *The House of Leo* on your world.

"I'm familiar with the study of our star systems and their meanings." Olena says, calmly letting The Magi know she doesn't after one hundred years need to be taught how to——as humans might say, *suck eggs*. The solar system from Olena's world mimicked Earth's in what some might call a *parallel* universal way. Except their daytime hours never really fell fully on the light side of her world and the sunlight barely even grazed where true darkness dwelled.

"You will enter a maze devised purely for the challenges set by us." The Magi say collectively as a wicked gleam of amber orbs flash from the depths of the black hood worn over the short levitating entity's head.

Your friends shall be placed inside the maze——held captive by individual guardians in three separate chambers. It is *your* job Olena to free them one by one as a reflection of courage, valour and wit——all things required to prove yourself worthy enough to obtain the first dagger. Be warned——should you fail, then the timeline will be reset without you or your people.

*Yeah, yeah blah! Blah! I got the gist already.* Olena thought to herself immediately regretting it in case The Magi should be listening intrusively into her thoughts again. If they were however they don't make it known, and this relaxes her somewhat.

"All this fuss over one stupid human being zapped out of existence!" Olena exclaims——fear and trepidation seeing to it that her mouth goes into action before her brain can stop her speaking out.

"That *stupid* human would have played a pivotal role in changing the course of human history. We are not at liberty to say how but——the timeline requires he live for history to play out the way the Powers That Be intend. This slim chance of you redeeming yourself and your people is at their discretion——don't forget that." The Magi's collective voices state——sounding like acidic venom dripping from a viper's fangs.

"Please, forgive me——I find myself in this body unable to control my emotions. How will we obtain the dagger when——*if,* I and my friends manage to overcome each of the guardians you speak of?"

"All will become apparent in due course." The Magi say raising a cloaked arm——causing Olena to call out, making The Magi pause momentarily.

"I...would like to know——*please,* is there anything you can tell me about these guardians, who they are at least?"

The Magi say nothing. They conjure up a rush of spinning wind that makes Olena's stomach swirl as she clamps her eyes shut to save her getting any grit or dust in them. Her body spins round and around in a spin she feels may never end. Momentum sends her rapidly skyward before mere moments later has her fall (not too hard) onto her feet. Dusting herself off, Olena can see once her eyes have adjusted to having been transported to a dimly lit stone corridor with braziers lining the walls. Directly in front of her is a stone archway.

Wasting no time wishing to be reunited with Nathan and co sooner rather than later Olena strides ahead propelled by adrenaline——as her heart presently pounds out a beat akin to that of a thousand galloping unicorn hooves.

Perspiration has broken out all over Olena's face and body as fear and uncertainty tear across her central nervous system. While her mind makes up all kinds of unhelpful deadly scenarios to run through it, her usual Vampire self would be more composed she felt. The alien terror she was now experiencing was all but diabolical. Olena swore right here and now that should she ever feed off of a human ever——when her fantasies finally did come in regarding they were all successful getting the daggers to reset time. That she would take into more account the fragility of the human condition on a deeper level.

Even though there is light being emitted from braziers mounted at intervals along the stone walls——in Olena's mind it wouldn't matter if she had been plunged into complete blackness, seeing as she had no map or navigation of any kind to help point her in the right direction. What she was certain of however was that could mean certain death may befall her at any moment. She pondered briefly on whether or not that would be such a bad thing if it meant all these horrid feelings and sensations were to cease——but she knew too many people were counting on her to win at this quest and her parents had always raised her to do things to the best of her ability and if she were unable to do so——to not even bother starting in the first place, otherwise (they would say) what would be the point if you weren't set on putting your all into a challenge or task.

Venturing a little further along the seemingly never-ending stone corridor, Olena is relieved to finally come across an alcove where inside are two unblemished wooden doorways standing side by side.

The door to her left Olena notes has a bright golden lion-headed knocker holding onto a gold metal ring inside its mouth with menacing looking ruby red eyes

——the other door off to her right is a brightly polished silver metal rat knocker with just as wicked a gleam to its amber eyes.

Taking a deep shaky breath feeling unsure of what to do here Olena takes an unsteady few steps forwards. The Lion and Rat stir to life making Olena startle ever so slightly with what she would deem to be embarrassing *eep!* sound. Annoyed at herself for being such a scaredy cat, Olena tells herself to get a grip.

"Olena Lupescu! Welcome to *The Trials of Leo*! We have been expecting you." The rat says with a surprisingly powerful booming voice for such a little character. The vibration alone sends mini shockwaves that has the stone walls and floor of where she stands to shake ever so slightly. An evil glimmer crosses the rat-head's beady yellow eyes ensuring that Olena feels she ought not trust either of the entities——at least not right away.

"Hi——So, *what's* the deal here?" She asks figuring the doors represent some sort of fork in the road. One door leading her on the right track, whereas the other one could lead perhaps in a wrong direction or worse ——certain death.

The lion-headed door-knocker opens his proud golden mouth wide in a yawning gesture which sends the metal ring clanging to the floor loudly before it blinks out of existence before Olena's very eyes.

*Illusionary Magi-magic* is all Olena can think of here.

"Feels good to get rid of that ruddy thing. We were frozen until you turned up——as were the enchantments put upon us both by The Magi. Your task here is simple, you simply decide which of our doorways you wish to step through. One leads to the path that shall take you into the maze grounds whereas the *other* door shall lead you——

"Let me guess, certain death?" Olena asks cutting off the Lion head which in turn makes the Rat face wrinkle its ugly pointed nose in clear distinguishable distaste.

*"I'm going to enjoy watching this stupid contender fry."* The Rat whispers to his Lion counter-part——not realising that Olena's hearing is just as sharp as it was when she was a Vampire so heard just such a sentiment. It caused her blood to begin simmering beneath all that fear she'd previously been feeling, and a welcome warmth spread throughout her body——where previously she'd begun to feel a chill as the perspiration dried up causing her skin to cool suddenly.

Growling, Olena stomps up to the rat making his eyes go wide with terror. She's as mad as a giant bee which are about the size of Earth's giraffes and can kill with their stinger and venom with one huge jab. No-one messed with giant bees in her world.

"Let's see how *stupid* I come across now!" Olena says hotly as she rips the rat door-knocker clean off his mount with surprising ease. He yelps in fear opening his mouth to protest but any words die in his little silver mouth, as Olena proceeds to open his doorway——launching him inside it. A small explosion follows, pushing Olena backwards.

Dusting herself off for a second time Olena exclaims she will be walking on through the Lion's doorway.

Shock and alarm register clearly on the now less proud looking lion faced knocker.

*Good! He should be scared of me. I may be human but from where we're all from, in our world I will be revered and feared as if I were still my true wicked Vampire self. My body may be pure flesh now but my heart will always remain true to who and what I am——a Vampire.*

Marching right on up to the open doorway wearing a wicked grin across her pale Vampire face, Olena's confidence starts to tick up a notch feeling the nostalgic waves of what it meant to be a true Vampire.

Swiftly, while on a roll with old feelings resurfacing of who she used to be. Olena raises a hand grasping a hold of the Lion's head. Ripping him clean away from his door mount with a pleasant metallic pinging sound. Raising him up she'd planned to also throw him through the rat's doorway too wondering if the booby-trap may work a second time around now that the rat's doorway was pretty beat up.

"WAIT!! I can...can...*help* you. I know the maze—— let me be your guide. You have five friends you need to rescue——correct?" The lion says while quivering like a cub, in Olena's cool hands.

*Oh shoot! Now he's gone and said that, I'd best hear what he has to say——it'd had better be good or it's the big sleep for him. I'm not in the mood for suffering fools.*

"Go on, I'm listening. You seem to know about this *challenge* set by The Magi otherwise how else would you know about me and my five friends? ——what else do you know?" Olena says affixing her living red eyes to his bright ruby stone ones. Using her power of observation here to seek out the truth, as had been taught to her by her Vampire detective dad——Manix.

"I know which direction you need to travel in to find them. This would halve the time and save you having to blindly attempt navigating through the sea of traps laid out by The Magi." The lion says in steadier tones.

"Ok, say I trust you——what's to say you won't lead me straight into a trap and have me killed?"

"I——well, this may come as a surprise but I wasn't always a glorified door knocker you know. One minute I'm at home hanging out with my family the next—— *poof!* I'm here under order of The Magi. They told me and my rat friend you just killed, all about our *duties* here. They also informed us both we needn't bother about ever expecting to return home again as we're expendable. Anyway, for some reason when we were placed onto our individual door mounts it was as if we downloaded the entire map of the maze into our minds. I can't see exactly what is beyond each chamber where your friends are being held but for some reason I just *know* where they are. If I help you——well the timeline gets reset doesn't it? ——oh yes, we've been told all about your little *incident*. But I want to assure you that you have my full support. After all, if the time line never gets reset I'm going to be stuck like this——forever. The prospect is rather gloomy I'm sure you'll agree. If, however you wish to throw me through that other doorway, and be done with me——I won't bear a grudge, it will end my torment being stuck in this annoying metallic head.

"Hmm, sounds plausible enough. Ok——I will bring you with me, but even try to double cross me just once and you're toast——*understand?*" Olena says opening the satchel she was thankful to have been wearing before The Magi zapped her down to the maze, to slip the talking lion-head inside of it. It crossed her mind to ask exactly what the lion-head was normally when in his usual form but with time ticking away and pressure mounting she found herself neither caring nor wanting to know.

"Th-thank you. I promise you won't regret this." The lion-head says in muffled tones through the leather fabric of her satchel.

"*Famous last words.*" Olena says to herself before striding on through the doorway that transports her immediately to a most unexpected scene.

"Hot gangle-bangers! Where the fuggleducs am I!" Olena exclaims which even earns her an audible gasp from the lion-head, as she's used yet more crude swear terms from her world.

## Chapter 36

Olena blinks rapidly as bright sunlight hits her full force in the face. Making her wish to be back in the dimly lit stone corridors as sunshine is a huge point of anxiety for her given her Vampire history.

*Must have been a portal doorway.* She surmises while still adjusting to the unexpected sunshine blasting down upon her pale Vampire skin——which gives it a pearlescent glow as the rays cheerfully bounce off her exposed forearms and face. Turning she can see that the doorway behind her has vanished and as her vision clears some more——can also see bright green rolling hills all around her. directly in front of her lies a shimmering silver pathway.

*Guess this is a one-way trip.* She ponders.

Something tickles her lower leg making her squeal and jump side-ways while giving out a little kick. Looking down Olena notices small and sickeningly sweet looking, fluffy white bunny rabbits hopping about all over the place. Adding to that the scene of colourful flowers and trees——birds singing everywhere, has Olena feeling positively stupefied which is new for her as being no stranger to the powers of illusionary magic and portal travel——has to date never seen anything set out quite like this.

Lifting a foot, she shoos away the offending rabbit that had caused her to squeal. The cuteness and brightness of everything has her skin all but itching with discomfort, as her world is all about darkness and muted emotions.

"Excuse me——Olena." The muffled voice of the lion-head speaks from within the darkness of her satchel.

Reaching inside Olena lifts the golden, ruby eyed lion-head out to sit comfortably in the palm of her hand.

"Speak!" She orders the still scared looking lion-head, whose name she doesn't know and couldn't care less about as it would run the risk of her forming an attachment to the creature.

"If you head on straight down this silver pathway, you'll eventually come across a wide green archway cut into a neatly trimmed wall of hedgerow. I promise to the best of my newly acquainted knowledge I can see no traps along here." The lion-head says as confidently as his voice will allow——which isn't by much as the tremor still lingers.

"Very well——this better be safe or Hades help you!" Olena hisses, roughly dropping the lion-head back inside her satchel before following the silver pathway that also boasts fancy trees bursting either side of it with blooms of varying vibrant coloured trunks and blossoms.

Luck seems to be on the lion-head's side. As described, Olena is soon greeted by a tall standing wall of well-kept vibrant green hedgerow. At the direct end of the pathway sits a tall green archway——with some sort of short gnome looking person sitting inside of wooden booth just off to the left. A sign adjacent to the booth reads (in English) reads: **Welcome traveller to The Trials of Leo maze - *in Wonderland theme.***

Stepping up to the booth warily, Olena startles as the odd-ball looking fellow abruptly barks out

"*Name*" as she wanders up for closer inspection.

Olena can see that the gnome like person has sepia toned skin, and is wearing a tweed waistcoat over long white sleeved shirt with gnome styled black hat atop his head and tight fitting itchy looking dark brown trousers.

"Err——Olena."

"Err Olena." He brusquely repeats writing this down.

"No, sorry, just Olena."

"Fine. What do you identify as?"

A pregnant pause sits here until Olena realises what the gnome is referring to.

"Well, usually Vampire but I guess for now——*human*."

"I'll just put half-breed, shall I?" The comment immediately has Olena's blood running hot——but thinking better of it, and figuring to argue with such a creature would be pointless, lets his snide comment go.

"*Pssst! Psssst!*" The sound from within her satchel disrupts proceedings——as the lion-head once again aims to grab Olena's attention.

"Excuse me a moment will you." Olena says taking a few strides away from the booth.

"Whatever. I'm here all day——everyday——*eternally*." The gnome says in grumpy fashion wriggling himself back on the uncomfortable looking wooden seat ——folding his short plump arms across his stout tummy.

Flipping open her satchel Olena asks what it is the lion-head wants.

"Bribe the gate keeper with fruit from that tree over there. You should receive a *hint* in return. Don't ask me how I know this——it must be like my knowledge of knowing all about this maze. The Magi appear to have filled me with all kinds of useful information regarding your quest—— possibly never contemplating or predicting that you and I should join forces." The lion-head says more confidently, feeling here that the more he helps Olena out the better his situation will work out——in so far as he won't end up dead or worse, perhaps mangled or half melted.

"Oh...well, thank you for the heads up." Olena says cagily, as she stalks on toward the tree plucking the biggest juiciest apple-looking fruit she can get hold of.

Lifting the fruit to her nose in curiosity once she's extracted it from the tree, Olena all but drops it recoiling at the sheer awful stench it emits.

"*Eurgh*! I can't give him *that*! It smells positively

rancid!" She exclaims recoiling in disgust——glaring at the lion-head who shoots her a wary glance.

"I assure you he will love it. It's a *ponky-apple* tree. Gnomes *love* this particular fruit. As our friend here can't move from his station one might suggest he is to be forever tormented by that of which he desires most—— *that* fruit. He must have done something very naughty for The Magi to punish him so severely. Best you, be *careful* around him." The lion-head warns, thankful to see Olena wearing less of a scowl now and more of a contemplative look.

"Ok, but if this doesn't work and I don't get a hint ——deal's off and I'll just leave you to get better acquainted with Mr manky pants over there——for all eternity." Olena says making the lion-head's eyes go wide as she drops him back inside her satchel hearing what she can only imagine must be silent prayers by her annoying metal-headed guide.

Wasting no further time, Olena spins on her heal taking the fruit right up to the gnome placing it under his small button styled nose. Instantly and to Olena's amazement the gnome all but leaps out of his tiny wooden seat trying to grab the fruit from her hand. However Olena's reflexes prove to be faster as she yanks the fruit away.

"Ah—ah——ah. Not so fast. If I give you this, you'll owe me a *hint*. Is that correct?"

The gnome's mouth falls agape at how possibly a human would know any of any such thing——but nods all the same in confirmation, his mouth all but dripping with stinky breath saliva.

"Fruit first——then I'll give you the hint."

Knowing he is in no position to make demands. Olena simply gives the gnome a *look* to where he huffs his annoyance. Agreeing reluctantly to hand over the hint before being in receipt of the goods.

"Fine! Take the third left, second right, fourth right, then a left——

"I don't need directions! I need help! Give me information on the challenges set by The Magi."

Rolling his eyes, swearing. The gnome tells Olena of the first chamber's challenge and that she will need to be quiet and stealthy as an Earth mouse to succeed with this particular challenge. He also goes on cryptically to warn that *Death is as Death does here*. But doesn't broaden the scope on what that could possibly mean.

"Do you have a name?" Olena asks as she mulls over the most unhelpful information.

"Flitwick." The gnome states greedily holding out his hand indicating for Olena to place the fruit inside it.

"Well Flitwick, I'll leave this right *here*." She states crouching down to place the stinky apple-fruit down by her feet on the ground just out of reach of Flitwick's greedy palms.

He all but yells obscenities at Olena which she ignores, grinning wickedly as she heads on through the tall green archway of the maze. Sensibly the lion-head kept thoughts of how harsh she had been to himself. Unbeknown to Olena the lion-head has an agenda and needed her to complete the missions——so he may have a chance to become his old self——for then things would be *very* different indeed. Grinning with relief that she has actually bought his sob story act, the lion-head can only smile, unable to believe his luck. While celebrating in the gullibility of one Olena Lupescu.

"Come on feet, let's get this show on the road." Olena exclaims as she half trots——half skips down a stone pathway this time, following the gnome's directions cautiously——just in case he decided to pull a double cross and get her skewered by a pit of stakes or something as equally nasty.

"You know, I might be more helpful out of your bag?" The lion-head calls out. "Also, being wrapped in a dead animal's carcass is making me feel rather queasy ——it might, throw my concentration off and we wouldn't want me making a mistake, now would we?"

"Shh! I can smell danger, and my senses although not firing off on all cylinders——are at least helpful. In fact, so much so I reckon if I leave you here I can still complete my mission. Perhaps I don't need you after all." Olena says beginning to put her hand inside her satchel to where the lion-head nips at her fingers.

"Ouch! For that you can forget going one step further with me." Olena exclaims shaking her hand, cursing under her breath.

"I...I don't like loneliness. Please do not leave me *alone*. I am a lion after all. We are a pride animal, it's not normal for us to be without companionship." The lion says in mock sadness, hoping to tug on those human heartstrings now enveloping Olena's usually stonier vampiric heart.

"You, my friend, are no pride animal, at least not by human standards."

"You said friend——so we're at least…friends then?" The lion-head says trying every which way to ensure Olena does not leave him alone in the maze.

"*Relax,* I'm not gonna leave you." Olena says to the lion-head's relief. "You know" She says carrying on "considering this all started in Egypt, it's all very fairy tale for me. Why, I thought I'd be faced with pyramids, and other Egyptian themed scenarios. Not white fluffy bunnies and rolling green hills!" Olena states, shivering at the sickly sweetness of the world around her. With its well-manicured emerald green grass, white bunnies, and bright coloured flora and fauna. The sunshine she hopes isn't set to permanent in this illusionary world and that there will at least be night-time at some point.

"I wonder…" The lion's head said drifting off into what sounded to be like a dreamy tone.

"What's the matter now?" Olena asks, her patience fast wearing thin.

"You wouldn't be interested. You've already made up your mind——I'm no use to you."

"Speak lion-head or forever sit here lost in this maze." Olena says all but ready to leave him behind this time.

"Well…I might be able to help relieve you of your clear discomfort with this *wonderland* themed maze. Here, hold me up to your eye level." The lion-head instructs trying to gain some sort of control over a situation he has absolutely no control in.

"No tricks." Olena warns.

"Cross my lion heart——wherever it may be." The lion says smiling.

Rolling her eyes, sighing. Olena holds up the lion-head to where her eyes lock onto his ruby ones.

A blinding flash of red light makes her momentarily drop the lion-head onto the ground where he yelps in pain.

"Sorry." Olena says automatically as she rubs red dots from her eyes. "Oh...my...how is this even possible?" She says in sheer astonishment once her sight has returned. Looking around her she appears to be back inside the underground stone corridors with dim lighting from braziers.

"I don't pretend to know how or why the Powers That Be do what they do." The lion-head says while still lying on his side looking up at the befuddled Olena. "But I do know that I have the capacity to show you either illusionary scenario. There is only this one or the bunny one——pick whichever one you like but I'm guessing this would better suited to your liking? Perhaps The Magi formed the other world scenario just to torment you some more." The lion-head suggests unhelpfully.

"Won't you get into trouble for breaking the illusion?" Olena asks while bending down to pick up the lion-head.

"Oh considerable, and please won't you call me by my name——it's Chance."

"Ok, I'll call you *Chance*——seeing as you've saved me from those awful bunnies and that bright sunlight." Olena says finding herself warming to the lion-head while still remembering to be wary of him. Had she not done what she did with his rat friend back at the doors——well she may very well have chosen the wrong one to walk through meaning he would've spent eternity as he was ——a knob. This begged the question for Olena, just how trustworthy did that make Chance then.

A giant roar jolts both Olena and Chance. The sound causes a shiver to race down her spine, wondering what on Hades black underworld could've made such a wild and threatening sound. It was loud and unfamiliar to anything she'd ever heard on her world.

"What in the sweet frizz was that?!" Olena says swearing in her native tongue.

"I believe that dear Olena is the sound of a *Knarled-Knackle-Fagger*." Chance says as if its common knowledge.

"Okay, first off don't call me *dear* its patronising and unwarranted. Secondly——what is one of those Fankle Kackers or whatever they're called again?" She asks annoyed at herself for portraying the persona of someone who should be by now clued up on almost every species from her world.

"Just some mind bending porcine-type creature that's extremely fast, strong and from the sounds of things——*hungry*." Olena gulps audibly as Chance reels off his understanding of just such a creature.

"What exactly does the KKF eat?" Olena asks shortening down the beast's name to mere letters——knowing she would never get used to pronouncing such a complicated ridiculous sounding name.

"That's smart, how you shortened the name down to initials. Well! A KKF eats everything and anything that falls into its path. I doubt your friend will have been eaten however otherwise what would be the point of this suicidal rescue challenge The Magi have sent you on? I suggest we both use our combined powers of scent and hearing to seek out your friend for this one——word of advice, keep speech to a minimum. The KKF has exceptionally acute hearing."

"Well I guess this is your lucky day seeing as you're still useful to me...for now. Try any funny business however and I won't think twice about feeding you to the beast myself." Olena threatens, holding onto Chance outside of her satchel this time, in the hope it might help heighten his sense of smell.

## Chapter 37

The KKF roars again, this time sounding a lot closer as both Chance and Olena have followed the creature's scent to where it must be residing. While focusing in Olena's heart skips a couple of beats to also catch the faintest whiff of Nathan's scent on the air.

"Might I make a suggestion that you take one of those fiery sticks along. There are vast dark spaces inside this maze and I don't know about you but I'm not too good at seeing——well, much of anything in the dark." Chance says in what Olena is fast appreciating to be a fancy pants sounding English tone. People from her world speak their mother tongues as well as Earth's languages, having been so heavily intertwined with Earth since its humble beginnings. So, hearing Chance's voice of choice comes as no surprise to her.

Olena does as suggested picking up a brazier. Chance was soon proven right as the further they wandered toward the smells of the KKF and Nathan, the darker and somewhat narrower some of the passage ways became.

The further they ventured, the stronger Nathan's scent became causing Olena's blood to sing in her body as her heart kicked up a notch——driven by the wild emotions she was feeling as vivid memories of their bedtime tango resurfaced. Cut with his usual spicy and heady scent were tinges of clear fear and frustration——she thanked Hades that she still obtained her strong Vampire sense of smell where it was possible to sense out not just aromas that the living emit but also their emotions.

"Look out!" Chance barks out the order giving Olena just enough time to drop to the stone floor, as a swinging axe all but nearly takes her head clean off.

"Did you not *hear* me telling you to watch out for traps!" Chance grumbles annoyed, knowing only too well if Olena loses her head, then he'd be well and truly stuck down here *forever*. The thought makes what little he has of his physical self, prickle uncomfortably.

"Sorry——my bad. So why do you think The Magi gave me an illusion of *fluffy bunny land?*" She asks feeling more annoyed than puzzled as to their tortuous angle with this whole sordid ordeal. Wasn't it bad enough The Magi punished her by turning her human while also erasing all the people she loved and cared about from living memory——as well as her entire species.

"To throw you off balance, giving them an upper hand. I presume you already have the feeling this *second* chance at redemption is not from the kindness of their demonic hearts?" Chance says vocalising exactly what Olena had been wondering herself.

"Yeah...I did think that. I suppose if I fail——quickly, their job is done and they can move on from this magical administration headache. I's get dotted T's crossed and its *business as usual* for them and the Powers That Be——only minus us Vampires. I really hope myself and the guys can figure this all out and get every one of those daggers. I feel just terrible for my mistake with the genie, in so much as he got blown up. I'm less sympathetic about that stinking *human* that got wiped out instead of Nathan———I'm talking too much aren't I, seems to be a habit of mine in this human form." Olena admits unsure of why she now feels comfortable opening up to Chance more and more——hoping he isn't trying to put some sort of magical whammy on her.

"Let us continue on, perhaps with less conversation hmm? It's not just traps down here but monsters awaiting in hidden pockets of the maze to ambush us."

Olena lets that last comment about rogue monsters wishing to ambush them sink in before responding with "Hopefully it's not too much further until we reach the KKF and Nathan." Just as her legs begin to cry out in protest from all of the days walking.

"Just a few more turns to go I promise." Chance says keeping back thoughts that she'd be lucky to find Nathan alive if he was in an area with a KKF beast. They didn't hang about with prey, and he wondered what kind of state Olena might find herself in emotionally should she discover her love interest torn to shreds——whatever may be remaining of him if there was anything beyond bones and teeth.

"Ok, I'm trusting you so I really hope you're not trying to set me up for certain death because then I'm gonna be really pissed at you."

"I assure you fair maiden I am not playing any such tricks." Chance says in his rich aristocratic English accent that's starting to grate on Olena's nerves.

"Cut the crap——you're not going to score brownie points with me by being all nice and endearing. Just call me Olena ok? O-l-e-n-a there I've spelt it out for you. So stop with your damn *Dears* and *fair maidens.*"

"I apologise, Olena." Chance says waiting a moment to give her a directional instruction. "Head on straight down this corridor until I say otherwise." Olena huffs as she walks forwards, absolutely hating the fact she is reliant on such an unworthy, patronising——door knob.

———

Nathan backs up against the cool stone wall, surrounded by three sets of metallic bars trapping him in place. The metallic sheen from the bars flashes iridescent light in the dimly lit room he's in and he wonders if the bars may be charged by some sort of electrical force field.

The creature pacing around in front of him——is as large and mean looking as one of the dinosaurs he grew up learning about on the tv. Feeling frustrated at being trapped and unarmed, all he can do is await rescue. Not knowing if or when that might happen. His mind practically spun on the notion that one minute he was with his comrades and Olena in a comfortable setting——the next *poof!* He was jettisoned elsewhere——where ever this *elsewhere* might be was anyone's guess, but figuring it must be to do with Olena's quest——worries Nathan as much as what may become of him and those he loves should she fail.

Watching the big pig type beast manoeuvre around in front of him, an idea suddenly strikes Nathan of how he may evade both this cage and the monster before him.

"Here piggy, piggy, piggy." Nathan says waving his muscular arm that only just fit, tentatively through the bars (just in case they had been charged but relaxed on contact, pleased to feel he wasn't zapped) taunting and tempting the enraged boar-like creature so much so that it charges, smacking its tusks and face hard against the thick steel bars of the cage missing Nathan's arm by mere millimetres as the creature moved with unnatural speed. Pleased with the preliminary test that the bars were not going to electrocute him and that he could at least taunt Mr Piggy in front of him, Nathan began to figure a way in which he may escape.

*Maybe if I can knock the damn animal out by getting it to charge at me hard and fast enough then——hey wait! Are those keys around its huge neck? Yeah, deffo keys. Ah-ha! At last a glimmer of hope.* Nathan thinks to himself excitedly before going right back to taunting the creature again.

Olena and Chance round another stone walled corridor unhindered by any nasty surprises waiting for them. So much so that neither of them can believe how easy the first rescue appears to be going.

"Hey! Will you cut out making that stupid sucking teeth noise." Olena says to Chance who looks quite confused as to what she's getting at, as he's doing no such thing.

Realising once she looks at Chance's lion-head that it's not him making the sound both stare off behind them to where this now tip-tapping, click sound accompanies the sucking noise.

"*Run.*" Chance whispers as Olena needing no need to know what it is——because if Chance says to run it must be very, *very* bad, spins on her heel beginning to sprint forwards towards another bend in the corridor.

Glancing behind her, immediately regretting her decision———a silent scream presses along the inside of her windpipe unable to emanate as sheer terror locks it inside. A massive arachnid type creature accompanied with a million smaller ones is now galloping toward her and Chance. Fear, swirls inside of her gut——even as a Vampire she'd hated the Spider-Climber community. Her heart hammered against her chest, as for once she wished her hearing wasn't so acute as to hear the hungry clicking of the spider's fangs.

"When I say leap——you leap." Chance says as Olena nods silent in her acknowledgment of his instruction. If a Spider-Climber bit her, the venom in her human form would instantly paralyse then kill her——rendering the mission well and truly over.

"*LEAP!*" Chance roars to which Olena does, over quite a huge gap in the ground where at the bottom are hundreds of razor-sharp barbs ready to pierce any unlucky person who might quite literally *miss the gap.*

"Shizzle-twitters! I dropped the brazier." Olena says having landed on her stomach causing the wind to become loosely knocked out of her. She's also skinned her knees and grazed the palms of her hands but she's still alive—-as she glances down into the pit of metal spikes illuminated by the mess of smashed embers from the hot brazier she is no longer in possession of.

"They're still coming——*keep running*! I'll guide you." Chance shouts above the now much louder, much closer din of clicking, clacking sounds emitted from the sharply pointed legs of the arachnid type critters. Venom drips heavily from the largest Spider-Climber which all but sizzles as droplets hit the stone floor.

"Left, ok go straight. Right——no wait!"

Too late. By the time Chance realises his fatal mistake, both of them have hurtled head long into a dead end.

"What do we DO?" Olena exclaims becoming almost hysterical, her red tinted eyes look wild and her clothes are soaked through with perspiration. Panicked, blind with fear——she sets about pressing her stinging grazed palms against solid stone wall with no clear way out.

"I——I...

A roar of a different kind, ripples the air around them shortly before the ground begins to shake. The Spider-Climbers spooked, about turn and scram.

"What was that?" Olena asks now terrified that whatever the Spider-Climbers were fleeing from was clearly worse.

"Ahhhhh!" Nathan's voice rings out in the darkness as he sprints directly towards Olena and Chance in the pitch blackness.

"Nate? Is that you?" Olena calls out.

"Olena? *Woah*! This beast's after me!" He yelps running directly toward the sound of her voice as air burns his lungs with the effort of sprinting.

"Be careful there's a pit ahead, you might still see it illuminated by a brazier I dropped in there——you need to jump across it."

There is no sound and as Olena squints hard in the dark to see Nathan, she asks Chance if he can see what's happening.

"Hang on, hang on. Ok...he's clear." Chance says having witnessed the entire ordeal with his sharp and precise night vision he'd decided to keep as an ace bargaining chip for later on should it be required.

A short while later a puffing and panting Nathan appears, all but crawling towards them. Sweat pours off his face and body as he trembles uncontrollably with adrenaline still coursing through his veins.

"I'm guessing...your friends The Magi are responsible for this? Given the hole in my memory of how I ended up in a huge cage guarded by some kind of pig beast?"

Nathan says wiping at his sweaty face with the bottom of his dirty, pig beast saliva stained shirt.

"Yeah…The Magi orchestrated this whole elaborate maze. With the odds so hugely stacked against us I can't help but feel this is a fix. A sort of 'they're being seen to be doing the right thing'——giving me a *second chance* and all, when really, they just want this whole charade done and over with so they can go back to meddling in universal world matters. The crux being that *the Powers That Be* wholly recognise this wasn't all my fault and so there has to be an opportunity for this so-called redemption."

"It does appear as if the odds have been stacked heavily against you. But, if I can escape and find you amongst all this chaos without so much as a compass or a torch then——maybe we have someone looking out for us up there." Nathan says making Olena ponder on the different angelic realms, and what little she knows of them and their mystical powers of balancing lives and energies.

"Apart from feeling totally fried and I'm guessing in pain looking at your knees and palms———

Nathan's voice is cut off as Olena grabs hold of his grubby shirt pulling him close pressing their lips together. He tastes salty and a little rough around the edges but she doesn't care. He is heavenly in her mouth, as warm fuzzy feelings erupt throughout her body instantly switching her mind from primal survival mode to that of just wishing to get laid. It's all she needed to take the edge off her *fried* mind, as Nathan had so aptly put it.

"The worlds are doomed." Chance says to himself having been faced upward on the ground, getting a full painful view of them lip-locking. "If I had my stomach back I'd be vomiting right about now. Can we *please* get on with the mission?" He says a little louder.

"Hades you taste so good." Olena says as they part, all breathy while looking all doe and stag eyed at one another.

"I'd kiss you again but I don't think your friend here would survive an R-rate experience. Question——how *does* something made of inanimate metal become sentient?" Nathan asks as if it's the most reasonable thing in the world.

"Magic?" Olena offers in place of explanation before both she and Nathan are falling about laughing.

"Oh sure, laugh it up at my expense ha bloody ha!" Chance says not in the least bit amused.

"Right, come on it's about time we were heading off to locate Frank and the rest of the guys. Apparently, you were all placed in varying chambers in this maze. Oddly though there are only three chambers to locate and break all of you out from. The Magi I'm guessing know of my romantic interest in you and more than likely wished to put you alone putting you at greater risk. Probably just to piss me off more ——don't ask and don't mention fluffy bunnies, sunlight or green hills to me." Olena says cryptically which only deepens Nathan's want to know what it is she's speaking of.

Knowing he won't give up the ghost that easily——Olena babbles on explaining her weird illusionary dimensional experience with the strange gnome creature, while Chance guides them back to the edge of the pit with razor sharp spikes.

"I don't think I have the energy for another run up and jump. This human body seems to tire quickly compared to what I'm used to." Olena admits which stings her ego, as she knows she's outwardly expressing to feeling weak.

"While you were both talking, I ran through my memory bank and remembered a panel here on the wall ——to your right." Chance says which has both Olena and Nathan looking and feeling about for just such a panel.

"There is some writing above which says if you press it, a sliding walkway will appear." Chance goes on explaining the rest of the instructions.

"How do we know you're not tricking us?" Olena asks just as the last glowing embers from her dropped brazier go out plunging them completely into darkness.

"I guess you'll have to trust me. If anything happens to either of you I don't get my body back. Come on, hurry up will you. I believe your next closest friend on the map could be in greater danger then your friend Nathan here." Chance says injecting just the right amount of pressure in his statement to have Nathan press the panel.

The ground beneath them vibrates slightly before the sound of scraping stone can be heard.

"Be *very* careful here——I will guide you. The pathway is flush to the left wall——face the wall and side step along, but watch your footing." Chance says telling a bit of a porky-pie lie. The pathway did in fact cover the entire gap of the pit, but seeing the pair gingerly navigate the route was comedically amusing for him and gave him a boost to his own ego. Nope, they needed him and he felt more assured than when he and Olena had started the journey that she wouldn't be ditching him anytime soon.

# Chapter 38

A weird screaming had filled the previous stone room he'd found himself locked inside of. It would take a mere minute for Frank to realise that had been his own scream emanating from his tiny human mouth——in comparison to the Jackal-man's much larger, broader mouth.

Frank had been searching his mind in the dark trying but failing to figure out who this individual was——but being that Frank was not very up to date on historical characters, outside of British history——found himself well and truly stumped. Egypt has always shown wall art of ancient half human-animal hybrid creatures but the name and identity of this one evaded him.

The Jackal-man had thrown Frank into this room to eventually get him to stop screaming. The darkness at first was comforting but that comfort was now fast turning into a nightmare as Frank's mind raced with thoughts of "What if I'm left here to rot" among other hair-raising scenarios running amuck through his usually much more well put-together mind. Practicing his box breathing that he'd learned back in his military days helps to calm the racing thoughts down to a better controlled simmer.

"Everyone will be looking for me. Clearly whoever it is that has captured me needs me alive otherwise why am I still breathing? Yes, that's good Frank——very good. Keep to the common sensical, leave fear at the door." Inward chatter like this carried on until Frank found some sort of soft thing on the floor that felt like a duvet or blanket. Gingerly he had been exploring the blackened space on hands and knees——movement also helped keep him busy enough as a distraction away from fearful thoughts that if allowed——could swallow him whole making his entire mind break open like an egg. Having seen plenty of battlefield action——Frank was not averse to deny himself the knowledge that the real danger lay with himself and his mind. Soldiers came home battered and bruised and sometimes mentally broken. Some came back from that——others didn't and spent decades or longer on meds or worse, in mental institutions—— designed to keep the unstable and dangerous inside their concrete boxed prisons where many would never get out.

Climbing onto the nice soft material, Frank closed his eyes just for a moment. A scent of something pleasant drifted up his nostrils and before he could think any more on it was fast into the land of nod.

Anubis raged at The Magi. Demanding to know answers as to why *he,* God of the Egyptian Hades had been dragged from his realm to be stuck in a silly game concocted by themselves over a pathetic wrinkle in time.

Knowing how much beneath them and the Powers That Be any God or Goddess is, The Magi simply explain ——once Anubis has calmed down, that failure to comply with this mission would see his immediate removal from his present position as God in charge of the dead. Everything and anything placed into existence from all of their creators, could be snuffed out in an instant but this was seldom done due to keeping timelines as neat and tidy as possible. The fragility of the cosmos in any quadrant of space and time meant that rules had to be applied and obeyed. Knowing this truth Anubis eventually swallows any further retorts, opting to silently grumble as he takes a position on a giant stone throne, leaning his giant jackal chin upon his giant human hand.

Instructions were given that Anubis was to watch this human man until his friends came to rescue him ——if at any point in the challenge should they fail, Anubis would be relieved of his position. The Magi sounded fairly confident the maze's challenges would see to it that Olena did indeed fail meaning they could all go back to their work and home stations forgetting the whole sordid ordeal ever happened. Anubis asked what he was to do with this Olena human being should she manage to succeed——to which The Magi's amber orbs gleamed beneath their collective cloak before they simply said "Then you must annihilate them both——her and the man she will have rescued. We doubt very much she will have got past the *Knarled-Knackle-Fagger* but on the rare chance she has succeeded she would still need to navigate all of the traps set within the maze of which there were hundreds." With all of the twisty turns and bends, and having no map——The Magi gave Anubis the clear impression he was simply to sit tight before everything righted itself again.

"Fantastic! I'm *king* of the underworld and have been reduced to...babysitting duties." Anubis growls, looking at the closed door leading to where Frank's being held and presently——sleeping like a baby.

The Magi, having no knowledge of the help Olena is receiving as the talking lion-head named Chance appears to be a blind spot they never considered, leave Anubis to get on with more important duties——such as punishing the wicked and blessing the good. Oh yes, The Magi don't just deal out harsh punishments, there has to be balance in all things. What anyone gives out whichever universe or realm they may herald from——it normally always doesn't come back to them three-fold in some fashion or another.

———

"Ok, so going by the memorised map in my head, we have one turn to the left——two more to the right and then...we should be there." Chance says reeling off the directions happily now he's not subjected to the dark cramped conditions of Olena's ponging leather satchel.

"I'd be lying here Olena if I didn't admit that your little friend here is pretty trippy to look at. I mean Goblins, Vampires, Genies, Fairies——it's all things I grew up with listening to fairy tales but——*A talking lion-head?* ——nah! You couldn't make this shit up." Nathan remarks, making Olena wince at the sudden use of foul language, understanding what the word in human language translated to.

"Good sir, might I remind you that my *name* is Chance."

"Yeah——Chance, sorry mate."

"Shh! Both of you...*listen*." Olena says holding out a hand stopping Nathan in his tracks.

"That doesn't not sound good chaps." Chance says making Nathan quirk an eye-brow up at him at the use of the word *chaps* in perfect aristocratic British English.

"I'm never gonna get used to this fella." Nathan says listening with Olena to see what's up.

"Sorry, I don't hear anything?" Nathan says turning to Olena whose ruby eyes flash in the flame-light of the wall braziers.

"I think we're good. Ok Chance, what's the plan from here——we're at the last right turn so going by your directions where we need to be is straight down this stone corridor——correct?" Nathan asks looking straight into Chance's ruby coloured eyes a little freaked out that both the lion-head and Olena share this in common.

"Indeed."

"Cool, you want me to go on ahead——check things out before joining me?" Nathan asks Olena who finds his offer incredibly tempting——but none the less can't find the strength to have him leave her side. Should anything happen to Nathan she could only imagine all manner of unwanted emotions bubbling to the surface while also being back it being alone the thoughts made her shudder.

"No need, hang on." is all Olena says before raising Chance and launching him straight down the corridor and out of sight. A metal clang alerts them both that he had landed and nothing untoward had happened——no booby-traps.

"Would you mind *not* throwing me in future——and put my eye back in please." Chance protests as Olena can see indeed one of the rubies has popped out to leave a small golden hollow.

"Here you go buddy, good as new." Nathan says finding and popping back the ruby into its proper place again. "Say, do we get any sort of a weapon against this next assailant?" Nathan asks feeling naked going into a potential battle un-armed.

"Afraid not, from what I can gather if The Magi were so averse to giving me a map or any clear clue what I was meant to be doing with this maze——I doubt very much they'd be helping us defend ourselves. They wouldn't want to slow this process down——they want us dead and gone so life can go back to normal for them——wrinkle in time or not." Olena says grimly which elicits a small shiver to be expelled from Nathan as if someone just wandered over his grave.

"Wonderful." Nathan says, his voice dripping with sarcasm.

They reach a huge stone wall at the end of the corridor with two giant metal doors embedded into said wall. Hieroglyphics here appear to meld into English words the closer they get.

"Read the doorway, I don't have my glasses with me." Nathan instructs Olena as they've now reached the better illuminated end of the stone corridor.

"Oh...*Anubis*."

"Oh...dear." Chance says. "I suggest I do not enter this room with you. The Magi may be watching and it's clear they don't know I'm helping you. If you would be so kind as to put me down over there——near to the light, I'd very much appreciate it." Chance asks Olena who without arguing does as is requested of her.

"Word of advice——*DON'T* let Anubis so much as *smell* either of you inside—— it wouldn't end well, for either of you." Chance says affixing the couple with a grave stare through glinting almond shaped ruby eyes.

"Ok...got it, straight in, grab our friend and remain out of sniffing distance——I don't know about you Mr Jones but I don't fancy ever getting that close to our Jackal headed God friend." Olena states having placed Chance carefully near a resident palm plant and much brighter brazier light. As around this particular junction of the maze are tall-ish palm plants, a small drinking-fountain type thing built into the stone wall of the left-hand side with crystal clear water trickling out through the mouth of a mini stone Anubis head.

"How do we get in here?" Nathan asks looking but not finding any sort of handle or mechanism to open the door.

"Translation indicates it has to be the old-fashioned way——we knock." Olena says raising a hand to do just this.

The sound is muted and barely audible. Nothing happens for a few seconds but then the stone doorway slides effortlessly and almost silently open.

Sticking to the shadows as much as possible——they both take in the room before them. Tall sandstone pillars, palms, hieroglyphics that shimmer along stone walls, flitting between magical Egyptian text and English and back again. A giant seated statue of the God Anubis can be seen perched atop his mighty stone throne. Like ants, feeling they may be squished at any moment, both Olena and Nathan scuttle one behind the other praying Anubis cannot spot them among the dancing shadows.

Sneaking silently around the outside of the pillars, staying out of any and all light cast about the gigantic throne room from enormous braziers, both Olena and Nathan dive toward a corner when the huge statue of Anubis arises. He strides towards the open doorway causing the ground to tremor ever so slightly. He is following the sound of a lion's roar——Chance's lion's roar. A huge golden spear is carried in one of Anubis' giant hands attached to one of his giant tattooed, arms.

"Help! Somebody help me! I'm here——I'm in here!" Frank is heard yelling on the opposite side of the room.

Making the most of Chance's distraction Olena and Nathan reach the hidden doorway made to look like a stone wall. Hurrying to translate the door opening sequence——Olena rapidly knocks three times sending the doorway sliding silently sideways.

Frank was lying motionless in the dark, wondering if perhaps he may have gone blind and how that might be better so he wouldn't have to lay eyes on the enormous God-like beast again. He'd seen the movie Stargate plenty of times when a woman he'd dated long since gone now, had a young boy absolutely fascinated by the story. Frank understood the theorised idea behind interstellar wormhole technology and Egypt Gods not being the types of creature humans found themselves to be sometimes worshipping. But to have this whacky experience in *real* time——well it all but fried his poor overloaded older man's mind. Memories of happier times with his ex-girlfriend and son floated forwards—— just as a square of golden light appeared in the doorway filling the darkness ——causing Frank to squint. Terror filled his tummy as he realised this must be it——the end, time for his execution, God style. Although he supposed being killed by a God might not the worst way to go out of this world ——after all no ne he knew could attest to that. But he was still terrified none the less.

Dazed and disorientated, Frank stumbled forward falling into Nathan's arms. Both Olena and Nathan help him remain standing and just as they intend to turn and make a run for it does Frank once again scream aloud.

---

Nathan sprinted across Anubis' throne room floor like he was dodging bullets. Bits of broken off stone, some fallen pillars and other things like cracked stone urns peppered his pathway. His lungs were on fire and his body all but screamed at him to stop but he just kept on running. Leaping and climbing over everything and anything in his way. This only amused Anubis who was drawn to full height and watching Nathan with admiration——wondering if he should use a foot of the bottom of his staff to squash him to death. The God was watching something to the equivalent of a human watching an ant run for its life. To the ant perhaps that was very fast but to something so much bigger, taller and stronger then it——why Nathan may well have been running through molasses for all the good his effort was costing him.

Anubis grins maniacally with fierce glowing blue orbs for eyes, wearing a wicked scowl. His booming laughter makes his entire throne room shake causing Nathan to lose his footing which pitches him forward and headlong into a lump of stone. Stars spring out inside of his field of vision as mild concussion jangles his brain, balance and mind.

"You cannot outrun me tiny humans, and however entertaining it is for me to watch you try like ants to escape——If you carry on **running** I'll only make your deaths slower and a lot more painful. You've caused me a great inconvenience not being stationed at my regular post for the dead. Now, if you give up, I'll make your deaths all very fast and painless then we can all travel back to my underworld together." Anubis says in a tone that matches that of someone who might well have informed a scratch card player they'd won the jackpot prize.

None of them listen however to the booming overhead voice of the Egyptian God, as all focus remains on reaching the main entryway. As Olena and Frank catch up to Nathan, ducking and diving better fallen stone and other debris——it is here Olena has a quick and sudden brain wave.

"Of course! Frank, get Nathan outta here——I have a plan. *Trust me.*" Olena says gripping hold of Frank's forearm as he shoots her a very worried look of concern. But with no time to consider an alternative agrees, heading on over to the still dazed and confused Nathan Jones.

"Ok, but hurry!" Frank says struggling to keep a limping Nathan upright and mobile. A gash across Nathan's forehead is releasing blood making it trickle down his face and into his eyes.

"I will."

These are the last words Olena speaks to Frank before she watches them both disappear out of Anubis' throne room. As he'd been laughing so hard he had not been paying attention and being too high up couldn't hear anything the humans had been discussing while plotting an immediate escape. To watch the two human males dash out his throne room knowing he was bound to remain, had Anubis all but stare now in utter disbelief.

---

"Goddammit Olena!" Nathan says aloud as Frank props him up against the wall closest to Chance while trying to tend to the head wound.

"Where is Olena?" Chance asks shakily, knowing if she were to be killed or otherwise that they would all be stuck as and where they were——forever.

"*Apparently* she told my buddy Frank here that she has a plan." Nathan explains through gritted teeth as Frank tends to his very sore open wound.

"Lucky for you I still have my pack *and* stitching kit inside my mini first-aid pack. Frank says almost pleased at being so well prepared. "Where is your pack?" Frank asks realising Nathan has nothing to hand.

"The beast keeping me caged tore it from me. After eating the contents, it bolted after me. I wonder how Donnie, Jamie and Pete are getting on. I pray they'll survive until we can locate and rescue them." Nathan says, his breath easing a bit once Frank has administered the final stitch.

"You mean to tell me that two big burly chaps such as yourselves left a poor defenceless *human* woman to face the God of the underworld——*alone?*" As Chance says this both men can only carry very somber and guilty expressions.

"Cowards!" Chance says much quieter as Nathan takes a few sips from the water trickling through the Anubis styled side wall fountain to where Frank also follows suit.

All they can do now is sit in the hope this plan of Olena's works.

## Chapter 39

"You tell me your name is Olena Lupescu?" Anubis says having taken quite a firm hold of a horrified Olena. "Hmm, well I can certainly see the resemblance from your mother Valeria's complexion. Oh yes——I know of all your kin downstairs in my usual humble abode." Anubis says and it is as if someone has slapped Olena. Knowing in one form or another——be that ghostly or otherwise, her parents, her people are for want of better explanation still in existence.

"I thought everyone I knew was lost forever because of my stupid mistake with the genie."

"Where did you think all of your kind went when they met their eternal death?" He says getting all of Olena's attention now.

"I guess I...figured they'd just been erased like The Magi insinuated."

"Well let me assure you they are all safely tucked away inside the underworld. Word got around about what happened down there, between you and that 1000-year-old genie. Shame, they're quite rare these days——genies I mean." Anubis says in hypnotic waves——that has Olena struggling to keep her eyes from closing.

"Please Anubis great God of the underworld——can't you——

"Can't I what? You're in *no* position to make any sort of demands of me, *little human.*" Anubis says annoyance lacing his voice as he cuts Olena off.

Unbeknown to Anubis, Olena had deliberately allowed herself to be captured. No sooner had Anubis lifted her up in one of his human crushing sized hands, did Olena stab him with a baby Spider-Climber fang laced with poison. It wouldn't have dropped Anubis right away which is why she stalled for time. Her father always stressed she should carry an ace up her sleeve——however this time it was a fang, hidden out of sight by one of her khaki combat styled trouser pockets.

"What——what's happening….to *me.*" Anubis says as Olena hoped in slurred tones meaning the venom was indeed taking effect. Just one drop would be enough to drop a full-grown dragon or giant. It appeared the venom also worked on Gods.

"Spider-Climber venom. My gift to you——ensuring you go right back from whence you came. Oh, and by the way…I'd be *very* careful on how you tell The Magi about this failed attempt on our lives. After all it wouldn't be a good look for you as *God of the underworld*——explaining how a tiny *little human,* brought your sorry arse down." Olena says relishing in getting to throw back the earlier insult to Anubis before his legs buckle sending him sprawling to the ground, his fingers loosen and Olena half wiggles half jumps free, landing safely on a square boulder of stone before running toward the exit doorway.

A fizzing sound begins as Anubis' body begins to break down and dissolve into the sand. Olena bolts for the doorway as the whole space begins to disintegrate.

"Wait!" Olena spins around, a small squeal escaping her lips to see standing before her——a more human sized height Anubis who now is just in pure spirit form.

"Well done on defeating me Miss Lupescu. Take this, it should help with the next stage of your journey.

I'll be sure to take care of your parents and people. Keep going, I'll be rooting for you." Anubis states having pressed a small purple pouch into Olena's hands before disappearing in wafty smoke fashion.

The doorway slides open and on the other side is a wide eyed worried looking Nathan who all but pulls her through to safety as the rest of the throne room disintegrates and collapses, destroying the entire illusion as it had never existed in the first place. Hugging her close, walking her away from the door, they stop by the small stream of drinking water allowing Olena to grab a quick slurp using her hands.

"Nate, Nate...I'm good, I'm all good. Look see, not a scratch——I'm fine." Olena says pulling away from his vice like grip once he'd pulled her to him as she finished her drink.

"Hells bells Olena! You took down a God." Frank says grinning broadly.

"Yeah...guess I did."

"What's that?" Chance asks, and Olena crouches down to pick him up.

"It's something Anubis gave me for the next challenge. I'll open it later but first; can we try and find some food I'm starving." Olena says feeling weakness once again washing over her as the most recent bout of adrenaline wears off.

"I know just the place." Chance says re-capping to himself where all the hidden and secret doorways reside within the stone maze walls. The undisclosed doorways can take a traveller to anywhere they want within the city above ground. This time he takes them to the doorway that will lead them straight back to The Blue Pharaoh hotel. Olena had mentioned in a brief conversation to be staying here. It is Chance's hope in giving them an easy passage back out of the maze to freshen up and get food and drinks in comfortable familiar surroundings, will earn him some huge trustworthy brownie points with Olena.

---

"Woah...are we?" Nathan asks once they exit out of a side doorway that leads them straight out and into the reception foyer of The Blue Pharaoh. His head spins from the sudden transition yet it is the tamest experience he's had in recent hours so doesn't feel too shocked.

"Hold up." Frank says putting an arm across Nathan's chest before they step forward and out into the foyer from the concealed entryway. "Notice anything *suspicious.*" Frank says affixing Nathan with a knowing stare, familiar among special forces guys.

Scanning the space Nathan clocks on that Brax the *permanent* receptionist is now nowhere to be seen. In his place is a very concerned and flustered looking Monnie.

Magical folk come and go across the expansive floor space none the wiser that three humans and a talking lion-head simply watch on in astonishment.

Turning to address Olena and Nathan, Frank grumbles audibly, swearing under his breath to see Olena striding on up to reception without saying a word it had been her intention to do so.

"What is she up to?! Frank says annoyed and through gritted teeth. He didn't deal with insubordination well and although not officially Olena's boss, Frank thought perhaps naively that she would learn to fall in line like everybody else——clearly this was not the case and so he made the mental note to have words with her later.

A surprised almost relieved expression crosses Monnie's face as he spots Olena——wasting no time ushering her forward with one of his monkey hands.

"I suggest we go on after Olena before losing sight of her." Frank suggests marching out into sight of *Gargoyle40121962.*

The big animated stone figure strides up to them in a threatening manner. A determined stare is written across his face which reads *I must stop them at all costs!* Frank and Nathan make evasive manoeuvres until Gargoyle40121962 gets entangled in one of the tall indoor palm trees which sends them crashing unceremoniously to the hard marble floor.

"Come on, hurry it up will you! Brax is sick and Monnie can't disclose details up here, so we're catching this lift down to a lower level——are you coming or what?" Olena exclaims wondering what the holdup had been.

Oh yes, she and Frank would most *definitely* be having words later about her conduct or her lack of.

Crammed into the shoebox sized service lift making Nathan and Frank feels all kinds of claustrophobic—— where even the gentle musical notes drifting across the condensed space don't do anything to quell the rising tensions inside. After what seemed like forever, the lift eventually stops and blissfully the doors open bringing in a punch of much needed fresher air. They all practically shoe horn one another to make it out in one piece.

"Jesus wept Nathan!" Frank says as he and Olena along with Monnie dry heave upon exiting the lift.

"Sorry——I'm nervous." Nathan admitted his cheeks burning red with embarrassment.

"I'll consider myself lucky here at not having a sense of smell. Would someone care to explain what we're all doing down here——in the basement? Did no one consider this may be a trap?" Chance says, his bemused face at seeing the three amigos almost vomiting——gone his expression back to being that of a hard-set gold lion face.

"No trap I assure you. I glamoured Monnie into telling the truth of Brax's whereabouts——sorry Monnie but I can't take any chances I——*we,* still have friends relying on us to rescue them."

"That's quite alright, I'm sure Brax will be glad for the company of familiar faces. I must leave to man the desk; those check ins and outs won't happen on their own." He says in feigned cheerful tune——before a more somber expression crosses his usually bright smiley face. As he steps back inside the lift Olena could swear he even wiped a tear away but she didn't ask or pry.

Alone in the darkened basement area the four comrades head on toward what looks to be bog standard front door.

"This place will never cease to amaze me." Nathan says quietly which earns him an understandable look from Frank as Olena stares ahead seeming not to have heard him.

"Hold onto your butts folks, this could be an inter dimensional portal doorway." Frank says now holding onto Chance in place of Olena.

Rolling her eyes and reaching out a hand, Olena twists the brass doorknob and voila——it opens and inside is normal looking house porch way.

Nathan whistles wondering why a creature such as Brax would need such humble human-esque dwellings. Didn't Minotaurs usually live out in the woods? Or was he thinking of Centaurs from Parry Trotter? He continues to ponder this as they head on deeper inside of Brax's home.

## Chapter 40

"Monnie requested that we please don't touch anything and that to find Brax he'd be in his room second door on the left." Olena says as gingerly they take one careful step at a time. Having just come from a place full of booby-traps none could be too careful as to what kind of home security system a magical Minotaur might have.

On entry to Brax's home, like the rest of the basement it's extremely dark with only candle-light for companionship. There is an immediate foul odour that assaults all their sense of smell——once again making the small group wretch and heave. Covering the lower half of their faces with their tops seemed to be the only way to help them acclimatise to such a stinky atmosphere.

"I'm guessing by your reaction here that there is some unpleasant stench about us?" Chance exclaims thankful again not to have his sense of smell in full working order.

"How observant of you. And yes, there is a rather pungent stench down here——you don't think Brax has *died* do you?" Olena asks voice muffled by the fabric of her top as she turns to address Nathan with the question wondering if the smell of death mimicked that of those who died out on the battlefield.

A weird gurgling sound hurtles from Frank's body making Olena and Nathan turn to look at him with shared puzzled expressions.

"Oh god——not now." is all he manages to utter before turning and sprinting for the door.

"Never took my boss to being the sensitive type around death, which can only mean one thing—— Frank's unwell." Nathan says looking at Olena with grim expression. "As for the smell, I don't know what the cause is but I suggest we don't linger inside here longer than necessary." Nathan says biting back his own waves of nausea, as every time he speaks wafts of the stench enter in through his mouth hitting his gag reflex.

"Well I hope if he's sick it isn't catching." Olena says quite cruelly having witnessed many a sick human person when on hunts with her parents. They were to never feed on the sick only the young and thriving, so to stave off any cross-contamination for although rare illness could afflict a Vampire from time to time.

Olena's foot catches on a small wooden table near to the entryway sending her momentarily sprawling forwards with curses flying freely from her luscious lips that Nathan enjoys kissing——*very* much. Landing on her knees, the stinging sensation instantly brings tears springing to her red tinted eyes. Nathan horrified at seeing the woman he's growing fond of injured—-however mildly, holds out a hand to help her up. The unplanned contact with Nathan that usually sees Olena's heart rate soaring and body humming——does nothing to dim the rising nausea attacking Olena's sense of smell, as her top slipped from her face mid-fall, causing her to retch again.

Thanking Nathan for his help once better composed ——Olena turns spotting Chance, grumbling to himself on the floor. She assumes that Frank must have left him before making a hasty retreat. Picking the unamused Chance up, lightly dusts him off to place him atop a mantlepiece she spies off on adjacent wall. He protests but can do little about where Olena puts him as options seem limited here.

"Should Frank return or anyone else enter, do us a favour and make some noise." Olena instructs Chance struggling with every word, as each time she opens her mouth she can taste the rancid pong in the air. She ignores his response to not being a glorified guard hound.

Olena and Nathan continue their way through Brax's dimly lit living quarters. Olena unconsciously has wrapped a wary arm around Nathan's and giving it a squeeze causes him to smirk under his shirt. Thoughts of having her in bed again start to surface to which he expertly packs away using his military training. His mind then focuses in on Frank and what might be the matter with him, reassured only that the Blue Pharaoh have capable medical staff on site to help him if need be.

They come across a big green doorway with dull brass knob. The smell has intensified so both Olena and Nathan share a look that this could very well be Brax's bedroom. Having been distracted by Olena's fall and the overwhelming stench——while navigating in almost pitch-black conditions, made the seemingly simple task of locating Brax's bedroom doorway more than a little challenging. Turning the knob, glad to see it is unlocked. Pushing it open, instantly has Nathan and Olena lurching backwards to throw up. Nathan has slamming the door firmly shut again until they can both recover.

"I think it's...safe to assume...our buddy Brax in there might not be...in the land of the living anymore. Want me to go in alone to check it...out?" Nathan says struggling against wanting to throw up again now the original stench is mixed with both the smells of his and Olena's stomach contents.

"I...think...I'll manage. I...want to know...I'm no stranger to death...as hello *Vampire*." Olena says loosely trying to lighten the atmosphere with a joke.

Nathan grins at her attempt quite pleased to see her injecting humour into their tense situation.

"Ok...lead on then...oh deathly one." Nathan mockingly bows to where Olena playfully punches him on the side of an arm which to his surprise actually dings quite a bit.

*Hadn't Monnie said he had just spoken to Brax? What on Earth is going on here. Is it a set up? Has Monnie killed Brax wishing to trap us down here——oh Hades! I can feel the claustrophobia clawing up my throat. Stay calm, be cool, The Magi wouldn't allow for such sabotage——unless they requested Monnie do this for them. Oh Farcey-Fazzle-Cankers!* Olena's mind whirs with fear on a level she knows she will never grow accustomed too.

As they walk further into Brax's presumed bedroom Olena finds a candlestick combined with three half melted candles sitting atop of a wooden chest. Checking the drawers is relieved to find a box of enchanted flints (small multicoloured stones that when rubbed between two fingers (or whatever appendages the user has), create a flame to light candles. Unlike human candles however many magical ones are created from the donated fat of Boar-Orc warriors. Huge burly, brutish creatures with no empathy and a tenacity for violence and war. All armies and wars need to be funded it appeared, whichever universe you hail from and so the fat was a product they sold to candlemakers for just such a purpose. Other candles are created from plant-based materials or waxy substances created by The Magical realm's equivalent of bee-type species.

Candle ignited all but has Nathan's eyes standing out on stalks——seeing the entire magical process occur. Shaking his head, reminds himself here that this isn't Earth as he knows it and the thought somewhat grounds him again.

"A fireplace! Finally, we can create some decent light in here." Olena says brightly although muffled through the top she is wearing covering the lower portion of her face again.

Glancing down with the illumination of the candles

helping them both to see better. Olena and Nathan spot big globs of blood-stained gelatinous blobs dotted about the floor which explains where the awful stench is coming from.

Olena makes fast work to light the fireplace but a sound makes her jump back alarmed——causing her to slip on one of the stinky blobs on the floor. Nathan fortunately had been stood behind her and so prevented Olena toppling to the floor for a second time.

"Haha haha! So sorry my dears but haven't been lit in such a long time and well——It tickles!" The animated fireplace explains.

"Figures...you're a *magical* fireplace?" She exclaims now standing solidly on her own two feet again.

"Certainly am. I was one of the unfortunate ones who missed the spell being broken at Master Beast's castle. Belle ever so kindly sought out all displaced enchanted items to bring them back to the castle but...I was taken to auction before my rescue could be concluded. Brax bid on me and won. Belle on locating me asked if I was sure I wished to remain under Brax's care to which I said I was. Of course, Master Beast and Belle have long since passed now...then what with happened to Master Brax and not seeing him in such a long while——or anyone for that matter and...well it gets awfully lonely down here." The fireplace with female voice says giving the fast, ugly version of what her life has become.

Olena makes a mental note to come back here once the time-line is reset to take the fireplace to her own family's home where she will be well looked after. The human empathic twinge going unnoticed by herself, as Olena becomes more human and less Vampire in memory——with every moment she remains as one.

"That's terrible, I'm so sorry you've been through such a lonely ordeal. Shall I...put you out?" Olena asks knowing how important it is to make friends with those you wish to obtain information from. A lesson well taught by her Vampire detective father.

"Hang on——Beauty and the Beast?" Nathan inquires unsure the fireplace was talking about the same Beast and Belle he knew from human fairy tales.

"Well, she didn't much like the term *beauty* as of course Mistress Belle was her official name." The fireplace explains as if Nathan should already be abreast of such head-spinning knowledge.

"Ignore him——he's human and I'm...well by nature Vampire but——I had a little *accident* at work and so until I can fix it, my punishment is to remain human." Olena explains not wanting to give too much detail away in case the fireplace may take offence to learn her lonely predicament could yet be reset.

"Oh...how *interesting* and well beyond the realms of my understanding. A human coming here, seems almost impossible——preposterous even, but I suppose stranger things have happened." The fireplace goes on amused.

"How come you didn't alert us to your presence right away?" Nathan asks unable to stop automatically firing off questions bred from suspicion.

"Since Master Brax was cursed to an eternal desk job

——I half wondered if I was not hallucinating you both. I get so terribly lonely back here on my own." The fireplace admits miserably.

"What is your name? Mine is Olena——this is Nathan." Olena says fast changing the subject keeping things friendly while silently praying Nathan can rein in his *macho* military attitude.

"The name's Shurlee. I was——*back in the day* a proud maid for Master Beast and Mistress Belle in their grand castle. Alas it appears not all fairy tales have a happy ending. Being a few thousand years old——perhaps I'm cynical these days. Anyway, you need anything I'll try to help to the best of my ability. I can hear all manner of conversations through the pipes in this room. So I do sort of already know who you are and perhaps why you're all here but don't you worry——Shurlee's the word." The fireplace named Shurlee says in place Nathan feels of the old adage *'mum's the word'* from his world. "Oh——I can see that stinky stuff on the floor affects you both quite negatively. Feel free to slip it into my fire and it should make quite a difference for you both." Shurlee suggests and needing no second invitation to do so sees Nathan rapidly grabbing a small black metal shovel-shaped device hanging off to the side of Shurlee with a range of other poker type items, to do just this.

The blobs fizzle and smoke slightly before disappearing into ash as Shurlee makes her fire extra hot.

"Thank you." Nathan says pulling the top away from his face as Olena follows suit. There is now a far less prominent stench to the air which makes breathing so much easier on them both.

"Master Brax is through those doors over there." Shurlee says indicating the two wooden sliding doors each fitted with amber coloured glass panels, off to their right.

"Well Shurlee, it's been a pleasure to make your acquaintance." Olena says turning to head on toward Brax's room keen to see if he's alive or dead.

"Oh...sure, it's been a pleasure. Glad to have helped." Shurlee calls out after Olena who's already stepping through the doorway.

"Yeah——thanks." Nathan mutters before following after her.

"They've de-hoofed him!" Olena all but wails at the mangled sight of their newly acquainted enchanted friend.

"I think I'm gonna be——" Nathan bends at the knees as memories of the gelatinous lumps recently burned, come to mind——making him realise these were Brax's hooves.

"Nathan look at me. You're not going to be sick." Olena says, rapidly glamouring Nathan which works only because he was caught unawares of what she was doing.

The nausea stops instantly as Nathan shakes his head, momentarily losing his train of thought.

Brax is incoherent while in so much pain. His big Minotaur eyes roll inside of his bull like face as his breathing comes in rapid hefty wisps.

"Hey! MAGI! I know you can hear me! I request an audience with you——*NOW*!" Olena says using the rising anger she now feels to bolster her request.

"Now just one minu——

Nathan pauses mid-sentence as he is frozen in place as is Brax.

"Do not presume Olena to being able to make requests or demands for our attention." The Magi say threateningly, causing their words to ring out inside of her head while momentarily appearing in painful scratches all across her body——the pain of which brings her to her knees.

"S...sorry. I just——why was this done? Has Brax not taken good care of us? What has he done that is so wrong?"

"Brax has been punished again for helping aid you in your quest. The communication devices——the maps, he shouldn't have interfered. The only job this disgusting beast has is to take care of your survival needs. Food, Water, comfort——just as he sees to all the guests here."

Olena feels her stomach rolling, to know their action of simple request for maps and anything to help keep them connected has seen Brax tortured in such a traumatic fashion.

"I apologise profusely your high sirs. Please——we promise never to request anything from him ever again. We did not know this was a breech to the terms of the quest. How can he be made well again?" Olena says trying very carefully to choose words that won't make The Magi consider making Brax suffer further pain.

"Very well——we didn't think you would care anything of this useless beast. If it will hamper your focus to know of his plight——we agree to reversing the punishment." Before The Magi even finish speaking Brax vanishes from sight and his huge four poster bed goes back to being made as if never slept in.

"Th-thank you. I shall try to never call upon you again." Olena says warily, sure to not look up into those creepy amber orbs that occasionally flash in place of eyes.

"See to it that you don't."

The Magi disappear causing Nathan to become re-animated again.

"Minute." Nathan finishes, looking about confused. "The Magi?" He asks now pleased to see no sign of a distressed injured Brax, and to smell nothing of rotting flesh but in its place stale musty air akin to that of a dusty room unused in a while.

"Let's go see if he's back at reception." Olena says once more bolting away from Nathan who has to jog to keep up with her.

Shurlee says a rushed goodbye asking them both not to be strangers unsure if either of them heard her. Silently the corners of her mouth droop down and tears threaten to spill over——until that is Nathan pops back briefly to assure Shurlee that she will see them again and perhaps if all goes well with their mission, to return with more of their friends. This makes Shurlee brighten inside as hope flares in her heart again to being in good company after too long alone.

Olena has already called for the lift as Monnie makes

an appearance as the door open. Rushing inside Olena wastes no time asking if all is well with Brax, and before he can answer right away Nathan steps inside.

"Brax is back on duty, he doesn't remember anything so myself and all the staff have decided not to bring it up. Which floor can I take you to?" Monnie asks stepping right back into the role of lift operator.

"Lobby please." Olena says wearing her best fake smile——before turning away from Monnie and Nathan to cry silently in the far corner of the lift. Nathan gently rubs her back before drawing her close for a hug. Olena recovers, managing to compose herself just as the doors ping open. Thoughts of screwing up and perhaps without even knowing her errs, much like the genie incident——turns Olena's insides to ice.

*"Try not to worry. Anxiety is all part and parcel of being human——you sort of get used to it."* Nathan whispers to Olena, having clearly picked up on her sense of unease from her firm hold of his hand.

*"Yeah but I bet if you make a mistake as a human you're not threatened with being turned into some other creature while having the rest of your entire race erased from existence!"* Olena whispers back hotly.

*"Well, when you put it like that...I guess you're entitled to feel what you're feeling and to cry when need be. Sorry ——I've been trained to keep such expressions of emotion inside of me at all times when not in private or alone. It's a British 'stiff upper lip' philosophy. They don't instil it so much now but——Sorry I'm waffling."* Nathan says beginning to feel pretty nervous himself as to the power

these mysterious Magi forces wield. If they could make Olena feel scared to the point of crying——a normally ferocious predator (if the storybooks and movies were anything to go by on Vampires), then he deemed them wary adversaries indeed. The thoughts of what they were all embroiled in caused his own stomach to feel unsettled.

## Chapter 41

"Good evening Olena and Nathan. How may I or my staff be of service to you tonight?" Brax asks in usual formal fashion. "Oh, and before you answer me——I believe *this* belongs to you." Brax says handing a very cheesed off looking gold lion-head over to Olena, who looks aghast to having forgotten him.

"I'm so sorry Chance, in all the confusion of everything I...*forgot* you were there." Olena says cringing inwardly at actually admitting she had forgotten her newly acquainted lion-head friend. He simply rolls his eyes and harrumphs as she carefully places him inside of her satchel.

"Do you happen to know where our friend Frank is? He left us in a hurry, looking quite *unwell*." Olena says placing a hand on Nathan's forearm to silence him, having seen his lips part as if he were about to *waffle* some more.

"Frank is presently being tended to by Mortina our chief nurse in his bedroom. Would you like me to call for an update?" Brax asks giving both of them a fixed look over his half-moon spectacles——that look Olena decided, ridiculously dainty upon his massive bullish face.

"Sure, that would be great. Also, we'd like to request to have supper down in the...*basement*. We sort of got lost and ended up in a place with a talking fireplace of all things——*Shurlee* she said her name was." Olena says playing the role of clueless guest expertly.

"Oh——I see. Of course, consider it done." Brax says, barely holding it together as waves of revulsion wash over him——to having forgotten his enchanted fireplace companion, after so many decades serving his eternal sentence. Quietly he makes a mental note to see his staff have her taken away——and placed in a nice busy household with lots of company so she may never be forgotten again. The loneliness itself must have all but crippled her. Brax couldn't help but think which made putting on a front to Olena and Nathan that much harder.

"Shurlee explained at how *isolated* she felt and was keen to have us dine with her." Olena says gingerly realising to have appeared to have touched on a sensitive subject with Brax.

"It's no bother——I'm glad she has the two of you to keep her company tonight. Any special requests for your meal?"

"I don't know sweetie——what do you fancy?"

Olena says in her best *bright as a button* tone of voice which all but makes Nathan's head swim.

*Sweetie!* He exclaims to himself.

"How about a veggie lasagne and chips, a beer for me and a Diet Coke for Olena." Nathan says reeling off food names so fast Olena can all but look at him in awe.

*He just seems so...well put together. How did I get to being so lucky in finding such love and warmth during this heinous time of my life? Now I know what love feels like I worry how this may affect me should be successful in our quest and I be returned to my old Vampire self.*

"Olena...? Hello?" Nathan says waving slightly in front of Olena's glazed over expression.

"Oh I'm sorry, I was just talking to myself——you know, up here." She says pointing animatedly to her head with a big goofy grin. "That food you've ordered all sounds delicious to me. You've managed not to offend my human taste buds so far so——I trust you know what you're doing."

"Ok, that order has all been put through for you. Do you still want me to call through to Frank's room for you?"

"Yes, please. I'd be very grateful to know how my friend's doing." Nathan says trying but failing to keep the nerves out of his voice as he wonders if Frank isn't struck down with some magical sickness or disease, that might be wreaking all kinds of havoc on his long-time boss and friend's body.

Checking his computer Brax can see that Frank has

been transferred to one of their private on-site medical rooms.

"It appears your friend has been transferred to one of our private medical rooms. It says here on a note left by Mortina——to tell you that Frank's suffering mild effects of what humans call a stomach bug. They're giving him fluids and plenty of bed rest."

"Isn't that a relief to know Frank's going to be just fine? Tell you what, I'm going to go and be with Shurlee for a little bit, you go catch up with Frank. I'll meet you down in the basement for supper." Olena says giving Nathan a chaste kiss on the cheek before turning and hurrying away, flagging down Monnie as she went to request an escort. Fortunately for Olena, Monnie had just emptied out the lift and got a colleague nearby to step in for him.

"Whatever Olena is having——I want some." Brax says in rare joking fashion.

"She sure is peppy this evening. I'd best put an appearance with Frank——is there someone who can take me?" Nathan asks his head still feeling fuzzy at the complete 180 on Olena's behaviour. One minute she seems terrified and worried the next all but bursting full of beans like a giddy school girl on a sugar rush. Then again, he wondered how difficult it must be for her going from Vampire to human and guessed were roles reversed ——he may too be struggling to navigate and accept how his body and mind may feel becoming far removed from everything he deemed to be normal, so far as in what it meant for *him* being human.

"Certainly——Cuprella, please escort Mr Jones to our medical wing, room 25." Brax says catching the attention of a passing elf-lady who Nathan guesses stands to be about 4ft tall and dressed like Tinkerbell.

"Of course, right this way please Mr Jones." The fairy elf named Cuprella says and it's here as she passes Nathan that he can see pinky-green iridescent wings fluttering speedily behind her.

*Of course, a fairy-elf woman. Why am I not surprised?* Nathan thinks but soon regrets this as she turns to look at him with guarded expression as if to silently relay to him the message that she can read his thoughts.

———

"Hey Monnie, you know it's odd, Brax never acknowledged to having ever lived down in the basement or owning Shurlee——maybe in his many centuries manning the desk he somehow forgot elements of his old life." Olena says wondering if she herself is now *waffling* as Nathan so eloquently put it. For some reason with this sense of unease and butterflies in her stomach——it makes her just want to talk perhaps a little too much.

Monnie simply turns back giving an awkward smile to acknowledge Olena before turning back around to face the panel of buttons and lift doors.

To Olena's utter amazement and delight upon re-entering Brax's residence. She can now see it has been well lit and looks positively spick and span. There's no funky or nasty smells of half dead rotting carcasses. Peach toned candles mounted on the wall give an ethereal warm and cosy feel to the place. Unrecognisable scents wash over Olena like a slight summer-night's breeze would, bringing with them a sense of calm and ease.

Heading on deeper inside to where Shurlee is situated ——Olena can see her full beauty here. Shurlee's marble has been polished, the seat of her fire looking spotlessly clean and gleaming. Shurlee's aquamarine marble eyes sparkle whereas before they had looked dull and sad. Before forgetting him this time, Olena reaches inside of her satchel to take out Chance and places him carefully on top of a shelf right next to Shurlee. He is still refusing to speak to Olena.

"Hello my new friend, how do you like the place *now?*" Shurlee says giving Olena a wink. "Your little companion there isn't very chatty, is he?" She says indicating to Chance by moving her eyes to the right.

"It's beautiful, ——oh, Chance is a beast of *few* words. Best to just ignore him. Nathan will be joining us promptly, he's gone to visit our other friend who's a bit unwell."

*How on Earth was this place cleaned up so fast?"* Olena thinks quietly to herself, because even by magical standards this had been accomplished ridiculously fast.

"Oh dear I hope it is nothing serious."

"No, as far as I could gather he has what some humans call a...*stomach bug?*"

"Oh poor fellow, let's share a drink and make a toast to your friend Frank's fast recovery. Please, take a seat." Shurlee says indicating to the gorgeous laid out table for two, adorned with crisp white cloths, roses and a candelabra making it look very romantic.

Soothing music plays out from somewhere unseen and Olena almost jumps when seemingly out of nowhere a handsome topless male with rich Egyptian coloured skin tone, wearing loose fitting shiny blue and golden trousers, steps forward to help Olena into her chair before setting her napkin atop of her lap and asking if she'd like a glass of wine.

"I think I'll stick with the *Diet Coke* drink Nathan recommended for me——thanks."

The handsome butler simply clicks his fingers over his golden tray and a can of Diet Coke appears.

"When you're ready to order or if you'd like a top up, simply ring this bell and I'll be here instantaneously." The man says before vanishing in a smoothly done poof of smoke, having placed a tiny brass bell on top of the table.

*I'm so jumpy these days.* Olena thinks quietly having startled when the male who'd served her disappeared. She fiddles with her napkin to have it sitting neater on her lap.

Conversation is soon underway between Shurlee and Olena and before too long Nathan arrives to join them.

"This sure is different from before." Nathan says unable to keep the surprise from his voice. "I wonder how staff managed to get everything so——*clean* in no time at all." Nathan says echoing Olena's earlier thoughts.

Nathan runs his index finger atop of Shurlee's mantlepiece making her laugh ever so slightly.

"Oh, sorry." Nathan says pulling his hand back as if he'd burned it.

"Don't worry my dear, and to answer your question The Blue Pharaoh houses up to fifty million dust ball cleaners——tiny little unassuming balls of fluff with big personalities and a ferociousness to want to clean everything and anything——sometimes *anyone.*" Shurlee says winking at Nathan, making him take a nervous few steps away from her.

Olena rings the bell and the semi-nude butler appears again. He wastes no time taking Nathan's drink order before confirming their food preference for this evening and once again vanishing in a tidy wisp of smoke.

"Who's he when he's at home?" Nathan asks affixing Olena with a look as if she were to know what species the butler is from.

"Our delectable host this evening is called Emanet. He is a descendant of one of the oldest desert wizard tribes. He used to tend to Brax and this place before... Brax's trial and punishment were rolled out. Emanet is a little shy around new people, and I imagine quite floored to being pulled into service again. Anyway, let's eat I'm starved." Shurlee says taking Nathan by surprise to actually being able to eat and drink food. "Oh alright——you two eat I'll just enjoy watching." Shurlee adds seeming to have read Nathan's mind given his puzzled expression.

"How's Frank?" Olena asks just as their food arrives.

"He is good——has a touch of this magical virus

which to humans presents as a stomach bug——but it's not very contagious so the nurse doesn't expect any of us to come down with it." Nathan quickly adds while shovelling forkfuls of food into his mouth in a fashion that'd make anyone think he hadn't eaten for days.

"Slow down there young man——you'll give yourself indigestion." Shurlee playfully scorns as Nathan blushes before placing his knife and fork down——struggling to chew the large mouthful currently masticating inside of his mouth.

The three of them spend a couple of hours enjoying each other's company. Nathan is surprised to learn the true goings on inside of the real Beauty and Beast fairy tale castle——at least from those who served the castle behind closed doors.

"It's been a wonderful evening, thank you for sharing the time with me. Brax has kindly put in for a transfer for me——I'm to be placed with large family where its guaranteed I'll never be lonely again. I have to admit I won't be sorry to see the back of this room when I go. Brax couldn't help abandoning me and who wouldn't forget things after centuries at a desk job. I hold no grudge against him. Anyway, you'd best get some sleep, undoubtedly you have a busy day ahead of you in your quest to seek out this Ruby Sunrise Dagger. I wish you all the best." Shurlee says bringing their evening to a close.

Olena and Nathan say obligatory goodbyes and wish Shurlee all the best with her new home placement. Emanet never re-appears but Olena calls out a loud thank you all the same. She also makes a mental note to come back once the timelines restored seeing to it Shurlee gets to again be re-homed. Spotting Chance this time on the shelf she picks him up and puts him once again inside of her satchel——his eyes are closed a mini snoozing sounds can be heard emanating from his shiny golden mouth. Olena thinks he looks really rather cute here.

---

Satiated from good food, for the first time since entering the world of magic and mystery——Nathan is glad to be feeling relaxed and more than ready for sleep. Olena places a gentle hand against one of his firm buttocks but instead of subtly reacting——conscious that Monnie stands in front of them manning the lift controls, Nathan lifts her hand up to his waist.

As they enter Olena's enchanted bedroom she whips her shoes off keen to feel the grass against the bare skin of her feet.

"Sorry for shunning you in the lift——I'm dog tired and more than ready for bed." Nathan says in way of explanation that sex was off the table for the next few hours.

"Oh——it's no bother. I'm happy just to cuddle with you." Olena says immediately reeling from the words.

*What am I saying?! CUDDLE?!! Were I my usual Vampire self——had I so chosen to have my wicked way with this mere mortal——tired or not I'd have had my way and then some. Here I am trotting beside him like a little fawn in heat, rolling over to his will, that because he doesn't want sex——no sex will happen! What is wrong with me! Hades dammit——where's my tenacity?!* Olena's blood begins to simmer as the heat coursing through her body which she doesn't realise is classed as being *horny* to most human beings, makes her feel borderline feral. Wondering here how long she will be able to remain pleasant with Nathan with these powerful sensations coursing through her——for his sake she hopes Nathan falls asleep promptly for both their sakes.

Accidentally she drops her satchel onto the hard wood floor of the yurt making Chance yelp and swear. Rapidly she goes to take him out apologising again but it appears of no use as he now glares at her before going back to ignoring again. Gingerly she places him atop of a soft cushion on a chair facing the yurt entryway (just in case she and Nathan do end up rubbing bodies together).

## Chapter 42

Within minutes Nathan is deep asleep into the land of nod but annoyingly for Olena and her hot and frustrated body——sleep seems to be evading her.

Throwing the covers off her side of the bed unable to switch off, Olena sneaks off wrapping a lightweight emerald green blanket around her before stepping out of the yurt to cosy near the campfire——lighting it with a mere click of her fingers. Much like sound activated lights in *smart* homes, this fireplace was also ignited.

In her hands she has brought with her the pouch Anubis handed to her. Curiosity getting the better of her starts to undo the threaded material at the top of the pouch.

*Olena...wait...*a ghostly voice speaks close to her ear.

Turning, a surprised expression crosses her face having half expected Nathan to be standing right behind her——but a chill zips down Olena's spine at seeing... no one.

"Ah!" Olena squeaks as looking down sees within the flames of the camp-fire the translucent image of Anubis' head.

*When the time is right——not before...be patient.* He whispers out before disappearing.

Huffing at not being able to sneak a peek. Olena suspects Anubis appeared to her using flame communication (an extremely old and archaic way to talk to one another in The Magical realm) so as to not arouse suspicions with The Magi. With her curiosity bubble well and truly burst, and feeling like the first real waves of tiredness starting to wash over her. Olena clicks and stands up to walk the short distance back to the yurt where she discovers a still sound asleep Nathan.

"My hero." She exclaims silently to herself, sliding back into bed.

Nathan having felt the mattress move, turns toward Olena wrapping his arms around her pulling to bring her closer to him.

"You wandered off, I went to look and saw you by the camp fire——you ok?" Nathan asks taking Olena by surprise that it was she who had not noticed him and not the other way around.

"I——err...can't sleep with all of these hot *feelings* running through me." She admitted sheepishly, keeping the subject of Anubis to herself.

Nathan says nothing in response to Olena's explanation——he simply rolls her gently onto her back while starting to make long slow love to her. From this wonderful new experience of human tenderness, Olena finally manages to fall into a very deep state of sleep.

---

Olena finds herself transported inside of Anubis's temple situated in the underworld. By the hieroglyphs and statues, she can tell immediately this is where he resides. It's a lot brighter and less threatening then she'd imagined, but then also reminded herself this was just a dream so not to take too many of the details to being factually true.

Anubis floats into view a few feet in front of Olena in the form of a black cat so as to not intimidate or overwhelm her.

*'Olena, I am sorry I could not say more while in the fire. At least here in the land of dreams The Magi cannot spy on us.'* Anubis explains.

*'Are you controlling this dream, or am I?'*

*'Forgive me, it was I——guiding your sleeping subconscious mind here to my temple space. Battu one of my female Seers helped me with this process. There is not a whole lot of information I can pass along regarding the remainder of your quest——As a God I have ways of spying while remaining undetected. The Magi however are keeping their cards very close to their chest with your——mission. All I can tell you is that your friends will be found in plain sight——but you shall be blind to them. That is when you may use the power within that pouch which I've gifted you. Your parents are here——waiting for you.*

*There isn't much time left so make the most of this experience.'* Anubis says opening a dream doorway gently nudging Olena through with his cat nose. Once across the threshold the doorway closes before Olena has time to thank him but in her dream state Olena's sole focus now is seeing her mum and dad.

Anubis knowing Olena will forget the dream upon awakening is banking on her human subconscious memory to prompt her when required to use and open the pouch when the time is right. The Magi did Anubis a dis-service using him like a puppet in this little dagger game of theirs and so he had no qualms about helping Olena and her friends because of this.

Olena sees her parents and wastes no time hurrying across to them. They are in a big bright garden with flowers, birds, trees and looking abnormally——*human* and happy to be bathed in this spiritual dream sunlight.

Valeria and Manix understand what transpired and hope all goes well in Olena's mission to set things right. They tell her they are not mad at her but instead very proud of her. The three of them then go to meet and greet other Vampire spirits——some of whom are Olena's long-time friends from school. Seeing everyone she knew during her time living as a half-dead Vampire in nothing but darkness——finds the experience of seeing all her kin happy in sunlight more than just a tad trippy. The underworld was not the dark and gloomy place she suspected it would be——knowing only of it what had been taught to her in school.

Soon Olena feels the pull of awakening grasping her and

not wasting a second grabs hold of her parents giving them the biggest hug of her life before her awakening human body brings her well and truly back to the land of the living.

---

Groggily Olena awakens with predictably no memory of her dream. Nathan she sees is already fully clothed, and gently nudging at her to awaken fully.

"*Mmm*, what time is it?" She says sleepily while rubbing her eyes.

"It's early. I thought it best not to sleep too long as we need to make a start on today's challenges——whatever they may be." Nathan says handing Olena a cup of sweet English tea.

"Good idea, thank you for the tea."

"I'll leave you to get yourself sorted. I have arranged a breakfast picnic by the camp fire. Brax organised for room service staff to bring me the ingredients I required while you slept."

"That is so thoughtful of you, thank you. Right I'd best get myself a shower and then I'll meet you for breakfast I'm so hungry I could eat a——

"Hippo?" Nathan says cutting her off.

"Sure, one of those."

Nathan smiles, turning to exit the yurt but not before glancing back to sneak a cheeky peak of Olena's naked form as she slips from beneath the covers. Catching him she playfully shoos him away while grabbing a forest green coloured dressing gown to wrap around her.

———

Olena freshly showered and clothed heads on to join Nathan for breakfast. She smells of wind mint and lavender from the smelly pink and purple bottles of gloopy stuff labelled shower gel, shampoo and conditioner inside her designated jungle shower. Nathan makes a nice comment about how wonderful she smells and also looks taking in her chosen outfit for the day. An open coffee coloured shirt, with a turquoise coloured tight-fitting t-shirt beneath it. On the bottom Olena is wearing tight fitting black shorts. Nathan would have insisted they skip breakfast and head back to bed but his duty to his friends left inside of the freaky maze keeps his mind focused on the job at hand.

The pair of them enjoy tucking into platefuls of fried bacon, scrambled eggs and sausages. Olena can't get over how delicious everything tastes. Nathan has even made toast campfire style which he always thought tasted much nicer then bog standard slices put in an electric toaster. There was an almost earthy flavour to the bread which brought nostalgic waves from his outdoor training days in the military.

"That was *so* yummy, thank you." Olena says, her cheeks rosy pink from the rush of calorific nutrients.

"I'm glad you liked it. I've put together a pack with

basic essentials. Water, snacks, emergency first-aid kit——

"Lucky me for having a solider boyfriend then——huh?" Olena cuts in as Nathan's serious face falters and he can't help but grin broadly at her.

*She called me her boyfriend! I wonder if she knows the actual semblance of the word. Ah hell——what does it matter anyway. It's all just a fantasy for now, soon we'll forget either one existed and——who knows who we'll end up with then. But damn, if I were not to lose my memories of her——I know in a heartbeat I'd choose to become a Vampire just so I could be with her.*

"No, Olena, it is me who is the lucky one." Nathan answers before gently kissing her on the mouth licking at a splodge of egg on the edge of her plump red lips.

Olena says nothing in response to the kiss because the way her body feels right now——is saying enough.

## Chapter 43

Frank enters Olena's enchanted forest bedroom. Stealthily he creeps up on both the young adults as they appear to be in a lip locked dance.

Quietly he sneaks close to Nathan just as Olena clocks him sending her eyes wide. Frank says a quiet *boo!* Which all but has Nathan sprawling backwards, away from Olena with sudden fright. Then annoyance clouds his face before embarrassment sets in.

"If you two have finished fooling around——Monnie said he can take us back to the spot we exited out from the maze. I'll leave you to clean up your *mess*. Meet you both in the lobby——pronto! and before you ask I already ate——with Mortina." Frank grumbles turning to stalk away——secretly smiling, that he can still put the wind up his guys when needed.

"Woah he seems *pissed*." Olena says stating the obvious.

"You think? Well cat's out of the bag now——about

us, being an *item*. Guess we'd best hurry and bite the proverbial bullet——oh don't forget Chance, we'll need him to navigate." Nathan says busying his hands getting to work on re-checking his pack for essential items as Olena hurries off to collect Chance.

———

Olena and Nathan walk rapidly across the lobby to meet Frank who's sitting near to the reception desk.

"Boss, I'm sorry for you finding out this way, about me and Olena...it's just——

"Don't sweat it. I'm not going to bust your balls over this——but please remember to wear your seatbelt I've seen Twilight and the last thing any of us needs is to have little Vampires running about. Also keep things discreet ——*no* PDAs. I can't be having the rest of the men distracted when we've relocated and rescued them. It's none of my business or theirs, and so long as it doesn't affect your focus in regards to this mission then you have my blessing to do *whatever*. Now can we please just get on with the day seeing as you've both finished massaging one another's lips." Frank says, standing while catching eye contact with Monnie, signalling to him that they are ready to leave.

———

They re-enter the maze through the same hidden stone doorway they had exited out from. Chance has requested that Frank be in charge of him from now on——not trusting that he won't be forgotten again by Olena. The request stings but only momentarily as this means she can hold hands with Nathan as they follow along behind Frank who's now listening intently to all of the instructions given by Chance. Gone were all of Olena's worries and concerns about Chance potentially double crossing them as more sensations and feeling of love for Nathan poured forth like an uncontrollable torrent.

"Olena, my hand's getting a little achy do you mind if we let go for a while?" Nathan asks beginning to see the tell-tale signs from Olena of wanting to literally begin clinging to him.

Hearing Nathan ask this makes Olena's heart sink a bit as she second guesses perhaps his own feelings for her.

*Aching hand? Isn't he supposed to be some rough and tough soldier——yet holding my hand causes it to...ache? Oh for fracking Hades' sake——get a grip. What is the matter with me?! Why can't I focus. This can't be happening! I'm going all gooey over a man——A HUMAN MAN!* Olena all but yells to herself of the sheer absurdity of the entire situation with Nathan and the anger she feels at herself is enough to break the heady spell of lust——putting her well and truly back in the game.

"I'll take Chance now if you don't mind Frank. I still don't one hundred percent trust him——how we met is...part of my reasoning." Olena says having marched ahead of Nathan whose skin now feels all itchy to think there's going to be an atmosphere of weirdness between him and Olena.

"Jule, go right ahead. We'll discuss *later* on how it is you don't entirely trust our golden headed friend here." Frank says while glancing back to Nathan giving him a very old-fashioned look.

Taking over as lead from Frank, Olena demands that Chance carry on giving her the directions. He makes an unwise quip about something being the matter with *lover boy,* leading Olena to give him a threat that one more word like that and she would indeed leave him on the floor of the maze where she stood——reasoning that she now had two expert navigators with her. Chance didn't know anything of soldiers from Earth so couldn't bank on Frank and Nathan not doing a good enough job to see Olena through the rest of the maze. Swearing under his breath he apologises and agrees to never bring up the subject of her love life again to which she corrects him it's a *non-existent* love life.

Nathan tries to make small talk with Olena feeling bad about the hand holding comment earlier, realising how pathetic it sounded——but she simply shoots him down, asking for silence to better concentrate. Frank having grown fond of Olena much as a father might a daughter, looks murderously at Nathan telling him quietly that they shall be having words later if they succeed with today's mission.

The trio walk on in relative quiet for what feels like a couple of hours. Perspiration is starting to soak through Olena's clothing while sweat soaks both Frank and Nathan's.

"Get ready——we're close to your next challenge." Chance says abruptly.

Olena, Nathan and Frank take this to mean they can all take five minutes to get water and sustenance on board.

"Sorry it's not much. I packed a piece of fruit for us all, some water, bread and a few biscuits." Nathan says handing Olena her portions.

"It's plenty——thanks." She says biting into her warm green apple.

*follow the sound of my voice.*

"Woah! Did anyone else hear that?" Nathan says jolting suddenly which makes the hair on Frank's neck and arms stand on end as both he and Olena now share wary glances.

"No——I didn't hear anything...did you Frank?" Olena asks closing the lid of the small container carrying remains of her food to hand them back to Nathan.

"Sorry mate didn't hear a thing then again——don't have my hearing aids in." Franks admits taking a swig of water.

"If you all look to the walls I think you'll find a hint as to what possibly spoke those words." Chance says—— a silent admission to having heard what Nathan had.

"Parry Trotter eat ya heart out." Nathan exclaims ——seeing the snake pictures running along the walls combined with hieroglyphs looking to tell a story. One where if the pictures were anything to go by showcased humans getting devoured and mutilated by a massive snake-like creature.

"Oh no." Olena says dropping her plastic water bottle in shock.

"Oh no what?" Frank and Nathan echo back in unison.

"Out next challenger is——Ouroboros" Olena's voice comes out in barely a whisper as fear sends her heart rate sky-rocketing. "Nathan, I need you to hold me. Quickly——put your arms around me." Olena orders him as Frank watches on most confused.

"Olena, now isn't the time to cud——

"Shhhh, just like that. *Mmmm* that's nice." She says pulling Nathan's arms tight around her until she can zone in on his heart beat. Breathing rhythmically to the sound finds her own reducing in speed allowing her focus to come back online.

"Ok, I'm good. Ok Ouroboros is the snake that eats its tail——only *this* one; the *real* one...well they eat... people."

There was no way to sugar coat what they would be up against. Although the way Olena described how Ouroboros was a snake she hoped didn't paint a picture that it was just a normal sized Earth snake. This thing was gigantic and could and had swallowed entire village loads of people in its past.

"So...just out of interest——what exactly did this voice say?" Frank asks trying to keep objectivity up among them.

"It instructed us to follow the sound of its voice." Chance says rolling his eyes and yawning.

"Oh...I see. Well then, I guess we're...*following* the

sound of its voice" Frank says hearing no argument from Olena or Nathan.

As they gingerly navigate the twists and turns of the maze——with snakes being depicted everywhere Olena stops suddenly having successfully translated a portion of the hieroglyphs on one of the walls. This roots her to the spot as a glazed expression wanders across her face and the blood in her veins turns to ice.

"Olena whatever is the matter?" Nathan asks noticing she is now no longer leading but rather lagging behind him and Frank.

"This portion of the wall translates as this." Olena says beginning to read aloud the inscription.

***Ouroboros resides here. Snake, killer, devourer of human flesh. Ruler of all things wicked and insane - Soul eater.***

***Be warned this chamber brings all who enter certain death.***

Running her hand over the cool stone snakes and hieroglyphics, Olena's spooked reverie is broken as Nathan weaves a strong masculine hand through hers, giving a gentle squeeze. As they all begin to digest the information held in Olena's translation - the creepy slithering voice returns only this time——a lot louder.

*"Join me for a little supper, won't you? I insist. The pitter patter of your feet tell I am to be a fat and happy snake before the night is out!"*

Chance urges the group forwards at a speedier pace through the increasingly narrowing pathways, checking his memory bank at every turn to ensure there aren't any traps.

"STOP!" Chance calls out as suddenly his mind doesn't just go blank——it goes completely dark. "I believe we have entered the arena of your next challenge." Chance goes on by way of explanation. The three of them turn looking around at the walls as all of a sudden, the portion of maze they stand in is plunged into darkness, and when the braziers come back to being lit——Olena, Nathan and Frank find they are now alone, having been separated, but are now also it appears... *invisible*.

## Chapter 44

'*Jamie! Pssst! Where are you?*' Donnie says hoping he'd be close enough to his friend not to lose him *again*. The pair had briefly found one another in the dark but Ouroboros wasn't about to let them stay that way and seemed to have a good knack of keeping the men apart.

Both Donnie and Jamie are presently navigating narrow tunnels in pitch darkness. The ground at times feels slimy and at others feels dry and littered by what each man from touch alone, knows to be bones from past living things that clearly haven't made it out alive. The only light administered appears to be that of an electrical blue glow from the huge snake beast——much like electric eels have an electric field around them.

The only saving grace for Jamie and Donnie is that the snake beast does appear to require rest from time to time giving them also time to rest between constantly crawling about to avoiding the glowing blue light when it appears. When they had first found each other, it was only because Donnie had literally bumped into the back of Jamie's hunched over body. The men made too much noise with relief which brought the snake beast hurtling toward them with the speed of a freight train. Since then both friends had failed to find one another again as they continually tried to navigate to a place of safety until the next time the snake came close again. Each fearing the worst had happened to the other.

Olena, Frank and Nathan are all standing in individual circular stone rooms. Each room is lit with braziers and has smooth curved walls save for a final entry exit way point that will lead them on into the maze of tunnels. Egyptian paintings of pharaohs and snakes with warnings of Ouroboros and how he hunts to kill an devour his prey covers each of the room's walls. It didn't take long for any of them to realise they were invisible as none of them could see their own usually visible limbs.

Trying to ignore her rising panic Olena takes a moment grasping her satchel which is still around her shoulders. Inside she is relieved to find that Chance is at least still with her. Lifting him out of the satchel and before he can yelp at seemingly being made to levitate by some invisible force——Olena quietens him by stating it is her holding him.

"Any ideas about what I'm supposed to do here?" Olena asks her golden faced friend who looks just as puzzled as she does.

"Afraid not. Where are the others?" Chance says having noticed Olena is by herself.

"I haven't a clue. One second we were altogether the next everything went black and then I was here——alone and...*invisible.*"

"Well not quite alone——at least we are together and my mother always did say two heads are better than one." Chance says in such a calm tone it helps Olena to relax a bit more while she thinks about what they should do.

"Ok so——clearly I am meant to go inside...*there.*" Olena says invisibly pointing to the only low down curved archway that has no light coming through it.

"It would appear so. I suggest keeping me hidden ——The Magi could be watching." Chance reminds Olena as she rapidly places him back inside her satchel.

Steeling herself to crouch low enough so she can enter the small exit way, she takes a moment to still her racing heart and ringing inside her ears——Olena then crawls forwards. Once her entire body is through a whooshing sound can be heard behind her as the only seeming way out is closed off. Claustrophobia claws at her insides as panic races through her veins.

"I can't breathe! I——Can't——

"YES! you *can.*" Chance says almost barking out the words hoping it will shock Olena into getting a hold of herself.

It appears to work as he then gives her clear instructions to take carefully placed movements forward. The floor beneath Olena's hands and knees trembles and she figures that must be Ouroboros. Her mouth runs dry wondering how the others are getting along and how in

Hades they are going find each other in the darkness of these tunnels.

After a while Olena finds the darkness to be quite comforting. Imagining she's crawling along the floor of an expansive tunnel——laying low to stay out of sound of the huge snake. A sound off to her right makes her stop dead as she painfully listened in pulling on all her ability of heightened sense of sound to see if she can get even a hint of where anyone might be.

*"Olena! Oleeeena!" Ole*——

Nathan's whispered yell comes as a huge surprise and relief to her. About to open her own mouth to sort of shout in whispered tones back——Olena rapidly shut it to see a blue glow starting to head straight for her and within that blue light is the large terrifying face of the snake Ouroboros.

Quickly she scrambles about trying to find some way of going left or right as the snake fast descends upon her its forked tongue getting ever closer.

*"Mmmmm a female! I can taste your sweetness on my tongue."* The snake says in terrifying slithery tones.

"Hey! Asshole! Bet you can't find me!" Nathan shouts momentarily startling the snake into stopping his pursuit of Olena to turn and zip down a side passage way.

As Ouroboros slithers away his blue light illuminates a nearby left tunnel——which Olena wastes no time utilising as it takes her in the opposite direction from the huge scaled beast. Crawling at speed Olena also yelps when she bumps into something both hard and soft at the same time.

*"Is that you Olena?"* Nathan whispers having smelled the scent of lavender from her earlier shower.

*"Oh Hades! Nathan!"* Olena says in hushed tones as she fumbles to feel for Nathan's torso where she hugs him tightly. *"I thought you were somewhere else as the snake moved away."* Olena asked puzzled as to how Nathan is here instead.

"I found some tiny hole things on the inner walls. It appears to send your voice somewhere else——I imagine like some weird old telephone system. Here listen." Nathan says as he whistles through a hole Olena can't actually see and it sends the sound somewhere that sounds quite far away.

"Won't Ouroboros know about that trick? When they realise you're not where they heard you——won't they come back here?" Olena says anxiously.

"Good point. Best we get moving. Boy I sure do remember playing murder in the dark and sardines but ——this is like a weird mash of both games put together." At the lengthy silence that followed Nathan's statement he goes on to explain "Childhood games I used to play with Felicity and friends at home for birthday parties etc."

"You used to *murder* in a game?" Olena asks incredulous to the idea of human children being so barbaric and if it were the case then how had she never been taught about it.

"No not for real. We'd all have to hide in the dark

——one person would be challenged to seek us out and when they did we *pretend* played that the person was *murdered* with blood curdling scream."

"Oh...and *sardines?*"

"I'll explain more when we hopefully get out of here but first——let's find the others and plan how to take down this electrified snake." As Nathan says this he hears no argument from Olena. "You still there?" He asks while indeed still feeling one of her hands on the back of his calf muscles.

"Yeah, still here." She says as they continually creep forward together.

"Excuse me——would now be a good time to tell you both that I appear to have the gift of——*night vision.*" Chance says only just thinking of how this might help them.

"Do you know something, I think I'm really starting to like you Chance." Nathan says as he hears Olena fiddle with her satchel which is swiftly followed by a muttered curse as Chance slips from her hands——clanging loudly to the floor.

"*Ohhhhh farts.*" Nathan exclaims as the ground immediately starts to tremble as the pair pick up the pace.

Following Chance's directions to the letter eventually the couple manage to duck into a side tunnel as Ouroboros rushes past having become so hungry and angry, not locating a single tasty morsel yet that he loses the scent——angering him further.

"Hang on a second. Yes! Yes!" Chance says excitedly. "Nathan if you reach forward you should feel the remains of someone. I can see they wore some sort of jacket and inside that jacket I can tell you is a way to make fire. I'm sure you'll know the item when you find it." Chance says not having the words to describe the item he can see gleaming through holes in the jacket pocket.

"Oh——hey! He's right! It's a lighter." Nathan exclaims excitedly but quietly to Olena.

Once he has the lighter in his possession Nathan flips open the top of the metal lid and to his utter amazement and a great bit of luck it lights immediately. Using the light from the flame to look closer at the tunnel they're in, Nathan sees a tiny groove with some sort of black liquid running through the tiny smooth crevice that appears to run the length of the tunnel they're presently inside of. As he takes the lighter for closer inspection he jumps as much as the cramped tunnel will allow——as the flame from the lighter ignites the black liquid sending a surge of fire forward that carries on illuminating not just their own tunnel but beyond. The effect reminds him of a film he watched as a child called *Tron* where in place of thin flames there were these beams of almost laser style lights that outlined walls and floors of this gaming matrix some guy got sucked into. The reason the flame wouldn't burn him or Olena was that it was inside of a deep but tiny groove and so the smooth stone edges prevented any clothing or skin from making contact.

"Well hush my mouth and slap my thigh——you really *are* a good luck charm Chance." Nathan says unable to see the look of utter delight and relief to cross

Olena's face at finally having sight of where they're going. Being *night blind* seeing as she no longer had her own night vision capabilities hurt more then she'd care to admit it did.

"I wonder how it is we managed to find each other so fast? Perhaps we all entered the maze close to one another? If that's the case then Frank may be close by too." Olena says optimistically. Impressing Nathan to think she might not be too far off base.

"Smart thinking." Nathan says reaching a hand behind him an indication for Olena to take it so he might give her a reassuring squeeze.

---

Olena and Nathan locate Frank as Olena suspected——quite quickly. Quietly at varying intervals they called out his name until he responded. When Ouroboros felt through vibrations he was getting closer, Nathan and Olena utilised the small holes in the walls of the tunnel to disorientate and confuses the giant snake.

"You kids ok? Damn am I glad to see both of you. I'm ashamed to admit that...this has been by far the *most* terrifying experience of my life. Give me hijackers, kidnappers, terrorists and flying bullets any day over this insane situation." Frank admits glad he can't see Nathan's expression as the three of them creep along together down twisting tunnels in the hope eventually they may find a way out or at least become reunited with Donnie and Jamie.

"Shhh! I think I can hear...yep, that's definitely Jamie and from the sounds of things he may have found Donnie." Nathan says enthusiastically——making sure they all remain quiet enough to try and locate which direction the echoes are travelling from.

*"Mmmmm you all smell...divine. I can tell you are in groups so eating you will give me double the pleasure—— I'm only sad my hunt for you all will be over soon——this has been the most entertainment I've had in a long time! Oh well no bother."* Ouroboros states making Olena's flesh literally crawl with the idea of becoming food to such an abhorrent creature, who's clearly at the bottom of the food chain considering even Anubis wouldn't take him into the underworld.

"Hey, I just had another thought. Ouroboros clearly rests from time to time right going by his movement patterns? Well what if when he goes rest it's at the centre of this maze where possibly there's a...way out?" Olena says quite impressed at her dad's problem-solving training shining through her here.

"You sure are one smart cookie Olena." Frank says in an almost proud fatherly tone.

"Thanks Frank. I suggest we start stalking our friend Ouroboros here to see if he will lead us to wherever it is he goes to rest. With any luck it may well lead us to an exit——if we find Donnie and Jamie en-route then I'd say that's a bonus."

"Olena——in case I forget to tell you later...you have all the makings of a great leader." As Nathan says this he is unaware of the rise in colour his statement has brought to Olena's lips and cheeks.

A sniffling sound can be heard as Olena cries silently overwhelmed at knowing how proud her parents——especially her father would be to have heard those words in evaluation of her character.

"Thanks——you've no idea how much that means to hear those words. My dad being a Vampire detective and all." She says which strikes up a continuing mushy conversation seeming to turn into an almost competition of who can outdo the other on complimenting one another. The sound makes Frank want to be sick.

"Will you two cut it out. I can't listen for our friends or that sodding snake with your waffling whispered notes firing off every five seconds!" Frank says his ire all too clear in the tone of his voice. No apology is spoken and thankfully Frank is glad to hear flirtatious babbling replaced with glorious silence.

"I can hear them again——they sound *closer*." Nathan says before calling out in fast whisper. "Hey guys! Where are you?"

"Nate! Is that you?" Donnie calls out aloud forgetting from the shock of hearing Nathan's voice of where they are.

"*Idiot*." Frank exclaims angrily under his breath as the ground vibrates violently this time, with Ouroboros having pinpointed exactly where Donnie's voice came from and so wastes no time in heading straight toward that direction.

"Quickly start yelling through the holes in the wall

——hopefully if we make enough sound we might just save Donnie." Nathan says as the three of them begin in vain to yell, squawk and make all manner of noises——creating a cacophony of eerie sound waves. Ouroboros might be blind but his hearing was like that of a bat. No matter how much Donnie and Jamie's friends might try to distract him—— Ouroboros now knew *exactly* where his prey was sitting.

---

Donnie having relocated Jamie for a second time the pair decided to make a rope from the dusty clothing of a dead humanoid's skeleton. Donnie while extracting the garments to make strips of fabric before binding his wrist to Jamie's——was thankful he couldn't really see the bones of who the clothing had belonged to but he was pretty sure he felt bony protuberances that felt very much like *horns*.

"I'm so sorry man, I didn't think. I was just so *happy* to hear Nate's voice that I...forgot myself before calling out." Donnie says as sweat pours down both their faces.

"Apologise later——first we got to get ourselves out of here." Jamie pants out——urging his friend onward as they try their best to creep at speed away from their present location while the giant man-eating snake can be heard and felt through vibrations inching ever closer.

---

"Please...I need a moment...to catch...my *breath*——sorry...I'm slowing you both down. Maybe you should find your friends without me." Olena says coughing through dust being kicked up into her face by Nathan's feet while panting hard——as bile rises up uncontrollably, threatening to make her vomit from the sheer volume of exertion she's putting onto her human body.

"It's ok——we can rest." Nathan says as he hears just up ahead of him Frank mutter silent curses under his breath.

"Are you sure? I feel bad...what if Donnie and perhaps Jamie if they're together get eaten because I'm too slow?" Olena asks terrified she could be the direct cause of them missing a chance to save Donnie and Jamie's lives.

"If I know my friends, then I can guarantee that if they're together then——they'll be just fine." Nathan says holding back the admission that he too was feeling tired enough to warrant a rest.

Olena reaches inside her satchel to take Chance out but it is here she suddenly remembered something——the pouch Anubis had given her.

"Erm, guys——I'm not one hundred percent sure but...I kinda of got this *gift* from Anubis after the last challenge and well——

Olena gets momentarily cut off from what she is saying when Frank makes a weird guttural sound like something stuck in his throat at the mere mention of the name Anubis. The shock of having been in the presence of a real God appearing to still overwhelm his sensitive fragile psyche——no matter how much war time he'd seen.

"What is it? Can it help us defeat the snake?" Nathan asks shocked that Olena would only mention this now.

"I——well, don't know *exactly*. Anubis told me I was *not* to open the pouch until the time was right. He assured me I would know when that time was——only... now I'm thinking is it the right time?"

"Yes!" Frank and Nathan both say in unison.

*When the time is right you will know what to do.* Anubis' words run through Olena's mind as she slowly takes hold of the pouch, fumbling about in the semi-darkness to undo the tightly bound threads. Once the knots are clear she closes her eyes taking in a deep breath before——opening it.

## Chapter 45

A bright purple light pops out of the pouch covering the three friends in spooky violet hues. The tunnel they were previously all squashed inside of suddenly grows in size——allowing them chance to finally stand up and stretch their legs and bodies.

*Finally, some fairy godmother magic. Mmmm feels good to be able to stretch out again.* Olena thinks suspecting there must be some fairy godmother involvement as they were Master manipulators of many things. Such as the sheer feats of magic told by the Cinderella and Sleeping Beauty stories.

"So...*what* is it?" Frank asks directing his question at Olena as he contemplates the purple light being.

Dusting his khaki combat trousers off Frank isn't fast enough to stop Nathan reaching a finger toward the glowing orb——gently touching it.

"Hehehe! That tickles." The light says doing a little dance around him. Relief floods through Frank quickly replaced with ire at how stupid Nathan's actions were. Touching *anything* in this whacky world could be extremely dangerous and so Frank made a mental note to have *words* with Nathan later——if there was a later. That thought threatened to depress Frank so he pushes it away.

"Of course, it'd be a *talking* glowing purple ball of light." Nathan says having learned, it's easier just to accept this world of crazy mayhem that defies the laws of *all* human physics, then to question it.

"Hey! I can *SEE* you as in really SEE you!" Olena says excitedly. "Wow!...*Hands.*" Her voice carries with it a dreamy tinge as she wiggles her fingers before patting at her well-toned stomach and chest.

"What are you again?" Frank asks, his mind feeling as if it is on the verge of melting out through his ear holes ——unsure of how much more strangeness he can witness or accept.

"I am a Will-o-wisp!" The bouncy floating ball of purple energy says proudly, in teeny-tiny high pitch voice.

"Of course! I learned of you all in my ethereal classes. You're tasked spiritual guides and advisors to Anubis and his most senior staff." Olena says as the Will-o-wisp giggles with delight at having a sudden friend. "These little guys are made from babies of any and all species who are either never born alive or who sadly...*don't* make it very long in the land of the living. Younglings——

that's children to you and Frank, who pass away from violent crime, illness or disease, accident etcetera they too become these little blessed light beings. Those who have a particularly violent passing have their memories wiped ——so you'd be hard pressed to ever find a sad or unhappy Will-o-wisp." Olena explains allowing the happy ball of purple light to rest on her shoulder. She deliberately withholds that fact it is indeed fairy godmothers who make child spirits into Will-o-wisps as she figures looking at Frank's face it might just be enough to tip him mentally over the edge.

"Anubis gave me strict instructions that I am to help you and your friends defeat Ouroboros. He is a very *mean* beast and Anubis dislikes him intensely. Apparently, the higher Gods and Goddesses wanted to banish Ouroboros to the underworld eons ago——but Anubis wouldn't take him and so The Magi and *Powers That Be* agreed to have Ouroboros trapped here in this maze for all eternity." The Will-o-wisp explains.

"The Powers That Be seem to like handing out a lot of these...*eternal* punishments." Nathan says as a scream jolts them all back to the urgency of the situation.

"Right——your friends. Be right back, stay here." The Will-o-wisp says before zipping away, out of sight.

"Ah, it feels good to see me again, and you——and you." Nathan says running his hands over his upper body to then stretch tall popping his shoulders and back. Having relieved the tension Nathan then further celebrates by pulling Olena close for a kiss.

"Gross guys——come on no PDAs! I'm *serious*!"

Frank barks as Olena and Nathan ignore him, now peering into one another's eyes. Nathan gently pushing back loose tendrils of Olena's hair that have escaped from her hair tie.

"God——Gods——ah hell! ——Anubis himself ——*give me strength*!" Frank exclaims as he swears to hearing an eerie almost inaudible voice whispering *You have my sympathies...*

———

Ouroboros can taste that his prey is within swallowing distance as he lines up Donnie and Jamie——their scent on his tongue strong enough to give him stomach cramps in anticipation of devouring the two tasty morsels in front of him. Opening his gaping snake mouth wide as venom and saliva drip from his enormous fangs—— Donnie lets out an almighty scream, as he and Jamie bunch themselves against a dead end too exhausted and frozen with fear to attempt finding yet another opening to a maze tunnel that appears to go nowhere.

"I love you man." Jamie says through streaming tears.

"I love you too brother." Donnie exclaims as the two comrades hold one another tightly as they lie side by side in each other's arms.

The Will-o-wisp arrives before Ouroboros gets to enjoy his meal. Fortunately for the youthful spirit, time can be slowed down or sped up——as time usually has no meaning to the dead. Spirits are not bound by the same laws of space time.

"Zip-zoom-zip-zip-zoom." The Will-o-wisp hums as they first bring Donnie and Jamie into full view and then get to work enlarging this portion of the maze before making a wall appear between Ouroboros and the men they are protecting. As the maze is made up of illusionary magic this enables the Will-o-wisp to morph it anyway they deem fit. Similar to that human movie *Inception*——where the dreamer is in charge of the construction or deconstruction of their surroundings.

"Sorry fangs——these two are *not* for you." The spirit says in a sing song voice as they place themselves back into a speed of time that matches human perception.

***THUD*!**

"What was that?! Hey wait——We're *ALIVE*! No snake and——and I can see you! Can you see me?! Jamie exclaims as the loud thud had made both open their eyes. Jamie and Donnie then realise they have a lot more room to manoeuvre around in while still gripping onto one another.

"Woah! What is *that* thing." Donnie says as the men pull apart starting to gain their bearings in the new larger surroundings——and the fact both are now visible to one another with no sight of the man-eating snake beast.

"I'm a Will-o-wisp. Follow me I will guide you back to your friends. No time to explain——I must leave and return to the underworld soon." The little glowing ball of purple light explains not waiting as it bobs away at a pace Donnie and Jamie can keep up with.

On very shaky legs both Donnie and Jamie struggle to keep up with the friendly light.

"Dude! What is that smell did you——oh." Donnie's voice trails off as he realises Jamie has indeed had a little *accident* as in——relieving his bladder.

"Hang on a second dude." Donnie says noticing a slumped skeletal figure leaning against a wall of the tunnel.

"Mate I am *not* wearing some dead dude's pants!" Jamie exclaims aghast.

"That's cool, wear mine and I'll wear this...funky guys baggy pirate styled trousers." Donnie says already stripping.

"Yo! Purple light thing——wait up!" Jamie calls down to the dwindling light as the Will-o-wisp almost vanishes from view.

"Hurry! I don't have a lot of time left outside the underworld——I'm needed elsewhere." The Will-o-wisp says urging the men to hurry.

———

As Donnie and Jamie stagger into view, Frank and Nathan rush over to give their long-time comrades hugs as they reunite. Olena hangs back for a respectable beat, not knowing them that well.

"I must go——Anubis is calling me back. The Magi have been causing problems so he requires me to relay my findings here to the Powers That Be——proving you are at an unfair disadvantage. Sorry I cannot stay——goodbye——

"Wait! how do we defeat Ouroboros?" Olena asks fast hoping to get at least a hint before the Will-o-wisp leaves them.

"I am not allowed to interfere in *that* part of this challenge, sorry." With that the Will-o-wisp blinks out of sight.

"Olena come on——group hug." Jamie exclaims holding out an open arm inviting her to join them, she notes here how his usually well uniformed mop of fiery red hair——sits dull and full of dust, dirt and grime atop his head.

"Donnie! What happened to your *trousers?*" Frank asks in a stern tone having noticed how unkempt and dishevelled his soldier looks wearing anything but military combat suitable attire.

"It's a long story. Boy am I glad to see all of you. Wonder how Pete's getting on seeing as he's the last one we need to locate." Jamie says wanting to fast get off the subject of pants and his little *accident.*

"Where's the ball of light gone?" Nathan asks realising there are now no purple hues surrounding them.

"The Will-o-wisp...has done all they can. Anubis required them to return to the underworld. There was nothing they could tell me about how to defeat Ouroboros——we're on our own with this part of the challenge." Olena says sounding deflated.

"Excuse me everyone——I believe I may be able to help you with Ouroboros." Chance says through Olena's satchel. "It appears I've just had my memory bank updated——to see *everything* as in where the centre of this maze and its exit is." As Chance says updating the group with a bit of good news.

*Just another little push before I regain my full power and strength.* Chance thinks keenly to himself almost chuckling with joy at the gift bestowed upon him.

Olena considers this information dubiously and wonders if it is true about Chance only just receiving these memory updates regarding maze passageways. The Magi as far as any of them know have no knowledge of Chance and how he's helped to aid her in her quest alongside Frank and Nathan. Having no choice but to trust Chance for now——Olena makes a mental note to pump him for more information——much the same way her father used to do when he was an acting Vampire detective interrogating suspects. For her to be able to have that opportunity however meant they would first need to take down Ouroboros.

"Lead on little lion friend." Jamie says in a tone that instantly grates on Olena's nerves. How he can be so trusting of Chance she wonders isn't why humans are considered mainly food to her kind——when not being utilised as servants or sex slaves.

"You're all close to the maze's centre but Ouroboros is mad with rage and starvation. Should he catch a whiff of any of you——like lightning he'll strike." Chance's words put them all on edge as they pin their ears back taking note of exactly what directions Chance is giving. The previous humour in Jamie's tone evaporates as he too becomes silent and focused. The transformation in Jamie's no-nonsense serious attitude makes Olena regard her newly acquainted red headed friend with fresh eyes.

*Of course——how silly of me to forget that at all of your cores you are...trained killers.* She thinks which brings a dangerous smile to her rosy red lips that normally cover her own main killing tools——her *fangs.*

## Chapter 46

Ouroboros can be heard swearing in magical mother tongues——shrieking at the sheer frustration of not having yet eaten the living beings scurrying about inside of *his* lair. The enlarged tunnels have also disorientated him——making navigating his home turf much more difficult. The centre of his maze however through scent alone——insures he will always find his way back to it.

Small sounds cause Ouroboros to stop slithering momentarily as he uses his sharp hearing skills to listen in. There are *echoes* close-by and he realises one thing——his prey is *close*.

———

The group locate Ouroboros' central lair within minutes. It appeared Chance was still very much on their side as he seemingly helped navigate the way with his newer updated memories of the maze with ease.

The central part of Ouroboros' maze was stunning. It was brightly lit with a tall, domed-glass ceiling made from what looked to be rock crystal. Glancing up, nighttime stars twinkle down at the group. The walls are immaculate with clear unblemished painted Egyptian images and hieroglyphics telling stories of sacrifices, bloodletting and the feeding of one——once free Ouroboros. He accepted regular sacrifices from villagers as part of an agreement; so long as he was kept well fed, he wouldn't destroy and devour everything they had built and relied upon to thrive.

Braziers light the room giving welcoming balanced relaxed candlelit vibes. Odd Olena contemplated, considering this is the ultimate death trap for any who enter while also pondering on why Ouroboros might need so much light given he was blind.

"From what I can decipher, the pictures on the wall tell of a scroll contained somewhere inside this room. We only need speak the words to save ourselves. The maze is ——circular." Olena says carrying on her translation "and use of the correct enchantment *will* set Ouroboros to return to their static state——circling the inside of the tunnels swallowing its own tail——for eternity. Once Ouroboros is reset to their docile state——we can get out of here as an exit doorway should reveal itself." Olena explains causing Frank, Nathan, Jamie and Donnie to begin dashing about in their pursuit of the scroll.

After much searching around behind pillars and looking for any kind of secret hidden wall vault——coming up empty handed they all sit together feeling beyond tired and defeated.

"Well——it was worth a try. Maybe someone else already located and used the scroll, ergo losing it. Any other ideas?" Nathan asks catching his breath as sweat pours off his reddened face. Looking across to Olena sitting on his right he can see she to is just as exhausted and so reaches a hand across to give hers a gentle squeeze. She smiles back at him in appreciation of the reassuring gesture.

"Afraid not——I'd suggest killing the beast but we have no means of doing so." Olena replies watching Jamie stand to have another vain search of Ouroboros' lair.

"For pity's sake man——will you sit down! We can just as effectively brainstorm from a seated position." Frank shouts out at Jamie who appears to have a sudden flourishing of the jitters.

**Crash!**

Jamie collapses sideways as exhaustion and dehydration take over.

"Donnie——

"On it boss." Donnie says jumping up with Nathan to head on over to the now unconscious Jamie who's managed to spectacularly cut his head on one of the braziers knocking the mini Inferno to the stone floor, where the coals scattered everywhere.

As the men sort Jamie out, Olena looks across to the coal littered floor, startling to glance the fast appearance of Anubis' face——which flashes instantaneously in and out of visibility within seconds. As he vanishes from sight, a small scroll appears looking to catch alight on the coals, prompting Olena to move at speed toward it.

"What happened?" Frank asks heading to where Olena now crouches down. Turning to give him a look of glee. Frank realises why when she presents him with the scroll in question.

"Miss Lupescu, you——young lady are most definitely a good luck charm." Frank says relief replacing his tense and tired expression.

"Gentlemen, I believe we have found our scroll." Olena says excitedly turning to address the rest of their group.

As everyone comes close to get a better inspection of the scroll, Olena glances up but the scream never leaves her throat before Ouroboros——who has slithered in, silently and with lightning reflex——swallows Olena whole.

Nathan stands paralysed a moment before he hears Frank clear order ring through for him to grab the scroll Olena has dropped and get away from the snake.

"HEY! SNAKE-EYES! *Oooops*! wrong choice of words." Jamie says taunting Ouroboros who grinning from the first meal takes the bait and launches his enormous triangular face in Jamie's general direction striking out for him.

Diving behind a pillar decorated in hieroglyphics. Ouroboros misses Jamie by a hair's breadth as he instead slams headfirst into the pillar becoming visibly dazed. As the tunnels had grown in size so too had his lair making spatial awareness almost impossible now.

Shrieking wildly in frustration, Ouroboros deliberately hits the pillar for a second time——smashing through it which sends huge boulders flying——one of which almost takes Jamie's head clean off had it not been for Donnie grabbing the front of his shirt pulling him down at the last second.

"Dude! I hate to hurry you in reading the incantation but I don't fancy being pummelled to death by the giant man-eating snake. Could you hurry things along?" Donnie calls out as they all continually duck and dive to avoid being either eaten or knocked out by flying debris as Ouroboros continues his aggressive tirade.

"I can't read any of this! I don't know what to say!" Nathan shouts in panicked response.

Jamie seeing an opening——leaps clear onto the back of Ouroboros, instantly regretting his decision as the snake immediately bucks and rolls. However, Jamie holds on for grim death having slipped the fingers of each hand into the snake's scales. Changing tactic Ouroboros unable to shake Jamie off instead uses his tail to wrap around Jamie's waist pulling him free from his body while proceeding to squeeze.

Jamie can feel consciousness slipping away as his rib cage starts to crack and his insides feel they may burst out of him any second. His friends' yells become fainter as the light in his eyes starts to dim. Death racing up to meet him until in one fell swoop Ouroboros roars——dropping Jamie, before diving head long into a wall of the temple entrance. Whatever happened sent Ouroboros whizzing away back into the maze of tunnels ——out of sight.

"Jamie! Are you ok? Talk to me! Say something!" Nathan exclaims rushing to his friend's side to cradle his head in his lap. Tears falling freely with the grief of already having lost Olena pouring out of him——as he silently pleads with the Gods above for one of his military brothers to pull through.

"Is that you Auntie Em? I had the weirdest dream. And you were in it and you and you." Jamie says quoting Dorothy's response from The Wizard of Oz when she learns it was all just a bad dream.

Nathan grins glad to see his friend appears well enough to at least crack a joke.

"Come on big guy, up ya get." Nathan says helping Jamie to stand.

"Well, I have to say. Out of all the fubar situations we found ourselves in during our time in the military——this one certainly tops the lot." Donnie says bent double ——panting.

"You've no argument from me brother." Nathan says as the pair half walk-half hobble to sit on a stone slab from one of the destroyed pillars.

Frank says nothing just goes to join his comrades as they sit in quiet contemplation regarding their fate.

"What shall we do? Sit and wait for the inevitable or ——do it ourselves?" Jamie says which has Nathan sobering up very quickly at the mere mention of them even contemplating suicide.

"Dude we are not *offing* ourselves. There'd be no honour in that. No——I say down the hatch just like Olena suffered." Donnie says defiantly which is met with grim expressions from the others. As they ponder what sort of an end being eaten alive by this snake may bring them. Would it be fast or slow? Did the snake have stomach acid and if so would it be like lava——fast acting. Or would they all perish slowly and oh so painfully.

"So...anyone care to tell what made the snake disappear so fast?" Jamie asks still flummoxed as to where and why the snake on the verge of devouring the, decided to suddenly piss off back to the tunnels.

"Come to think of it——we don't actually know." Frank says as this anomaly suddenly dawns on the men.

"Perhaps——she gave him what for inside his stomach before...you know." Nathan says bravely, trying to stem the flow of fresh tears as both relief of Jamie being ok and grief of losing Olena hit at the same time ——pushing him to the verge of what he feels could be sheer hysteria.

"I'm sorry about Olena man——that sucks. We all kind of know you held a soft spot for her so..." Jamie's vice is cut off with a yelp as something or someone taps him on the shoulder. Nathan, Frank and Dominic having been looking to the floor in solemn keeping with Nathan's somber mood, all look up——and *smile*.

A panting, soaking wet Olena stands before them. She's covered in vile smelling sticky fluid wearing a wicked triumphant grin.

"Did you miss me?" She asks as Nathan pulls her to him, un-caring whether or not she's filthy and stinks to high heaven——as he embraces her. Kissing though even for him is a step too far as he sees gelatinous snot coloured goopy stuff dabbed around her mouth.

"I'll take that as a yes." Olena says struggling to get the words out as Nathan holds her tight.

"Nate! Will ya let the little lady go. Jeez——she looks like she can barely breathe." Jamie exclaims in his bad American put-on cowboy accent.

"Don't ask how I got out of Ouroboros. Let's just say the inside of the snake is more cavern less digesting stomach. It appears as if Ouroboros is itself a portal which would explain the whole swallowing of its own tail. The beast is basically like a tube of tunnels with a personality. I'm all gloopy because as I passed through I dunno its throat I'm guessing——it's pretty fleshy and gunky."

"Yes, no need to thank me either for helping re-direct you out of that awful monstrosity." Chance says flatly thankful to have at least been shielded from Olena's now destroyed satchel which saved him getting a dousing of stinky gloop.

"Here wear this." Nathan says all but tearing the shirt

from his back leaving him bare chested as he offers it to Olena.

"Thank Hades! Yuck! I'm seriously gross right now —-Thanks." Olena says carefully placing Chance and the scroll into Frank's hands, tossing the remnants of her sodden satchel away.

"Before you put that on, use mine to wipe yourself down." Donnie offers chivalrously so that Olena now has two extremely delectable looking gentlemen standing semi-naked in front of her.

"I believe I'm feeling better already." Olena exclaims winking at Frank who makes an awkward coughing noise.

The scent of Nathan so close to Olena's skin makes her body rush with warmth and *other* sensations she makes a mental note to see to when they return to her yurt bedroom.

"Can you please read the inscription now so we might——get out of here." Jamie exclaims just as the ground begins to start vibrating again indicating their hunter was on his return toward them.

"May I." Olena asks Frank as she holds out a hand for the scroll just as Ouroboros bursts back into his lair once again——sending blocks of stone and dust spewing everywhere——wildly thrashing around blindly, clearly disorientated with the much larger dimensions of his once cosy and comfortable lair.

Starting to read the words aloud as Nathan, Jamie, Donnie and Frank all rally together collectively keeping

Ouroboros occupied. Olena given enough time manages to speak all of the resetting enchantments.

As the last word is spoken there is the sound of a large elastic band snapping making everyone's ears ring, as Ouroboros vanishes from sight. The entire room shifts and shimmers until every speck of sand, dust and stone is back to its original position. A big bell sound tolls which presumably signals the trial to be over. Gentle rumbling occurs again putting everyone on edge until it becomes apparently that the inner walls of the temple are retracting into the ceiling. The entire walls of the maze drop to below knee height showing a clear pathway out. Much the same Nathan muses as one of those mini maze games where you roll the silver ball around until it drops into the exit point.

With the walls gone——everyone can see that the now inanimate Ouroboros, peacefully circles the outside of the maze——seemingly happily swallowing its own tail.

"Guys, I don't know long this *reset* is likely to last. I suggest we hot foot it out of here while we can." Olena suggests as they all promptly head toward the clear glowing exit-portal, just a few strides ahead.

Across the threshold——exhausted, Olena collapses to the ground on all fours. The escape from Ouroboros' inner tunnels and using a magical enchantment as a human had taken a lot of energy from her. This surprised Olena as she was no stranger to doing enchantments having attended a magical school. They never even so much as made her yawn when she had been a Vampire.

The thought of once again how weak she was in this human state threatened to overwhelm and depress her——that is until those wonderful strong arms of Nathan Jones helped lift her up off her feet to carry her.

"*Shhh*, you've done good——Rest now." is all Nathan can be heard saying to Olena before she falls into the blissful peace of unconsciousness.

"Ow!" Olena exclaims as a sharp prick is felt on her upper arm.

"Don't concern yourself——it's only a vaccination. Humankind require special injections to protect themselves from illnesses and diseases that might otherwise kill them. As you've never received a vaccination in your life I have to administer two more. One in your leg and another in the other arm."

"Are there any side effects? Are they permanent?" Any thoughts of lustful pining after Nathan evaporate as Mortina has grabbed Olena's full attention administering the foreign fluids inside of her.

"Perhaps a headache, some mild aches and pains. Honestly they're perfectly safe——so much so that even human *babies* have these vaccines administered." Mortina says assuring Olena all is well.

"Oh...right...well, I guess I'd best stop being a *big baby* then and relax."

"*Exactly*! I'll go let your friends know you're up for having visitors now. Apart from some scrapes and bruises I'm happy to give you a clean bill of health." Mortina states as she jovially heads on out to inform the guys that Olena is fine but will require a few more hours rest before they leave the hotel again.

"Olena——after your friends have been in to see you...I wonder if I might have a quiet word. It's important and what I have to say may give cause for The Magi to suspect you're receiving help——outside the realms of what is possible for *humans* to do." Chance says which immediately sends Olena's heart racing with fear over yet perhaps further punishment by the mystical forces that have caused her so much pain already.

Olena goes to respond but gets cut off as Nathan strides inside the yurt swiftly followed by Donnie, Jamie and Frank.

---

Frank took the liberty of ordering Chinese food for everyone——which they enjoyed inside of Olena's yurt sitting at a small round wooden table, as Olena and Nathan ate from trays on her bed.

"I'm happy for you two——being a *couple* and all." Jamie says finishing the last few mouthfuls of his Thai cuisine.

Nathan just rolls his eyes and sighs at Jamie already beginning with the sarcastic jibes.

"Yeah, yeah keep 'em coming——like I haven't been ribbed for having a *girlfriend* before."

"Ok, time to leave these two——*lovebirds* alone." Frank says making shooing motions with his hands indicating for them all——bar Nathan to vacate the yurt. Nathan looking on at his long-time boss and friend in total disbelief, that he'd fan the flames of such teasing by adding *lovebirds* into the conversation.

"Don't keep her up too late. We all need to be in good condition for tomorrow's jolly old jaunt back into this twilight zone. Wonder how Pete's getting on." Donnie says stretching his arms up to pop his upper back and shoulder joints.

"Good point——hey Chance there's no *chance* you can see Pete anywhere in the maze is there?" Nathan calls across to the less than amused golden lion-head.

"I'm afraid not——it's all rather black and gloomy again." Chance replies in bored tones.

"Worth a try, but you do know where he is right?" Donnie asks before stepping outside of the yurt.

"If you ask a stupid question expect a stupid answer." Chance says beyond exhausted at all of the recent jovial atmospherics going on around him. Donnie says a silent curse under his breath as he leaves.

"Finally! I thought they'd never leave! Please, take all my clothes off and ravage me." Olena says instantly switching on Nathan's primal sexual switch in record speed.

"Stop! Don't you *dare* fornicate before removing me well out of hearing range." Chance exclaims as Nathan gladly picks him up to launch him across the illusionary forest floor paying close attention to where he lands.

"Wait! Oh fuggle-figsticks! He had something *important* to tell me." Olena exclaims mortified at having forgotten Chance's request for a quiet word.

"He can wait. Sex first——conversation later." is all Nathan says before putting all of his focus back onto Olena.

*"Ohhh."* Olena lets out a heady moan as Nathan touches all of her buttons. "Then wait he shall." She exclaims threadily, lying back on top of her bedsheets ——enjoying every single pleasurable sensation and climax Nathan brings to what feels like her very soul.

Fully satiated Olena sends Nathan out to find Chance and bring him back so he can speak to her about his information.

Once Nathan has done this he agrees to leave Olena the rest of the night——ensuring they both get in a good few hours of sleep. If he stayed with her he'd just want to make long languid love to her——urged on with the fact they might die tomorrow and being a very much *seize the day* character, Nathan knows with Olena fast becoming his own personal brand of addiction——that a little bit of space right about now would be a very good thing.

———

Re-entering his and Frank's room, Nathan is unprepared for what he is about to witness.

Frank——pleasuring Mortina atop of both their beds that have been pushed together. Stepping back suddenly with the shock of just such a sight, Nathan bolts silently back out of the room hoping and praying he wasn't seen.

———

"Nathan?! What are you doing back here? I thought we agreed——

"Frank's having sex with Mortina in our room so..."

his voice trails off as the shock still registers clearly across his face.

"Oh...I see, well——can I tell him?" Olena says turning to look at Chance.

"Tell me what?" Nathan asks sitting down fast into a wooden seat at the round table——unable to erase the image of Frank's naked body with his head situated between Mortina's legs——clearly doing something that had her throwing her head back and groaning with desire.

"Chance said the enchantment I spoke aloud to reset Ouroboros——won't work with non-magical individuals. Therefore, because it worked, and I am now human ——The Magi may well suspect that someone or something is helping us."

"Crap. Want me to...assemble the guys?" Nathan asks ——unsure he could bear heading back to his room not knowing if Frank might have finished having fun with Mortina.

"Let's...leave it a couple of hours. I'm exhausted—— we'll figure it out tomorrow."

As Nathan goes to lie next to Olena a thought suddenly hits him.

"Wait——so The Magi must have been banking on us all failing this part of the challenge because even if we found the incantation——it wouldn't have worked? How is that fair?"

"It isn't——I doubt they'll wish us to know of this piece of information. Let's keep our cards close to our chest and see what happens when we go to rescue Pete and finally retrieve the first dagger." Olena says as if success were guaranteed. Nathan simply didn't have the heart to try to prepare her for potential failure as the odds were seemingly and massively stacked against them. Then again——he mused, Olena had taken on the God Anubis, and won so perhaps the odds were not as stacked against them as he first thought.

"Ok, let's not mention this to the others yet. The less people who know means the less chance The Magi will find out we know that Ouroboros was set up to be a suicide mission. Let's sleep on this." Nathan says leaning across Olena kissing her before turning away. She snuggles in close to Nathan's back as the pair fast fall into peaceful slumber.

Chance, sitting quite literally as still as a statue on a shelf——takes note when The Magi materialise at some point during the night——while Olena and Nathan gently snore. Fortunately, there are lion styled accents around the yurt as well as other animals and so The Magi completely miss him while doing a quick search of Olena's room. He absorbs to memory the angry exclamations and arguments for how they should just kill them both where they sleep and be done with it. Then one of The Magi reminds the others they are under constant surveillance from the Powers That Be. It is only when The Magi disappear that Chance is sure had he need breath to live that he would have let out a hefty sigh of relief.

*That was a close call——too close, but at least it confirms my suspicions. The Magi must be going out of their minds at not being able to locate my whereabouts. Perhaps if they stopped trying to destroy Olena and her friends they might very well have noticed me. I wonder if they shall replace me now it's a sure thing I'm not where they first left me——I do hope they'll keep up their end of the deal, I have missed my body——oh so very much.* Chance muses to himself in the darkness, as light snoring can be heard from the bed.

*Soon...everything will come together——just as I'd hoped and planned it would.* A malicious grin spreads across Chance's face as he imagines his best-case scenario playing out.

## Chapter 48

The following morning, they all rise early, preparing daily rations before re-entry to the maze——in the hope of a successful rescue of Pete and retrieval of The Ruby Sunrise Dagger.

"I have news." Frank announces aloud heading inside Olena's enchanted bedroom with Mortina in tow.

Frank only had to glance up at Nathan's face to know that *he knew* about his and Mortina's impromptu romp a few hours ago. Flustered Frank coughs mildly as if clearing his throat before helping Mortina to a seat at an oblong wooden table—— situated between the little ravine and Olena's yurt. There were only six chairs but with Mortina's magical help she was able to conjure a seventh.

"Sometimes I forget where I am and how *fantastic* you are." Frank says all gooey eyed which makes Nathan feel unwell——as Jamie and Donnie fortunately unawares, chat among themselves over by the camp fire.

Mortina gazes at Frank with *come to bed eyes* that this time have Nathan clearing his throat as the vivid memory of seeing his boss in the throes of enjoy kissing Mortina on her *other lips* comes roaring in to the front of his mind making Nathan almost want to gag. Of course, he and Olena enjoy one another's bodies but seeing Frank in the midst of love making was gross——like watching his own dad doing the deed——something no child should have to suffer be they an adult child or otherwise.

Donnie and Jamie saunter across from the camp fire taking up the remaining two empty seats.

"Ok! Hit us boss man——what's the big news?!" Jamie exclaims before drinking the remaining dregs of his camp fire coffee that had been sitting in the bottom of his metal mug.

"Now that I have us altogether...word is——according to Mortina that Pete has been seen by local folks to being transferred...*beyond* the veil——back to humanity's——*our* side of Egypt." Frank explains which makes the guys' faces brighten and Olena's blanch.

"Yes! *Finally*! No magic or mystery this time. *Hallelujah*! This should be a cake walk——so come on, don't leave us all in suspense. What's the challenge?" Jamie asks having punched the air in jubilation——not quite realising the absolute shit-storm of a problem Frank was about to dump on them all.

"Its...not so easy as that. The Magi may have had Pete *smuggled* out by a group of——sorry hun what are they called again?" Frank asks kicking himself over his slip-up on the use of the word *hun*. Anyone who knew Frank knew that *hun* was not used in his vocabulary unless he was with a *serious* lady friend.

"Scuttlebug trolls" Mortina reminds Frank as the idea of trolls existing begins to sink in for Nathan, Donnie and Jamie.

"You——*okay*?" Nathan whispers to Olena, who's porcelain features have turned powder-white.

"Scuttlebug Trolls" Mortina begins "skin humans alive, making clothes and products much the same way as your people would make leather goods from cows or similar animals. Occasionally they will do a recon and kidnap humans to place in their wild jungles——purely for the pleasure of hunting and killing them. They also... wear human teeth as trophies around their necks, wrists and ankles. If your friend Pete is even still alive...he'll more than likely be at an illegal leather market——being readied for auction."

By the time Olena has finished explaining all of this you could have heard a pin-drop in the illusionary forest.

"Well shit." Nathan says feeling weak in the knees ——so glad to be sitting down.

"Nate! You ok brother? You look...*ill*." Jamie asks having noticed the sweaty pasty-pallor of Nathan's skin.

"I'm afraid everything Olena has just described about Scuttlebug Trolls is all true." Mortina says grimly.

"What is it about magical creatures wanting to eat humans every five minutes?!" Donnie exclaims angrily. "Olena who normally equates as a Vampire——equates us with being food. Ouroboros also wanted to eat us—— these trolls I can't say I'm surprised turns out want to eat us too! I'm getting a bit fed up of being constantly on someone's menu." He goes on as the reality sinks in for everyone.

"Yes, but you're forgetting that I too am also on the menu now." Olena says as if to imply they're all in the same boat——which from the sounds of both Jamie and Donnie's silent exclamations, rubs them up the wrong way.

Olena fears that as time goes on and more attempts are made on all their lives——if Nathan's friends will keep wanting to help her in retrieving all seven daggers ——or give up which would mean all manner of loop holes opening up in favour of The Magi. It wouldn't mean anything to them to simply wipe Vampires forever out of existence and tweak the time-line in keeping with what the Powers That Be so desired for it to play out as. No, she had to keep them all on her side for the sake of her people and humanity. Olena said a silent oath she would not fail in her mission to put right her mistake.

Frank gives out all of the details regarding the information he'd been told via Mortina regarding the Scuttlebug Trolls and where their trading markets would be located. Olena squirms under the scrutinising glances thrown her way by Donnie and Jamie as their silent curses release one after the other. Mortina has created a virtual map using magic for Frank to point out where these markets are.

"So what are we saying here? That Pete's more than likely been turned into leather boots?!" Jamie says, unable to concentrate as he stands to pace——raking his hands through his short fiery red hair.

An argument erupts and as much as Frank tried to prevent the predictable from happening, sits back waiting for everyone to cool down.

Donnie turns——marching toward Olena. His white blonde hair was strikingly bright against the stark contrast of his beetroot face.

"Woah! Just what do you think you're doing?" Nathan exclaims angrily, already het up from the insults being thrown in both his and Olena's direction——for being the direct cause for the fubar situation they all now find themselves a part of.

"Nothing like stating the obvious bro——but fighting like this, come on, both of you know of we don't work this out right now then it could put Pete's life in greater jeopardy." Nathan says trying to diffuse the flaring tempers from two of his closest friends.

"That's if he's even still alive *bro.*" Jamie spits back before sitting back down arms folded like a petulant teenager.

Donnie takes a bit longer to consider what his next move will be until he also goes to sit back down.

Using the argument as the perfect cover for her to sneak away. Olena grabs the pack Nathan had put together, resting by her feet before covertly leaving them to it.

Mortina spotting Olena just as she disappears through the doorway says nothing instead choosing to follow in hot pursuit. She doesn't want a reason for anyone else to give her yet more grief. Mortina's heart aches for Olena's situation——having all of her race wiped out of living memory and being turned into the very object of what Vampires would normally consider food——Olena's reality made Mortina's skin crawl. Having all the information about their mission to hand via Frank, Mortina cast a memory spell on herself to recall Vampires, who and what they were and as the memories flooded back——it was the defining moment where Mortina decided to help others remember about Vampires. So far Brax, Monnie and in-house staff were all being worked on to recall Olena's race. Some magical species felt sorry for Olena whereas others were only too thankful not having Vampires in existence. Mortina also requested that mages she knew in Cairo work to get the memories bleeding through into the general public's psyche——and if possible beyond. Fortunately, Mortina was also quite clued up on magical law, studying ancient law more as a hobby than anything else. Speaking to a local professor before attending this morning's meeting with Frank, Mortina put in a special call just to double check what she was doing was above board and as it transpired——after the professor had a brief conversation with an archangel (refusing to mention which one), everything checked out.

"Olena...wait up. I have something to tell you." Mortina says catching up with Olena.

"Thanks for...helping everyone here to remember my people but as for the others arguing in there." Olena says gesturing with a thumb toward her room. "Save your breath. The Magi want to divide and conquer but these nit-wits seem to be doing a grand job of it all on their own. I'm not welcome in their little group of *solider-boys.* That's pretty obvious and I'm just so fed up of the constant blame game. We don't have time for arguments if Pete is indeed in the hands of Scuttlebug Trolls. If you want to truly help me the please give me the location of where to find them and I'll be on my way." Olena says giving Mortina a look to know her mind was well and truly made up.

"This would not be wise. You see...my sources tell me that although they are sure they've seen the gentleman in question with Scuttlebug Trolls——there is no proof they have him and also he...may well be *elsewhere* and not with them at all——it could be a deliberate ruse to throw you off base." Mortina stresses, hoping her point has come across clearly enough for Olena to reconsider rushing off alone.

Having neither the patience nor energy to fret upon this new information. Olena decides heading off alone is exactly what she must do to try and locate Pete——without the hindrance of a group of grumpy men who would only slow her down. Olena felt confident in her capabilities on stalking humans that even as a human herself now figured the method was still pretty much the same——just as her parents had taught her.

Mortina watching on in horror as Olena catches a ride with Monnie down to the lobby——races back inside the enchanted bedroom to give the men a piece of her mind, while also hoping they catch up to her before it's too late and she's vanished out of the hotel——out of sight.

As Olena reaches the lobby she wastes no time hurrying on out of the entryway without looking back. It was no secret among her people from The Magical realm ——that the smartest of human men and women—— were attached to establishments such as the British SAS. They were if nothing else——expert trackers and so with time against her Olena sets off at a rapid pace. Entering the rising sun and scorching temperatures——she kicks herself for forgetting a face covering or protective skin cream Nathan had mentioned from time to time. There was no chance for her to check the pack for just such a cream, as she feared she'd be located by the others when right now what she truly needed was all her focus ahead in the search for Pete. Perhaps if she could locate him and bring him back——Donnie and Jamie might stop with the arguments and venomous jibes that on the surface don't appear to affect Olena that much——but deeper hurt a hell of a lot.

———

"She did what?" Nathan all but roars as spittle flies from his mouth upon Mortina's rushed explanation of where she's scurried off to.

"I hope you two idiots are both packed and ready to leave because we're going, *RIGHT NOW!*" Frank states firing his order directly at Donnie and Jamie who appear less angry and more sheepish. Nathan has already made it to the door and rushed on out.

"Jeez, the man can stride a distance." Jamie utters to himself as their boots on marbled flooring echo all around the extensive hallways. The lift already in use as it carried Nathan down——meant they had no option but to use the stairwells.

"Hey! Nate! Wait up. I'm old!" Frank calls out as the three of them reach the bottom of the stairs just as Nathan marches on toward the exit and out of sight.

Mortina tried in vain to keep up with the men but instead zaps herself down with magic. About to follow them all out into the day's heat——she is prevented when Brax calls her back for a *quick word*.

As the three men exit into the blistering sunshine and heat——there isn't a sign of Nathan anywhere.

*Damn you Nathan Jones!* Frank thinks knowing that splitting up right now is the worst possible thing any of them could have done. It also went completely against all of the training they'd ever received. Golden rule being *especially* on foreign territory that you stuck by and with your military brothers and sisters come hell or high water. Nope——Nathan's ass was going to fry once Frank caught up to him and the others——whose asses were also gonna fry!

# Chapter 49

Olena having flagged down an enchanted camel merchant all but throws coins at him before hopping on her ride and galloping in the direction of the edge of the veil. Nathan having just caught sight of her——isn't in possession of any coin but remembers his tattoo and so flashes this to obtain use of a camel. The merchant fires off rapid instruction on how to make the beast go faster or slower and so needing to go much faster Nathan gently pulls on the right ear of the animal to where it suddenly jets off at speeds much faster than a galloping race horse. Nathan's stomach lurches and he all but almost becomes unseated——until managing to grasp the edge of his saddle as the camel rapidly follows in hot pursuit of Olena's camel.

Keeping some deliberate distance between them——Nathan slows his camel just before the threshold to the veil. Once across it he cautiously monitors Olena's much better controlled ride. She's thrown on a black shroud which covers her head, lower face and body. There are many women wearing much similar shrouds and so Nathan starts struggling to keep his trained military eyes on her. His blood sings with adrenaline and annoyance for once he pins her down she will have some fast explaining to do.

---

Jamie stops to catch his breath having reached the same camel merchant where Olena and Nathan had arranged their rides from.

After badgering the merchant for a ride——where the man apologetically stated that he was clearly out of camels. Jamie, flashing his butt tattoo to the vendor manages to secure a form of transport that's perhaps a little bit unorthodox. The man thanks Jamie for his custom and begins walking to his large tent for a rest during the hottest hours of the day.

*Eey-orr eey-orr* the animal brays as it trots onward, protesting perhaps at the sheer weight of the man sitting upon its back.

"Come on Gonzo." Jamie says calling the donkey by the name on its identifying tag hanging around its neck.

"*Eeey-ooore*" Gonzo brays in response.

---

Having spotted Nathan in her periphery——Olena allows for him to catch up to her.

"You're pretty good at camel riding." Olena quips ——letting Nathan know she's identified him.

"We learned out on tours of the Middle East." Nathan says wrapping his head in the shemagh he's thankful to have on him as a vicious wind starts whipping up.

"Where are the others? I'd have thought you'd all stick together."

Olena says kicking her camel onward into a canter, wishing to get through the annoyance of the minor dust storm faster.

"Let's just get to Pete yeah then concern ourselves with the *others*." Nathan answers deflecting away from knowing just how much trouble he'd be in with Frank once this was all over——if they even survived.

"Fine. I suggest we travel in silence from this point onward so as to save us both swallowing sand."

Nathan unable to think of something to ensure he has the last word, simply mock salutes Olena in agreement as they ride onward toward the nearest set of stables.

Both camels end up leading the way as visibility gets to almost zero. A young stable boy rushes out to greet them——his face heavily covered and protected from the sand. The stables are of course for enchanted animals only, so the boy is quite happy being tipped handsomely in magical Egyptian currency as he leads them inside the tall barn style building and out of the raging hot winds.

Nathan, too busy ogling Olena forgot how to dismount off a camel. As the beast drops its front legs the unprepared Nathan gets sent sprawling head first over its ears. Startling first the boy and then Olena who promptly bursts out laughing.

———

"Let me get this straight. We're to get Pete freed from wherever it is he is being held——only to have him transported back into this trial whereby we *all* have to risk life and limb once again to save him?" Frank asks Brax who's now looking quite uncomfortable at the human man's rising ire. He'd been just about to dash off after the guys when Mortina managed to get him to come back so that Brax could fill him in with the updated information.

"May I remind you sir that had it not been for our *friends* out here——then you would be further into the dark on this mission then you realise. So please, enough with the yelling and dramatics——you're frightening the other guests." Brax says smiling reassuringly to a female with two offspring.

"Yeah...I know. Sorry, it's not your fault. I'm just so damn frustrated. My guys are normally better *organised*. This chaos is unacceptable——heads will *roll* when I catch up to them all." Frank promises more to himself than anyone else. Because sure as eggs is eggs——he knows before long all will be forgiven long before he's had a chance to speak to any of them.

"If it helps, one of my wisp-nurses tracked your

friends heading towards the veil. She can lead you directly to the point they exited out from. Perhaps then your tracking capabilities can help you locate Olena and the others." Mortina suggests having overheard everything Brax disclosed to Frank, while keeping a respectable distance.

"That certainly would help me. What about transport? How do you get around here?" Frank asks Mortina whose face instantly brightens on knowing she can be of better help here.

"Take my little Bee-Bee." Mortina says excitedly while handing Frank a set of very normal looking car keys.

"Mortina! Are you sure that's a...*wise* decision?" Brax asks warily.

"Absolutely. She won't let you down, just——speak kindly to her ok."

"Right. Sure, I mean I've always given names to vehicles I've owned in the past." Frank says which earns him an almost comical expression from Mortina. "Why don't you lead me to this *Bee-Bee* of yours."

---

"This is...*surreal*. But why am I surprised? Everything here is surreal." Frank exclaims as he claps eyes on all of the weird and wonderful looking animated vehicles with clear *personalities* inside of the hotel's private garage.

A racing car with a bull's head which snorts and stamps its wheels as they walk by.

"Bee-Bee!" Mortina calls out to where the low

humming and buzzing of approaching vehicle can be heard.

What appears before Frank's very eyes is a low to the ground sand buggy that's all yellow and black. In place of a windscreen is a large looking bee's head and on each wheel are sharp barbs protruding outward. Mortina explains how these can shoot out in defence should he require back up.

"Her key works the same as a human's car does——as in you put it into the ignition. This turns on Bee-Bee's inbuilt solar charging system. She never runs out of energy but can become slow if not charged fully with sunlight." Mortina explains as Bee-Bee demands a fuss from her mistress.

"What about…people seeing me beyond the veil?" Frank inquires.

"Oh, well you see Bee-Bee has cloaking technology. You can remain hidden so long as she has her day's sunlight. I've not had need to give her a run so I'm sure she will appreciate being out and about. You'd best be off if you're to catch up with your friends——there are not many daylight hours left." Mortina says letting Frank and the wisp nurse climb inside the stinging dust buggy.

"This is so cool she even has a roll cage!" Frank notes, giving Bee-Bee's dash board a gentle rub, which earns him a buzz-purr sound in response.

"Best of luck, I'd better hurry on back up to my medical station. My wisp light I've placed upon your shoulder." Mortina says as Frank now notes the tiny little blue light pulsating atop his shoulder.

Bee-Bee drove like a dream, she was fast, smooth and with the help of the wisp-light, knew exactly where she was meant to be going. Frank had to do relatively very little as the two magical entities continually conversed heading toward the veil.

All of a sudden Bee-Bee came to a grinding halt puzzling Frank as they were still surrounded by miles of sand with seemingly no shimmering veil around.

"There is a human male a few feet over there——is he with you?" The wisp light says addressing Frank for the first time since they had set off.

"Oh——I'm not sure. Let's take a closer look." Frank says not feeling threatened to hear this person is at least another human. "How do you know they're human?" Frank asks just to make double sure this isn't some sort of weird hijacking trap or something.

"I have the capability to scan big swathes of land—— much like human GPS technology——oh yes we wisp-lights are spiritual tech gurus from *many* different worlds and cultures. Much as your maths is a universal language ——so too is that of most technology."

"I'll just agree with you on that. Wait here, I'll be right back." With that Frank climbs out of Bee-Bee's roll cage, cautiously heading toward the almost invisible lump on the desert floor.

"Who——who are you?" Donnie says jumping up to take a fighting stance, wondering if he's not so dehydrated and overcome with heat exhaustion to not be hallucinating the figure in front of him.

"Relax will ya! It's me Frank. Come on no time to

explain here——I'd give you the third degree but there is no time and going by your terrified face I'd say you've suffered enough." Frank explains handing Donnie his flask of water.

Once inside Bee-Bee, Frank gives Donnie the fast version of how he came to use such an enchanting vehicle while also introducing him to the wisp-light. Unsurprisingly Donnie doesn't have much to say after his ordeal in the desert. He sits back and tries to rest while they journey onward in search of Olena, Nathan and Jamie. Exhaustion eventually wins——sending Donnie into a light slumber. Frank grins at his sleeping charge, remembering how utterly scared he and Jamie had been when they were first assigned to him with what would turn out to be the last group of soldiers he'd train before leaving the military.

---

Frank lets Bee-Bee and Wisp-light choose the perfect parking spot for enchanted vehicles——once they're all safely across the veiled border between human reality and magical. Sunlight floods through the designated parking spot. Beside Bee-Bee is a dragon ride which is an enchanted mechanical dragon. A couple of levitating scooters and other mystery modes of transportation——charging with solar energy while parked, flit and move about which is a sight to behold. If anyone ever watched Roger Rabbit they'd get the idea of how *looney* everything looked to Frank and Donnie's human eyes.

"Thanks very much friendly bee-car." Donnie say's clambering out from the roller caged stinging beastie.

Bee-Bee has grown to like Donnie and Frank as she buzzes in equivalent cat purr-like fashion to show their appreciation of a little head scratch administered by Frank.

The wisp-light floats in front of the men before bravely transforming to show her true self. Donnie considers how similar the wisp-light resembles one of those blue characters from a famous movie about avatars. Complete with braided magenta hair and tribal tattoos.

"My true name is Freya. I don't believe you or I have met officially." Freya says going to shake both men's hands.

"Charmed my dear." Frank says trying to hide the fact he finds a blue tinted female quite bizarre.

"I shall not blend in well with my natural colours ——please excuse me while I rectify this issue with some Jingle-berry juice." Freya says taking a tiny vial of silvery liquid from a pouch around her waist.

Before their very eyes——Freya turns very human-like. Her skin is cream coloured with a light bronze hue. And her hair——dark brown is styled back into a plait. On her bottom half are khaki shorts while her top is dressed in a green tight-fitting strappy top that's certainly grasped Donnie's attention among her many——*assets*. Freya's feet don thick white socks inside of heavy set looking hiking boots.

*"Clara Croft——eat ya heart out!"* Donnie exclaims earning him a groan and eye roll from Frank——as he

quotes the name of his favourite female computer gaming character.

"Shall we?" Donnie says holding out an arm from Freya to take, which she graciously does as Frank can only watch on totally dumbfounded. Then reminds himself that Donnie always did have fast luck with women so wasn't overly surprised to see Freya taking an instant shine to the blond-haired dare-devil.

"Freya, you may wish to find a way to cover your head and perhaps most of your body. Although you have us to protect you——let's just say men view uncovered western women…like——

"Good point." Donnie cuts in remembering the horrific attack on an American journalist who got caught up in a mob of jeering Egyptians who saw fit to pull her away from her bodyguard and cameraman to do all manner of unpleasant things to her. Naively she had been uncovered and so was seen as free game.

"Oh…I forget myself——in my world attacks of any kind on females are very rare——Earth sure can is a cruel world." Freya says working her magic to transform into the epitome of what would be deemed a respectable Egyptian Muslim woman.

Donnie's heart momentarily sinks at seeing hardly any part of Freya now uncovered, but when her foot momentarily touches his and he glances down——Donnie grins to see Freya still wearing the hiking boots and so imagines the same clothing underneath the black robes.

"We had better make haste if we are to reach the

markets and make it back before sunset." Freya says already marching ahead.

"Come on *lover boy.*" Frank says rolling his eyes as Donnie takes in Freya's form from behind——even if now it is respectfully covered over and then some.

*Give me strength.* Frank utters under his breath as they jog to catch up to Freya. Both thankful the winds have died down making visibility a lot easier to navigate the path forwards.

———

Olena and Nathan are hitting the back-alley markets now that the sandstorm has passed. Chance guides them the best he can——recalling the map Mortina had pulled up earlier. It appeared Chance could not only have memories of maps randomly installed by some seeming invisible force——but could also photographically remember details quite clearly and for a prolonged period of time.

"Any signs were close to where the Scuttlebug Trolls and Pete are?" Olena asks pressing Chance for clearer directions.

"This is definitely the street where magical folk come to do *livestock* business." Chance says trying to convey optimism that they are in fact on the right track.

"I guess this answers the age-old question where most *missing* people end up who are never seen or heard from again." Nathan says somberly as the smells of body odour begin assaulting his nasal passages——bringing with them a sense of dread because mixed with the unmistakable stench of living human body odour was also the scent of——*death*.

"These are what your people might call black markets." Chance explains

Which does nothing to reassure the rising dread within Nathan's now mildly trembling body as adrenaline drips thickly through his veins——ready for action at a moment's notice.

Groans and pleading voices among yells of pain alert Nathan and Olena to the path they now need to take. Blood stains the ground and the smells become heavier making both of them momentarily wretch.

As they head deeper into *livestock* territory nothing could have prepared either Nathan or Olena for what they were about to be faced with.

In front of them is a towering circular building which Chance says is an arena where all kinds of species are pitted against one another and beasts. The slaves or livestock that are insubordinate get thrown into the arena with usually the odds stacked hugely against them.

"How do you know all of this?" Nathan asks as Olena find herself also wishing to know how Chance suddenly knows so much about these black markets.

"I'm centuries old———I might not be so clued up on geography without the use of maps but historically——I can tell you nothing good ever happens here to those in chains."

"Agreed." Olena says as they enter the main throng of buyers and sellers.

Fairies, dwarfs, elves, and other indistinguishable

creatures Nathan sees——look crestfallen and as if all hope has left them as they are bound by heavy set chains linked together in long rows awaiting to be what looks like some processing system, with long tables at the end with armed personnel stamping paperwork or waving a hand to mean the prisoner is take away which causes deep upset and a lot of yelling and pleading as the individuals are unlinked from fellow prisoners before being dragged toward the area.

Turning away so as to avoid confusion among guards and owners of the chained-up individuals——that Olena and Nathan are not captured. They duck into a quieter side alley to catch their breath and minds.

"I hate to state the obvious here but——trying to locate your friend with so many up for auction, with the time that's already passed I'd say there is a good chance he's already been moved on. If this is the case we may never find him." Chance says wishing nothing more than to be away from such a grotesque situation. One thing he loved most about his life before The Magi turned him into a door ornament——was his solitude.

"We're not leaving here without giving this place a thorough going over——we've got The Magi's tattoos so that's got to count for something——right?' Nathan says as Olena can only look at him with eyes full of sorrow.

A huge commotion can be heard with very loud crashing, bashing and yelling sounds.

"Err——I think we might have found the trolls." Olena says glancing up at the sheer magnitude of the beasts.

"I believe." Nathan says taking a moment to gulp down his swallow "you might be right."

The trolls are enormous brutes——all carrying stereotypical clubs and other manner of heavyset skull crushing weapons.

"Olena, to gain information from Scuttlebug trolls you must show a commanding presence. No fear, otherwise they will see a weakness in you and might attempt to tear you limb from limb before eating——either of you." Chance says beginning to sound nervous himself which does nothing to fill either Olena or Nathan with confidence.

"Wait here——I excelled in negotiation training. Might as well try something, no use both of us ending up troll poo." Nathan says putting an arm across Olena indicating he's deadly serious for her to stay up of harm's way and before she can argue any point——as words simply fail her here, Nathan strides on out to make his presence seen and felt (no matter how puny he appears to be.)

Olena and Chance watch on in horror as one of the trolls' glances down laughing as he proceeds to pick Nathan up with two fingers by the scruff of his shirt collar. The troll shakes him around——slamming Nathan into the ground a few times before with no effort at all hurtling him back down the alleyway towards Olena and Chance.

Magical folk scatter as Nathan's body comes barrelling through, landing on thankfully a pulled-out awning of one of the market stalls before crashing into a load of pallets full of what look to be nut type things and berries. The force of Nathan landing on them sends the goods flying off in various directions like mini pellets as various creatures duck and dive for cover. The nut type things become embedded into walls and from the sounds of yelps——people.

"Nathan! Are you ok?!" Olena yells above a cloud of dust as a growing group of angry merchants closes in.

The troll that had thrown Nathan laughs before stomping toward them with two of its friends which fortunately cause the merchants and everyone else in their path to run for their lives.

*"THIS WAY!"* Chance all but roars as he leads them both out of the veiled enchanted market and across to a pavement area——in full view of human Egyptian shoppers and tourists. The slight commotion of Olena and Nathan bursting forth from seemingly nowhere makes people turn their heads but as its very busy between markets stalls——no one bats an eye-lid.

"Ah-ah! I think I've bruised or cracked a few ribs." Nathan exclaims aloud in clear agony. Olena responds by rapidly lifting his partially torn shirt up to check underneath. There are indeed nasty looking purple welts starting to form around his rib cage.

"We need Mortina or some form of medical aid——any suggestions Chance?" Olena asks as Nathan's breathing becomes more laboured before he groans and collapses onto the ground.

———

Frank, Donnie and Freya reached the entryway point to the hidden black market just as there is the commotion of Nathan collapsing. Frank having his attention momentarily pulled away to where the noises came from ——glances Nathan's shirt and saying a silent oath, heads on over.

"Hey! Boss! Where are you going——market's this way?" Donnie calls out but it appears is not heard. Sighing and swearing under his breath he and Freya follow Frank in hot pursuit until it becomes clear exactly why Frank had diverted away.

"Looks like we caught up to you just in time." Frank says as the reunited friends let worried passers-by know in Egyptian that they are fine——their friend has had too much sun.

Managing to get Nathan up onto his feet with the aid of Frank and Donnie either side of him, locate a local bar across the busy street and head on inside where Frank requests a table for them to sit at.

"Who's your friend?" Nathan asks having noticed a new woman with Frank and Donnie.

"Oh——Freya meet the bane of my life Nate, Nate this is Freya——our guide for this jolly Pete finding jaunt." Donnie says unable to see the blush he elicits on Freya's face beneath her veiled head and face.

"Hello Mr Nate——

"Just Nate will do fine." Nathan says interrupting the cool eyed female giving her a brief shake of the hand before wincing again.

A waitress comes over to take an order of drinks and

gives a disapproving look——noticing Freya with her hands placed around Nathan's mid-riff as he tips his head back and moans. She hurries away and Frank realises that the act could be mistaken to be a PDA which is a big no-no out here. At the risk of sounding paranoid he ushers everyone back outside before the waitress can report them all. Freya never breaks contact with Nathan's skin.

"Woah——I feel *woozy*." Nathan exclaims as their group shuffle along and out of sight down a relatively quiet alleyway situated between two restaurants.

"I've given you a hefty dose of healing magic. I can confirm you had fractured ribs and a cracked spine but..."

Freya's words die on her lips as she collapses to the ground.

"Don't worry about her, it's a faint. When wisp-lights use their magic to heal they exhaust themselves quite quickly. Have any of you got any means to contact Mortina? Freya has done her job in getting us here——she needs rest and it would be safer back at the hotel." Chance says as Olena thinks of how to contact Mortina.

"Its...its...ok...I can——call on her...just make sure... we're out of sight." Freya says, her voice breaking with the effort talking now takes from her.

"Ok, you do your thing calling Mortina——we'll cover the entryway into the alley." Frank says sending Donnie and Nathan to ensure no one can discover them.

Telepathically Freya sends out a weak signal to Mortina who materialises within mere moments——aghast at seeing her wisp-light in such a sorry state. Frank makes his apologies as he and Olena explain what happened. Mortina accepts the apologies before gathering Freya into her arms and zapping them both out of sight.

"Hey look——if it ain't our buddy Jamie! Fortune has smiled down upon us fondly today friends." Donnie says as Nathan can only groan at what it could mean to have the dynamic duo back together——annoying the hell out of himself and Frank.

"At least this means we can all enjoy a stiff drink *together* while deciding our next move." Nathan exclaims warily before stepping back out into the afternoon sun already over the unrelenting heat, dust and sand.

He notes that Jamie's red hair is a mess jutting out at odd angles, with his blue eyes out on frightened stalks ——as he actively seeks them out.

Nathan not wanting to prolong his friend's clear agony at being alone any longer, jogs on ahead to gently tap him on the shoulder.

"Woah! Buddy it's me——Nate." He exclaims ducking to miss Jamie's right hook.

Jamie says nothing but just throws his arms around Nathan's recently healed mid-riff making him unconsciously tense at the recent memory of his injuries.

Donnie, Frank and Olena with Chance safely tucked into her satchel——all head towards where Nathan and Jamie stand.

"Let's go inside that Cobra bar over there——I'm in dire need of a beer." Jamie says making everyone smile.

"I should all bash your heads in for rushing off like that——but it looks like you punished yourselves enough by getting lost out here." Frank says bursting Donnie, Jamie and Nathan's mini celebration bubble.

"Sorry boss." The three men all mumble to varying degrees. Olena has to stifle a laugh at how under the thumb they all are.

They all enter a bar called *The Hooded Cobra*——situated right near to where their world meets the hidden veil of The Magical black market. Fortunately, the waitress from the previous establishment looked to not have caused a fuss——as no one official could be seen actively seeking out *criminals* who just did what looked to be an outrageous display of PDA. Olena reckons there must be a plethora of disguised magical folk inside the bar and cautions the others to be on guard.

"How do these women survive in this get up. I feel like a Bracka-bird stuffed in the hottest oven of Kilnmire ——a place where dwarfs congregate to smelt and forge all manner of weaponry etc." Olena explains as Nathan and co give her quizzical expressions.

As a waiter brings them their drinks Frank leads a toast to honour Pete.

"To Pete, wherever he may be let us hope he is at least alive——and also *well*."

"To Pete." They all raise their glasses and as Olena brings her glass of non-alcoholic Diet Coke to her lips she splutters as Chance calls out to her from his hiding place inside her satchel. None of the others noticed nor did the staff or customers nearby.

"Please excuse me I have to...got to eh bathroom." Olena says placing her drink down to stand.

"Good idea, I'll join you——as in walk you to the loos." Nathan says as wary glances shoot toward him at the mention of going to *join* Olena in the ladies' room. Clearly there are Egyptian people inside who understand English.

What Olena and Nathan failed to admit to the others was that Olena had gently squeezed Nathan's leg to indicate she possibly had something to tell him.

"Ok, so what's up?" Nathan asks as they reach the separated men and women's toilet doorways.

"I don't know yet——Chance has something to tell me, about Pete. I'll go in find out what I can and then you and I can decide how best to tell the others——for I fear the news...is not good."

"Ah hell! I've lost friends in the past to firefights during battle but...any of these guys——they're my family——brothers."

"I know and I'm sorry but——I'd best make use of the bathroom being empty."

Olena doesn't wait for a response before slipping inside the ladies' room.

Nathan stands in front of the door alerting women that it's out of order and to use the men's which he diligently checks each time to make sure it's empty of male customers as that could cause a right raucous.

Olena eventually exits which Nathan is relieved about——as he moves aside to let a female waitress inside the bathroom——his ruse about it being out of order going unnoticed.

"Ok, so spill——what's happened to Pete?"

"I ——well, there's no easy way to say this." Olena says with unreadable expression.

"Just spit it out will you. He's dead, isn't he?" Nathan's voice says beginning to crack, wondering how he will break the news to the others.

"No!...*no*. Pete is very much alive." Olena says hoping to quell the rising tension in Nathan's voice.

People are beginning to notice their heated discussion so Olena rapidly tries to relay what Chance just told her as they make their way back toward their table.

"Freya telepathically linked to Chance. Some of Brax's spy-scouts that have a keen sense of smell. Scented Pete to an——avian market."

"Right so he's...with bird merchants?" Nathan asks puzzled as to where this is going.

"He's not just with bird merchants——he is a bird." As Olena says this Nathan's legs give way slightly and he knocks into a waitress who curses as fortunately empty glasses and plates get sent sprawling.

"I need——fresh air." Nathan says bolting for the entryway into the bar.

———

Having no means to pay the establishment and noticing Nathan and Olena's rapid exit——Frank signals for Donnie and Jamie to stand and leave. As the place is bustling their table gets taken up immediately giving them time to skulk away before it is noticed they've not settled the tab.

"Everyone keep walking, head toward the veil." Frank says barking out the order as everyone does as he says.

Once just on the inside of the veil and cloaked from view of humans Frank demands to know what the bloody hell is going on.

"Sir...Donnie...Jamie...you're going to want to brace yourselves. Turns out not only is Pete alive and well but ——he's now a bird——

"A Crocking-Wocka-Backa bird to be exact." Olena finishes having interrupted Nathan.

"Oh." is all Jamie says before speedily passing out from shock.

Tutting Donnie places him in the recovery position as magical folk seemingly come and go, passing them by through the veil without so much as batting an eye-lid ——for those who *had* eyelids.

"Chance has been given directions telepathically by both Mortina and Freya. If we hurry we can reach the market where enchanted birds are kept and rescue Pete before he's transferred on the next lorry load out from there." Olena says grabbing everyone's attention.

"You go, I'll stay here with Mr weak constitution." Donnie says ushering for Frank, Nathan and Olena to leave.

"Ok, but if anything kicks off this side you're to head on out of here back to the human side——no questions." Frank orders to where Donnie simply mock salutes him in response.

"Ok, this way, come on let's hurry. Next lorry load of birds could be shipped out any minute." Olena says beginning the journey through weaving market stalls as Chance rapidly fires off instructions of where to go.

"Slow down! We can't afford to become separated." Nathan shouts to where Olena tuts rolling her eyes as she waits anxiously for him and Frank.

"Boss——you don't look so hot, maybe you should——

"Yeah, ok——I'm going back but please, just get Pete so we can get the heck out of here and figure out how to turn our friend back his usual human self." Frank says showing clear signs of fatigue, not being able to move as fast as he used to. The stomach bug he suffered earlier sapping his strength on top of everything else.

"We will, now come on." Olena says not hanging around any longer——as what she failed to mention was the mere fact the birds up for transportation were in fact akin to that of how battery hens are farmed. They're for the food chain. So although Pete may not have been skinned alive before being consumed——he may yet still be someone's supper.

*Looks like Donnie had a point before——I guess magical people really do like having human beings on the menu——even if not in the traditional form.* Olena muses while continually hurrying along through cramped alleyways packed with merchants and buyers. The sights, smells and sounds a cacophony of confusion ——overwhelm Olena's fragile human constitution—— made only a little easier to navigate through from Chance's called out directions.

"Just when I thought this fubar situation couldn't

become anymore fubar then it already was——you deliver the news my long-time friend and brother is now a bird!" Nathan says huffing at being sardined in among a throng of various strange looking creatures, beasties and species that also bring with them a surge of smells. Sometimes pleasant and at other times make Nathan want to throw up. One minute roses pass him by——the next putrid boil smells.

"I'm sorry——I don't know what else to say. you're either gonna have to suck it up or bow out. Either way right now we have just one mission and that is to retrieve Pete." Olena says taking Nathan aback at how much of a leader she just sounded like. Frank better watch his back ——Nathan mused or Olena might just give him a run for his position as their elected boss.

## Chapter 51

Olena and Nathan reach the bird market stalls just as the transporter lorry parks up to take on new crates full of squawking protesting beasts ranging from minute in size——to that of a human nine-seater vehicle. Nathan was unsurprised to see the vehicle in question materialise through what must be a vehicle portal. One minute there's nothing——the next a reversing vehicle approaches.

"Woah! These beasts are *angry.*" Nathan notes as he marginally misses getting a finger bitten off having attempted to pet an unassuming docile looking fluorescent-pink bird. Not to dissimilar he thought from a flamingo.

"Suck elves and jump off a gorge!" The bird yelled at him causing Nathan to remember most things from Olena's world———including animal looking beasties, could also talk.

"Sorry——so sorry." Nathan says to the bird who

simply huffs before turning its fluffy-plumage behind on him.

"I'd suggest *not* trying to touch these guys. They all have intelligent personalities——many will have been kidnapped or sold by evil owners." Olena says while listening into Chance to figure out how hot or cold their position is in conjunction with Pete.

"There——over there by the stack of Raven-rangers." Chance exclaims through two little peep-holes Olena added to her satchel, meaning she didn't need to keep lifting Chance out so could remain well hidden.

Overhead squares of thin material create a protective canopy helping keep the blistering sun from everyone's heads——as people come and go through the narrow pathways checking out which birds they wish to obtain as pets——or produce.

A person shrieking can be heard before an almighty crash follows along with anxious shouts for those nearby to *grab that Crocking-Wocka-Backa!*

"I'm not a gambling woman——if I were however, I'd say we just found your friend Pete." Olena says as they hurry forward toward all the commotion.

"There, he's on top of that crate of bee-stingers!" Chance yells to ensure he was heard above the din of excited and angry merchants as everyone now tried to grab the rogue Crocking-Wocka-Backa bird.

Boxes much the same as bee-keepers might have on the human side of magical veils——could be seen bunched together where a separate lorry had already started loading them on.

The bird in question——now sat atop of the boxes as they buzzed angrily from within. Nathan noted how the bird was a stunning shade of fluorescent green with vibrant pink and yellow plumage and darker tail feathers of violet and indigo hues.

"Pete! Pete! Down here——it's us! Nathan and Olena!" Nathan called out but felt this was in vain as there were too many people and voices surrounding them now.

"We need a better distraction——you thinking what I'm thinking?" Olena says indicating to the bee-stinger boxes.

"Prepare to run." Nathan says as they both grab one of the boxes out of sight of the cyclops busily loading them onto his lorry.

"3...2...——

"Hey I didn't say 1!" Nathan said annoyed as he jumped out of the way of the released insects that were individually about as big as the average human foot with a stinger as long as a shin bone.

"In here!" Olena yells pulling Nathan behind a covered area——out of sight of everyone now running around screaming as bee-stingers look for victims to puncture and maim.

Looking through a small crack in the fabric Nathan huffs at not being able to see the bird anymore——that is until it flies directly toward them.

The fabric parts and a small dust cloud gets kicked up as the Crocking-Wocka-Backa bird says aloud in Pete's voice for them both to follow him.

Frank, Donnie and Jamie had to move out and away from the veil after a large commotion all but saw a mad rush of magical folk to sprint out and away from The Magical black market.

With Jamie fully recovered from the shock of learning about Pete's fate the trio managed to find a quiet spot to sit down in as they awaited the return of Olena and Nathan hopefully with Pete in tow. As luck would have it they didn't have to wait long, for as all The Magical folk began to clear came Olena, Nathan and some extraordinarily vibrant bird bringing up the rear.

"Run! Frank, guys——get up, it's time to go." Nathan calls out just before he, Olena and Pete reach them.

Turning to see what's chasing them means the men need no further explanation as they watch in utter terror at enormous bee creatures buzzing angrily toward them. However, upon exiting The Magical veil——all that can be witnessed is disguised magical folk now looking very human running away from normal bee sized creatures. It appeared the other side of the veil shrank the creatures to respectable sizes. Still, the now much smaller cloud of bees was still angry and so caused the group to carry on fleeing until they could find a safe spot to catch their breath. Pete also appeared to have shrunk to look more like a parakeet then a phoenix.

"Well——that was fun!" Pete says sarcastically as Jamie faints once again.

"Best we get him back to the hotel——perhaps Mortina can help us turn Pete back into a human." Olena says with no argument from any of the men who all look relatively shell-shocked.

"Great idea. Come on bud——let's get you fixed." Nathan says trying but failing to sound confident and reassuring as Pete comes to rest atop of his shoulder.

"Squawk——Polly wanna cracker." Pete exclaims swiftly followed with an apology. "Sorry, I couldn't help myself, you have to agree though, when will any of us be able to say we cracked that joke as a literal bird."

"Careful what you wish for. You may end up remaining as a bird for the duration of this quest——*if* we can't get you changed back." Olena says dubiously while keeping to herself the fact with transfiguration comes more often than not the added complication an object or person changed one way may not so easily be changed back to their original form.

———

They reach The Blue Pharaoh Hotel just as the sun dips down behind the *real* pyramids. Mortina with Brax arranged for better transportation to bring everyone back safely which included her beloved little Bee-Bee.

"How did Bee-Bee run?" Mortina asks Frank——approaching them all with caution as she notes the tired, grubby and worn-out look each of them is wearing.

"Like a dream." Frank confirms handing the keys back as the others step out of a literal driverless cat-bus.

The doorway which meows wide as they disembark. The strange vehicle then leaves purring, alongside Bee-Bee as they head toward the hotel's underground garage.

"Oh you poor love——you've over done it. Come on, I'll accompany you to your room and give you a full check-up." Mortina says as she ushers Frank onward up the long marble steps leading into the hotel lobby before he or any of the others could protest.

"Hey Olena, mind if me and Donnie catch a swim in that gorgeous lagoon of yours before grabbing a shower and some grub?" Jamie asks having already discussed on the cat-bus ride back how he and Donnie planned to unwind upon their return.

"Sure——it's no bother. By all means feel free to stay in the tents by the campsite too. I'm sure you and Nathan, Pete and Frank have a lot to discuss. I know I'm included in your discussions but...truth be told I'm actually feeling pretty beat myself. I'd hoped to grab a shower ——some *grub* as you call it and get my head down for a few hours before we figure out what Pete's original part to play in all of this should've been." Olena says, looking every bit as exhausted as she'd admitted to feeling.

"Oh sure——meanwhile I'll just continue being stuck in this bird body, shall I?" Pete says instantly making the others pull grimaces to having almost forgotten Pete was with them in current format.

"It's ok bud——join us for a *bird* bath. I'm sure we can get Brax to arrange some birdseed for you." Jamie jests—— earning him a dollop of poo ejected from Pete's bottom as he circles over their heads.

"Jeez bro! Gah! That is gross!" Jamie says trying and failing to get the wet excrement out of his hair making it worse as he rubs with his hands.

Olena, Nathan and Donnie unable to cope with the absurdity of Pete's predicament any longer——burst out laughing.

"Thanks for nothing guys." Pete says flying on ahead inside the hotel.

As luck would have it Monnie is just letting guests out of the lift and with no one standing around waiting to board——Pete flies in instructing Monnie to take him up to the top floor. There is a reluctance on Monnie's expression wondering if this bird could pose a danger to their human guests. But as Pete fires off who he is—— Monnie remembers the discussion he'd overheard between Brax and Mortina about Pete being turned into a bird.

"Ah——so *you're* the guy all the fuss had been about. So sorry you've been changed into a Crocking-Wocka-Backa." Monnie says offering his condolences.

"Why are you sorry? What's so bad about that?" Pete asks nervously just as the lift doors close and they begin the ascent to the top floor.

"I'm not sure if I should mention anything but...its common knowledge that those who get turned into other things——rarely make it back to their original forms."

"You mean, I could be stuck like this...*forever!*" The thought make Pete feel suddenly unwell.

"Like I said——I'm sorry."

The rest of the lifts journey is done so in icy silence.

---

Everyone settles around the campfire. Pete has forgiven Jamie for his earlier bird bath and food jibes as they all now enjoy hot-dogs and hamburgers grilled by Nathan, Donnie and Jamie. The news Pete may not be so easily returned into his human self was something they were now all coming to terms with.

Tentatively Pete was fed tiny morsels of meat in case human food didn't now agree with his magical bird digestion but fortunately for him the breed of bird he had been turned into could eat pretty much anything.

"Wanda Farkun Narkles!!" Olena yells as everyone but her becomes frozen.

The Magi appear with a furious fiery glow about them this time making Olena swallow any further retort she was thinking of spitting out in their direction.

"Olena Lupescu, well done! You have made it to the final round of trials for The Ruby Sunrise. We *apologise* for the unforeseen kidnapping and transfiguration of your *friend* Pete. We know accusations have been fast and loose when implicating our involvement with just such an operation——we assure you any rumour or hearsay spreaders have been dealt with. May the rest of this journey go a lot smoother for you. *The Powers That Be* have given our internal...*systems* a complete overhaul due to this mis-hap. Rest assured no other interference should be expected for the duration of your quest in obtaining all seven daggers. Expect to see little to nothing of us in future. So mote it be!"

The Magi flamed out of sight as quickly as they had arrived making Olena's head spin.

"Going by that look our *friends* The Magi have just turned up——haven't they?" Nathan says out of earshot of the others as he passes Olena a plateful of food. The queasy feeling he's learned to associate with The Magi showing up——only just starting to ebb away.

"Indeed. They apologised for the mistake and apparently have been *re-programmed*. Which means nothing to me for I know next to nothing how any of that higher spiritual real stuff works.

"Pity they couldn't see fit to return Pete to his human state." Nathan says sounding more than a little cheesed off at The Magi having got away with causing trouble——*again*. Making the quest's challenges an unfair advantage against them all.

"Yeah but——at least we're all back together again." Olena says resting her head upon Nathan's shoulder as they sit side by side watching the campfire flames dance in front of them.

Mortina and Freya have also joined in for the evening meal which could potentially be their last one at the hotel. Comments are passed around at how delicious all the food tastes and before long Mortina and Freya are saying goodnight to everyone. Nathan ensures Frank knows he has the room to himself tonight——which is code for he and Mortina have time to be romantic should they so desire. Frank takes the hint as he and Mortina leave ahead of Donnie and Freya——who'd made the excuse she wished for Donnie to escort her back to her quarters as she felt unsafe walking there alone.

"Looks like I'm crashing here *alone* tonight." Jamie says sounding a little crest-fallen.

"You've still got me buddy." Pete says coming to sit on Jamie's shoulder.

"Much as I love you bro——sometimes a guy just needs a little lady-friend attention." Jamie admits standing to head off to his chosen tent for the night.

The two of them carry on the conversation in muted tones as Olena and Nathan share a long languid kiss by the fire before retiring to her yurt.

It has escaped everyone's attentions that Chance is now——*nowhere* to be seen.

## Chapter 52

Stretching awake——yawning aloud, Olena is puzzled when her out-stretched arm feels nothing but air.

"Hey...good morning sleepy head." Nathan's voice says while Olena is still trying to get her bearings.

"What——is going on?" She asks as opening her eyes seems difficult given the bright blinding light bearing down upon her.

"It appears as if at some point during the night we were all transported...somewhere else." Nathan says gingerly——appreciating that Olena is not fully in the room yet.

"Pah! Transported is one way of putting it. I didn't even get so say goodbye to Freya. Bet she thinks I just waltzed on out of her room after we——

"Keep the details to yourself please." Frank orders from nearby, cutting Donnie off.

Feeling more awake now, Olena can see through

squinting eyes that she is sitting up on the dusty floor ——-inside of a colossal open-air circular stone space. The walls of a hollowed-out tower rise high above her. There are gaps in the walls that look similar to that of the Italian colosseum.

Bright sunlight beats down atop of all of them making Olena's nerves stand on end. Had she been a Vampire there would only remain a pile of ashes where she now stood.

"Ok, seeing as you are more awake now——I must tell you. Pete and Chance are both...*missing*. I know The Magi turned up yesterday evening as we discussed but...is there anything that could explain their disappearance?" Nathan asks a stressed looking Olena.

"N-no...they just made their apologies and left."

"Hmmm, well from what we've gathered taking a look around——we appear to be in some sort of colosseum structure. Without weaponry or any means to protect ourselves——I fear we might be about to meet Anubis down in the underworld——*prematurely*." As Frank gives Olena the low down of their situation the ground hums a little with small vibrations before a loud guttural roar is heard echoing around the circular space.

Donnie and Jamie stand back to back waiting for whatever might be about to attack them. Frank and Nathan both go to stand closer to Olena as everyone glances around nervously.

A zap of wind draws attention away from where everyone heard the initial roar——as Mortina materialises in front of all of them. She is barely visible and as an elemental mage explains quickly how she is able to disguise herself as wind so to help them all while not being seen by The Magi.

*"Try not to draw any focus or attention my way."* Mortina starts in barely audible tones as her voice sounds quite literally like a whispering wind. *"Nathan, I gift you the broad sword of needle Vikings. Frank——a bow for being such a sharp shooter. Jamie, I gift you the pummelling action of a mace and Donnie may your heart be protected by a spear of truth. For Olena I gift a set of katanas——forged in the metal of miltith. You are all to receive protective heat resistant armour——made of blazing dragon skin. By the highest lords and ladies may my will be done!"* As Mortina speaks her words, each receives their weapon of her choosing while also donning the snug fitting fire-retardant armour.

*"Best of luck my dears. I must return to my station at The Blue Pharaoh."* Mortina whispers having created the illusion of a dust-devil to better conceal her aiding them so that at least the odds a about who they were going to face were better evened.

The ground rumbles a lot more violently than before and the roar makes everyone's ears ring with pain as before them materialises a beast that cannot exist——a *Manticore*.

"Oh Jesus! What is that thing?" Jamie can be heard with a voice laced in panic.

"I believe it is a *Manticore*. Head of a human, body of a lion and the tail of a scorpion. It may also breath fire——

As Olena explains the beast's characteristics a huge flame erupts from the Manticore's mouth as if to prove her point.

An evil laugh escapes the Manticore's lips as the beast brags of being Chance——in his true form.

Jamie unable to cope, drops his mace to grasp at the sides of his head. Repeating over and over again how he *can't do this.*

Donnie has neither the time nor patience to coddle him, as Frank barks out the clear order for everyone to get themselves together.

Olena holds up her katanas in fighting stance ready to take on Chance as Nathan stands behind her to cover her back. Frank and Donnie partner up unable to stop Jamie from wandering around like an unhinged asylum in-patient whose mind looks to have finally cracked open like an egg.

"So you were in on the ruse all along? What are The Magi giving you for cementing our fate Chance?" Olena spits out angrily——annoyed at herself for not listening to her true gut instincts about Chance from the very first meeting.

"Why I'll get my freedom of course. This colosseum is my domain but...I need to branch out——see the world——*eat* better food." He says in a voice that makes Olena's skin prickle with apprehension.

"If we can beat Anubis and Ouroboros——what makes you think we can't also defeat you?" Olena calls out as Chance climbs up the walls, disappearing inside one of the open spaces.

Her body quivers as adrenaline surfs throughout her central nervous system. Perspiration pours down her face, neck and chest. Olena listens intently, honing her Vampire sense of hearing just in time to realise Chance is going straight for Jamie.

"There! He's going to launch from over——

Olena's voice cuts off as Chance does indeed burst forth out from one of the spaces in the hollowed out circular stone structure. Her alert gave Frank and Donnie just enough time to reach Jamie——tugging him out of the way of Chance's ferocious talons.

Annoyed at having missed Jamie by a hair's breadth, Chance roars——once again making all of them wince as pain zips through all of their eardrums. Cursing loudly, Chance grimaces——as before their very eyes gigantic dragon styled wings sprout outward from his body. He laughs menacingly before thanking The Magi aloud for such a huge advantage over his prey.

"Great! Now it can fly!" Nathan yells above the roaring downdraft caused by Chance's giant dragon wings.

"Err-guys, I think we should head inside the structure." Olena advises as she starts ahead toward one of the entranceways leading inside the circular stone building.

Nathan, Donnie, Jamie and Frank all hang back to take a better look at what Olena had seen——that caused her to run away. As Chance circles up high once before re-aligning himself to come back down——their puzzlement is soon answered as a jet stream of liquid napalm gets blasted down toward them.

"Fuuuuuuu——-

Nathan's swearing is cut off as Donnie runs into him jolting Nathan out of his stunned frozen-shock and back into action.

"Move! Move! Move!" Frank yells as the four of them race to reach where Olena had been seen entering the structure.

Fire blasts through no sooner has Jamie made it inside. Frank pulled him off to the side where they all now bunched together to avoid being flambéed.

"Any ideas what we should do?" Olena calls out from her own hiding place.

"Yeah! If we split up perhaps we can disorientate the beast. He can't put all his efforts onto all of us at once if we spread out——it's the best bet don't you think Frank?" Nathan calls out above the screeching roars and continuous blasts of fire.

"Good idea! I'll head to the top——perhaps I can hit him with some arrows. Nathan you and Olena take the east side, Donnie and Jamie you guys take the west. We need to keep moving however so run rotationally when you can and stay apart. If we get too close to one another it makes Chance's job easier. On my count——*move!*" Frank races ahead to the first flight of stone stairs. Adrenaline helps him so much but he also has the distinct feeling that Mortina may be lending some of her energies from further afield as he feels almost teenager-like again.

"I think we'll do better apart. The more widespread we are the harder it makes things for Chance. What if...I run out——attempt to climb up him using the katanas?

If I make it up his body I can aim for his head." Olena shouts as Chance turns away from the group having his attention now drawn to Frank who's firing off arrows one after another. What no-one but Frank realises is that his arrow quiver appears to re-fill itself with unlimited arrows every time he uses one.

"That's actually not a bad idea I just——wish I could go in your place. This sword is far too heavy for you——I don't mean that in a sexist way it's just, I'm having a hard time carrying it myself." Nathan says agreeing to Olena's fast thought out plan——appreciating there is little time to argue or re-think a different tactical manoeuvre.

"Ok, well in case I don't make it——I think I love you Nate." With that Olena rushes out into the arena. His tail hangs low enough to the ground that she can jump up and grab it before jamming the first katana in. Chance bellows his protest beginning wild bucking, ducking and diving movements but Olena thrusts the other katana in for good sticking measure. It takes her a while to find her rhythm but before long she's able to make her way up to Chance's newly acquired dragon wings.

Chance twists, blind with rage clawing at Olena with his huge lion talons. Fortunately, she has slipped just out of his reach as talons miss her by millimetres while Olena clings onto one of the embedded katanas for quite literally grim death. Getting her bearings between Chance bucking through the air——Olena manages to balance ——pulling herself up then using the katana as a foot hold as she reaches a bit higher up for the other one embedded into Chance's body. Ripping the katana higher up——free from his side Chance lets out an ear-splitting roar. Wasting no time and before he can try for a death roll. Olena jumps across to his left dragon wing in the hope her added weight would stop him from being able to roll, duck and dive so easily.

"Frank! Aim...for...his...*wings*!" Olena yells hoping Frank can hear her calling out.

Chance too focused on trying to rid himself of Olena ——doesn't hear her much smaller voice as to him it sounds more akin to that of a mouse squeaking.

Frank proves he heard Olena's instruction loud and clear however as he aims and fires two arrows in fast succession directly through the thinner skin of Chance's wings——dropping him to the ground like a stone——along with...*Olena*.

## Chapter 53

Olena's body is slammed full force into the hard ground below. Dust kicks up covering her entire now motionless body from head to foot. Nathan having watched the disaster unfold races down to the arena floor——yelling for the others to get ready and if possible for Frank to hit Chance's other wing.

The Manticore's breath comes in huge winded gasps. Blood seeps from the puncture wounds made from Olena's katanas——turning his lion's fur from dirty gold to dark angry red.

Donnie and Jamie race across the open ground where Nathan is rapidly trying to extract an unconscious Olena from harm's way. All they can see is dust and blood as Nathan lifts her light weight frame easily into his arms.

Chance catches his breath, his human manticore face widening into an evil grin, that could have rivalled that of

Mr King's 'It' Jamie considers——while silently swearing under his breath, to never being able to sleep again after coming face to face with such a monstrous beast.

Nathan rapidly barks out orders for Donnie and Jamie to split up, taking positions away from one another and to wait for his signal to strike when ready. Nathan then sprints, arms laden with Olena heading toward an alcove leading into the hollowed out stone structure.

Spotting Donnie and Jamie running in opposite directions across the open floor arena——Chance having recovered from the latest hit——starts spinning, whipping his scorpion tail around the open-air arena space ——marginally missing both men as they jump the tail several times before reaching the structure's wall. Donnie and Jamie press both their bodies flat against the smooth stone's surface——a mere hair's breadth from the sharp poisoned tip of Chance's scorpion tail whizzing past. Edging sideways, both men eventually make it through one of the lower level alcoves taking them back inside the temporary sanctuary of the colossal structure.

The building has been designed in such a way that sound easily travels right the way through. As Nathan calls out to Donnie, Jamie and Frank——they in turn can be heard responding with ease. The only thing hard to pinpoint, is the exact location where each of them is situated.

"I have Olena safe——when I make a break for the arena ground, Donnie, Jamie you follow my lead but we *must* stay separated from one another. Frank——keep doing what you're doing with the arrows." Nathan calls out hoping Chance cannot hear their plans but even if he could——Nathan knew from their point of view, as proposed ambushes went——having four of them and one of him meant the odds could be stacked in their favour.

Collecting himself——using the box breathing method he was taught during his time in the military. Nathan is able to calm his breath and mind long enough to switch back on into focused mode, disallowing adrenaline and fear to take charge. No, he needed to be in the driving seat. Taking all the knowledge from his training Nathan grips his broad sword and strides on out.

Chance, with his back to Nathan can be seen lazily licking his paws. The blood that had been actively bleeding from the wounds inflicted via Olena's katanas have since stopped——leaving dark red matted globs of clotted blood——where fresh ran mere moments before.

"Human, I can sense your puny body so if you had thought to sneak up behind me——think again." Chance says whipping round to face Nathan——putting his human masculine face a bit close for Nathan's comfort. His breath stank like rotting bones, eggs and prawns. "Tell me——*who* gave you such weaponry? I ask because The Magi promised me this would be no different to being fed like the carnivores at a petting zoo." Chance says coolly while sitting on his haunches—— picking up one of his giant paws looking at it as if to consider it. The sight of such talons continuously extending and retracting, make Nathan's head feel woozy as he imagines the damage a single one of those could do to human flesh.

As Chance drones on about how unfair everything appears to have turned out for him and that all of them have become rather bothersome——Nathan takes his moment to slip from Chance's peripheral vision. Carefully he gets close to Chance's scorpion tail and without hesitation lifts his broad sword up——slamming it with all his might, down upon the wretched looking thing, slicing it clean away from Chance's body.

The Manticore throws its body around wildly as it tries and fails to lick the site of the now excruciatingly painful, stinging stub-end where his scorpion tail used to feature. Nathan runs wide of Chance as he flails around clearly in a lot of pain. Roars ricochet loud enough to almost burst Nathan's ear drums and that he guesses of his comrades.

Catching the eyes of both Donnie and Jamie——Nathan indicates with the use of special military sign language what his intended next steps are.

Venom drips from the tip of Chance's dead scorpion tail and seizing the opportunity Nathan runs his broad sword along the stinging tip dousing the metal in venom. Like a tag team once Nathan has anointed his sword he runs wide as Jamie comes close to cover his mace before retreating, allowing Donnie to then take some venom to rub onto his spear.

Chance eventually stops writhing in agony but before he can fully recover——Olena has arisen from her shielded position inside the stone structure. Valiantly she calls out grabbing all of the manticore's attention onto herself, drawing him close. Before Nathan or the others can protest, Olena throws her katanas——dart style at both Chance's eyes. One after the other they hit their mark as wild screams echo their loudest causing everyone to drop to the ground grabbing the sides of their heads ——covering their ears the best they can. Blood streams down Chance's human face as his giant eyes have been reduced to empty hollows after ripping the katanas free from his face——leaving gelatinous globs that used to be his eyes——skewered onto the middle prong of each katana.

The effort it had taken for Olena to move herself let alone carry off two such precise strikes have all but taken any energy she had remaining, out of her——and as her batteries go flat, she crumples once more to the ground.

———

The sound of an arrow whistling through the air reaches Nathan, Donnie and Jamie's ears as Frank takes expert aim firing another arrow through the second dragon wing. Chance barely wails this time or moves as pain has led him into a shock state.

Lying on his side, Chance huffs heartily with difficulty in breathing.

"Take...the win." is all Chance utters as he indicates with a paw to his broad muscular chest for a strike to his heart. "You'd better not miss...because then...I'll *really* be mad." He carries on, accepting defeat.

Nathan gives a look to Donnie as he and Jamie move Olena and themselves out of the blistering heat from the sun——and away into a shadier patch of the arena's grounds now that the sun has moved round.

Using the remaining energy he has left, Chance manages to get into a sitting position once more——exposing his chest ready to welcome death.

"You're all worthy adversaries. As for the dagger——find it tucked safely inside my heart."

*Thump!*

Donnie hits his mark straight and true. He had always been very good at javelin in high school so using his spear much the same way has been able to give Chance a fast, painless end.

Walking up to the huge dead Manticore's body. Donnie pulls his spear clear and as he does so, The Ruby Sunrise comes out with it.

*Whoever thought I'd end up being the hero of the day.* Donnie thinks nonchalantly, bending down to pick up the dagger before heading on over to meet with the others.

"Well done everyone." Frank says as they now sit together in the shade.

"The dagger is in our hands but——no Pete." Donnie says somberly, fearing the worst.

No one responds, the men just sit in quiet reflective silence——hoping for the best but preparing for the worst.

Olena groans as the feel of strong hands pull her up into what she guesses are Nathan's arms. Small movements registering but with the intense tinnitus and throbbing head pain bringing with it blurred vision——little else gets through as Olena struggles to focus on much of anything. The human heart inside of her chest ——beats hysterically, soon becoming a soothing internal lullaby as its rhythm decelerates sending Olena into the clutches of unconsciousness——her last lucid thought being that if she were to die right now——she would welcome death.

———

*Some time later...*

The men are tiring of being left hanging around with nowhere to go.

"I thought The Magi would at least have put in an appearance——I mean we got the dagger, didn't we?" Jamie whines which instantly starts to get everyone's backs up.

"Shut up man——seriously I have a thumping headache and——

"Oh *sure*, pick on the guy who never so much as got to use his weapon——Mr *I'm so special because I killed the beast.*" Jamie says cutting off Donnie to poke fun at him.

"Oh for pity's sake! You're really going to turn this into a pissing contest?!" Donnie spits back annoyed.

"Keep your knickers on *Prince Valiant* I was only——

"Enough!" Frank shouts causing them both to quit

their quarrel. "*Listen*" he says as the men tune into any sounds they may now hear around them.

"Woah! Pete! It's Pete!" Jamie exclaims punching the air, as indeed their newly *feathered* friend makes a grand entrance doing a loop-the-loop before pooping on Jamie's head, before coming to perch on Frank's shoulder as a matter of safety.

"Man! That's disgusting! And what the hell have you been eating to give you purple shit that smells like cheese-ass?!" Jamie says wiping the mess from his shoulder.

"*Cheese-ass*" Donnie echoes back as Frank, Nathan and he all burst out laughing.

"Yeah-yeah, laugh it up fellas. I still might yet turn my hand to tasting pigeon one of these days——hey *pigeon* yeah! That's now my new nickname for you Petey-boy!" Jamie says quite pleased with himself for having found what he feels is the ultimate way to wind his friend up, bird or not.

In a fit of rage Pete flies from Frank's shoulder going feet first toward Jamie's face while flapping his wings ferociously——demanding he retract that statement.

"Alright——*dude* I said alright!" Jamie coughs out through mouthfuls of stray feathers.

"And I think your new nickname should be chicken." Donnie says having seen how ridiculous Jamie now looks with a head and face full of fluffy-tufts bits of feathers.

Olena murmurs drawing everyone's attentions onto her and away from the two squabbling best friends.

*Olena...Olena hun...it's time to wake up now.* A familiar voice says sounding so far away from her.

*I'm having the most wonderful dream——must I truly wake up?* She thinks.

Olena is in a fairy garden dream——when all of a sudden, a dragon interrupts, attempting to eat her and burn everything in its way——sending fairies fleeing for their lives.

"Ahhhh!" Olena yelps, jerking awake to smack Nathan unsuspecting on the forehead. He'd been leaning over his fallen angel——concerned she may never wake up.

The force of impact after having already had a bump to the head, makes Olena dry heave on all fours.

"I don't...feel so good." Olena says rubbing her own forehead while trying to stand.

"Should you——

"Quiet! Or I can't hear the voice." Olena explains cutting Nathan off as he can only look at her in stunned silence as he helps her up to standing. When she goes to head off for some privacy and he tries to follow her Olena bats him away with her hands. The only reason Nathan's happy to let her go is he knows she won't go far and that presently there appears to be no threat to them past dying of hunger, thirst or boredom.

"When we get back to London——Olena should be checked over, *thoroughly*." Frank says with concerned sigh as it was clear Olena showed signs of brain damage.

"You don't think she's...*permanently* damaged do you?" Nathan asks, a feeling of deep uncertainly pooling in the pit of his stomach. Watching as Olena paces back and forth making wild hand and arm gestures——almost as if she's speaking to an invisible friend.

"No one would blame you for cutting your loses if these *changes* in Olena's brain chemistry are to be *permanent*." Jamie suggests, placing a hand on Nathan's shoulder.

"Stop that!" Nathan growls at his friend as he stalks closer to where Olena paces in frustrated fashion.

*Perhaps much like an epileptic I should just let her rage on to the imaginary person/s.* Nathan contemplates as he closes the gap between them.

———

*"Ok, I've heard from the Powers That Be——well a messenger of theirs I should say. It turns out The Magi have been taken in for further...'rebooting' apparently the first attempt didn't go as well as they'd hoped."* Mortina relays telepathically to Olena.

*"When can we go back to London? And what about Pete——will he ever be human again?"* Olena asks thinking of gaining answers to questions on the lips of Nathan and everyone else.

*"What I can tell you is...there's a new set of rules being drafted up. Brax has been instructed to wait for the parchment to arrive and then I'll bring it here. You'll all need to agree to the new terms and conditions prior to your being released. The Powers That Be sent their apologies via angel messenger to myself whilst during a meditation——and*

*before they left assured* me to let you all know from this point on everything should be a fair challenge——I imagine that to mean if whoever you battle has powers or weaponry so too shall you. Meanwhile Is everyone ok? Do you require any healing?"

"I...banged my head and it's hard to breath." Olena admits making a mental note that Mortina ignored her question regarding Pete's bird state.

*"Goodness! Hang on I'll be right there——*

"You're kidding me. You mean you could have been here this entire time? They're all probably thinking I've gone round the twist!" Olena exclaims annoyed, glancing back to notice the nervous nods and smiles cast her way.

*Sorry, I had to make sure you'd finished the task in hand before attempting any form of communication again.*

**'POP'**

The sound of a loud balloon bursting is heard second before Mortina makes her appearance. Olena is about to be checked over by Mortina, when Frank out of nowhere appears to have grasped his second wind as he dashes across the sand and dust laden ground——where upon reaching Mortina pulls her in close for a wild passionate kiss.

"I err——I'll just go wait over there until you guys are...finished." Olena says awkwardly as she hobbles across to where Nathan, Donnie and Jamie all sit looking agape at Frank ad his sudden boost of youthfulness.

———

Mortina fixes Olena's wounds before tending to the others. A sound like a computer gamer who's just won at a level pings out from nowhere as a piece of rolled up parchment falls from the sky——wrapped in silk red ribbon. A tag attached reads **Compliments from The Powers That Be.**

"This is your new contract. As I explained to Olena the higher ups have done *another* reset of The Magi seeing as the last one didn't quite go as well as they'd hoped. I don't pretend to understand how any of that works——so don't shoot the messenger. Anyway, if you all agree to the new terms and conditions laid in this contract and sign——you can return home." There is a sad note to Mortina's voice as she vocalises the last part about them returning home.

"That means..." Jamie's voice trails off having stated the obvious.

"Yeah——we must part company my dear." Frank says turning to Mortina with tears in his eyes.

"Oh for pity's sake!" Olena says snatching the parchment up from the ground. "Magi! I know you can hear me! I demand an audience with you——*immediately.*" Olena says unable to bear the painful expressions in both Mortina and Frank's faces any longer. It makes her heart sickeningly ache for them.

Time stops as the cloaked figure emerges.

"*Olena. Please excuse our previous transgressions we The Magi are glad to hear of your great success in defeating Chance the Manticore.*"

"Yeah——yeah, enough with the pleasantries. Can

you add into this contract that Mortina can accompany us? I feel she will make a valuable asset to our team——being a medic and all that." Olena says stating her case.

"*Very well——consider it done.*" The Magi say in almost cheerful notes which immediately put Olena's back up. She didn't care what sort of reboot or reset had been done to them——she still would never trust them as far as she could throw them.

Glancing down at the parchment Olena can indeed see a new paragraph inserted stating that should she choose to Mortina may also accompany them all in the quest to retrieve the rest of the daggers.

Signing before they can change their minds, time then switches back into normal mode as Olena passes the parchment complete with golden winged pen to Nathan who then passes it to Frank, then Donnie, Jamie——even Pete who with a little help from Jamie is able to print two little bird feet at the bottom having had some ink placed on them. When they think they're finished Olena announces how Mortina must now decide if she would like to join them.

Everyone's stunned faces——especially Frank and Mortina's come as no surprise to Olena. As they re-read the terms where it does indeed state Mortina can now choose continue the journey with them or stay behind.

With barely a pause to think Mortina snatches the pen from Jamie, eagerly scribbling down her signature. She then yelps, flushing red while holding a hand to her bottom——as a tattoo, courtesy of The Magi gets slapped across one of her arse cheeks.

Once all signatures are accounted for the parchment disappears along with winged pen——as if by magic. Below everyone's feet small rumbles can be felt as they all cling to one another for support——just as beneath them a portal gateway opens, and they all go tumbling through.

## Chapter 54

The portal doorway worked similarly to special effects seen on popular television shows such as *Stranger Dimensions*——where a group of school friends end up discovering weird monsters and an underworld they call the *upside down*.

"That is some *serious* vertigo." Nathan exclaims dusting off his shoulders as he reacquaints himself to the living room——his living room, he reminds himself as the jarring effect of having been in mystical Egypt one minute and home again in the blink of an eye make his brain feel momentarily funky.

"So...this is your home then?" Mortina asks as the group turn to watch her take in the lavish surroundings of book shelves and plush furniture.

"Actually this is Nathan and his sister Felicity's home. We just err——pop by once in a while to you know...hang out." Frank says wondering how Mortina might adjust to being so far flung from everything she's ever known seeing as her signature on their new contract, meant it's a done deal that she's now stuck with them for the duration of this dagger retrieval quest.

"Look everyone, I'm glad we're all back safe and sound but would anyone mind if I hit the hay——I'm absolutely bushwhacked." Jamie says the look in his eyes all too apparent in proving his extreme fatigue.

"Sure, go right ahead——I'm not sure if Rosa's been in but yours and Donnie's usual guest room should be ready none the less. As always help yourselves to any food and drinks from the kitchen." Nathan says as both Jamie and Donnie lope away down the hallway to the guest quarters.

"Right, Mortina and Frank——there's plenty of room upstairs as well. As we had such luxury at The Blue Pharaoh it seems only befitting I should offer you the same grace. There's a Master suite far room on the left. It was originally my parents but Felicity and I have since had it re-decorated. In my opinion it's the best room in the house with sprawling balcony overlooking the garden. Anyway it's yours if you so choose to occupy it mind you——

"Nate, it's perfect. Thanks for the offer." Frank says placing a hand on Nathan's shoulder before pulling him in for a hug, patting him heartily on the back.

"Ah stop that——can't be going all *gooey-eyed* on the missus, can I?" Nathan says winking at Olena, as Frank steps back.

Yawning Olena also attests to feeling incredibly tired

while also reminding them of Pete's condition and where he should sleep.

"Pete, you have full roam of the house, fly and sleep wherever you like. Please let me know if you're ever hungry and what you might be in the mood for——I've never owned pet birds so I'm a little out of the loop on caring for——*pigeons.*" Nathan has to stifle a laugh as he mentions the word pigeon.

Pete flies off the shelf he'd been perched on to gently prod at Nathan on the tip of his ear with his beak.

"Ow! Alright—alright, no more jokes——*tweety pie.* Ok, ok, I'm sorry that really was the last one." Nathan says as Pete brandishes his feathers directly in front of his face.

Flying away for a comfortable place to roost for the night. Pete opts for an empty golden birdcage situated in the library come lounge room. The cage was chosen more for aesthetic design by Felicity, then to actually house a bird. But Pete manages to open the small unlocked cage door with ease before climbing inside shutting it firmly behind him. Being so small he feels vulnerable and wonders if some innate bird self-preservation might be kicking in as he automatically thought of how the cage would offer him some protection should a predator try to eat him in the night.

"Poor guy." is all Nathan can think to say as Frank and Mortina excuse themselves for the evening leaving Olena and Nathan alone.

"Considering I'm so far removed from home and everything I knew before this extraordinary human life

——I have to admit, coming home to creature comforts like this, it ain't all bad. I can see where you get the attraction to chase having *nice things* as a species." Olena says sleepily.

"Right missy——its bedtime for us, and not to sound offensive but do you mind if we lay off doing the bedroom tango tonight——I'm sorta dead on my feet."

"I hear you. But can we at least shower first?"

"Oh absolutely——Rosa would absolutely kill me if I were to fall in bed carrying half of the Sahara with me."

"Hey——who you callin' a desert." Olena quips back at Nathan.

"Woah! Miss Lupescu I do believe you're also a comedienne in the making." Nathan says while heartily laughing at her effort for a joke. "Jamie would've been proud." He adds.

"Now I know you love me if you're equating me to that simpering idiot."

"Ouch! Those grapes are sour."

"Better than the cheese you just added with that repost."

The pair carry on joking right the way into the shower——where it was inevitable that they would undress, get wet and make slow passionate love from catching a second wind of energy before falling in a tangled romantic twist between heavenly clean sheets.

# Epilogue

The Ruby Sunrise Dagger sits inside of an antique glass display case——— hidden inside of a metal compartment. To view the dagger a correct code must be entered for the case to rise up and be witnessed.

It has been two days since their return home and not so much as a peep has been seen or heard from The Magi.

———

"Still nothing from our friends?" Nathan asks as Olena lazily saunters into the kitchen donning one of his sister's oriental red and gold silk robes.

"Afraid not——sorry everyone." She says addressing the room where the others are all enjoying a breakfast of various delights.

"Olena, perhaps I can contact Brax to see if he can get

the attention of a messenger angel? It might help give you the information you need?" Mortina offers gingerly as she still gets acquainted with the group and her new living situation.

"Can you not——do that yourself?" Olena asks concern crossing her face to notice the sadness in Mortina's eyes.

"It appears for whatever reason I am not yet able to access my powers while here in London. Perhaps it is to prevent any little magical mis-haps from occurring. I hadn't noticed any such mention of a ban in the small print. It is my hope that when we reach the next veiled country——I shall be able to use my magic again...as it stands I am much like yourself——very much human from this point on."

"Those bastards!" Frank exclaims through gritted teeth. "Always a sodding loop-hole not unlike our own scheming government." He carries on, remaining hidden behind his newspaper as he takes what sounds like an angry slurp of coffee. Mortina gives his thigh a gentle squeeze to let him know she's ok but he silently continues to fume none the less.

"Say——where did Jamie, Donnie and Pete skulk off to?" Olena says noticing the now absent chairs and mini bird perch that Rosa had set up for the new *pet bird*.

"Oh, well actually they've been helping get bird-sized armour fitted for Pete. And have also been helping him to learn tricks with his new form. Things like how to spy, checking out how far he can hear——which apparently is quite some distance. So good for eavesdropping. He can now also pick locks with the right combination of tools and balance." Nathan says sounding quite impressed.

"It'll keep them out of trouble I suppose." Olena says heading toward the coffee machine unsure of how it all worked.

"Ah! You want your *hot chocolate* fix. There's already fresh water in the back of the machine, just open the box that says chocolate-pods and——here let me show you."

Once Nathan has shown Olena how to get her morning liquid chocolate fix as well as re-educating her on how to use the toaster. Mortina asks for a bit of quiet and privacy so she might attempt to telepathically link in with Brax for an update.

Frank, Nathan and Olena head for the conservatory attached to the kitchen. Sun shines through the glass creating explosive fragments of rainbow light that Olena plays with between her fingers.

"I shall miss this——the sun, when…everything goes back to *normal.*" As she says these words it is near impossible for Olena to keep the somber tone from her voice. As she knows it will inevitably mean their relationship would end.

"Come on——no sad subjects. Let's just snuggle and wait for——

Before Nathan can finish his sentence Mortina bursts through the doors breathless.

"Thank Hades you requested me to check in! You *all* should have been in Hawaii——*YESTERDAY!*"

"*Ohhhh* farts! Seems The old Magi are still up to their dirty dogged tricks of attempting to sabotage our success. Frank, go get the lads——it's time we packed...for *Honolulu*!"

***This story continues in book two***
***Race For The Tangerine Sapphire***

## Also by Emma Bruce

Pink Club series

Pink Club

Dreams in Pink

Pink Passions

United in Pink

Sinful Seven series

Midnight

# About Emma Bruce

Emma Bruce is a feisty 30 something Sagittarian who lives by the motto "Never give up" She lives with her family, the love of her life Matthew and their four beautiful children.

Her first book 'Pink Club' was received so well by the general reading population that there was a sudden big demand for her to complete the second book in her mini series to which she has aptly called "Dreams in Pink".

Emma (When not chasing after her children, picking out stray Lego bricks imbedded into her feet, cleaning pen from the walls with a magic sponge, among a plethora of other jobs being a mother and housewife entails), enjoys in her quieter hours both reading books as a form of escapism and relaxation alongside working on her own written projects.

For more information please check out Emma's website

www.emmabruceauthor.com
http://pinkclub.site

# About Morticia Gayle

A quirky Aquarian cat 'slave' to a fiesty tortoiseshell. She can be found lurking in her local coffee shop with a large mocha and her nose deep in the latest paranormal/cosy/thriller downloaded to her ereader. When not people watching, she can be found in the kitchen baking or dreaming up the next weird adventure with her partner-in-writing Emma Bruce.

# Acknowledgments

Proofreading by Agent M.

Email agentmproofreader@gmail.com

Agent M Proof Reading A qualified proofreader and beta reader. I can proof your theses , dissertations, fiction and non-fiction manuscripts. I am also available to discuss plot and character development. I have assisted in the publication of two works of fiction so far. I will also type up handwritten manuscripts if you provide a data stick for the finished project.

I'm a fifty something coffee snob who likes nothing more than curling up with a good book on a cold, rainy day with my tortoiseshell cat Blaze beside me. Hobbies include baking and debating the merits of a Victoria sandwich cake over a fruit cake when reading a historical murder mystery. I enjoy many different genres and can be found in my local coffee shop, people watching while reading a good book. https://agentmproofreading.com

Marie-Louise Bio:

Marie-Louise specialises in branding, design and Canva for SMEs. She offers a range of logo and design 121 services, Canva group training and is an official Canva Creator.

With 20 years industry experience and a degree in branding and packaging, she's created everything from logo designs, social media templates and website design in the digital space, to printed brochures, book covers, adverts, banners and packaging.

She loves to work with entrepreneurs, coaches, marketing experts and virtual assistants to create consistent content that's on brand but with the flexibility to evolve over time.

Her design process is focussed on collaboration, meeting on Zoom and using great tools like Canva, to bounce ideas and bring the design to life before her clients' eyes.

https://lovelyevolution.co.uk/

Photo credit: Jo Blackwell Photography

Printed in Great Britain
by Amazon